Austentatious

Austen*tatious*

Alyssa Goodnight

KENSINGTON BOOKS
www.kensingtonbooks.com

KENSINGTON BOOKS are published by

Kensington Publishing Corp.
119 West 40th Street
New York, NY 10018

ISBN-13: 978-0-7582-6743-6
ISBN-10: 0-7582-6743-6

First Kensington Trade Paperback Printing: February 2012
10 9 8 7 6 5 4 3 2 1

Printed in the United States of America

For Zach and Alex, who totally get that a good writing day
means more video game time and, quite possibly,
fish sticks and Tater Tots for dinner. Win-win!
And for Jason, who never fails to impress me.

ACKNOWLEDGMENTS

I would like to extend my effusive thanks and giddy appreciation to the following people who were instrumental in turning my story into a full-fledged book:

My exceptionally sweet and savvy agent, Rebecca Strauss, who loved this book from the very beginning and then charmingly helped me make it even better.

My excellent editor, Megan Records, who is cool just by virtue of owning a Jane Austen action figure, but in lots of other ways too.

My conscientious copy editor, Stacia Seaman, who caught all my Austin-related errors and inspired future research trips to the original *weird* city.

All the fabulous authors whose books inspire me to write mine even better, most especially the incomparable Jane Austen.

My awesome, ninja-cool blog regulars . . . you know who you are! Your smart, funny, encouraging comments put the sparkle in my day.

My mom, who introduced me to Mary Stewart's romantic suspense novels and also set a stellar example of recreational reading, and my dad, who always squeezed in a trip to the bookstore (not to mention a Tex-Mex lunch) amid all our weekend errands.

My mother-in-law, who probably hyped my first book more than I hyped it myself, and my father-in-law, who didn't say a word when his wife insisted on buying copies for every one of their friends.

And for my family . . . my boys. You get me, and that makes all the difference.

1

Miss Nicola James will be sensible and indulge in a little romance.

As the song goes, there are "miles and miles of Texas." Miles of desert to the west, miles of piney woods to the east, miles of highway and byway streaking every which way in between, and Austin, the sparkling jewel nestled at the center, a kaleidoscope of color and movement . . . and *weird*. Those of us lucky enough to move here from Houston, Dallas, and beyond hung on like runner weeds, determined to stay whether we really belonged or not.

But who could say, really, who belonged and who didn't—conformance was a dirty word here in the capital city, where the unofficial slogan, emblazoned across T-shirts in all-capped, bold white font, was "Keep Austin Weird." I didn't own one of these shirts. Not yet. I'd held off, waiting for the moment when my own personal weirdness factor justified the purchase. Otherwise, I'd just be a poseur, part of the problem. Geeky not being synonymous with weird, I'd been under the impression I still had a long way to go. But as of approximately ten seconds ago, I think, just maybe, I might have crossed over into the realm of "weird."

Having lived in this city for eight serious-minded years as somewhat of an outsider, skulking on the fringe in T-shirts from Old Navy, you'd think I'd be excited, giddy even. But honestly, I was getting more and more panicky by the minute. All because of a journal.

The journal had been intended as the perfect Austenesque birthday gift for my vintage-obsessed younger cousin. I'd found it lying alongside a worn copy of *Pride and Prejudice* in a quirky antiques shop down on South Congress and simply couldn't pass it up, hobnobbing, as it was, with greatness. I had a bit of a soft spot for Ms. Austen and all she touched. The book was even inscribed with a quirky and rather perplexing dedication in an old-fashioned script:

> "... I dedicate to You the following Miscellanious Morsels, convinced that if you seriously attend to them, You will derive from them very important Instructions, with regard to your Conduct in Life."

Charmingly vintage, with its elaborately detailed antiqued brass key plate and burnished doorknob affixed to the front, not to mention its slightly batty hint of shrewdly dispensed life advice, it seemed a perfect choice for a secret diary. I figured the absence of clasp and key could be remedied with a good hiding place. Evidently mine hadn't been nearly good enough. But then, I'd never planned on needing one.

My delight in finding the perfect gift had lasted all of five minutes—long enough to treat myself to a chai tea latte and settle into a café chair to admire my purchase. Slightly envious, I'd splayed my fingers over the bumpy black leather cover and even gone so far as to dip my unpolished, trimmed-short fingernail into the tiny keyhole. I'd instantly felt an unexpected little zing that had sent goose bumps chasing each other up my arms and nerves spiraling down like a roller coaster into the pit of my stomach. Startled, I'd jerked back, jostling my full-to-the-brim cup and sending a cascade of warm, spiced tea down onto the little book, staining the pages, buckling the edges, and rendering it ungiftable all in one fell swoop.

I'd chalked the whole situation up to general journal incompatibility and carted my newly ruined journal home with me, not having any clue what I'd do with it. I'd always been more of a clip-board kind of girl, and not much had changed recently. After four years of engineering at UT–Austin, and another few getting my MBA, I was anxious to keep the momentum going. Having just purchased my first house, a little fixer-up bungalow in the city's über-hip West Sixth Street neighborhood, I was now gunning for a management position with its boost in salary and prestige, and I was spending my weekends on carefully planned and executed DIY projects. Men were a distraction. They were also the meat and potatoes of journaling, and for the time being, I was dieting. Looking back on it now, and ever so modestly casting myself as Elizabeth Bennet, I could see that discovering this journal had been like the arrival of the Bingleys: a call to adventure. And, in my own clumsy manner, I'd answered. Eventually.

The charming little book had sat, waiting patiently on the shelf with my own, marginally less dusty, treasure trove of Austen novels until I could no longer resist the allure of that miniature door and those tea-stained, cinnamon-scented pages. Clearly I'd jinxed myself.

Glancing somewhat nervously toward the kitchen timer digitally counting down the seconds . . . *9:56 . . . 55 . . . 54 . . . 53* . . . I shifted my gaze back to the seemingly innocuous book that was quickly becoming quite the little nemesis. With cupcakes in the oven (my signature contribution to next door's weekly karaoke shindig), I had time to kill . . . and no legitimate excuse not to take another look.

One wide-eyed glance was all it took—now I was *officially* freaked. The page looked exactly the same as it had fifteen seconds ago but distinctly, disturbingly different from the way it had the day I wrote it. And therein lay the rub—not to mention the weirdness. Because *how* could it be different?

Goose bumps cropped up on my arms as I tried to focus on the scattering of words remaining. As I read them in order, left to right and down the page, my heartbeat kicked up in my chest, deep, ominous thuds. There were twelve words left.

Miss Nicola James   will
be
sensible
and indulge in a   little romance.

It was either an extraordinary coincidence . . . or not. And the "not" was what scared me.

I had to admit, I hadn't taken particular notice of my choice of words when I'd penned the one and only entry almost a week ago, but now that they were gone, I wanted them back. It was the damn *principle* of the thing! Well, that and the creepiness.

I forced myself to slow down and think calmly. I peered more closely at the page, running my fingers over its unmarred smoothness. Tilting the little volume back and forth, I noticed nothing but pristine blank paper spanning the gaps the missing words had left behind. There was nothing—no marks. No smudges, smears, eraser marks, *nothing*. No sign that the rest of the words had ever been there. My words—some of them anyway—had completely disappeared. But *how?* And equally curious . . . *why?*

I skimmed ahead a few pages, just checking—for what, I had no idea—and then suddenly, rabidly obsessed, whipped through every single page, searching for any sort of marking at all. Common sense didn't bother to kick in until I'd finished. What was I thinking? That somehow my words were playing hide and seek, waiting for me to come searching?

8:13 . . . Timing myself definitely wasn't helping!

Focus. What did I know? I'd written a single entry, stashed the journal in the bookcase to be guarded between the Misses Bennet and Woodhouse, and it had been hijacked.

I think that about summed it up: Basically I knew absolutely nothing other than this was my journal, and somebody was messing with me—and doing so at their own peril. But who? No one knew about the journal, and no one of my acquaintance had the skill set necessary to pull something like this off. They'd need dodgy breaking-and-entering skills to get the journal (having somehow first discovered its existence), an impressive knack for wordplay, and access to *Mission Impossible*–style office products to obliterate all superfluous words into mind-blowing nonexistence. By now, I was leaning heavily toward adopting Vizzini's "Inconceivable" mantra. (And it *totally* meant what I thought it meant.)

7:22 . . . Think . . . think! It occurred to me that Nancy Drew would have had this case solved by now, so what was I, a top-of-my-class engineering major and MBA grad, missing? I let my eyes roam around the room. This wasn't the sort of place where unexpected, magical things happened. Everything that happened here was practical and preplanned. And until tonight, it all made complete sense! I needed a connection, an explanation . . . basically a "Why Me?"

I dragged my eyes back to the page to scan it yet again, and this time, I made myself focus on the words themselves.

Ms. Nicola James will be sensible(!) and indulge in a little romance?

It would seem that the journal had been soaking up inspiration as it sat, unsupervised, alongside my much-loved collection of Austen novels all week long. Now I just needed a single man in possession of a good fortune, and I was good to go. To continue the metaphor likening the appearance of the journal to that of the Bingleys, this snarky bit of commentary could be viewed as the introduction of Mr. Darcy, spouting off unnecessarily.

Forgetting for a minute the stranger-than-fiction details of this whole situation, I was offended now on a whole other level. I was *nothing* if not sensible, but I wasn't about to be prodded into "indulging" until I was good and ready. And yet, perversely, I was impressed. I didn't remember using half of those words in my own entry, but obviously I had, because there they were, big as life, taunting me in my very own handwriting.

A glance at the clock had me thudding back into a near stupor of helplessness. The antiques store was a no-go until tomorrow afternoon. Surely there was something I could be doing about this predicament right now. . . . Then it hit me: I'd re-create my original entry and get it back, fully intact. How that might help, I couldn't imagine—I was simply driven by a desperation to put things back the way I'd left them, the way they made sense.

Thrilled to have a specific task to perform, I scrambled to get a pen, then changed my mind and grabbed a pencil instead—one with a good chunky eraser.

My ringtone blithely sounded off from the kitchen counter, and I jerked nervously away from it. Glancing at the journal, my decision was instantaneous: I was sooo not telling anyone about this. Scrabbling for the phone, my greeting came out as something of a croak.

"Good, I caught you." As usual, Gabe was oblivious. I could hear his fingers clicking over a keyboard and assumed he was still at work. My gaze shifted curiously to the timer yet again.

Gabe was my best friend, and maybe that should have entitled him to a juicy divulgence, but he was also an engineer, not to mention a coworker, and his mind worked, more or less, the same way mine did. Seeing as I'd already classified this whole situation as un-freakin'-believable, I really didn't need, and couldn't stomach, his second opinion. I decided to stay mum, perched against the counter, a watchful eye on the journal.

"I assume you're aware that South by Southwest kicks off tonight," Gabe continued when I hadn't spoken.

"Aware, yes; indifferent, also yes." I wasn't the type to get excited about the city's annual movie slash music fest, no matter how prestigious.

Gabe ignored me. "So the music part of the festival doesn't start till next week, but some of the bands arrived early and scored some extra gigs."

I'd tease him for using the word "gig," but I needed to speed things up here.

"So . . . ?" I heard myself asking, my feigned interest the closest I intended on coming to any plans he might have for me that evening.

"So I'm heading down to Fadó with a couple of expats and a guy in from Glasgow, and I thought you might like to come. It's a Scottish band." With Austin nicknamed Silicon Hills and Glasgow dubbed Silicon Glen, many companies operated sister facilities, here and across the pond, creating somewhat of a foreign exchange program for the high-tech set.

"You are *not* trying to set me up." Less of a question, more of a stern reminder.

"God no. I'm just offering you an evening of men with accents."

And here I'd thought my best chance of going international tonight was a lawn full of lesbians salsaing to a karaoke rendition of "Livin' La Vida Loca."

"I think I'll pass, but you get points for a good, solid effort."

"Ah, come on, Nic—don't pass. You can't expect to earn a Weird shirt by missing eight consecutive years of South by Southwest."

"Why not? In this particular instance, I'm the epitome of weird." My eyes skimmed over the journal and quickly darted away. "Who else would choose questionable backyard karaoke over a legitimate Scottish band?"

"You're going next door?" Cue massive sigh.

"Of course. I've got cupcakes baking as we speak."

"Never mind that you need an intervention more than you need another cupcake." I started to react, but it quickly became clear that this was just his starter jab. "You're. Not. A. Lesbian. Nic. And you wouldn't karaoke for a hundred bucks." That was true. Sad, but true. "So what in the hell are you doing over there every Friday night?" And *then* he lapsed into absurdity: "Are they brainwashing you? Luring you into some sort of sexual cult? Should I come over?"

I rolled my eyes and responded accordingly. "Don't worry—it's nothing I can't handle. Just a little girl-on-girl action."

After a couple beats of uncharacteristic silence, Gabe eventually surfaced. "Okay, I'm getting a sarcastic vibe here, and it's throwing me off."

"Wishful thinking doesn't make it so, Gabe. Remember that."

"Damn. I thought not. So how exactly do the weekly lesbian potlucks fit in with the Nic James Life Plan?"

By now immune to Gabe's (and everyone else's) disdain for my carefully considered, down-to-the-detail life plan, I answered matter-of-factly. "It's actually a rather elegant solution. As you've just pointed out, I'm not a lesbian. As a result, I'm relatively immune to their charms. So no strings attached. Ingenious, huh?"

"I guess. Define 'relatively.' " I ignored this too. "Are there gonna be any guys there, trying to coax a few back to our team?" He sounded positively titillated over such an opportunity.

"Nope. And I consider that a definite draw." My patience was drying up.

"Are men even allowed?"

"Only for the occasional ritual sacrifice. Now I really—"

Gabe's laugh blasted back over the phone line, and I imagined him throwing back his head to punctuate the jocularity. For someone so obviously opposed to my attending these Friday night get-togethers, he seemed vicariously enthralled.

"Gabe, I gotta go."

"Okay, but I hear these guys are good. If, as you claim, you are still playing for our team, maybe they could get you off the bench."

The corners of my mouth began to curl despite my best efforts. "I'll suit up next season," I parried, nudging a spatula through the bowl of ganache sitting beside me on the counter, looking dangerously delicious.

"Are you telling me that men are on your agenda for next year?"

"I thought I was being lured out for a night of Austin culture and camaraderie?" As opposed to a night of *Austen* culture and camaraderie with my traitorous journal.

"Just sayin' . . ."

"Anything's possible," I allowed, suddenly distinctly uncomfortable with that admission, given what I'd been dealing with for the past quarter hour. "Bye, Gabe. Have fun tonight." I hung up before hearing his reply, just as the timer went off.

Retrieving the cupcakes, I set them on the baking rack to cool, swiped a finger through the ganache, and dropped back down at the kitchen table. I glared at the offending journal page and its few remaining survivors and underlined each of them with a short, sharp motion.

Then suddenly I remembered. My one-entry stint as a journaler had sprung from plans to attend a coworker's wedding this weekend—tomorrow, in fact. And the reality that I'd been going alone.

Miss Nicola James, 1 will attend.

Tentatively at first, I let my mind play through some possibilities. I mouthed the words and tapped my pencil over the page, checking the spacing. Within seconds, I was feeling very déjà vu.

I'm going solo.   As per The Plan. Sure it'd be kinda nice to have a date, but I'm not sure I'm ready for the complications just yet. Besides, I'll do just fine on my own.

Dateless, I was a free agent. I didn't have to stick close to anyone, entertain anyone, or worry about anyone—I could leave when I was ready. I actually loved weddings. And just like that, it all started coming back to me. . . .

A wedding is the perfect opportunity to dress up in frilly, feminine clothes and far-from-sensible shoes,

Not to impress anyone—just for me. Well, maybe one other person . . .

to mingle and indulge in a plate of fancy little hors d'oeuvres, and enjoy the ~~blurred at the edges~~ heady sense of romance without getting tangled up in any of it myself.

That last part was a little vague (not to mention over-the-top), but I'd remembered the general gist, and it fit the space, more or less, so I wasn't going to worry about being too precise. And I suppose the rest of it really didn't matter, as no words beyond "romance" had been deemed keepers. There'd been a vague mention of flirting, but that was it.

Tipping the book up off the table to read away from the glare of the pendant light, I slowly scanned the words. Definitely close enough.

It felt slightly cathartic, as if things were marginally back to normal. And yet . . . they were sooo not. Twenty minutes into this little mystery, and a logical explanation still escaped me. I didn't have a hypothesis, a theory, or even a guess. All I could claim was a shifty version of the original entry, and it didn't comfort me nearly as much as I'd imagined.

Thrumming my eraser on the table, I decided to lay a trap.

Flipping forward a page, I started with the prompt I'd been offered.

Miss Nicola James will be sensible and indulge in a little romance. . . .

Not with a man, with a dress. A fabulously out-of-character peacock blue party dress, complete with a flirty skirt and a daring neckline that, miracle of miracles, provides just a hint of cleavage.

This was starting to sound a little like a J. Peterman catalog, but honestly, it was just that kind of dress. It was a whim of fancy with an almost audible siren song. It had cut in on my long-standing arrangement with my little black dress and impelled me to buy it—and the matching shoes too. Both were impractical, but I couldn't seem to help myself.

She'll go bare-legged and carefree, sliding her whimsically painted toes into the cramped but vamped sequined sandals that she miraculously found on sale.

Okay, the whimsical toes were probably a stretch, but if a girl couldn't live it up in her journal, then what was the point?

Nicola is bravely ignoring the unpredictability of March weather in Austin and will no doubt end up shivering in her spaghetti straps, frozen as a Fudgsicle. At which point her cleavage may just get its big break. . . . She's kinda hoping it does.

A quick reread, and I was done. It felt a little weird referring to myself in the third person, but no weirder than sparring with a journal.

Take that, Mr. Darcy.

I flipped back a page, just confirming that my recent rewrite hadn't disappeared, and then realized that I should probably re-copy today's entry somewhere else, just to be on the safe side. Evidently you can't be too careful.

After dashing off the entry on the back of that week's grocery list, I shut the journal with a snap. Then, counting out ten Mississippi-seconds, I whipped it back open, tussled with the pages, and held my hand flat down on page two, staring at my still-familiar words, all of them still intact.

Edging out a relieved little smile, I tipped the book closed and stood to replace it on the shelf, because I definitely didn't want to leave it out—*exposed*—on the kitchen table. Then again, I wasn't certain I wanted to slide it back in amongst The Collected Works either, given the parallels my overactive imagination was busily drawing between my own situation and Elizabeth Bennet's. Giving my options for a new hiding place some quick and serious thought, I decided to be cautious and stash it between a couple of favorite cookbooks. Crazy as it was, it helped. I felt marginally better, having moved past frantic to the problem-solving, data-collection stage.

Even so, the only thing keeping me from curling up on the couch with the entire bowl of chocolate ganache was the fact that these cupcakes were expected next door.

Cupcakes, with their happy little faces in tidy little packages, usually centered me. Not tonight. Work was driving me crazy—I was tired of my efforts being rewarded with catchy phrases, shoulder squeezes, and personalized glass statuettes. I'd taken the job right out of grad school with the intent to learn the basics of the business before earning myself a place on the management team. Well, I'd mastered the basics—mastered them so well, in fact, that management wanted me to train all new engineers hired into our group. Not *manage* the new engineers, but train them and, if necessary, shoulder them aside in an emergency. I was Wonder Woman without the deflective wristbands and red knee boots, and it wasn't damn near enough. I indulged myself in a deep, all-suffering sigh and a finger swipe of dark, minty chocolate. I was truly hoping everything would be different after my performance evaluation on Monday.

My attention strayed, catching on last year's Christmas gift from Gabe. It was a Jane Austen Quote-a-Day calendar on a tacky little blue plastic stand, but I checked it every day without fail. Today's quote read, " 'Sense will always have attractions for me.' *Sense and Sensibility.*" A perfect mantra. (Honestly, "Inconceivable!" just wasn't working for me.) I repeated it for each cupcake I frosted and felt marginally better.

In three calming minutes, I'd transferred the finished cupcakes onto a white stoneware platter and pulled off my apron to hang it on the hook behind the door. Mantra or no mantra, I still had the heebie jeebies. Sliding into a belted sweater and ballet flats, I was more than ready to make my escape. I figured there was little point in primping—the girls either wouldn't notice, so why bother, or they would, and that had the potential to get a smidge uncomfortable.

The phone rang just as I stepped out the door, but I ignored it, sparing one final glance at the bookcase before pulling the back door firmly shut behind me and locking it. With the platter heavy in the crook of my arm, I walked through the brisk March chill and headed next door, already wondering what might be happening between the pages of my journal and how many cupcakes I'd need to distract me.

Glancing up at the inky night sky, only the brightest stars winking back at me, I felt disturbingly out of my depth. Here I was, on the thrilling cusp of weirdness, and I couldn't help but consider it wretchedly overrated.

2

In which Fairy Jane
makes an appearance

Karaoke nights at Laura and Leslie's had that homey, sprawling family reunion feel. Well, the sort of reunion you might have if the menfolk had been plucked off your family tree and kicked over the fence. And by the end of the workweek, that was just perfect. I'd missed the weekly shindig only once since I'd moved in six months ago, despite that first Friday night eye-opener. As a new neighbor, a.k.a. innocent victim, I was treated to the grand tour, complete with running commentary. Which is exactly how I'd come to discover their true feelings on TVs and penises: both were unsightly and arguably unnecessary.

Fresh from a viewing of an astonishingly diverse vibrator collection, Leslie had introduced me around in whirlwind fashion, and by the end of the evening, everyone had my number. (By that I mean they knew I wasn't a lesbian and that I didn't karaoke—no one *actually* had my number, no thanks to Leslie.) And despite these shortcomings, I'd been warmly welcomed ever since.

It was occasionally necessary to put up with Leslie's matchmaking attempts and know-it-all attitude (we suspected she viewed her doctorate not so much as an advanced degree in one particular subject area, but more as the staff of a modern-day god-

dess of wisdom), but Laura's cooking was amazing (although of-
tentimes overly optimistic), and there was never a dull moment.

I'd only just tucked my feet up under me in the most sought-
after seating on the deck, ready to calm down with a cupcake,
when Leslie walked up, trailed by a woman I'd never seen before.
Leslie is a frosted blonde, her eyes smoke blue, and I suspected
both colors were being helped along. She's a professor of women's
studies at the University of Texas, smart and savvy on the clock, a
little wacko during time off, and intimidating in every situation,
probably because it's impossible to know what to expect. Her
companion was about a foot shorter with a pert face and tight,
shoulder-length curls that looked like a tangle of copper wiring.

My eyes narrowed from the cradle of the purple papasan, and I
shook my head ever so slightly in warning. I was starting to feel a
little fidgety. As if we were all just pretending there wasn't a crazy
weird journal waiting for me at home. Waiting to psych me out.
Trying to set me up. Leslie could afford to take the night off. I must
have been sending out a shock wave of back-off vibes, because
Leslie sailed past me, pulling her friend along in her wake. But it
wasn't long before she circled back.

"She's cute, isn't she?" Leslie said, holding a tortilla chip edged
in guacamole, arching her eyebrows in question. "UT grad—does
some sort of networking thing. With computers," she added,
around a mouth full of chip.

"I'd say above average for tech support." I was feeling that particularly itchy combination of frenzied urgency and studied nonchalance and was ill equipped to deal with Leslie's matchmaking
schemes. "Let it go, Leslie. I'm not in the mood." I took a long-
awaited bite of cupcake and sighed as a bit of the craziness of the
last thirty minutes fell away. It was like a little taste of normal in a
world gone weird.

"You may have a 'Plan,' sweetheart, but life has a way of trump-
ing it. And all the clichés are true: 'it's not fair,' 'it's a bitch,' and
surely you've heard, 'it's what happens when you're busy making
other *plans*'?"

I nodded agreeably and started planning my escape, hoping she'd lose interest in our little chat given her abysmal chance of success in luring me into a lesbian romance and away from my Plan.

Everybody mocked The Plan, and it didn't faze me one little bit. A certain journal, on the other hand, was fazing me big-time. I took another bite of cupcake and reminded myself that I knew, better than anyone, what I needed. I'd come up with the Nic James Life Plan, Version 1.0, when I was thirteen, and very little had changed since then—I was currently living out Version 3.5 and doing a fine job of it, if I did say so myself. Except for that damn journal. I polished off the cupcake and felt my nerves clamoring all over again.

When I was a kid my dad had always had big plans—huge, wild, exciting plans that honestly would have wowed anyone. We were going to explore every subterranean inch of New York City; we were going to ride wild horses and camp on the beach; we were going to follow rainbows and go on real-life treasure hunts; we were going to be mushers in the Iditarod. And the plans and promises got wilder every summer. I believed in all of them and was disappointed again and again. There were always reasons we couldn't go—the timing, the money, a mysterious dog allergy— and one by one, each idea faded from our conversations and day- dreams, only to be replaced by a fresh new one. I had stopped believing at thirteen and vowed to escape into books. Definitely not the sort where kids were having adventures—I wasn't ready for such flagrant unfairness—I martyred myself with one of my mom's dog-eared romances.

And so began my love affair with Jane Austen. *Pride and Preju- dice* appealed to me from the very first pages because I admired Elizabeth Bennet as much as I commiserated. I was comforted by the idea that if a person was clever and sensible—maybe a little charming—things could, even without any bona fide adventures, turn out all right. And while that certainly wasn't my ideal—I had a clipboard list of ideas and dreams and things to get done—as a backup plan it wasn't too horrible.

So I'd made my Plan and promised myself that *I* would follow through—I would *do* things. And if I didn't, well, then somehow I'd make it work on my own terms. But I wasn't about to go haring off in pursuit of a man at the bullied urgings of "Mr. Darcy" and a lesbian version of Mrs. Bennet. So I just let Leslie's jabs roll right off me as I awkwardly stood and moved casually toward the buffet table.

Still, she seemed smugger than usual tonight, and I couldn't think why. I was inching even farther away when it hit me: Could she know about my journal? I'd left her and Laura with a house key over Christmas when I'd headed home to Houston—could she have had it copied and then used it later for a little casual snooping? Could she even now be using it in an elegant yet unethical scheme to prod me into a little lesbian experimentation? I turned to stare, slightly horrified and a little overawed. *God, I hope it hasn't come to this.*

I grabbed a tortilla chip, vigorously crunching as my thoughts raced over opportunities, possibilities, and unlikely scenarios. They all screeched to a halt at the sound of Leslie's voice, at the need to listen for clues.

"I don't plan to stop introducing you to the fabulous women who pop over here—you'll just have to buck up your willpower." Her knowing smile started the warning drums in my head, making me wonder: Just what *does* she know? How to make words disappear without a trace? How to really mess with a person's head? Was it possible I'd been too hasty in assuming Leslie's innocence? Well, I suppose technically speaking, I'd really only assumed ignorance and incompetence. . . .

Leslie winked as she walked away, sending me into a veritable tizzy.

Laura snuck up behind me as I stared, wide-eyed with worry, at the fajita buffet sprawling over the white mosaic patio table that had been crafted literally from the broken pieces of Leslie's short-lived marriage (or at least her wedding china).

"Did you try the tofu?"

A ponytailed brunette perpetually outfitted in workout clothes and athletic footwear, Laura owned a fitness store right off the running track snaking along Lady Bird Lake, and as far as I could tell, her life goal was to exorcise a person's every self-indulgent tendency before shoving them bodily down the path toward total fitness. Odd that she'd partnered herself with the greatest lover of Hostess Ho Hos the world had perhaps ever known. Their relationship was one of life's great mysteries.

"Maybe I'll try it later," I stalled, sidestepping away.

"Are you chicken?" Evidently she'd forgotten that I didn't do dares.

"Well, I'd *like* some chicken," I tossed back at her, filling a tortilla with black beans, guacamole, and pico de gallo. Honestly I just wanted a drink, but didn't think the cupcake I'd wolfed down could hold its own against the alcohol. I grabbed a hard cranberry lemonade and headed for my still-vacant chair. Once the soursweet buzz of the lemonade began to swim through my veins, the karaoke would start to sound a lot better—this I knew from experience. And maybe if I was really lucky, the liquor would make a magical journal seem like a *good* thing.

Despite the nip in the air and because of the knot of nerves in my stomach, I stuck it out for another couple of hours, and through it all, there was Leslie, blithely mingling with her Shiner Bock and her outside voice. Solid alibi . . . should any further suspicions arise.

Now, with everyone either going or gone, I was just trying to work up the gumption to face my journal with the headache drumming behind my eyes. I'd almost rather karaoke . . . Almost. My buzz had definitely faded, and a certain magical journal was once again a blight on my well-ordered life.

As I was prepping myself for the papasan extrication process, Leslie sauntered into my field of vision with a stack of leftover containers. She hovered a moment over the remaining cupcakes on the table before selecting one and peeling back the wrapper. Excellent. Leslie was infinitely more predictable with her mouth full.

I watched, slightly envious, as her eyes closed on that first decadent minty bite. "Mmmph. It was a good crowd tonight. Did you see Ginger up there, braving it out?"

"The redhead? I did." I knew exactly where this was going and figured I'd rather duke it out with the journal, much as I'd been dreading it. I stood awkwardly and haphazardly folded the blanket that had, at least for a little while, been a refuge.

"You can't be a karaoke voyeur forever, Nic."

I heard myself snort, but I refused to take the bait.

"Come on, Nic. Just try it once," Laura urged softly from her crouch beside the karaoke machine.

Before I could respond, Leslie was turning toward me, one hand propped on her jean-clad hip. "It isn't about the singing at all, is it, Nic? I think you can't put yourself out there just for the hell of it and take a chance, go crazy, and have a little fun. Karaoke is not, after all, in 'The Plan.' " She made the air quotes look more like a dance move from "Thriller." "Or maybe you really do suck—I guess we'll never know."

Feeling that this was all a little uncalled for, I simply stared before finally bumbling out with, "You're a real . . . *peach*, Leslie." In my head it came out as "bitch" and felt so right.

"And you're the pit, my dear."

And here we go. . . . Rubbing my arms against the pervasive chill, some of which I knew was mental, I headed for the buffet table to retrieve my stoneware platter on my way back home.

"Ease up, Les," Laura warned.

"I'm just trying to make a point here," Leslie backpedaled. Her voice softened slightly, and a little of the tension eased out of my shoulders. "You're the pit to my peach because while I'm out there on display—for better or worse—you're hiding from everyone, following a preprepared, preemptive, *preposterous* plan that doesn't make room for anything. I'm getting the nicks, the cuts, and the bruises, but I'm also getting the nibbles."

Don't think about it. Don't picture it.

"Nobody's making a cobbler out of you, honey," she tossed off before popping the last of the cupcake into her mouth.

"And the bad news is . . . ?"

"Honestly? You're starting to remind me of Tattoo from *Fantasy Island,* but with you it's 'De *Plan,* de *Plan!*' Let me just say, it's not a good look for you."

I couldn't help it—she had me smiling a little now.

"I say screw 'De Plan,' and have a little fun. Chances are everywhere, Nic. Reach out, grab one by the horns, and ride that baby. Sure, you might be thrown, things could get ugly, but you'll get up with a flush in your cheeks, a smile on your lips, and the courage and confidence to try the next big thing."

"Cowgirl up."

I glanced at Laura and shot her my best "not helping" look.

Leslie stepped closer to me, and there was no escape.

"What about Elizabeth Bennet, hmm?"

Now she had my attention, in a *what the hell?* kinda way. "What about her?" I said warily, a little weirded out at the *P&P* mention, given my current situation.

"*She* was a wild woman, and she ended up with a man women still fantasize about." Overly smug, she snapped the lid on the left-over guacamole.

"A wild woman? *Really?* Are you referring to her snarky attitude, her scandalous walks in the rain, or her refusal to accept a shoddy proposal? Because if that's all it takes to keep you off my back, I can handle any one of those."

"Well, that was plenty two hundred years ago. I hate to tell you, but you've gotta up the ante a little, sweetie." She tried for an apologetic smile, but it slid away from her, pushed out by ill-concealed glee. "Keep your eyes on the prize, chickie."

"I'll see what I can do," I muttered, desperately wanting to add "Mrs. Bennet," but too chicken to pull it off. I grabbed the platter, slid the remaining cupcakes onto the table, and skirted around her on my way toward the gate. "Thanks for a lovely evening."

"Come on, stay for a while, Nic. If you leave now, things will just get awkward." Laura's voice slowed my retreat but didn't halt it.

"Inconceivable," I answered, still moving. Too late . . . things had gone way beyond awkward.

"Start small!" Leslie called after me. "Try sleeping naked tonight! I think it's a safe assumption that that would be new and different." The last part was muttered, but I could hear it ringing through the night air, just like I could feel the grudge starting to build in my chest. Little by little, I was moving away from the color and light, navigating the pavers into darkness.

Confidence bolstered, I called back, "You know . . . Elizabeth Bennet was content simply to be witty and charming. Meeting Mr. Darcy was just a sexy coincidence."

"Oh that we all could have such 'sexy coincidences,' " Leslie drawled, a regular Southern belle. "But you gotta play to win, sweetie. And a couple little changes could make all the difference."

"You are pulling out every cliché in the book," came Laura's murmured reply, but it barely registered.

Mental snapshots of my journal suddenly flashed in my mind like before and after photos, triggered by the echoing finale of Leslie's rousing little pep talk. Heedless of the perils of lumpy lawns and nighttime critters, I ran the rest of the way home, in a sudden manic dread over the possibility of "a couple of little changes" and who or what might have made them. Leslie would assume I was spooked by the very idea of sleeping naked. And with that funky little journal in the house, who could blame me?

The quiet at home was a little creepy, and the fact that my ears were tingling with cold and Leslie's parting words didn't help engender the feeling of normalcy I was really kind of desperate for. Plunking the platter down on the counter, I ignored the blinking message light on my answering machine and squinted toward the bookcase. If I was willing to ride out the metaphor to the point of ridiculousness, imagining that the journal was Mr. Darcy, then was this whole thing somehow my very own sexy coincidence? The possibility was a little bit terrifying, a good clue that maybe I needed to dial back on the *Pride and Prejudice* complex.

It occurred to me that maybe I should come up with some sort of game plan before I braved another look at the journal. Like what to do if nothing had changed versus what to do if *everything* had. But with my mouth drying up and my stomach roiling with nerves and the liquor from the cranberry lemonade, I couldn't think. Strategy eluded me, right along with common sense. I wanted to look . . . but I didn't. I wanted everything to be normal, and yet, perversely, a little mystery held a certain appeal.

Squaring my shoulders, I stepped out of the light in the kitchen and moved into the dimness of the living room. It felt like high noon in an old-time TV Western, except that I was facing down a *word*slinger closer to midnight. My fingers curled in and out of fists, and I gulped big breaths of air, as if I could somehow load up on normal before stepping into a bizarro world of unexplained and unsolicited matchmaking.

I cautiously reached between the preselected cookbooks and snagged the leather-bound volume with my index finger and thumb. Hotfooting it back to the kitchen, I dropped my catch on the table and sat down to face the situation head-on—whatever that might entail. With a burst of courage, I flipped back the cover. The journal's little doorknob thwacked loudly against the table, unleashing a new wave of nerves. So much for all my carefully built-up calm . . . there was no going back now.

Seeing the first page still intact, complete with rewritten journal entry and underlined words, gave me a fleeting moment of confidence—just enough to catch my breath. These words, at least, hadn't disappeared.

Spurred on by my thunderous heartbeat, I cautiously turned the page—and saw only white. Until the few remaining words came clearly into focus. At which point the curse words were falling off my tongue like an avalanche as I started to panic.

I really hadn't expected a second message. *One* could have been written off as a fluke or . . . *something*. But two was a definite situation. Particularly with Leslie off the hook with her airtight alibi.

Willing myself to pull it together, I read the remaining words.

cleavage

is

as   *cleavage*

does

Every bit of tension suddenly came crashing down in the face of sheer ridiculousness. Oh, I was still panicked all right, but at that moment I was simply bowled over by the unpredictability of the situation. There I was, dealing with someone who had the mind-boggling ability to send private messages by erasing selected words in a seemingly unremarkable journal, and he/she chose to use this power to spout off on cleavage and issue a call to romance? It was like I was dealing with a teenage techie with a crush. Although I had to admit, the element of ridiculousness made things feel a little less threatening and more just *odd*. Number one, I had no cleavage worth discussing, and number two, I'd learned long ago that it was impossible to strong-arm a romance because romance was like dandelion fluff, floating out there, everywhere. And while we all chased it, grabbed hold of it, and hated to let it go, it was fickle and flighty—and impervious to even the most careful planning.

The little dandelion analogy had come to me during a particularly loopy marshmallow-crème-by-the-jar sugar high right after the demise of my only really serious relationship. I met Ethan my first year in the MBA program. Like me, he was an engineer with big dreams, but unlike me, he had no plans on how to reach them—zero. I suppose you could say the detailed nature of my Plan (and his inclusion in it) freaked him out a little. As did my "freakish obsession" with Jane Austen—his words. So he'd dumped me, and truly, I'd been a little relieved to be dumped—saved me the trouble of dumping him. I didn't want a guy with no plans—I wanted a guy who had big dreams and the motivation to go after them. After that, romance had gotten postponed indefinitely. And *Pushing Daisies* had taught me that a to-do list wasn't nearly enough. The man I wanted would come with the schematics and tools to hotwire a Norwegian RV. I'd been content to wait.

But clearly someone—or something—wasn't. Someone besides Leslie.

I shivered, both from the chill in the air and the realization that, like it or not, I had a problem . . . a Big Problem.

I stared into the darkness of the living room, my imagination casting me in the starring role of a B-movie thriller. Who knew what was lurking, waiting . . . watching . . . ready to comment.

I stood quickly, the backs of my knees pushing my chair back in a loud screech. I lunged toward the light switch, flipping on the overhead light before tussling with the lamp beside the sofa. Right now I needed lights on and voices of reason. I glanced over at the blinking light on my answering machine and decided to take a chance.

My heart beating wildly, I played the message.

"Hi, Nic, it's Beck. I thought that since the pair of us is in a boyfriend slump—yours by choice, mine, not so much—maybe we could meet up for coffee or go troll for guys. They can all be for me. Call soon or I'll be left to my own devices—not pretty, I warn you."

I let my eyes shutter closed. Beck wasn't exactly a voice of reason, but she was available, and I needed a little distance from the evening's Snowball's Chance in Hell. She answered on the third ring, and I determinedly stepped away from the knife drawer—I wasn't that far gone yet.

"Beck? Hey, it's Nic," I said, plowing over the frog in my throat. "Still want to meet?"

"Definitely! How about Central Market? Good coffee and a full gamut of guys."

"I'm sticking with tea tonight. Meet you in the café in fifteen?"

I didn't respond to the muttered "party pooper" accusation.

Hanging up, I stared down at my generic jeans, nubby sweater,

and ballet flats, getting a "parent or guardian" vibe. In the interest
of avoiding further name-calling, I darted back to my room for a
quick fix, flipping lights on as I went, hurriedly trading my brown
sweater for a sleeker black one and my flats for heeled boots. A
wave of the mascara wand and a slick of lip color, and I was hurry-
ing out the door.

Then I remembered.

The journal was still splayed open on the table with all that
cleavage wisdom gracing its pages. I couldn't just leave it there.
The little Pandora's book definitely needed to be relocated, and
later, we needed to have a few words. Or not. I suppose that was always an option. I slid it back onto the shelf between *Persuasion* and
Sense and Sensibility, figuring that couldn't be any worse than shelving it with the cookbooks.

My life had gone seriously wacko. The whole evening suddenly felt
like a Vaseline-edged dream, and I desperately needed a squeegee.

3

cleavage is as cleavage does

I saw her as soon as I stepped into the café, her wild froth of hair bent over what was undoubtedly a decaf soy mocha something-or-other.

Beck was the intern assigned to me at work, and also, by way of some sweet-talking, my mentee through the University of Texas Women in Engineering Program. I'd signed up for the program last spring, viewing it as one of those great give-back opportunities that fit in nicely with a well-rounded life plan. Honestly, I'd envisioned myself as sort of a big sister, dispensing life advice along with gourmet cupcakes. Beck was content with just the cupcakes—cupcakes were the one thing we had in common, other than our chosen career path.

She had magenta highlights and a sparkly pink nose stud *and* a Weird shirt. Not to mention a healthy interest in all sorts of new-age stuff, a willingness to try anything once, and a never-say-die attitude. She was single-handedly turning the engineering stereotype on its head.

Weaving through the maze of tables, I came up behind her. "I'm gonna go order," I said, thumbing in the direction of the counter. "Back in a sec."

"Yes, ma'am," she said jauntily, glancing up through her lashes at me, her eyes twinkling in amusement.

"Don't make me punish you," I warned, heading for the counter. She knew I hated to be ma'am'd. I ordered a nonfat chai latte and had the barista add a pair of coconut macaroons dipped in dark chocolate to my order before turning back to the table.

Settling myself across from her, I guarded the cookies close and quizzed her. "What's the first rule of being a mentee?"

"Never call your mentor ma'am," she recited in a pseudo-sullen mutter.

"Good girl," I said, handing over the lumpy wax paper sleeve filled with macaroon.

"You're the best! Next time's on me."

Scents of cinnamon, nutmeg, vanilla, and coconut swirled around us in a yummy confluence while the café hummed with nightlife. I quietly sipped my drink and watched Beck forge a plan of attack against her mound of macaroon. I hadn't yet mustered the courage to ask the tough questions: *Do you have to stick your finger up your nose to change the stud? If you take it out while you have a cold, does goo ooze out the hole? What about the hair—why pink?*

Probably best if I didn't. My street cred, what there was of it, would take a definite hit.

Given my train of thought, I had only myself to blame for the trend the conversation eventually took.

Looking me straight, and curiously, in the eye, Beck launched with, "Can I ask you something?"

"Sure."

"Anything?"

Her intensity made me pause, but not for long. I didn't have any skeletons in my closet. My bookshelf maybe . . .

Placing her forearms on the table, she leaned in and quietly asked, "What's going on with your chi?"

"My *chi?*" That was unexpected. "Chi as in *tai*-chi?" Immediately I pictured myself on a hilltop, stretching and reaching, for what I had no idea.

"Minus the tai. Your chi is Chinese-speak for the life force flowing through you. The positive and negative elements should always be in balance. Yours are out of whack."

Direct hit! I could almost hear the air-raid siren. I set my cup down, troubled on two separate levels. Not only was my chi "out of whack," but it was enough out of whack for Beck to notice and address it! This wasn't good.

Feeling like an idiot, I asked, "How can you tell? Do I even want to know?"

"My roommate is into all sorts of stuff: crystals, chakra, tarot. Talitha taught me how to tune in to my own life forces and understand their effect on my world. Occasionally I practice reading other people."

"Awesome." When I realized my mouth was still hanging open, I immediately popped it shut. "So what exactly is my chi telling you?"

"Just that you're out of balance. Something's on your mind—something big—and it's affecting your aura."

"My aura?"

"Very Harry Potter, isn't it?"

"A little, yeah." I sat back, a little weirded out, and picked up my tea, hiding, scanning the café, looking anywhere but at Beck.

"You okay?"

My gaze slid back to her, and I couldn't help but think, *After the evening I've had, "okay" is just a pie-in-the-sky fantasy for me. I'm pretty sure it'll be a while before I'm okay again.*

"I'm just . . . surprised at how dead-on your reading is," I finally answered. Breaking off a bite of cookie, I popped it into my mouth, buying myself some time with a good-manners defense.

"Really?" She seemed very proud of herself. "Awesome. I don't suppose you want to"—she paused to shrug casually—"talk about it?"

My initial reaction was a polite but emphatic "no thanks." I'd known Beck for several months now, and we'd gotten to be friends beyond work and school, but I was supposed to be the *mentor* here, not the lunatic with the *issues*.

But maybe Beck had a karmic or astrological explanation for my situation. Maybe I was standing under the wrong planet rising. At that point, I was willing to listen to anything. And seriously, how judgmental could she afford to be?

I glanced at Beck, who was still peering at me encouragingly, waiting for my decision. Honestly, I was nearly twitching with the urge to let all the pent-up craziness spill out of me.

"I think that maybe I would like to talk about it," I finally admitted, oozing calm. "But it's a little bizarre, so I want to offer you an out—"

"I'm good, so whenever you're ready."

Lowering my cup, I did a quick assessment. She looked good—solid—like maybe she could handle my little nugget of news with no problem. Maybe even solve it for me. So I decided to give it a shot.

She dropped her chin into her raised palms and settled in for a good story.

"I'm just gonna blurt it out," I glanced around, suddenly self-conscious, and lowered my voice, "*quietly*, and we'll go from there. Sound good?"

"Great." She wasn't fazed at all. Evidently I just needed to get on with it.

Eyes closed, fists clenched, deep breath, and go . . .

"I bought a journal at an antiques store down on SoCo and wrote in it last week. I opened it today, and words were missing." I glanced up in the middle of my confession and paused for just the barest second, waiting to see if she was going to stop me or worse, scoff in patent disbelief. But her clear brown eyes were riveted and wide with attention, and her only change of expression was the slight lift of a single eyebrow as she waited for me to continue. I was impressed.

I took another breath and forced myself to speak slowly. "Not all of them are missing. A few are left, scattered around, and they read kind of like a . . . message."

Beck dropped her hands, straightened to perfect posture, and hitched up the corner of her mouth. "Do I get to hear what it is?"

"Um, I suppose so." I took a breath and chickened out. On the second try, I managed to get it out. " 'Miss Nicola James will be sensible and indulge in a little romance.' " I really hoped I hadn't made the wrong call here.

"Whoa! Like a personalized fortune cookie." Her eyes got huge. "The entry you wrote was condensed into that?"

"Right." I nodded and felt like a bobblehead.

She sat back in her chair and bit her lip, her eyes bright with possibilities I probably didn't even want to consider. I wondered if I should push my luck and mention entry number two and its hints about cleavage. None of this was mentor material.

Beck leaned casually forward and asked, "Is there more?"

"Um, yeah." That's all it took to get her hunkered down for the rest.

Her reaction was unfathomable.

"Aren't you the slightest bit fazed by all this?"

She shrugged. "There's obviously an explanation."

"Really?" I was suddenly on the edge of my chair, quivering with anticipation.

"It's magic."

My whole body slumped. I did *not* need to hear that. "Thanks, Luna Lovegood—that clears things right up." It came out a bit sharper than I'd intended. "Sorry. I guess you could say I'm not quite so open-minded."

"Well, what's your take on things?"

"My take is that magic is for prime-time specials and Las Vegas shows—none of it is actually real. There's always an explanation, a trick, a sleight of hand. I'm missing something—*I must be*—and tomorrow I'm going back to that antiques store to grill the shop owner for any useful information." I wasn't about to tell her that my confidence in this plan of action was waning with each missing word.

Beck slapped her hands palms down on the table, making little flakes of coconut jump and our drinks slosh in their cups. Her eyes flared with excitement. "When? When are you going to do that?"

"Around lunchtime."

"Can I come? Do you mind?"

Slightly baffled by her exuberance, but not opposed to having her tag along, I shook my head and offered, "Sure. You'll have to meet me, though—I'll be coming from work."

"Well, that sucks."

"Hell, yeah it does." I was *beyond* tired of going above and beyond.

"Okay," she enthused, "how about I meet you around one? We can get lunch, come up with a strategy before we go in."

"We need a strategy?" I was well on my way to being thoroughly gobsmacked.

"Well, this isn't exactly *Lord of the Rings*, but I think a little pre-planning would be good. Has the student suddenly become the master?" she teased.

"Okay, just so you know, strategizing is tough when you're in denial. In case you hadn't noticed, 'My Precious' is sort of throwing me off my game."

I couldn't decide who was crazier—Beck for coming up with the analogy or me for running with it.

"So, we need a strategy," she concluded. "Let me hear the rest of the story."

"I'll give you the condensed version." I paused before revealing, "I wrote back." Beck's eyes widened considerably at this little tidbit. "Earlier tonight. Then I was gone for three hours, and I got another fortune." I paused out of sheer embarrassment and then laid it on her. " 'Cleavage is as cleavage does.' "

Beck clapped a hand over her mouth, and with her eyes twinkling, it abruptly occurred to me that the little traitor was laughing! This was sooo not laughable. I propped my elbow on the table and covered my eyes with my hand. Oh, but it was. If this was happening to anyone else, it would be incontrovertibly hilarious. I made myself promise not to hold a grudge. But I did spear her with a glare.

"That is just so unbelievably cool. Not to mention ironic."

Curious, I lifted an eyebrow.

"That out of all the weird souls in Austin, you'd be the one to end up with a fairy godmother." She chuckled to herself.

That got my attention. "A fairy godmother? Get serious." I made a point of rolling my eyes for Beck's benefit.

She sat back in her chair and crossed her arms over her chest. "Uh-huh. And what's your *serious* explanation for all this?"

She had me there. I straightened my spine and scraped away imaginary crumbs, refusing to meet her eyes. "I haven't hit on a legitimate explanation yet. Right now, I'm still gathering data."

"You mean writing in your magical journal and waiting for your fairy godmother to answer?"

"I wouldn't describe my procedure in precisely that way, but . . ."

Now it was Beck's turn at the eye-rolling. But before I could counter, she had leaned forward, widened her eyes, and begun speaking in an urgent undertone. "Don't you get it? It makes perfect sense. Your journal is obviously magical—what other explanation is there—*seriously?* And who else but a fairy godmother would be giving you romantic advice? Think of her as a modern-day, matchmaking Jane Austen—Jane Austen in *Austin—Fairy* Jane? Given your obsession with her, this is like the mother ship calling you home."

I was momentarily struck dumb, but I rallied. "*That* makes perfect sense? Really? No offense, but speaking as your mentor, not to mention your boss, I'm not exactly getting a warm fuzzy here."

She inched back off the table and held her hands up, palms out. "Okay, fine. Let's pretend I didn't say anything. Let's pretend that you don't have a magical journal with a fairy godmother, and she's certainly not Fairy Jane." She tipped her eyes down casually and nonchalantly inquired, "Have you had a chance to try it out yet, see if it works?"

I stared at her with squinty eyes, giving no thought to the wrinkles surely sprouting on my forehead. "Try what out?"

"The advice!"

"Are you *kidding* me?" I lowered my voice, sparing a glance for the café's other patrons, wondering if they'd already gotten an earful, feeling just crazy enough to take them all into my confidence and hammer out a strategy right here, right now.

"What?" she shot back.

"Taking the advice *definitely* isn't part of my strategy."

"Aha! So you *have* thought strategy!" Before I could respond to this, she was off again.

"Seriously, Nic, what's to lose?"

"My identity as a sensible, rational human being?"

"It won't be lost. Just sprinkled with a little fairy dust."

God, I hoped she was teasing. But I felt the need to clarify. "Except that I don't believe in fairy dust. Or fairy-tale endings. Or magic in general. This journal is throwing a major kink in the works."

"Maybe it's supposed to—maybe that's exactly what you need, a little kink." She winked and then looked around behind her toward a table shared by three grungy college guys cramming for something. She then peeked over her other shoulder at a man alone in a suit, poring over his PDA and sipping an espresso. When she turned back, she whispered, "Pull your sweater open a little at the neck."

Certain I'd misunderstood, I leaned forward against the table, eyebrows raised, and murmured, "What?"

"Try to show a little more skin." She dusted some bits of coconut off her fingertips and then proceeded to reach across the table to deal with my sweater herself.

I slapped her hand away, wondering how the conversation had spiraled so completely out of control.

I leaned in farther and whispered harshly, "I am *not* taking cleavage advice from a journal, a nonexistent fairy godmother, or you. Speaking of which—"

I glanced up to see the PDA guy moving past our table. He was looking down at me, and I met his friendly grin with a distracted one of my own before turning my attention back to Beck.

Her eyebrow was winged up, and her smile was definitely smug. She shifted her gaze from my face to my chest, and I let mine follow. Sitting there, boosted up and pushed together by my hunch over the table and partially exposed by my recently adjusted sweater, my bogus cleavage was on display. Perfect.

Tipping my no doubt ruby red face back up to glare at a grinning Beck, I felt an urgent need to get back on familiar ground. Yanking my sweater closed, I decided to play the mentor card.

I sat back and shifted my shoulders primly. "Have you decided what you want to do over the summer—work, school . . . both?"

Beck's eyes went from fantasy to reality in a single blink.

"I was thinking I'd stay at Micro." Her voice sounded vaguely flat, but I hardly noticed. Not only was I excited that she wanted to stay on over the summer, but I was thoroughly relieved we were no longer talking about road-testing the journal's advice or fairy godmothers. Definitely a plus.

"I was hoping you'd say that." I grinned at her. "I'll need to get final approval from David, but I can't imagine them letting you go. Do you think you might want to transition to another project—try something new?"

"Yes, ma'am." Her voice had flattened further—like roadkill— and she was glaring at me, breaking Rule #1 on purpose.

I glared right back. And then, ever so slowly, her eyebrow creeped up, as if to say, *what's it gonna be?*

Hell.

I slumped down against the table, saw one of the frat boys turn in our direction, and jerked myself erect, now totally self-conscious, thanks to my pimp of a mentee.

"Can't we discuss any mentee-related topics?"

"Like minty-fresh breath? An absolute must for those romantic indulgences!"

"You're teasing me? I just told you the biggest, weirdest secret I've ever told anyone, and now you're teasing me?"

"Maybe a little. Does that bother you? Because I can *not* do that." Her mouth quirked up at the side and her eyes twinkled.

"*Can you?* I wonder." I dredged up a smile and took a deep steadying breath. "Okay, well, I'm done chatting about Jane Austen and J.R.R. Tolkien, so unless you have another topic in mind . . ."

She shook her head in the negative. "Nothing that could come close to this."

I checked my watch—just past eleven. "There's a sandwich shop down on SoCo—"

"Jo's? Definitely, let's meet there—perfect vibe."

"O-kay." I couldn't help but wonder what constituted a perfect vibe for *Lord of the Rings*–style strategizing over a magical journal. I guess I'd find out. "Jo's it is. I'll bring the journal." I crumpled up my wax paper sleeve, ready to pack it in.

She nodded, clearly delighted with the arrangement, and we walked toward the exit, tossing our trash in the bin by the door.

The trees in the parking lot were underlit by spotlights and seemed vaguely otherworldly. With a shiver, I turned back to Beck.

"Thanks for calling. It feels weird to have said any of that out loud, but I'm glad I talked to you, even if your idea of 'perfect sense' is a bit loco. At least you didn't freak."

She laughed. "That makes one of us. Just consider the possibility . . . And by all means carry on with the data collection. I'll expect full deets tomorrow: What *you* said, what *she* said. . . ." Her head was tipping back and forth, and the sparkly pink star in her nose was winking at me. She shooed me away. "Go home! And write juicy," she called back over her shoulder.

I rolled my eyes in the dark, deciding I wasn't a big fan of surreal. I'd had a mind-numbingly normal day until words had disappeared from my journal and my intern/mentee had announced that they'd been stolen away by a fairy godmother channeling the spirit of Jane Austen. And there was no end in sight, because as self-appointed sidekick, the mind-blowing Mulder to my strait-laced Scully, Beck was very likely going to crazy up my day tomorrow too. At this point, it was unclear—at least to me—which of us was the protégé in this fledgling relationship. I worried what that meant for the future.

4

In which "enchanted" collides with "not so enchanted"

Alone in my kitchen, I dropped into a chair, positioned the journal in front of me, and considered Beck's parting words, trying hard not to think about her other, "fairy" words. Juicy. She thought I should write juicy. She should know by now that my life was about as juicy as a prune. I was, however, exasperated to the hilt and not above responding to the journal's latest little gem of wisdom with a certain amount of snark.

Rummaging through the assortment of quirky writing implements stuffed into an oversized mug on the kitchen counter, I pulled out my black fine-line permanent pen. Wouldn't want to make things too easy for little Fairy Jane.

Cleavage is as cleavage does, huh?

Normally I'd feel ridiculous speaking this whole thing aloud, but in this situation, I couldn't seem to help myself.

Just for the fun of it, just for a moment, let's pretend that I have cleavage. In that case, I might possibly make a tiny effort to decipher this mysterious bit of wonky "wisdom." But since, in reality, it's a nonissue, I'm not gonna worry about it.

And just for your clarification and future reference, I'm not a lesbian, not even experimental, nor do I have plans for men in my near future, which is why I'm going to the wedding alone. That way I get cake but not complications. I think we might have gotten off on the wrong foot here— I'm not cleavage obsessed—I'm not. It's just a fact of life that in dealings with my boobs, right is right, and left is left, and never the twain shall meet.

I figured I should be totally honest—this *was* my journal, after all, like it or not.

But if I were looking for "a little romance" . . . I do have some standards, one of which is that if a guy is focused in at chest level, I'm through with him from the get-go (and he's probably through with me too). Just sayin' . . .

P.S. Who are you?

That last part just slipped off the tip of my permanent pen, so there was no getting rid of it now. No doubt it would disappear by morning.

Then again, maybe I'd get an answer.

Don't get me wrong, I was still sensibly opposed to chalking this craziness up to a fairy godmother, but it didn't escape me that viable, logical explanations weren't exactly lining up. And Jane Austen? Gimme a break!

Beck expected me to buy into the idea that Jane Austen herself was dishing out kooky romantic advice in my living room, nearly two hundred years outside her realm of expertise? That this magical *Austenesque* journal had somehow slipped through the fingers of collectors, historians, literary buffs, and Mr. Darcy devotees to find its way into a little antiques shop in Austin, Texas?

That last bit gave me pause. Weirder things had very probably happened in this town, I just didn't know about them. And honestly, that made a world of difference.

I shook my head, trying, I suppose, to make sure the crazy didn't take hold. Tipping the journal closed, I let my fingers and eyes rove over the worn cover, the scuffed and barely stained pages, and the tarnished hardware. Suddenly remembering the inscription, I flipped open the cover and reread the careful script lettering.

"*. . . I dedicate to You the following Miscellanious Morsels, convinced that if you seriously attend to them, You will derive from them very important Instructions, with regard to your Conduct in Life.*"

Okay, maybe they had a little bit of a Jane Austen vibe. But even if I caved and allowed for the *possibility* that just *maybe* some sort of Jane Austen–inspired fairy godmother had taken my journal hostage, it didn't change anything.

Okay, maybe that was delusional. Rephrase: I didn't plan on taking any advice or falling under anyone's spell. No matter how many times I'd lost myself in The Collected Works, or lusted after Darcy and Knightley on page and screen, that didn't give *Fairy Jane* a right to interfere in my life. The fact that I owned a copy of *Dating with Jane Austen as Your Wing Woman* and had tried shoe-horning more than one date into an Austen character type was immaterial. I hadn't signed up for this. I wasn't wired for this. And it was starting to show.

And yet, even imagining the *possibility* that the voice in the journal belonged to Jane Austen had gone a long way toward vanquishing my B-movie fears. I felt like I could treat the situation more like a weird mystery—or a funky BBC adaptation. The ominous feeling had dissipated slightly, to be replaced by a sense of doubtful wonder.

Quite honestly, I could have used a little magical interference in my relationship with Ethan. I would have fought it tooth and nail on principle, but if I'd somehow been railroaded into submission, it could have had its advantages. By the time I'd pegged Ethan for a Willoughby—thoroughly too good to be true—he'd pegged me as obsessive-compulsive and we were done. All those plans, wasted . . .

I shook myself free of thoughts of Ethan once again and drummed my fingers on the cover of the journal, certain this was not the same sort of situation at all. Ethan hadn't been hand-picked by a journal, and our relationship hadn't been strong-armed into submission—I'd picked him and made a mistake. It wasn't like I was all out of chances—it was still my choice, and I wasn't giving in to magic *or* a legendary reputation.

Had I really let go of logic in favor of a fairy tale? Was I just willing to accept that I'd somehow stumbled over a fairy god-mother, and this was the sum total of our relationship—cryptic, mildly offensive communications regarding my profoundly unro-mantic life? Seriously, where were the perks that typically came with fairy godmothers? A *prearranged* wave of the wand here or there, and I might be able to get on board—after a requisite freak-out period. But this? This was sucker-punching me when I was al-ready down for the count. It was bad enough that my Plan was under fire, but by magic? Fairies? That was just cruel and unusual.

I carted the journal down the hall to my room, with a vague plan of keeping an eye on it while keeping it away from my bookshelf and any questionable influences.

Five minutes later, I'd crawled into bed in a T-shirt and boxers, my toes curled up in garishly purple chenille socks and the journal clutched in my right hand.

I closed my eyes and tried to relax, tried to pretend it was any other normal Friday.

That little exercise proved an utter impossibility. My very lim-ited imagination was already under a huge amount of strain, and I worried if I pushed it much more I might crack under the pressure.

So I gave in a little. Settled against the propped pillows, my bedside lamp glowing golden, I tried to imagine an enchanted world where fairy godmothers existed with magic wands and fairy dust up their sleeves. Brownies were the solid, chocolaty base of the food pyramid, my A-cups overfloweth, and roaches worked like Roombas. I felt my lips curling into a smile as I imagined the impossible, but that entire impossible world disappeared in an in-stant as my eyes flashed open, and I remembered that it wasn't the imagining but the *believing* that got you into trouble.

I glanced down at the journal, still tucked innocently in my hand . . . the ultimate troublemaker in my once well-ordered life. What was going on in there?

Ominous horror-movie music suddenly screeched in my head, and I panicked. Wrenching open the journal, fumbling with its pages, I hurried to find my latest entry: the one about to go under the knife (or rather, the magical, mystical eraser). My heart was still pumping full throttle as my eyes flew over the page.

I slumped back against the pillow in a cathartic funk. Nothing had changed—yet. And yet, it suddenly seemed as if everything had.

This situation would be mind-blowing to someone who believed in the typical, arm-waving magical chicanery. But to a nonbeliever, a card-carrying skeptic, this went far beyond the realm of incredible, past preposterous and even inconceivable, all the way out to unthinkable. But like it or not, it was happening. As a huge fan of All Things Jane, you'd think I'd be thrilled. I wasn't—not at all. I was skittish and restless and just a little bit nervous about having this book in bed with me.

I woke up with my fingers brushing the journal's key plate and an undeniable need to pee. Crossing my legs under the covers, I flipped open the journal and squinted against the daylight streaming in through the sheer curtains on my bedroom window.

Rather predictably, my paragraph—my *permanent ink* paragraph—had disappeared, all that was left a few scattered words:

have your cake but meet him too

I huffed out the breath I'd been holding, a little vague on whether I was disappointed or relieved—I couldn't say I wasn't expecting this. The cheeky matchmaker was obviously here to stay, and it seemed she had no qualms about horning in on Tooth Fairy territory. Thank God I hadn't taken Leslie's advice and slept naked. I felt a shiver run through me and watched as goose bumps flared up all over my skin. *Try not to think about it—focus on the message.*

But what the hell? *Have your cake but meet him too?* Color me clueless. Still, I had to admit, if I was going to follow any of this journal's wacky advice, this was as good a Morsel as any, seeing as I didn't exactly need a reason to have cake. The "meet him too" part could get sticky, but seeing as it was anonymous—just a pronoun with no specifics—it seemed perfectly doable. Surely I'd meet someone at some point . . . somewhere.

I wasn't planning on jumping through hoops to earn brownie points with whoever was hiding in there, trying to call the shots like the Great and Powerful Oz. My life, my Plan was good just the way it was—I didn't need any help, romantic or otherwise.

The cake would be an experiment . . . and an overture. And if I was lucky, it would get me one step closer to solving this problem. I was *desperate* to understand what was happening here, and the fact that I was getting thwarted and outsmarted at every turn was turning the whole mess into a vendetta of sorts. I couldn't give up on this journal until I figured a few things out. After that, I'd have no qualms about severing our connection.

I gazed down at the journal, smirking slightly. Almost immediately I remembered I was nowhere . . . with no clues or leads other than cake. And perhaps a mystery man.

So much for my theory on advice by association. The journal had been tucked in with me last night, far from the influence of The Collected Works and the rest of my bookshelf, and still I was feeling an Austen vibe with this latest little snippet of advice—in fact, the voice in my head had read it with a British accent. If Fairy Jane was, in fact, the wit behind this little prank, then it was worth noting that she'd ignored my attempt to get acquainted.

Slapping the book closed and leaving it on the bed, I hurried into the bathroom, wishing I could leave it stashed at home today. No such luck. Seeing as it was Exhibit A at the antiques shop, it was going to ride shotgun and join Beck and me for a lunch of strategizing. It was going to have to wait in the car while I was at work, though.

* * *

Work was a waste of a perfectly lovely spring Saturday morning, but by noon, I was done. Desperate for a little fresh air and sunshine, I packed up quickly, blowing bubbles with a piece of bubblegum I found in my top desk drawer. Wending my way through the empty maze of darkened cubicles leading inexorably to the main hallway and the stairs down to the lobby, I opted for a quick detour. Instead of turning left toward the exit, I dodged right, helpless against the heady lure of a secret crush.

Ignoring the fact that I was already running late for my lunch with Beck, I followed the much-trodden path to his corner cubicle three rows over and six cubes down from mine. As I'd hurried out the door that morning, I'd paused a second to tear yesterday's page off the calendar. Today's quote, coming on the heels of the latest journal excerpt, had sent a nervous shiver running through me: " 'Something must and will happen to throw a hero in her way.' *Northanger Abbey*." I figured it couldn't hurt to throw myself in the way of a hero . . . or at least stop by his cubicle.

Brett Tilson. The Mr. Knightley of my imagination: self-assured, serious-minded, and sexy. I stared silently at the name plaquette Velcroed on the cubicle's outside wall and indulged in a little junior high style merging of his last name with my first, then moved on to a very adult curiosity about all the other merging that would necessarily go on if things between us were ever to move beyond a casual hallway hello. I may have been resigned to stalking, at least for right now, but I was willing to let my imagination tango.

Within seconds, I'd blown a whopper of a bubble that had begun swaying slightly in the chilly gust from a nearby air-conditioning vent. And then I heard the faintest creak. Blinking myself back to reality, I froze. My lungs stopped working, leaving the bubble trapped as Brett's head tipped back over the top of his office chair to look out into the hallway. The second his eyes locked on mine, the fragile, rosy pink bubble popped, leaving me to deal with the sticky spread of goo now covering my nose and lips. Lovely.

"Uh, sorry about that, Nic. Were you looking for me?"

His eyes, chips of sea glass rimmed by sexy tortoiseshell frames, were curious and slightly amused. And the rest of him was equally yummy. Too yummy. In the back of my mind I heard the silence dragging on and on.

What's the right answer here? I didn't come to see him—I came to see his cubicle. To hang out for a minute by myself and just imagine future possibilities. But I can't admit to that! And if I tell him I came to see him, what's my reason? Dammit! Why must my timing always be so shitty?

"Hey . . . Brett. No, not looking." Imagining how ridiculous I looked with bubblegum pink smeared across my face spurred me into a frenzy of dabbing and scraping. But without a mirror it was like a tactile game of Marco Polo. "I was just wandering." I aimed a rueful smile in his direction. "I just finished up on the test floor, and I'm overdue for some fresh air."

"I think I'm done for the day too. Wanna grab some lunch?" He stood and moved to the doorway of his cubicle, sliding his hands deep into his pockets.

The words "sensible romance" suddenly lit up in my head like a Las Vegas marquee. I seriously hoped they weren't shining through so that Brett could read them on my forehead. I squelched the words and consciously did not think about cleavage. "Sure!" I finally blurted. "That sounds good! I'm up for anything." Well, that just sounded desperate. Then I remembered. "Oh, no, wait! I can't! I'm meeting someone." It wasn't at all difficult to look apologetic.

He nodded in polite understanding.

"A girl . . . er . . . a woman," I added lamely.

"Oh—okay."

Oh God. Did he just peg me as a lesbian? Damn Leslie and her brain-washing potlucks.

"It's not a date," I hastily assured him, grinning slightly as I held up my hand to halt any conclusion-jumping that might be going on. "She's interning here—you might have met her. Rebecca Connelly."

"Don't think so," he answered, keeping his eyes trained on me while propping one drool-worthy shoulder against the metal cubicle support.

"Rain check?" Still me: talking, grasping . . . for *anything*.

"Sure."

"Great," I agreed, nodding as I moved closer to toss my gum into the trash can behind him before stepping back with a choppy wave. "Okay, well, bye."

He caught me the first time I looked back but not the second. And by the time I'd reached the car, I was feeling downright resentful toward Jane Austen of the Journal. Her ridiculous little scraps of fortune-cookie wisdom had started an avalanche of insanity in my life. I could no longer seem to function as a normal person.

As I shifted the car into gear, it occurred to me that there was a good chance Brett would be at the wedding . . . *have your cake but meet him too* . . . That I could definitely do. With pleasure. But on my own terms, and not for the brownie points. If her advice just happened to mesh with my own, admittedly farther-flung, intentions, I wasn't about to restrategize out of spite. And if it didn't, well, it was all in the interpretation.

Apparently I was destined to be late for dealings with Beck. When I finally snagged a parking spot and swung into Jo's, the journal tucked carefully away in my bag, Beck was perusing the menu in all her DayGlo glory. Today she was wearing a bright orange T-shirt hyping some university engineering event, white cargo pants, and deep purple Converse hightops with turquoise laces.

"So?" Beck's enthusiasm, far from being contagious, was actually a little overwhelming. I had to keep reminding myself that she was still a relatively new friend—who knew my biggest, weirdest, wildest secret. The jury was still out on the wisdom of that decision.

"Yeah?" I said, pulling out a chair, playing coy. I mean, what else could she have been asking about?

"Is that gum in your hair?"

I quickly raised both hands to search for bubble remnants, but Beck had already moved on, shaking her head to dislodge that particular curiosity before demanding, "Did you get a reply?" I could see the whites of her eyes *and* her clenched teeth.

"Yep—I'm the victim of another excerpting."

Having subsisted on only a breakfast bar for the last four hours, I was now starving, scanning the menu choices as I worked my fingers through my short, straight locks, hoping to find the rogue piece of bubble gum. Beck tugged gently on my jacket sleeve, but knowing she only wanted the "deets," I put her off in favor of ordering first. Still, it was only a matter of time before we were facing each other over our gourmet sandwiches.

"Still waiting . . . ," she reminded me in a singsong voice, draping her napkin in her lap and lifting her eyebrow in voyeuristic encouragement.

I smiled. I had to concede, at least a little, that her optimism truly was contagious and that confiding in her seemed to make everything less creepy, even marginally thrilling. "It said, 'have your cake but meet him too,' " I admitted before taking a huge bite of my roast beef.

Beck slumped in her chair, seemingly baffled by this latest snippet. "Okay, I love cake as much as the next girl, but it's not the stuff of journaling—no offense." I shrugged, not the slightest bit offended—it totally depended on the cake. Beck pressed on. "And who's 'him'? Whoever he is, there's your juicy, right there." She took a halfhearted bite of her tomato basil with cheese and chewed thoughtfully.

I figured I should probably clue her in. "I have a wedding to go to tonight. It's a coworker's, and I'm going 'stagette.' " I added the air quotes. "I've mentioned it—and cake, obviously—in my entries."

This new information immediately revived Beck's spark and spirit, and she managed to talk almost nonstop about possibilities and intentions—all in the same vein as last night—while I polished off half my sandwich.

"This is a big clue. Way to go—you aced the homework!" I offered up an amused smile as she reached across the table and gave my arm an exuberant squeeze. "I don't suppose you want a 'plus one' cramping your loner status, huh?'" Her expression was suggestive but resigned to the inevitable—she knew she wouldn't be tagging along. I shook my head, trying to appear marginally apologetic. "Not to mention sending out a lesbian vibe," she added, with a pointed look. "You'll fill me in later, right? I'm not above stalking."

Evidently something else we had in common.

"If there's anything to tell, you're first on my list." And coincidentally last too.

"Uh-uh," she said, metronoming her finger. "There is no 'if.' There's definitely gonna be stuff to tell, girl, and I want to hear it. Deal?"

"Okay, deal," I agreed with a laugh, seriously wondering if I should just let her tag along and be done with it. That idea got immediately squelched as I realized she would be the voice of insanity, whispering in my ear, prompting me, nudging me into who-knows-what. My guess would be a bout of speed-dating with a side of cleavage. No, thank you.

And besides, wouldn't Beck's presence be tempting fate or flying in the face of a fairy godmother? I was sufficiently out of my element here to be worried about this.

While Beck caught up on her sandwich, I let myself imagine how different lunch with Brett would have been. I fully intended to cash in on that rain check I'd written myself ASAP.

"Okay!" Done with her sandwich, Beck rubbed her hands together over her plate, clearly itching to strategize. "Let's get down to business. What's the plan?"

"We go in, I produce the journal, quiz the shopkeeper on its provenance, and then we skedaddle."

Beck's eyebrows turned down in disapproval at my apparent lack of imagination.

"What if she wants to look through it? Or wonders why you want more information? What if she's shifty-eyed and suspicious?"

"Or twirling the tips of her roguish mustache? I guess we'll just have to wing it then."

"That's not much of a strategy," she mumbled, her lower lip jutting out a little.

"What can I say? *This* part of the situation seems pretty cut and dried. But I'm open to other ideas. *Reasonable* ideas." It was always best to clarify.

Beck feigned affronted attitude for all of two seconds before her expression switched comically to "Oh my God!" Her eyes widened and her lips curved into a giddy smile. "I just realized—you've got the journal with you, don't you? Can I see it?" Her tone was tentative rather than demanding, and although I felt my heart rate kick up into a steady, thumping rhythm, I figured, what the hell? There were no remaining secrets, as far as Beck was concerned. So, wiping my hands on my napkin, I pulled it out and handed it over.

Beck shoved her plate away and scoured the table with a fresh napkin in preparation for her chance at the journal. She took it reverently, carefully fingering the edges with neat, square-tipped, metallic blue-painted nails before laying it gently on the table. With nothing to say and an unfamiliar clutch in my chest, I started in on the other half of my sandwich. No regrets. I was glad I'd told her—glad I'd picked her specifically. This secret was too overwhelming to hold alone, and she was the perfect foil for my cynicism.

She took her time, clearly savoring this opportunity, running her fingers over the key plate and knob, the covers, inside and out, and then each individual page, lingering over the ones left with fortune-cookie wisdom. Having been through the very same process myself, although admittedly with more frantic fingers, I could tell she was searching for clues. Just as I knew she wouldn't find any. They simply weren't there. And, oh, was that bugging me!

"Amazing. I sooo want one of these. You, my friend, are going to be the stuff of urban legend." It was clear I had just gone up a notch in Beck's estimation. I kept chewing; she gushed on.

"What if this is like *The Last Mimzy,* but instead of being a device to communicate with an alien culture, maybe you're communicating with the past, channeling the matchmaking genius of Jane

Austen! Or what if this is one of those 'artifacts' collected by the government and stashed in a warehouse in South Dakota, like that show on the SyFy channel. Or remember *The Gods Must Be Crazy*, with the Coke bottle that dropped out of the sky and changed everything. . . ."

"Okay, I get it," I said, holding my hands up to derail Beck's runaway train of thought. "Hollywood loves crazy, unexplained phenomena."

"You think there might be another one, a little matched set?" She shot me a mischievous smile. "Which shop was it?"

I answered just as my eyes finished rolling. "Violet's Crown Antiques, just a couple of blocks down on the other side of the street from here. Self-professed 'Purveyors of Curious Goods.' Truer words . . ."

"So you don't think she has another one? Well, then maybe you'll let me borrow this one after you 'have your cake but meet him too.' I can wait until the romance really gets going." Little smart aleck.

"How can you possibly need any help in this department?"

"I think it's the pink—and maybe the stud. I think it scares off the nerds, and I *adore* nerds."

"Who doesn't?" I agreed.

As I watched Beck pore over the journal, I fantasized about the many nerdy facets of Mr. Brett Tilson.

The walk to Violet's Crown Antiques was quick and in the thick of Austin "Weirdness," and the closer we got, the more I worried. Beck was wired, but relaxed enough for window shopping, whereas I was tense and fidgety, not at all ready for any more surprises.

"You ready, Mulder?" We were steps away from the shop, the source of my personal X-File, and I figured Beck would thrill at the chance to be typecast as the weird detective.

"Lead the way, Scully," she said with a grin.

I pulled on the brass door handle and thought to add, "How about I do the talking on this one?"

No answer.

A little bell echoed from some mysterious spot in the back as I walked through a mind-boggling mix of goods just as likely to have been fished from someone's trash as culled from an estate sale. I made my way toward a makeshift counter in the middle of the store. Lavender was thick in the air, vying with the smells of dust and old age. I smiled at the chignoned shop owner, reaching into my bag and fishing out my one-of-a-kind find. I held the journal face out, the fancy little hardware on display, hoping to spark a memory.

"I bought this journal here a couple of weeks ago. It was on the table with some old novels and brass candle snuffers . . . ?" Her only reaction was to lift the reading glasses hanging from a chain around her neck and settle them on her nose. "I'm not, by any means, knowledgeable about antiques, but this little book seems like it's something special." Talk about your understatements. "I confess, my curiosity is piqued, and I wondered if you could tell me anything about it—where you got it, any history, anything . . . special?"

I turned my head slightly, my eyes darting around in their search for Beck.

"I'm surprised I remember it." The words had me whipping my eyes back around to focus on the shop owner. "But I do. It was a bit of a stowaway, tucked in the drawer of a lovely boudoir table I purchased from an elderly bachelor over in Fredericksburg during Trade Days."

A muffled noise from Beck, behind me and a little to the right, had me shooting her a curious glance. She was petting a stuffed and smiling armadillo that was poised over a backgammon board with one white chip clutched in its claws. I turned back, smiling to smooth over the interruption, fairly drooling for more information.

The shopkeeper dragged her disapproving gaze from Beck and refocused it on me before finally shifting it down to settle on the journal. "As it was empty and rather nondescript, I assumed the seller wouldn't quibble to have it back."

She, in turn, hadn't quibbled about selling it to me for ten dollars.

"Could you tell me the approximate age of the table?" Not that it mattered—the journal could easily be older or newer—but I felt compelled to come away with a little something more than a stowaway that had escaped a bachelor in Fredericksburg.

"I dated it as early 1920s."

"What about the man? Do you keep records of that sort?"

"I assume you're not referring to his age," she inquired drily.

"No! No, no, no. Well, honestly, anything you can tell me might be helpful," I backpedaled.

"Surely there's little to tell about a small blank book." She was clearly puzzled—and cranky. I could see the tight little lines around her lips, where coral lipstick was fanning into a prickly mess.

Instinctively, I slid the journal under my arm, shielding it from view.

Tripping forward on the exposed end of a rolled-up carpet stashed behind a pair of French-looking chairs, Beck materialized beside me and blurted, "We were actually wondering if you had anything else like it, stashed in another drawer somewhere."

I jabbed my elbow into her side and smiled my friendliest trust-me smile. "She's joking." I stepped forward, hoping to draw the woman's doubtful eyes away from Beck. "I'd just like to talk to the gentleman in Fredericksburg. All I'd need is his name and number . . . ?"

"It's not really our policy."

"Just this once? As a 'Purveyor of Curious Goods,' you have to sympathize with someone curious about the goods, right?" Beck had stepped forward once again to present this ingenious argument, but the Purveyor was not impressed. In fact, she was frowning.

"This is highly irregular, and while I won't give out contact information, I will call and briefly inquire about the book. Who knows? He may even ask to have it returned to him." Now she smirked, and I had to dig deep to keep from sticking my tongue out.

Climbing down off her stool, her lips set in a disapproving line, she moved to the other side of the wraparound counter, her sensible heels clicking on the painted concrete flooring. Beck and I exchanged a quick low five and some facial acrobatics as she tapped away on the shop's computer. When she lifted the phone to dial, I gestured wildly to Beck to move closer and scam the name and number from the computer screen. Miraculously, Beck's awkward lunge away from the counter and subsequent tussle with an umbrella stand went unnoticed as the Purveyor replaced the phone in its cradle and turned grimly back to me.

"I'm sorry," she said, clearly anything but. "There was no answer." Her smile was so brittle I was afraid it might shatter. Clearly we wouldn't be getting any more help from her. At least not on the up-and-up.

With a quickly tossed-off thank you, I grabbed Beck's arm and pulled her toward the door, exerting a determined yank when she reached for the top volume of a stack of scuffed-up books near the door.

"What?" she demanded, after the door had swung shut behind us. "Why couldn't we stay and look?" She dusted her hands on her rear end, and I reached into my purse in search of antibacterial gel.

"I think it's a pretty safe bet she doesn't have another one, Beck." I offered her a squirt. "Armadillos are filthy," I said by way of explanation.

"A little wishful thinking never hurt anyone, Nic. Remember that," she said, holding her hand out.

"I'd like to see some proof," I countered, taking a precautionary squirt for myself. The pair of us walked down the sidewalk, rubbing our hands together like a pair of evil geniuses with a plan. Mwa-ha-ha.

"So," I prompted, "did you get the number?"

Beck tapped her temple. "Ten digits, all accounted for. Got a piece of paper?"

I reached back into my purse and pulled out a cherry red Moleskine notebook, handing it over along with a ballpoint pen.

"His name is Elijah Nelson," she said, handing back notebook and pen. "When are we gonna call him?"

Suddenly I felt a compelling need to ground us both in a little

reality. "You know he may be the next step in this spontaneous little scavenger hunt, but I have a feeling he's also the dead end. And
then that's it, it's over, because he's our only lead."

We walked in silence for a few steps, and then Beck dipped her
voice James Earl Jones low and intoned, "There is another," then
adding, "Nic, I am your mentee." I turned to look at her, a dubious
smile curving my lips. Apparently we'd moved on from *Lord of the
Rings* to *Star Wars*. She bumped her shoulder against mine and
cryptically suggested, "And it's totally up to you whether this
'other lead' fizzles or not."

"I don't get it."

"*You're* the other lead, Nic. The magic is meant for you. The
question is, are you going to do anything about it? Are you going to
follow this lead, take the advice, go crazy, and have a little adventure?" Before I could respond, she was at it again. "It's lookin' like
there's probably no logical explanation. You can admit that, right?"
I nodded halfheartedly in agreement, still fervently wishing for a
miracle. "So, you'd have to believe a little, take the whole mind-
blowing situation on faith. Can you do that? Because if you can't,
you're wasting it—the journal and your chance at a little magic."

Back in Jo's parking lot, Beck stepped away from me toward a vintage baby blue Mustang convertible parked a little askew. "Think
about it, okay? This is big, Nic—a whopper. Don't waste it."

I couldn't answer, could barely breathe at the urgency choking
my throat. Was she right? Was it possible that my future happiness
hinged on something I couldn't understand, believe, or even get
my mind around? It was like this was a test, and I didn't know the
answer. I'd *always* known the answers—I'd planned my whole life;
I'd been so meticulous, ready for every contingency, every detour.
And yesterday I'd had the rug—quite possibly the ground—pulled
out from under me.

Beck honked as she pulled past me out of the parking lot, calling over the motor, "You've gotta pick a side, Nic."

She was right, I did. I had to make a conscious decision to cling
to normalcy or cross over to the Weird side, backseat my skepti-

cism, and give the journal and its matchmaking Fairy Jane a fair, fighting chance.

It appeared I'd already made my decision, at least subconsciously. Because if not, then what was I doing? Why was I still writing out messages to a chatty little journal and then urgently checking for its reply? Maybe because I *wanted* to believe—just a little—that magic might be possible?

A reckless, fizzy zing skittered through my body, one part excitement, one part queasiness, and I wondered, fleetingly, if that was what magic felt like. In siding with Fairy Jane, I was letting go of both personal pride and "magical journal" prejudice, taking a chance on the unknown. I figured this was definitely "upping the ante," and should officially classify me as a "wild woman." I was still minus one Mr. Darcy, but maybe not for long.

5

have your cake but meet him too

I spent the duration of what I imagine was a lovely ceremony trying to control the volume of my chattering teeth, the chilly wind feeling me up, top and bottom. I really tried to appreciate the loveliness of the setting, the enchanting live oak canopy strung up with fairy lights against the backdrop of a miniature limestone castle . . . But it was hard to be gracious with a numb ass.

I barely noticed the bride's grand tulle'd and tiara'd entrance, but I wanted to cheer when she floated back up the aisle on the arm of her new husband, leading the way to the *indoor* reception. Thank God.

I'd lingered in front of the mirror, my bare shoulders urging me to consider that this was an outdoor wedding in early March, but I was unmoved. I couldn't cover up the dress. The *dress* was the whole point—I'd *journaled* about the dress! Twisting and turning, feeling very fifties Hollywood glam with the peacock blue glowing warm against my winter-pale skin, my pixie haircut offset by a sweep of chocolate eyeliner and ruby red lips, I caved just a little, unable to throw caution completely to the winds, particularly chilly ones. I'd grabbed a pale gray pashmina from the bottom drawer of my dresser and, cinching it with a chunky vintage brooch, had been positively thrilled with the concession ever since.

The little castle was considerably more charming from the inside, a fire warming the air and staining the limestone walls a sumptuous shade of gold. Indulging myself in a personal, private tour, it was only moments before I spotted the cake, set off in an alcove by itself, surrounded by trim little stacks of silver-edged china and forks spread out in a fan of invitation. So this was it. This was *the* cake. Conceivably. I mean, who really knew? Even if it was, it was still only half the equation. For things to go as Fairy Jane planned, I'd need the "him" too. I wasn't 100 percent certain that Brett was coming, or that he'd even been invited, or that I'd be able to drum up the moxie to give him my phone number. This was quite possibly *not* the cake to inspire an impromptu flirtation and a sensible romance. And yet here I was, clinging to a what-if, hoping to catch a little dandelion fluff.

Stepping determinedly away, swishing back through the maze of rooms, I paused at the coffee urn, willing to brave the bitterness in exchange for a little warmth and a caffeine buzz.

I wandered for a few moments, warming my hands on my coffee mug, hoping I'd run into Brett. My boss caught up to me near a stone fountain, his small talk a transparent gambit to confirm that I was wearing my pager. (On this dress? As if! It was in my bag.) After that there was a veritable parade of guys from work, each of them giving me the wide-eyed once-over, as if expecting I'd show up wearing my engineering lab coat and the hideous heel straps that prevent us from zapping the microcontrollers with static electricity. Made me wonder if they were just now realizing I was a girl.

And still, no Brett.

It was looking like maybe the sensible romance was still very much on hold.

I was leaning against the wall, slowly sipping my coffee, doing my best to suppress the cranky little twist of my lips after each bitter sip, trying to decide what to do next, when Brett materialized mid-grimace. I couldn't help but wonder if our timing would always be awful, but it didn't stop the warm fuzzy from sparking to life inside me.

"Aren't too happy to see me, huh?" A wry grin curved his mouth just beautifully.

"It's the coffee. Not much of a fan."

His eyebrow lifted, asking the obvious.

"I'm driving. And after forty-five minutes spent in fifty-degree weather wearing this dress, I needed to warm up." I let my pashmina slide a bit, mostly for Brett's benefit, but also because I was finally starting to get a little toasty.

He didn't seem to notice. "So were you planning to come upstairs?"

"There's an upstairs?" I had no idea.

"There's a spiral staircase just past the bar."

"There's a bar?" I teased, beginning to wish I had a designated driver of my own.

He took a sip from his dark-bottled longneck and slid his other hand into his pocket. I gave him the once-over, taking my sweet time. He looked business classy, like he knew what he was doing, both making and spending money. So sexy. Navy pin-striped suit, white dress shirt, and cornflower blue patterned tie—I just wanted to smooth my hands over everything. So instead, I curled my fingers around my warm coffee cup and tried not to let him see the whites of my knuckles. But I couldn't stop my steady perusal. His hair was a little more artistic today and really just needed a finger run-through to de-crisp it. I could do it—pick me, pick me!

"So you wanna go up?"

"What's going on up there?" Not that it mattered. He'd come looking, and I was more than willing to follow him, if for no other reason than to get a look at his ass in this suit.

"The party." In response to my blank stare, he elaborated, "The band and the dance floor are upstairs, along with most of the younger crowd. The guys kept coming up, saying they saw you, but you never appeared. I volunteered to come down here and snag you."

Ah, the group dynamic. The warm fuzzy I'd been stoking burnt out as I wondered if I'd ever be anything other than "one of the guys" to this man. I was oozing awkward with my tipped-down head, shy smile, and manic attention to my coffee cup. Maybe I would get that drink. . . .

"I had an ulterior motive."

My head whipped up, curiosity frothing beneath the surface.

"I wanted to be the first to ask you to dance."

"Oh," I said, the warm fuzzy having returned full force. "I'd love to. But first, I need to find the ladies' room." So I could do a private little victory dance. "I'll see you up there." Just before he turned, he let his eyes slide away from mine on a long, slow perusal of my girliness. And if I wasn't mistaken, his grin was very appreciative indeed.

The ladies' room was a stall tactic, but I took advantage of my chance in front of a mirror to touch up and adjust—and wonder if this could really be what all the buildup had been about. Maybe Fairy Jane was under the impression that I just needed a little nudge, and maybe I did. I flashed myself a confident smile before swinging out the door—*this* I could handle.

I decided to get a quick bite to eat before heading upstairs and was startled to see all that expensive food sitting alone, nary a wedding guest in sight. Feeling a bit intrepid, I finger-snagged a slick brown stuffed mushroom from a jewel-toned platter, let my head fall back, and dropped the little fungus into my mouth.

Well, that was what I intended. But somehow it missed, bumped off my chin, and tumbled ignominiously down the front of my dress. My head snapped up and started swiveling as my hand brushed the marinade from the tip of my chin. Seeing no one, I turned back toward the table, squeezed my arms against my boobs, and peered down into the cavern of my newly created cleavage. For a split second I considered pulling my bra away from my body and letting the little bugger fall to the floor. But if anyone were to see that, God knows what their imagination would conjure up. I'd get it out the way it went in. Figuring there was a good chance that the greasy little mushroom would slip through my bare fingers a second, maybe even a third time, I grabbed a napkin, spared a glance for the bride and groom's names joined in a tangle of hearts, took a deep breath, and plunged it down between my breasts, searching.

"I would've done that for ye."

A stinging whip of shock shot down my spine and ricocheted around in my stomach. I yanked my hand back out, somehow losing the napkin in the process. My eyes shifted in horror up to the man in front of me—a man I didn't recognize, a man with a Scottish accent that in any other circumstances would make me weak in the knees—and then down to the napkin point still showing above my neckline.

I could see the headline in the company newsletter now: STRAIT-LACED EMPLOYEE NIC JAMES CAUGHT STUFFING HER BRA AT THE WEDDING OF A FELLOW EMPLOYEE. ALCOHOL CANNOT BE BLAMED. *Perfect.*

Panting out a little puff of awkwardness—mortification really—I mumbled, "I think it's probably better if I just . . ." before turning away and diving in after the mushroom.

The second I did, I heard the click of fast approaching heels and looming voices.

"This is my daughter's wedding," a man's voice rumbled. "The doctor said I could splurge a little."

"Yes, by all means, splurge a little. But don't let me catch you eating the crab dip by the spoonful, Henry."

I stood, frozen in shock, staring at the archway, knowing they were only steps away from witnessing my embarrassing little search and rescue, and resigned myself to the inevitable.

But then, like a superhero, the stranger with the accent swooped in, wrapping his hand around to settle on my lower back and leaning close, blocking my little project from any and all rubberneckers. He leaned in, let his lips feather over the curl of my ear, and whispered, "Always happy to help."

I got that this was about chivalry, but it was hard to keep that in mind with him so close, smelling so clean and spicy, a warm glow spreading slowly from the imprint of his hand. The mushroom had slipped almost entirely from my mind, but sadly not my bra.

That moment passed quickly, and in its aftermath I performed the extraction quickly and efficiently. With the mushroom safely contained in the cocktail napkin balled in my fist, the stranger and I pulled slightly apart. But his hand, still settled beneath the pashmina, shifting against the fabric of my dress, stayed. Feeling tense and a tad weirded out, I squeezed the bejesus out of that fungus, wishing for a drink to take the edge off the embarrassment.

As my new friend made polite chitchat with the bride's parents, I let myself take a good long look. His dark brown hair was cropped close and standing up almost defiantly. His eyebrows were full, slanting over pale blue eyes, edged in sapphire and fringed with those impossibly full, dark, curled lashes that always seem to end up on men. He was clean-shaven, but I imagined the stubble was only hours away, and I had to stop myself from counting his faded freckles. Dressed in clean-lined khakis, a fuchsia oxford, and a navy blue blazer, he was a regular J.Crew poster boy. With a Scottish accent!

And here I was, the mushroom girl.

Eventually the bride's parents filtered back toward the buffet table, and figuring it was high time, I stepped away from that warm hand and murmured a grateful, rather bemused thank you, with the oddest feeling that the awkwardness was just beginning. Curiosity was eating me alive.

"Who *are* you?"

"Sean MacInnes, little-known superhero." He gave me a smile that hinted at something else right behind it and had me thinking of Sean Connery.

"Nicola James, impervious to the male ego." This triggered a megawatt grin, and it was impossible not to respond with a shyer version of my own.

"How about a drink?"

"I'm driving," I countered.

"Then how about a dance?"

I let my eyes slide away from him, poised to disengage myself.

"I really don't think—"

"So don't."

That pulled my eyes right back. "Don't what?"

"Don't think."

"If I had a nickel . . ." It was said deliberately under my breath, and I didn't expect him to hear it.

"I'm good for the nickel. And if you dance with me, I won't picture you with your hand down the front of your—"

"All right!" It came out much too loudly, and I lifted my fingers to my lips to get myself back under control. Goose bumps were rising up, yet I wasn't the slightest bit chilly. Readjusting my pashmina to hide all signs of my now-infamous bodice, I met his eyes and tilted my head to indicate he had me, but just for the one dance. "Just so you know, I'm not very good."

He took my hand, threaded his fingers through mine. I stared dumbly at all those tangled digits but didn't pull away. "A good partner makes all the difference," he beckoned. "And I'm *very* good." He winked, and my eyes strayed to the sexiest little dimple on his left cheek.

I was *so* out of my element here. He was literally zinging with that Cary Grant brand of charm that makes a girl feel not only as if she has a man's full attention but that she totally deserves it. Trouble was I wasn't sure I wanted it.

"If I hold you close enough, no one will notice any missteps— you'll move with me, and we'll be in perfect sync."

He whispered the playful suggestion disturbingly close to my ear just before shifting his hand to the small of my back and nudging me onto the spiral staircase ahead of him. I could feel the imprint of every finger all over again, and the spark of adrenaline had me shooting up the stairs ahead of him. Knowing his head was on level with my ass all the way up had me quickening further still.

6

In which "enchanted" gets upgraded to "full-out captivated"

Large round tables were packed efficiently into the tight space, and just past the shiny square of dance floor, the band was playing a slightly modern version of "The Way You Look Tonight" to an appreciative couples crowd. Within seconds, Sean had my hand tucked fittingly in his and a spot for us among the dancers. A tiny spot, just big enough for one person to stand comfortably—he was very close. Body parts were getting acquainted.

"You're not here with someone, are you?" Before I could answer him firmly in the negative, he was tightening his grip on my waist and leaning down to speak close in my ear. "Could get a tad awkward, explaining just how we met . . ."

As he pulled back, his eyes darting sideways to meet mine, I finally found my voice.

"No. I'm here by myself, and I thought that subject was officially closed." I lifted a single eyebrow, both in question and warning.

"You're right. No more talk of escapee fungus. A fellow proponent of the 'less talk, more action' philosophy. Excellent."

Oh. My. God. My synapses were slogging along here, unable to keep up with this man and his wealth of innuendo. Generally speaking I knew how to deal with men—I'd had plenty of practice walking the tightrope between "just friends" and the uncomfortable beyond. But this was definitely falling.

I was aware of every little brush of his body against mine—solid male against cowardly custard. Closing my eyes, I took a deep, calming breath and smelled peppermint, laundry soap, and spicy aftershave. It had been a long time since I'd been this close to a man. My grip tightened reflexively on his shoulder as I realized I'd really like to hang on to him for a little while.

My eyes were drifting closed in contentment when I noticed the little pewter pin flush against his collar. I inched closer, up on my toes now, to get a better look. It was an archer's arm encircled with some sort of belt and words that weren't English. I let go of him long enough to run my finger curiously over the pin's surface. His fingers tightened at my waist, and his head tipped down to watch me. Self-conscious, I licked my lips, suddenly struck by an almost irresistible urge to lick his too, to just do it.

Skank Alert!

The little angel and I were tight, but I wasn't used to having a devil on my other shoulder, throwing a kink in the works. What was I *doing?* Seriously thinking about licking this stranger's lips? That even *sounded* slutty. I let my eyes flicker over them one more time, testing myself. Okay, no good. Now I wanted to nibble.

Squeezing my eyes shut, I tried to regroup. The man was a stranger, for God's sake. The last thing I needed was to be fantasizing about his lips. Never mind that I'd been doing it with a vengeance ever since he'd whispered in my ear and they'd skimmed hot on my skin. It didn't matter—I planned to adopt the Las Vegas slogan for the entire evening: What happened at the wedding, stayed at the wedding.

That solution sounded stellar until the little devil spoke up again, reminding me that we were still *at* the wedding, and there were opportunities for the taking.

"What does it say?" I asked, glancing again at the little pewter pin and hoping to distract myself from further absurdity.

"Ghift Dhe Agus An Righ." My knees buckled just slightly, hearing the lovely, lilting words spoken in his deep, dark voice. "It means 'By the grace of God and King.' It's the MacInnes clan motto."

The man spoke Gaelic—at least a little. As sexy goes, it was a major draw.

"Do you wear it all the time?"

"Not when I'm naked."

My entire body went on full alert as I began to picture this eventuality, and there was suddenly a free-for-all in my head, with loud and urgent voices spouting off all kinds of inappropriate suggestions. "Can I arrange a viewing?" was my personal favorite.

"With Sean meanin' 'God's gift' and MacInnes 'Unique One,' it's a lot to live up to." It was impossible to tell from his grin whether he was teasing or serious.

I stared up at him, gaping probably, before my mouth eventually curved into the smile I reserved for that irresistible cockiness only certain guys could pull off. At that moment our song ended and was immediately followed by an up-tempo, brassy, big-band number. Giving Sean a sharp little shake of my head to warn that I wasn't at all up for swing dancing, we stepped off the dance floor, our fingers still entwined.

It felt as if my temporary fantasy was in a fuzzy, in-between, about-to-change-back-to-reality limbo. Instinct had me turning toward the stairs, pulling him along behind me as we spiraled our way back down.

In the darker, quieter calm of downstairs, I turned to face him with a catch in my throat. "Thank you for the dance—and your help with a certain never-to-be-mentioned mushroom incident. Now, when I snap my fingers, you will remember none of this, particularly the search and rescue." I caught his eye and snapped my fingers.

He let his eyes, twinkling with amusement, roam around the little castle, seemed to be considering, and eventually leaned down toward me.

I skittishly angled my lips away from his, just in case, but the closer he came, the more tingly I felt. And the devil was starting to get very persuasive . . . Before I could do anything truly mortifying, his voice settled over me, that lilting, lazy accent skittering up my spine.

"You've a bit of a thing for me, don't you?"

He pulled back just in time to avoid my head whipping around in shock. I stared wide-eyed at those long, long lashes curling around sparkling eyes, taking in his raised eyebrows and quirked lips. I couldn't answer. Denying it now would come off as childish, cranky, and patently untrue. Much as I hated to admit it, I kinda *did* have a little thing for him. Some wedding fluke of a thing that shouldn't even merit a mention. Sensible girls should never tell charming, accented men that they were powerless against them— it tipped the balance of power in precarious ways.

Besides, I was pretty sure it had been a rhetorical question, so I'd match him with one of my own.

"Do you have one for me?" *Sooo* not what I'd been planning to say . . .

"Isn't it obvious?"

Talk about your awkward situations!

"You don't even know me." I'd intended this to come out with just an edge of attitude, but he was so messing with my head that it came off embarrassingly coy. This had to stop.

"True, it's early going yet, but so far I'm smitten." Placing his hand on my elbow, he led me toward a private alcove, limned in candlelight.

"So far? You mean after our shared participation in an awkward mushroom incident and one casual dance."

"I don't think either of us believes it was casual."

I shot him a vaguely concerned glance before letting my eyes settle on the pewter pin once more. "What part of Scotland?"

"Near the Isle of Skye, if you know where that is."

With a soaring, overly optimistic feeling of possibility, I wondered if he could be one of the expatriots who'd come over from

Scotland's Silicon Glen to work in Austin's semiconductor sprawl. Maybe underneath it all, he was a geek at heart.

Not bloody likely . . .

"Why Austin?" I was fishing.

"It's the Live Music Capital of the World."

I held my smile in place expectantly, waiting for the rest. But it wasn't forthcoming.

"What else?" I finally prompted.

"South by Southwest."

Okaaay.

"Pretty serious music fan, huh?"

"You could say that."

I felt like I was missing something, so I crinkled my forehead in confusion and stared back at him, waiting.

"I'm with one of the festival's showcased bands," he confided, eyebrows raised, waiting for a reaction.

"Oh wow! Really? That's awesome. I understand there's some pretty stiff competition." I shot him a shy smile. "I've never actually met someone in a band." So much for the moratorium on flirting.

"Well, now ye have."

"What's the name of your band?"

"Loch'd In, with an 'h' instead of a 'k,' playing on the whole Scottish thing." He was adorably disarming.

"Ah, clever. How many band members?"

"Four, including me. Ian on drums, Simon on keyboards, and Connor on bass guitar. They all do backup vocals as well."

"What, no Scottish beauty with a killer voice?" I teased.

"Well, there *is* me, luv." How was it that he was always one step ahead of me, and I was always stumbling to catch up?

"So the band doesn't interfere with any of your jobs, or lives, or anything?"

"Not so much interfere as dominate."

And then, like a flash, I got it, and my body began to cringe, curling in on itself, shirking the incompatibility. No wonder I'd felt so utterly out of my element.

"Sorry. I'm slow—you guys are professional musicians, right?" Sean was smiling, clearly amused to see me floundering.

"Pub players," he finally answered. "And what about you, Ms. James?"

"I'm a product engineer at Integrated Micro."

"Ah, so you're one of those geeky girls." I could tell by his smile that this was good-natured payback. "I suppose I should have pegged you from the start."

"How could you not, given the circumstances?"

"I saw that mushroom go in, and my mind was wrapped around search and rescue. It's the curse of the superhero, I'm afraid."

Breathing deep, relaxing a little despite the dizzying frenzy of emotions ping-ponging inside me, I realized we were engaged in the clichéd wedding chitchat. Which made me wonder . . .

"Hold on. You're not a wedding crasher, are you?"

"Why? Are you?" After all the playfulness, his deadpan response took me a little off guard.

My eyebrow lifted all on its own. "You haven't picked up on the higher concentration of geekiness in the vicinity? Most of the guys here are engineers at Micro."

"So I'm sort of the odd man out."

"Ya think?" I muttered.

"I'm actually backup for the band tonight. One of the guys—an old friend—has a wife who's ready to have her baby. It's down to the wire now, and he's ready to bolt. He's wearing a pager and two cell phones."

"You can just step in and take over, just like that?"

"Pretty much."

This didn't seem like a big deal to him, but I was very impressed. I had no musical skills whatsoever, hence my "no karaoke" rule.

"What else can you do?" I asked, suddenly fascinated.

He blinked but took the high road. "I play the guitar, I'm decent on keyboards, and I'm told my singing voice is not too shabby."

"My next-door neighbors could really use you at their Friday night karaoke parties," I joked.

"So invite me," he flirted, sliding his thumb over the back of my hand.

With no clue how to respond to that, the suggestion ended up dangling awkwardly between us.

"Allow me to demonstrate," Sean said, clearly amused. "My band is playing Maggie Mae's Thursday night. Will you come for a listen? I can leave passes for you with the manager."

With the sconces above us flickering with candlelight, I opened my mouth to decline, but then glanced up at his face, letting that boyish grin melt me just a little. "Sure," I finally answered, a resigned smile curving my lips. I knew that seeing him again and letting my mind get all tangled up in him was probably not a good idea. And yet, it'd be a shame to miss the chance, because I suspected he had a very talented mouth.

The sound of silver ringing against crystal kept that image from pulling me under, and as conversation gently died down, the announcement followed:

"The bride and groom will now be cutting the cake, if everyone would like to make their way into the foyer."

My eyes met Sean's, the question clear: *Shall we?*

Rather than answer, he settled his hand possessively at the base of my spine, gesturing gallantly for me to proceed him, and we abandoned our alcove to follow the crowd.

Even surrounded by wedding guests, I was aware of only Sean. Standing behind me, he was out of sight, and his hand, tracing shivery circles mere inches away from racy behavior, was driving me out of my mind. My breathing was erratic to say the least, and then he leaned in, his breath skimming my cheek.

"If he knows what he's doing, he'll muck it up, miss her mouth completely."

His lip glided casually across my cheek, and my heart started to pound out a rhythm: *Oh. My. God. Oh. My. God* . . . I didn't even attempt a response.

"Real men lick the icing," he teased, his voice as velvety as his lips. "I'll snag you a piece."

Then he was pulling away, taking all his warmth and innuendo with him. And cathartic relief was vying with pervasive disappointment. I was just barely recovering when he was back, with one single sliver, which he handed to me.

I awkwardly offered him the first bite. He grinned wolfishly and leaned down to take it. I forked up the second bite and closed my eyes in pleasure as the feather-light cake and decadent cream filling melded on my tongue. Finally . . . *cake.*

Awareness snapped at me like a live wire. *I'm having my cake.*

Sean, who a moment ago had been intently watching me savor my first bite, was now looking at me curiously, probably wondering if my cake had gone down the wrong way. Sean, whom I'd just met.

Have your cake . . . but meet him too.

Oh my God! How did I miss this? I was just about to follow Brett upstairs, thinking he was him, *and then there was that damn mushroom . . . and Sean. Oh my God! Is it possible the magic—or voodoo—or whatever it is—isn't confined to the journal? Did Fairy Jane somehow flick a mushroom down my dress and finagle this whole thing merely to make me forget about Brett and . . . Shit—Brett! I totally left him hanging—I never went up—Oh. My. God. I did* go upstairs—*I went up with Sean, danced with him, drooled over him . . .*

"Nicola, are you all right?" The concern was clear in Sean's voice. But I couldn't handle this right now—I didn't want to think or explain. I just needed to go.

"I need to go." This time I said it out loud, my voice watery. I looked for a place to dump my plate. Even the cake no longer appealed, almost as if it was tainted.

Sean stepped forward, took the plate, and set it in a niche beside a beautiful bouquet of wedding flowers. And then his hands came around me, moving me off, away from the crowd.

"What is it?" His eyes had sharpened their focus and darkened with concern.

Forcing a smile, I made myself look into his eyes as long as I could before letting my own dart away again. "It's nothing. It's just that I'm cold and my feet are nearly numb."

As soon as the words were out of my mouth, Sean was generously shrugging off his jacket.

"Daft! Just distracted, I guess. I assumed you were warm enough wrapped up in your scarf. That's not to say that I missed even a single opportunity to ogle your lovely bare legs."

Now I definitely didn't need the jacket—I could feel the warm tide of a flush creeping up my neck and settling on my cheeks. But as he swung it around my shoulders, I put my hand out, brushing his raspberry-colored sleeve.

"Seriously, though, unless you're up for trading shoes, I should probably go. I just want to get out of this dress and these shoes and go to bed." I heard the way that sounded and thrilled just a little at his pained expression.

"Is this your way of letting me down easy? Because if so, you're failing miserably."

I let a laugh escape and stepped backward, away from temptation. "Thank you for the cake and the dance. And the company. And the superhero save."

"My pleasure. I'll walk you out." He stepped toward me, and in reaction, I stepped away.

"It's fine. You really don't need to—" I so desperately wanted to be out of there before I had to face Brett. Surely he'd come down at some point for cake—probably any minute now—and that could get downright awkward. Besides, a Band-Aid-style good-bye right here would really be best. I'd make a clean break and limp out the way I'd come in, and it'd be as if this whole evening was a dream.

"Ah, but I do." He wrapped his arm around my shoulders, his own spicily scented jacket now settled between us, and began to lead me through the almost empty hallways of this little fairy-tale castle. "How else do you suppose I'll snare a kiss?"

At this point in our acquaintance, his nerve didn't even faze me, but despite the runaway thrill that went coursing through me, I felt the need to call him on it. "You really have a knack for those one-liners, don't you? A perfect mix of charming and presumptuous so that a girl doesn't know quite how to take you."

"I'm not at all picky. Just take me."

My laugh slid out on a sigh, and the moment felt oddly bittersweet. Sean and I would never be more than strangers, crossing paths for one magical night. Disturbingly magical, if it came to that.

Reality whipped in with the tingly cold snap of wind as we stepped out of the castle, away from the reception. The temperature had probably dropped ten degrees since the ceremony, but snuggled as I was into Sean's jacket, inhaling deep breaths of spicy male, his arm wrapped snugly around my waist, I barely noticed the cold. After stumbling over a chunk of limestone and having Sean pull me more tightly against him, I decided to fake-trip all the way back to my car. He probably thought me an utter klutz. I preferred the term "go-getter."

When he took the key from my hand to unlock the door, I was charmed. When he started the engine and cranked up the heat, I was enchanted. And when he leaned in to me and hovered just a whisper away from my lips, I was full-out panting. I held completely still, afraid to move, to break the spell, desperately wanting this one star-crossed kiss. I could have leaned in myself, but that would have been rushing things, and I most definitely didn't want that. So I waited.

And then he shifted, just slightly, brushing his lips over the corner of my mouth before slowly pulling away. Not the cheek, which after the time we'd spent together would have been a bit of a letdown, and not technically the lips, which might have been just a little presumptuous. A perfect compromise. I'd congratulate his ingenuity, but I figured it might ruin the moment.

My fingers were itching to touch that little wonder spot, but I didn't give in to the cliché. Instead I hugged his jacket even closer, knowing I was just seconds away from giving it up.

With a little separation once again between us, he looked down at me, and I realized he must be getting an eyeful of my self-induced, chilly weather cleavage. I peered back up at him, unwilling to move.

"You have a dress under there somewhere, right? Let's have a look at it, shall we?" A nod toward the car. "Your heater's on, and you're going home alone. And I am a superhero."

"A superhero looking for quid pro quo?" I lifted an eyebrow and tried to hold back a grin, because I'd already decided to give him a peek. *Someone* should see the magnificence of this dress, and who better than him?

Or maybe Brett . . . *Not now, Nicola. Not now!*

Shrugging off his jacket, I offered it back to him, and shivered in its absence. Then I unpinned the brooch holding me together, shifting and rearranging until I was gripping the ends of my glamorous pashmina right in front of me. I closed my eyes and braced myself against the shock of cold air before yanking the ends open, waiting two excruciating beats, and swooping them closed again. Opening my eyes to sneak a peek at his face, I couldn't help but wonder just how nippy it really was.

"Bloody hell. Come back inside . . . ?"

It was obvious he didn't expect an answer, and I didn't offer one. Instead he held the door for me, and we shared our last moments.

"You've promised to come Thursday?" His tone was almost urgent, insisting.

"I did," I said, wondering even now if I'd manage it.

"Perfect. So this really isn't good-bye, just *au revoir.*"

"Definitely," I agreed, not nearly as confident as I sounded.

"Well, then. It was lovely to meet you, Ms. James. I very much look forward to the next installment in what proves to be a very interesting saga."

Saga? I couldn't tell whether he was being deliberately obtuse or merely his charming, playful self.

"Likewise, Mr. MacInnes," I countered, extending my hand for a businesslike shake.

With a twinkle of moonlight in his eyes, he took my hand, twisted it, and brought it to his lips.

And then somehow I was in the driver's seat. Having turned from the moon, Sean's eyes and face were dark, and it was slightly easier, like this, to shut the door.

Driving away, I watched him, watching me, his hands sunk deep into his pockets, until all that was left was to drive out of the woods, out of the fairy tale, back to the city. The stroke of midnight was still another couple of hours away, but Cinderella had definitely left the ball.

7

Cinderella, dressed in yellow, went upstairs to kiss a fella . . .

With the nursery rhyme playing over and over in my mind on the drive home, I couldn't help but wonder how long it was going to take to get Sean out of my thoughts. But it had been worth it—*so* worth it. And Fairy Jane had known all along. As predicted, I'd had my cake—and it had been melt-in-your-mouth memorable—and I'd met "him" too. And he'd trumped the cake, no contest.

At that point I was trying to balance being totally freaked that my journal could predict—or possibly manipulate—the future, jealous that it seemed able to make deliriously sexy men do its bidding, and *seriously* impressed with its exquisite taste.

I had no doubt that I'd met the appropriate "him." A fairy godmother worth her salt couldn't possibly have meant anyone else—he was even British! And dreamy and charming and funny and *sexy.* But it was just a chance encounter, a memorable one-night fling that never made it past first base. And what about Brett? Had I absolutely killed my chances?

I reached over and turned down the heat in the car, suddenly overwarm.

It could never work. *Shit!* My mind had dodged away from Brett and bounced back to Sean all over again.

It could *never* work, and yet it had all been leading up to this. All of it had been intended solely as a means to this particular end, this guy, this date. The first little snippet I'd found in the journal had been my invitation to the ball: *Ms. Nicola James will be sensible and indulge in a little romance.* The second—*cleavage is as cleavage does*—had set the scene for my encounter with Sean and eventually our very sexy good-bye. And the third—*have your cake but meet him too*—had been the good solid nudge I needed to keep from getting too distracted to recognize what had been right in front of me.

And now it was over.

A queasy roller-coaster feeling settled in the pit of my stomach, and not from the curves and dips in the road. But I was nothing if not practical, and Sean was about as practical as my dress for the evening. Okay, bad example, but I'd already given myself the "vanity working on a weak head" lecture. *Emma*'s Mr. Knightley had indeed been correct: It had most certainly brought on the mischief. My mind veered into memories of that mischief once again, and by the time I emerged, I was sliding into traffic going south on Mopac.

No doubt the UT tower was glowing orange with some sort of victory for the Longhorns. I, on the contrary, was actually feeling a little defeated, like I'd been on a scavenger hunt and all the clues had led nowhere. Well, I suppose in all fairness they'd led to Sean. My trouble was, I didn't know what to do with him—he was so far out of the realm of my reality that he might as well have been a fairy tale. Which fit right in with the rest of my life lately. I'd been imagining myself as Cinderella, so I should know that none of this could ever be real. The way things were going, I'd be lucky to get home before my car turned into a pumpkin.

As I swung onto the Fifth Street exit and navigated the snug, one-way streets on my way home, I let Sarah MacLachlan remind me that one missed step can ruin everything. I should stick with Brett. It seemed likely that this had all been merely a case of mistaken identity. The evening would have been perfectly orchestrated if Brett had been the "him" to have with cake, the man to notice my cleavage, and the target of a perfectly imagined romance. Perhaps I could nudge Fairy Jane in the right direction.

When I finally turned the car into the driveway, I was both relieved to be home and a little skittish. Once upon a time, everything here made sense. Ever since I'd—temporarily—conceded a little piece of the picture to Fairy Jane, she'd been wreaking havoc all over the place.

Stepping out of the car into a gust of frigid March wind, I could see the novelty lights lit up next door dancing in the breeze, and I could smell the wood smoke wafting over onto my side of the fence. I'd need to be quick and quiet. I wasn't in the mood for an inquisition or a lecture tonight.

Letting the car door fall gently closed, I bumped my hip against it and heard the lock click into place. Poised on the balls of my feet, I darted up the driveway and over the dew-moist grass, up the steps to my tiny back porch, feeling the burnt orange glow of victory.

"Surely that can't be *Nic James*, coming home after dark on a Saturday night."

Two thumps sounded on the fence I shared with the Ls, and then two faces appeared over the top, grinning like goons in the near darkness.

"Ooh, she's dressed up too. Hubba hubba."

"Good night, ladies," I called, clutching the edges of my scarf, closing in on the back door.

"Come over for a sec," Leslie cajoled. "We've got a fire going, a bakery bag of chocolate croissants, and a thermos full of Baileys hot chocolate."

"The karaoke machine has the night off," Laura added. "And we have wheat germ cakes and Earl Grey too."

Gag.

My key was literally kissing the lock, but with a heartfelt eye roll, I straightened my shoulders, adjusted the scarf so that my hands were bundled, and clopped back down the steps on my way to the side gates. If I conceded this round, maybe it'd smooth over last night's flare-up, and at the price of a little discomfort, it was well worth it—one less grudge to contend with.

By the time I got over there, they had the purple papasan pulled up next to the fire bowl and a Pendleton blanket at the ready. I made quick use of it, swaddling myself so snugly I could barely move.

They were huddled around a laptop, a rosy coral Fiestaware platter sitting between them, golden croissants oozing chocolate sharing space with what appeared to be mini hay bales.

"What are you guys doing out here? It's freezing!"

Leslie flashed a crocodile grin and tilted the monitor out of view. "Funny you should ask. I propose a little 'tit for tat.' " Her eyebrows shot up. "You in?"

"Fine," I conceded, relishing the shock on their faces.

"Excellent." Leslie leaned forward to set the thermos and a cherry red mug in front of me. "We'll go first—get it out of the way. We're picking costumes for a friend's fortieth birthday party. It's going to be a masquerade."

Pulling my arms out of their cozy cocoon, I poured the cocoa, sloshing it slightly as I shivered uncontrollably. "Any good ideas so far?" The first sip snaked a warm trail down to my stomach, and the second and third chased away the cold.

"So far we're considering the two witches from *Wicked*, with me as the blonde. Laura looks better in green."

"Okay. Just so I'm clear. *You're* playing Glinda, the *Good* Witch?"

Laura laughed. "Typecasting is for Hollywood."

Leslie smiled sweetly and shot us the bad finger.

"So much for method acting," Laura teased. Leslie ignored her and finished out the list.

"Austin Powers and Dr. Evil is an option, but not my favorite. And our artsy-fartsy choice is da Vinci and the Mona Lisa. Laura can go longer without smiling, so she'd be the 'Woman of Mystery.' Good start, huh?" She was clearly ready to dismiss the topic altogether.

I tried to give it some thought but soon realized my brain was too full to come up with any really great suggestions. "What about a couple of cows out on the prowl for some Longhorns? Or maybe a couple of bats? That's very Austin, right?"

"That could be good, Les," Laura said, visualizing costumes. "We could even jazz it up a little. Get some fake teeth and be vampire bats."

"I'll add it to the list," Leslie promised, tipping the computer closed and shooting me an unreadable smile. "Okay, tit time is over. Your turn," she announced, reaching for a croissant. Laura slid a hay bale into place, just under her fingers. Skimming its dry texture, Leslie snatched her hand back in confusion before muttering "Horrid little things" under her breath and claiming the biggest croissant on the plate.

I made wide, innocent eyes at her and asked, "What sort of tat were you hoping for?"

"Oh, I don't know. Maybe we're curious as to what lured you out on a Saturday night in a skimpy dress, fuck-me heels, and some sort of fancy . . . swaddling."

"You think you're gonna be a good witch with that mouth?" I paused for a single beat, then hurried on when it looked like Leslie might start lobbing bits of croissant. "I was at a coworker's wedding. I went alone, came home alone."

"Hrrmph. Figures. Did you at least flirt? Dance? Toss anyone your underwear?"

"I danced one dance and flirted a little. My underwear remains intact," I countered.

"You danced?" By the tone of Leslie's voice, you'd think I'd lap-danced.

I nodded, letting the irritation show on my face.

"Coworker or stranger?"

"Stranger." This perked Leslie right up.

"Cute?" Laura chimed in, looking ready for a good campfire story.

"Very," I confided, letting the backyard fade for a moment as I remembered.

"Geek?" Leslie's face was clenched in preparation for bad news.

"Geeky like Jude Law." Okay, not exactly, but the analogy worked.

Leslie donned her professor face, pursed lips and penetrating gaze. "You're serious?"

My eyes shifted to Leslie's laptop as an idea occurred to me. I could Google him. Surely the band had a website, maybe even a few head shots. Flicking my gaze from Leslie to Laura, it occurred to me that a little privacy might be preferable to a gossip fest, but I didn't think I could wait. Nervous energy was building up inside me—I wanted to see if it was there, if *he* was there, online, *real*. I wanted one more look because I suspected I might not risk a second one in person.

Suddenly my mind was made up. Scooting forward in my chair, I commandeered Leslie's laptop.

"What are you doing?" She sounded miffed, likely imagining the inquisition was over.

"Just give me a minute," I insisted. Remembering the all-important "h," I Googled "Loched In," pausing for a single heart-thumping moment before tapping the Enter key.

I kept my eyes focused on the screen, vaguely aware of night sounds and the avid stares of the Ls. The search results were a mixed bag, and while there was a mention of home-buying in Scotland and even a Scottish thoroughbred, the band didn't get any hits. I held up a "bear with me" finger and shot the girls a smile. I was curious over a fine art print that had come up first in the search, and before tweaking the spelling for a follow-up search, I clicked on the link.

It was a gorgeous, ethereal twilight photograph of Eilean Donan Castle in the Scottish Highlands. Quickly scanning the description, I learned that it was one of Scotland's most visited castles, overlooking three lochs, and thus "Loched In." Blinking rapidly to pull my gaze and thoughts away, I hurriedly Googled "Loch'd In," without the "e" this time.

Second time was a charm. First on the list was a link for the band. Taking a deep, flutter-suppressing breath, I clicked over. Immediately a haunting rhythm began pulsing through the darkness, and the Ls, who had been quietly chatting up till now, turned to stare at me. As the page loaded, the music quickened and the volume rose to full-blooded rock. Startled, I searched frantically for the site's Volume Off button. Not finding one, I scanned the page, searching for what I needed right that minute: definitive proof that I, Nicola James, had participated in an evening of sexy seduction.

A hotlink for "The Band" looked promising, and clicking over, I was rewarded—there he was. All the guys were cute, but Sean was gorgeous, sending scads of butterflies swirling through me in a vortex of lust. I centered his picture on the screen, and as the music continued to pulse around us, I turned the monitor for inspection by my inquisitive, hard-sell neighbors.

"Oh my God, is that him?" Laura blurted, for once getting the jump on Leslie.

I nodded, remembering how I'd felt the first time I saw him. But as they stared, it occurred to me that men—even seriously sexy men—were not exactly their cup of tea. But even they had to appreciate this stunning specimen of manhood, didn't they? I waited nervously for the sure-to-come assessment, downing another fortifying gulp of cocoa.

This was sort of a first for us. In all the months I'd known them, I'd never really told them anything. Maybe because until now I'd never had anything to tell. Huh. Well, score one for Fairy Jane, I suppose.

"Tell me again why you're still wearing underwear," Leslie demanded, all squinty-eyed and serious.

"What is it with you and underwear?"

"It's a symbol—of sex and inhibitions, power and sensuality—"

"Okay." I held up my hand, desperately hoping to thwart an entire monologue on underwear.

"Not those plain white cotton Jockeys, Nic. I'm talking about the good stuff—"

"That's a topic for another time," I insisted. "Right now we're talkin' tat, and he's it."

"Who is he?" Laura seemed a little in awe. Pretty impressive that the man's jpeg could get a couple of lesbians hot and heavy. I'd gloat later.

"He's lead singer of a rock band called Loch'd In. They're a showcased act at South by Southwest this year." I was suddenly feeling very shy, staring deeply into my mug of hot chocolate. "He invited me to come to the festival and see him Thursday night, but I'm thinking I'll probably skip it."

"Sounds like he's interested," Laura said, gently probing.

"He seemed to be—a little—but anything beyond friends is pretty much out of the realm of possibility."

"Did he have a run-in with 'The Plan' already? Poor guy."

"You can nix the air quotes, Les. 'The Plan' actually exists. And it's not just The Plan—it's everything. He's everything I'm not." I reached for a croissant but didn't take a bite, choosing instead to busy my hands with flaking off tiny, crumbly bits. Within seconds they were littering my edge of the table. "It would never work. I can't be with a rock star—I don't have the rock-star mentality. And as you so often remind me, I don't even karaoke."

"You're definitely not a rock star." Apparently on that we could all agree. My lips had already folded themselves into a rueful line when Leslie continued, "But why should that stand in your way? Gwyneth Paltrow is a far cry from your average rock-and-roller, but she married Chris Martin and even tours with the band."

"Are you seriously comparing my situation to Gwyneth Paltrow's?" The woman was a college professor, yet every conversation I had with her seemed to make so little sense. I'd always thought it was her, but what if it was me? Not a comforting thought.

"Oh, I'm sorry. I'm having a little trouble hitting on a perfect celebrity matchup of Scottish rocker and repressed technology engineer."

"My point exactly." My smile was smug but surprisingly not all that comforting. The rest came out more as a mumble. "We have virtually nothing in common."

"Opposites attract, or hadn't you heard?" Leslie was laying heavy on the sarcasm tonight.

"Believe me, the man needs no help from a cliché. But attraction alone is not enough. Forget the insecurity, the clubs, the crazy schedule—what if he makes it big? And having met him, I have no doubt he will—then I'll need to contend with world tours and crazy-obsessed fans and . . . paparazzi!" All things to consider when determining the suitability of a career—or a boyfriend.

"Maybe getting just a little ahead of yourself there," Laura hinted.

"Just out of curiosity, how'd you manage to hook up"—seeing my glare, Leslie quickly amended—"*dance* with the one hot Scottish rocker at a reception full of geeky engineers? No offense."

"None taken," I returned, my smile a little catty. "And I have no idea. An odd twist of fate, I guess." Or magical interference. Tomato, to-mah-to.

Not wishing to pursue that topic any further, I disentangled myself from the blanket. "I think I'm ready to go to bed. I enjoyed our little tit-tat," I added, smiling.

"Sleep well," Laura said.

Obsessed with having the final word, Leslie chimed in with one more thinking point. "I know this is contrary to everything you believe in, but think about it, Nic. What's the worst that could happen if you gave him a chance?"

"I can't even begin to imagine," I answered honestly before hobbling away on my heels.

I was still pondering the question ten minutes later, tucked beneath the covers with my journal settled on my lap and pencil in hand. Having shoved the heels to the back of my closet and swapped my perfect, fairy-tale dress for an über-comfortable pairing of T-shirt and pajama pants, I felt almost back to normal. With Sean, I doubted anything would ever be normal again. And that was precisely why I couldn't take a chance on him—on us.

Flipping the pages of the journal till I reached the next completely blank page, I was poised to say my piece.

Little change of pace tonight . . . I went to the wedding, had my cake, and surprise, surprise—I met someone.

As you can probably imagine, I have some questions. Pretty much the basics, the five Ws:

<u>Who</u> is Sean MacInnes?

<u>Where</u> did you find him? And please tell me he isn't under some sort of spell.

<u>What</u> were you thinking? He's a Rock Star, for God's sake! This whole time I'd been thinking it was Brett—a much more appropriate, possibly even perfect match. He's the epitome of "sensible romance," so <u>Why not</u> him?

I will admit to being very impressed—swoony even. Sean is charming and sexy and adorable and just plain perfect, except that he's absolutely, incontrovertibly <u>wrong for me</u>. And I refuse to let a sketchy little arrangement, a big wow factor, and a little fairy dust trump my carefully thoughtout Plan—

Well, hell. I had to switch to pen. My pencil just broke under the pressure. I guess you could say I feel pretty strongly about people messing with my head . . . and my life.

It's been a long night. I'm going to bed now, knowing it'll be impossible not to think of him in a wistful, what-if sort of way. Just one more question:

<u>When</u> will tonight stop feeling so bittersweet?

I tipped the journal closed and laid it on the bed beside me. I'd pretty much resigned myself to the magical goings-on inside this little book, despite not having a clue how to explain or understand them. But I absolutely refused to bow under the pressure. Sean MacInnes was not a romance I planned to indulge in. I folded my lips into a determined line. *Take that, Fairy Jane.* As far as character types went, Sean was the epitome of handsome and charming bad boy Henry Crawford. Not exactly my match made in heaven.

And yet, with the lights doused, the darkness felt charged and mysterious, and despite my good intentions, I couldn't resist the flood of tingly memories. I remembered every second, every smile, every smirk and soft glance. In less than two minutes, I was flinging off the covers to keep from singeing the sheets. Eventually, in the private darkness of my own bedroom, I gave in and let my fingers trip gently over the spot he'd kissed, holding on to the memory, letting go of the man. After that, I slid into a dream involving a field of heather and some carelessly tossed skirts—it was impossible to tell whose, because he was most definitely wearing a kilt.

8

change of Plan—pencil him in.

Even a truly excellent dream couldn't take the edge off Fairy Jane's latest infuriating instruction: *pencil him in?*

Bossy, cheeky, impossible to get along with . . . No wonder Jane Austen had never married.

A little bitterness eased out of me as I realized that last jab wasn't fair. As far as I knew, this whole situation had absolutely nothing to do with the literary darling. Beck had broached the idea of Jane Austen as the voice behind the journal, and I'd latched onto her, the familiar in an outlandish situation, a writer who'd made a career out of impossible matchmaking and happily-ever-afters. Right now I was hanging my sanity on a Jane Austen obsession, because without a face, a name, a personality, there was nothing—it was all a nebulous mystery. And yet, it was almost as if Mr. Darcy of the Journal was warning me off the unsuitable Wickham, a.k.a. Brett Tilson. As if.

Goose bumps were popping up like pinpricks along my arms as I hurried down the hall to the living room and unceremoniously shoved the journal into the bookcase, hoping, I suppose, that this simple act would relegate these recent bits of advice to the realm of romantic fiction. Completely separate from me and my well-ordered life.

I stared at the journal's black leather spine, conscious of the fact that the little book looked pretty comfortable leaning on *P&P*, as if the two were gossipy old friends. I crossed my arms over my chest and turned away. This latest directive had left no room for interpretation. It was personal now—on a whole new level—and I was feeling pretty pissy.

I rubbed at the goose bumps, wishing this staggering feeling of vulnerability would disappear too.

How *was* it possible that I'd hooked up with *Sean,* a whirling dervish of mischief and charm, in a reception full of geeks? It boggled the mind. Unless Fairy Jane had truly conjured him—or meddled in whatever way that fairies do.

Quite the dizzying one-eighty for a girl who didn't believe in magic two short days ago. I didn't want to think about it. Not to mention the possibility that Fairy Jane might have stepped outside the bounds of the journal—I most certainly wasn't ready to deal with *that*.

I still needed to call the number we'd weaseled out of the Shop Nazi's computer: a Mr. Elijah Nelson. But nine on a Sunday morning felt a little too early to be discussing magical journals with strangers.

I needed something to keep my hands busy and my mind occupied. Today could very well be the perfect day for the Samoa cupcake recipe I'd stumbled across on a delectable little cupcake blog. Inspired by the much-loved Girl Scout Cookie, it involved a brown sugar butter cupcake spread with chocolate ganache, topped with a toasted coconut macaroon cap, and finished with a drizzle of ganache. I'd put off making it, slightly intimidated by its complexity. But today a challenge was exactly what I needed.

Tying on my apron, I did a quick check for ingredients and began pulling out the necessary baking paraphernalia and mentally breaking down the recipe into a series of mini tasks. I was sliding a tray of golden brown coconut back out of the oven when the phone rang.

"Wanna get brunch?" Gabe offered.

Glancing behind me at my cupcakes in progress and then at the clock, which read quarter to ten, I said, "What time?" Not being in on the Big Secret, Gabe was the ideal companion right now.

"Noon?"

"That'll work. Where'd you have in mind?"

"How about Moonshine?"

Perfect. Slightly upscale but down-to-earth.

"See ya there."

I glanced again at the clock the moment I hung up and decided to risk the temper of Mr. Elijah Nelson.

As the phone rang at the other end, I squared my shoulders and psyched myself up for an awkward conversation. On the fifth ring, I felt my shoulders slump a little in disappointment. On the tenth, I gave up on him having an answering machine and actually pulled the phone away from my ear. With my thumb poised over the End button, I was jolted back to attention as a gravelly old voice rumbled over the line.

"Hello? Hello?"

I slapped the phone back against my ear and stuttered to catch up, to be heard over the third, rather cantankerous "Hello?"

"Hello—hi. I'm here."

"Well, where the hell were you?"

Okay, so he was a little prickly in the morning. . . . "I was here, I just didn't have the phone up against my ear." Start out competent, that's the ticket.

"Well, you were hoping to talk to someone, weren't ya?"

"Yes. Sir. Yes, I was. Are you Mr. Nelson—Mr. Elijah Nelson?"

"Who's askin'?"

"Um . . . my name is Nicola James, Mr. Nelson. I'm up in Austin, and I got your number from the owner of Violet's Crown Antique Shop—"

"Violet who?"

I shook my head, trying to dispel the confusion. "No, sir, Violet's is an antique shop." I heard myself getting louder and tried to relax. "The owner recently purchased a lady's boudoir table from you."

I was really hoping this was enough to jog his memory.

"I got rid of plenty a while back, all at the Trade Days, before I moved down here to New Braunfels, and into Misty Glen. But I can't say as I remember who bought what. I never tried to pass anything off as a valuable antique. Don't tell me that Violet charlatan did."

"No, sir," I hurried to assure him. "She didn't." Or if she did, I didn't know about it. "I'm actually calling to ask about a journal she found in one of the drawers—it's black, with a fancy brass key plate and a little doorknob."

Silence.

"Is this ringing any bells for you?"

"Don't you worry, young lady, I can keep up just fine. I watch *Jeopardy!* every afternoon—I could give those contestants a run for their money."

My lips curled into a grin, but I kept silent, sensing he wasn't finished.

"Harrumph. So that's where that book was hiding. Good riddance as far as I'm concerned. And as for you, young lady, what is it they say? *Caveat emptor*—I think that's right."

My smile suddenly melted away, and I stood straighter, my lower back rigid against the kitchen counter.

"*Caveat emptor?* Let the buyer beware? Why do you say that?"

"All that magic mumbo jumbo. Cat would have done just fine without it."

"Who's Cat?" I felt breathless and urgent.

"My sister." The words sounded bitter, sad, and resigned. "Supposed to marry my best friend. Everything, all of it, arranged—until she stumbled across that journal."

He stopped there, and with no other choice, I waited. I wanted answers, and I was willing to forgo good manners and bust out the nosy curiosity, but first I needed to get my voice back. Because right now I couldn't speak. Couldn't get a single word out. All I could think was that I wasn't the first. This journal had belonged to someone else, worked its magic on someone else. I was, rather unbelievably, on the right track here—I just needed a little more information. Closing my eyes, I took a deep, shuddering breath and tried to inhale a little patience, a little calm to temper the piston firing of my heart.

"What happened then?" I finally asked quietly, reverently.

"Cat called off the wedding and hared off to parts unknown with big ideas."

"What sort of big ideas?" The words caught in my throat, but I forced them out. I needed to hear this story.

"The war was on, and Cat wanted to be where things were happening. In the thick of it, I suppose. Always was a busybody."

"And the journal?" I cringed inwardly, suspecting I knew the answer.

"When she broke it off with Tyler, she told me it was her journal's idea. I thought that was bullshit and told her so, so she showed me the page with the words, one little bossy instruction: 'Don't marry him.' 'Course I accused her of writing it herself. So then she slid the key into the lock—"

"Hold on. There isn't a key—or a lock. The key plate is just decorative." Could this possibly be a mistake? Was there another magical journal floating around somewhere between here and Fredericksburg? Beck would be thrilled.

"It's all part of the ruse," he assured me, an edge to his voice. "And once she turned the key, it was impossible not to believe her. Her words reappeared—and everyone else's right along with them—"

I heard a rushing *pop* in my ears, and my eyes telescoped, seeing only the journal, propped innocently beside P&P in the bookshelf. *Everyone else's?*

"And I read them. Didn't change my mind, but hers was made up. So she left, taking the book with her."

Now we were getting somewhere. . . .

"So how did you . . . ?" At this point I didn't even know which part of this whole thing to try to wrap my head around first.

"She died. In England. And that magic book of hers got shipped over in a brown box with the rest of her personal effects. Right about now you're probably wishing that book had been forgotten across the pond somewhere, aren't ya?"

"It's too early to tell," I told him honestly, determined not to get distracted. "So what happened to the key?"

"Oh, it came back too, but I never slipped it into the lock again—chicken, I guess. I take it from all the questions that it wasn't with the journal."

"No," I confirmed, slumping in my seat, a little defeated. "It wasn't."

My free fall back to ignorance came too fast, and all at once I was dizzy, my head spinning. Okay, deep breath, start again. "Any ideas?"

"I'd start with that Violet character. Best lead you got."

"You're right. Thank you very much for your time, Mr. Nelson, and I'm sorry to have brought up sad memories of your sister."

"Never mind that. It's past."

On impulse I asked one final question. "Just out of curiosity—was she happy with her decision?"

"Far as I know. Sent plenty of postcards from all over. Didn't seem to miss Tyler one little bit. Him, on the other hand, never stepped foot outside Gillespie County. But that doesn't prove a thing—Cat done gone and messed with fate."

"Yeah," I answered, my voice sounding faraway. I could relate to Tyler's situation. I'd recently come to the conclusion that my dad had planned Walt Disney World vacations around hurricane season and trips to Europe around the impossibility of scoring last-minute passports. Cat Nelson may have messed with fate, but at least she'd *gone* somewhere.

"Okay then. Good luck to you." He hung up with a click in my ear, and it barely registered, my thoughts were in such a tussle over this new information. Evidently I needed to go back, yet again, to Violet's and fend off the Purveyor long enough to find the key. A key that was likely to ratchet up the insanity yet another dubious notch.

The cupcakes momentarily forgotten, I unearthed my laptop and powered it up, crossing my fingers that Violet's was open on Sunday. It wasn't. My search was going to have to wait until Monday. I was going to have to sneak off to search for a magical key on the same day I hoped to be promoted to manager. Perfect.

As I turned back to the morning's cupcake distraction, I was conscious of the fact that I should call Beck. I knew she was waiting to hear from me, and I had plenty to tell her. But while I was confident she'd forgive me for rousing her so early on a Sunday, I didn't really want to go into the whole business right now. I'd call her eventually . . . or she'd call me.

I was assembling the cupcakes, my hands coated with gooey macaroon mixture, when the phone rang again. Of course it was Beck, a.k.a. Karma.

"Hey," I answered, the phone jammed between my ear and shoulder.

"Hey! What are you up to today? Wanna meet up?"

"Um, sure," I blurted, thinking fast. If I invited her to brunch, I'd only have to rehash the wedding details a single time. "How about brunch? I'm already meeting Gabe, and he's as avidly curious about my one-night solo social whirl as you are."

"Okay, sure," she enthused.

"One thing, though—he doesn't know about the journal."

"So you want me to keep Fairy Jane on the down-low?"

"Yeah, pretty much."

"Not a problem. As long as you promise to fill me in later."

"I'll do you one better. I'm meeting Gabe at Moonshine downtown at noon. Meet me there ten minutes early, and I'll catch you up."

"Gotcha."

With my afternoon satisfactorily arranged, I hung up the phone and returned to the task of forming little coconut caps on the cooled, ganached cupcakes, easily sliding into the unruffled calm that comes from mindless repetition. It didn't even occur to me to call Gabe to see if he minded a third.

Beck made an entrance in a swirly red miniskirt and turquoise sweater, her hair pulled back in a sparkly barrette, causing me, in my jeans and nubby sweater, to feel just the slightest bit drab.

Squelching that feeling, I waved from the bench seat beside the hostess station, and she hurried over, all giddy anticipation. She dropped a hug around my shoulders and then sat back, clearly ready to get right to it.

"So? Spill it, chick. Did you call the dude in Fredericksburg?" Seeing my nod, she continued, "Tell me about that first. Then the wedding, then whatever else you got."

"Fine, but as soon as Gabe shows up, we're nixing all journal-related conversation and sticking with the wedding replay, okay?"

"Got it."

I relayed the general gist of my conversation with Elijah Nelson amid a great deal of gasps and the occasional wild-eyed comment: "*Shit! There's a key? Wow—and she never came back?* Un-*freakin'*-believable." When I finally finished, she seemed confused. "And you didn't go back in to look for the key?" Her tone was distinctly accusatory.

"I waited to call him until this morning," I said, speaking slowly. "And it turns out they're closed on Sundays. Finding a matching key amid all that clutter seems like kind of a long shot, though. Unless the Nazi knows where it is and is willing to say." I raised my eyebrows to indicate my level of confidence in that turn of events.

"I don't know how you stand it. The suspense is *killing* me. Don't you wish life could be like the movies, all action without the filler?"

"Um, no. I'm a big fan of the filler." She cut her eyes over to me, clearly wondering if I could possibly be serious.

"What's your Plan B, if the key doesn't want to be found?" she said.

My eyebrows crinkled down in reaction to the ongoing *LOTR* analogy and I said, "A lot of the same: floundering around without a clue, hoping things start making sense on their own. But I'm not holding my breath."

Leveling me with a hard stare, she seemed to have no better alternative. "We'll deal with that later. Tell me about the wedding," she insisted, edging closer on the bench.

It was quite the novelty to realize that for once I wasn't the one living vicariously—I was the one with the exciting life. Or at least the exciting night. And already that one night was more than I could handle.

"So did it all come true? Did you meet him?"

"You don't want to know about the cake?" I teased.

She shot me a dangerous "very funny, but get serious" look and I straightened up quickly.

"Would you believe that they had the ceremony outside, under the trees, at dusk? It's March, for God's sakes, and *freezing!*"

Glancing pointedly at her watch, Beck warned, "Time's a-tickin', girl. Start with *him*, and go from there."

"Okay. Well, I definitely met *him*." Lust shimmied up my spine just remembering, and I could feel my lips beginning to curl up.

"And?" Beck's lips parted slightly in anticipation.

"And I had a *very* nice night," I admitted, my smile fully in place now. "But I definitely don't trust the journal's ability to make sensible decisions."

Beck's lips twisted in a wry smile. "Kinda seems like you skipped all the good stuff, Nic."

"Just wanted to make that clear."

"Okay, let's put *him* on hold for a minute. What happened? What'd Fairy Jane say now?"

"That . . . *fairy* . . . is a menace! The latest leftover was 'change of Plan—pencil him in,' but that's only part of it."

"I assume that 'him' is *him*, who, I might add, I've yet to hear anything about?" Her eyebrows crinkled down in annoyance.

"Seems pretty damn likely."

"Him who?" said a familiar voice a few feet in front of us.

Naturally it was Gabe, dressy casual in dark denim and a sharp-looking green polo, his hair gelled up into some sort of style. He reminded me of a blade of grass nudging his way in.

"No one important," I quipped, shooing the moment away and earning a smirk from Beck. Gabe and Beck had met previously but had had little time to get to know each other, as Beck's hours at

Micro were a little sporadic. I refreshed the introductions, gesturing first to Beck. "Rebecca Connelly—Beck for short—intern extraordinaire and über-hip chick, meet," and then over to Gabe, "Gabe Vogler, longtime coworker, self-professed geek, and all-around good guy."

With the introductions finished, I stood to catch the hostess's eye. When I turned back, Gabe was staring, quite possibly hypnotized as I'd once been, by the winking, blinking pink stud in Beck's nose. I snapped my fingers quick and hard as near his face as I dared, and Gabe whipped his head around in my direction, his eyes dark and distracted. I glanced at Beck, smudging her lips together, eyeing Gabe in all his nerdiness, and I couldn't help but wonder if my one wild night had already become old news. Not a problem.

Further conversation was put off until we were seated, Beck and I sitting on one side of the booth sipping Moonshine mimosas (both ordered by my just-barely-legal mentee) and Gabe on the other, sticking with iced tea.

"UT engineering, huh? What year?" Gabe asked, cautiously curious.

"Junior," Beck answered with a nod and a dimpled smile.

Judging by the tiny movements of Gabe's lips, I assumed he was doing the math, calculating that Beck was a good five years *his* junior. Evidently he wasn't spooked by the nose stud or the magenta hair—good for him. I smiled at him and kept one eyebrow raised, waiting for the numbers to click. When they did, he flicked a quick glance at me before determinedly turning his attention back to Beck.

"So how goes the mentoring?"

"I'm gonna let Beck answer that," I said, sliding out of the booth, heading for the buffet, and crossing my fingers that Beck could dodge the question.

The booth was empty when I got back, toting a syrup-doused waffle topped with strawberries and pecans. I glanced toward the buffet line to see Gabe leaning down to speak into Beck's ear, her shocking pink hair skimming the edge of his face. She looked up at him, her face glowing. It would definitely be interesting to see how this played out.

Once we were all settled back at the table, it was only a few bites before Gabe remembered what we'd arranged to discuss.

"So how was the wedding last night?" he asked, forking up a bite of chicken fried steak and letting his eyes stray to Beck, who was concentrating rather intently on buttering her cranberry orange muffin. I made a note to snag one of those on my next trip to the buffet.

"I left early."

"That can't be the best you can do," Gabe insisted. Beck's thigh bumped up against mine in an obvious I-told-you-so.

I bumped her right back, resisting the urge to turn and glare. Then I took a deep breath and launched right into things.

"I did meet a guy—a stranger," I added, preempting Gabe. "We talked, we danced, we had cake. Then he walked me out, he kissed me on the cheek, and that was that." It seemed a shame to encapsulate the evening like that, but also very sensible, all things considered.

"Did you give him your number?" The question came out slightly muffled, having dodged Beck's mouthful of muffin.

"Not exactly."

Suddenly it was a two-flanked stare-down as both Gabe and Beck stopped chewing to gaze at me, wide-eyed.

"What does that mean?" I imagined this was a joint question, but it was Beck who voiced it.

"He invited me out Thursday night, I said okay, we said goodbye."

"But no phone number?" Gabe fired this one, and it occurred to me that I was being tag-teamed.

"No need. I know where to find him if I want to," I told them simply. "And besides, he isn't 'the One.'"

I was conscious of Beck, frozen beside me, desperately wanting to press for details but holding it together because of Gabe.

"You didn't give him your phone number, but you let him kiss you?" Gabe demanded, clearly puzzled.

"Oh, he was *definitely* the one for that." I smiled, remembering with dreamy fondness that moment of weakness.

Gabe promptly turned to Beck and tattled, "This is classic Nic."

Glancing first at me, Beck swiveled her eyes back to Gabe and countered, "How so?"

"She has this perception of the perfect, sensible match, and if a guy doesn't look and act the part, it's all over for him from ground zero."

I took my time carving out another bite of waffle, swirling it in the syrup puddled on my plate. I answered before forking it into my mouth.

"He's an aspiring musician, and his band is being showcased at South by Southwest." I raised an eyebrow, daring either of them to challenge my decision.

"Are you kidding? That's awesome." This from Gabe.

Watching Gabe's face light up with interest, I was suddenly curious. "His band is Loch'd In, with an 'h.' Ever heard of them?" I asked casually.

"Loch'd In? You're kidding. That's the Scottish band we saw on Friday night—the men with accents? Pretty big coincidence. He was at the wedding?"

"He was a stand-in for the band's lead singer, who, apparently, was an imminent father-to-be." My voice was hollow and distracted. I was remembering Friday night: sparring with Gabe, having just discovered my journal's special bonus features. *Had* it been a coincidence? It seemed too big for that—too impossible to believe, as if worlds were colliding.

I couldn't look at Beck, couldn't risk meeting her eyes and losing it. Gabe, now focused on his plate and oblivious to the frenzy of unknowns clamoring in my head, asked. "So that's it then? He's out?"

"That's it."

"He's the *only* guy you met?" Beck asked. *"Him?"*

"Only him," I said, answering the unspoken question.

"You had to pick a guy with baggage—literally." Gabe smirked.

Huh? Before I could ask Gabe what he was talking about, he pushed on with, "You have a chance here, Nic, to play with the cool kids, and as an engineer and a self-professed geek, you should jump on it."

"I probably should object to that line of reasoning, but I've gotta side with Gabe on this one," Beck said, spearing a chunk of pineapple and quirking her lips in friendly apology.

"Except that I'm not looking for cool, I'm looking for compatible."

"Who's to say he's not?" Gabe was clearly rooting for this guy.

"Me!" Surely this should have been obvious. "We have nothing in common. And what about health insurance, a 401(k), job security . . . ?"

"First off, you don't know he doesn't have all that stuff. But even if he doesn't, so what? Not everyone is on the fast track to a cushy retirement, Nic. And I'm guessing your main objection is that he's not even on the *sensible* track. Face it, Nic," he persisted, his smile smug, "you're a snob."

"I am not!" And then I wondered. *Am I?* I decided to concede the possibility. "Okay, maybe I am, but I'm not going to apologize for that. It's *my life*." And just like that, the fight went out of me. "It's just not gonna work, okay?"

Gabe didn't argue, merely quirked his lips in a rueful smile. I glanced over at Beck. She'd stayed quiet since the engineer jab, likely forming hypotheses of her own based on her insider knowledge of the journal and Fairy Jane. Or else just distracted by Gabe.

"Okay, so we've exhausted that topic," I announced to the table at large. "Why don't you go reload," I suggested, gesturing to Gabe's nearly empty plate, "and when you get back we'll discuss the success of *your* evening. First date," I informed Beck.

Flicking a quiet glance at Beck, Gabe slid obediently out of the booth. "You two coming?"

Beck looked down at her near-empty plate, but before she

could answer, I swung my leg to smack against hers under the table, and like a pro, she looked up at Gabe and smiled. "Not yet." So Gabe trailed off alone, none the wiser.

He wasn't even a booth away when Beck whipped her attention back to me and whispered, "So is this true, a ruse, what? Tell me that you did not kiss a Scottish rocker, hand-picked by your fairy godmother no less, and send him on his merry way!"

"Shhhhhh! Yes, it's true, but as I explained, he can't have been the One. Fairy Jane must have been mistaken—or insane. Yes, he was charming and witty and sooo sexy, but he's completely, *inarguably*"—I drove this point home, hoping she'd concede the battle of wills before it began—"wrong for me."

"How do you know it was *him?*"

"Take my word for it—it was definitely *him.*"

Her skepticism was clear, but she didn't press it. "So really, that's it?"

I looked away, confirming Gabe's far-off location before falling back into the fray. "What do you mean exactly?"

"You're just going to snub Fairy Jane and to hell with your one-of-a-kind magical journal?"

"I tried to snub her, last night after the wedding. I wrote another entry explaining why things with Sean would never work, explaining about The Plan . . ."

"Oooh!" Beck had clearly put two and two together. "And she told you to pencil him in!" Her mouth fell open on a shocked smile. "I gotta say, I like the way she thinks. But how does she think you're gonna manage that? You didn't exchange phone numbers. Big mistake." Seeing my glare, she added, "I'm just sayin'."

"You're right, we didn't. Ergo, I will *not* be penciling him in. But I figure I'll give her another shot. I even tried to steer her in the right direction."

"You didn't!" Beck demanded.

"Didn't what?"

Beck and I jerked apart to stare up at Gabe as he slid into the booth with his second plate of food. He seemed to have an uncanny ability to horn in on secret powwows.

"You're back," Beck enthused. Her smile was winning, even in profile. "So tell me, where do you take a girl on a first date?" A little flirtatious drawl from Beck, and curiosity had clearly gone skittering from Gabe's mind. The girl was good.

"Depends on the girl." Very smooth, Gabe. "Last night we went to Eastside Café."

"And is there a second date in your future?" I asked, wondering about Beck's chances, pulling for them.

"All signs point to 'hell no,' " he admitted, with a wry smile and a self-deprecating shrug.

Beck laughed. "Ahhh, the Magic Eight Ball. Ours was a love-hate relationship. I loved to ask, but invariably hated the answers. Same sob story with the Ouija board too."

Gabe eyed her over the rim of his iced tea glass before informing us, "Well, you'll love this. She was obsessed with *The Amazing Race* and was screening potential matches up front for their able-bodiedness, just in case."

I couldn't help it: I stopped chewing and stared, and when Gabe moved to shove another bite of food in his mouth, I lunged across the table to block him.

"Wait! Did you put on a good showing?"

Gabe lowered his fork, careful to look sufficiently put-upon. "I'm pretty sure I passed muster in the able-bodied department, just not in the willingness department."

"You're kidding. I would have thought you'd be into that."

"I might have, but she was only interested in my body—and not in a good way. She all but pulled out a clipboard and measuring tape in the middle of dinner."

I felt a giggle bubbling up but forcibly suppressed it.

"And after the busboy cleared the table, she actually wanted to arm wrestle."

The mental picture this conjured was nearly too much for my self-control. I tipped my face down, feigning interest in my nearly empty plate.

"So did you?" Leave it to Beck to ask the million-dollar question. My head popped right back up again in my desperation to hear the answer.

Gabe swung his unreadable stare between the two of us, probably wondering how he'd ended up getting double-teamed, with hard-core participation from a complete stranger. Given what I'd just been through, I didn't have a whole lot of sympathy for the guy.

"No. There wasn't a lot of room, and besides, she's . . ."

"What?" Beck challenged. "A girl?"

I cut in. "Maybe in the interest of full disclosure, you should specify 'Unwilling to submit to feats of strength' in your profile," I teased. I forked up a last bite of waffle. "Have there been any other recent matchups?" I probed.

Beck propped her elbow on the table and dropped her chin in her hand, apparently just as curious.

"As a matter of fact, I'm in the question-and-answer phase with a doctor," he informed us, sounding distinctly stuffy. "And I wouldn't mind a second opinion." He grinned at his own pun, and with his eyes trained on Beck, it was obvious he didn't require a third.

"A second opinion on what?" Beck asked, clearly up for whatever this brunch threw at her.

"Her get-acquainted question."

"Let's hear it," she encouraged.

"She asked which three things I'd want with me if marooned on a desert island."

"Not too original, but lots of potential there," Beck allowed.

"I used to play that game with my grandfather," I interjected. "My three things were a playhouse with working kitchen and bathroom, my favorite blanket, and a suitcase full of clothes." I sipped my sour-sweet mimosa, proud of those long-ago, very sensible decisions.

"So math wasn't your strong suit early in life, huh?" Gabe said with a smirk.

"What do you mean?"

"It never occurred to you that your tally went way beyond three things? Why didn't you just tote along a luxury resort, complete with staff and swimming pool? Hell, why not a Super Walmart?"

"That's not the same at all," I protested, looking to Beck for a little backup. Her amused, slightly sympathetic expression told me I was on my own. "All right. What would *you* take, Jack Shephard?" I asked, laying on the sarcasm.

His teeth appeared in a flash of white—clearly I'd played right into his hands. "Okay, three things?" He propped his elbow on the table and made a show of ticking them off on his fingers. "One of those gadgets that can turn salt water into fresh drinking water, an inflatable raft—with oars, and an EPIRB."

"What's an ee-perb?" I asked, waspish even in ignorance.

"An emergency position indicating radiobeacon. It's a device that can send out traceable signals to the Coast Guard and other rescue teams."

I was speechless. For about two seconds. Then I blurted, "You know with the oars, you're over three."

Glancing over, I noticed that Beck was clearly impressed—with him—not so much with me.

"You're definitely a nerd," Beck said around a laugh, and I wondered if she was remembering her recently voiced opinion on nerds. "Very impressive," she added, in a tone that confirmed she was indeed. "*If* your plan is to get off the island. If you want to *stay,* I think I'd go with sunblock, a toolkit—if you get oars, I get a toolkit—and a change of clothes. Not a big fan of the coconut bikini. Still, between the two of us, we'd be pretty well equipped."

"What would the doctor bring?" I asked, interrupting the kick-off meeting of the mutual admiration society.

"She hasn't responded since I sent back my answer."

"Maybe a little EPIRB scared her off."

But by the look of things it wasn't scaring Beck, and Gabe definitely wasn't spooked by Beck's aura of pink. Leaving the love-struck fiends to discover just what it was they were dealing with, I excused myself to score a cranberry-orange muffin.

Without distraction, my own heady, inescapable infatuation came frothing to the surface, and I wondered, crazily, if I could really walk away from *magic*. This whole situation was like my own personal fire swamp—I just had to get my bearings before I was sucked in or tackled by the R.O.U.S.'s. Blinking away delusions of *The Princess Bride*, I grabbed a little pod of butter and turned away from the buffet.

When I got back to the table, it was to find that Gabe had moved his relationship with Beck efficiently into the question-and-answer phase.

"So, do you have any more piercings . . . anywhere?" You could almost hear the yearning—my guess was he was hoping for a belly ring.

"Not yet," Beck answered, letting the words trail off into possibility.

"What about tattoos? Like 'em? Hate 'em?"

I sat silently, riveted by this awkward mating dance of Gabe's, and ate my muffin.

Beck took a sip of her mimosa before answering and then licked her lips. Gabe stared, clearly enthralled with everything about her, and so did I, fascinated by the pair of them.

"I actually have one, but I don't think I'd get another one. It stung quite a bit, and I think I've outgrown it already."

She was *good*. She had Gabe and me both hanging on her every word, desperate to know *where* she was hiding her tattoo and *what* it looked like. I glanced at Gabe, wondering if he was man enough to ask her. If not, I'd do it myself, but I figured I'd give him first dibs.

Gabe was looking as if he wanted to lunge across the table for her right then and there. I was actually feeling a little third-wheelish and so leaned slightly away from them, trying to stay out of peripheral vision.

"Wh-what did you get?" His voice cracked ever so slightly.

"It's corny," she warned, blushing till she was pink all over from the neck up. "I got a little red heart with big billowy white wings."

"Really?" For some reason, this surprised me. Gabe just continued to stare, sort of slack-jawed now. "Where is it, or is that to remain undisclosed?" I teased.

"Lower back," she confided, her tone and expression clearly expecting censure. Not from this pair of awestruck geeks. Personally, I was of the opinion that tattoos could be very sexy in tasteful moderation (and on someone else's body).

"Can I see it?" I asked, fully content, in this situation, to be living vicariously.

For the briefest moment, Beck seemed startled by my request. Then her lips quirked in a mischievous smile as she reached around to pull the waist of her skirt down a couple inches to give me a peek.

"I like it," I told her, suddenly feeling a little surge of nerve and inspiration, poised for some pins and needles of my own. Figuratively speaking.

I'd weighed the pros and cons, *for* Sean and against, and there was no contest—I should walk away. But the pros wouldn't concede defeat—they were scrappy, devious little fighters, ceaselessly nibbling at my resolve, playing out the what-ifs like a Choose Your Own—*Potentially Very Sexy*—Adventure. And they'd won this round.

Schooling my voice to sound offhand around the uproar in my brain and body, I asked, "Either of you busy Thursday night?" Had me thinking about where their relationship could be by then . . .

An uncomfortable beat of silence passed as the two of them turned to gape at me.

"You're gonna go?" Beck asked, quick on the uptake and clearly ecstatic.

"You do remember that Thursday is a work night, right?" Gabe said.

Ignoring him, I pressed, "I'm not getting a good read here. Yes or no?"

"I'll go!" Beck offered enthusiastically. I was beginning to think that, regardless of the situation, Beck was always up for some crazy escapades.

I glanced at Gabe, daring him to say no now that Beck had

agreed to go. He was looking at her, his expression bland, but I could guess what he was thinking: If he went for it with Beck, would she hang on long enough for date number two? Hard to say.

"Okay, I'm in," he finally said. "If you tell me why we're going."

"Because he asked me." *And because I really want to see him again—just one more time—this wildly sexy rock star with a come-hither accent and an inexplicable "thing" for me.* "And because I'm not a snob."

"Reason enough," Beck agreed, staring across the table at Gabe as if daring him to find a flaw in this reasoning. "Maybe even because you want to give things one more chance?"

I shot her a quelling glare.

Gabe seemed content with that, and by mutual agreement, we turned the conversation back to the mundane. But when Beck casually presented her theory that there might be vampire bats living amongst the gargantuan urban bat colony beneath the Congress Avenue Bridge, it was obvious that Gabe was smitten, and for him, there would be no turning back at all.

Having both parked on a side street a block from the restaurant, Gabe and Beck walked off together post-brunch. I suspected Beck was both pleased and disappointed with this arrangement. I knew she'd love some extra face time with me to dish over the details of the wedding, the man, and the journal, but I got the feeling she'd like a little more time with Gabe too. The way things were going, the face time between them might shortly involve Gabe getting an up-close and personal view of that sparkly pink nose stud.

I'd probably be getting a call later, from one or both of them. But until then, I was actually a little relieved to be alone. I only wished I could escape the tug-of-war in my head. Cueing up a CD guaranteed to pry my mind away from my problems, I let KT Tunstall take me far away. To the extent that my turn into the parking lot of Waterloo Records was not a conscious decision.

And yet I knew exactly what I was doing there. Waterloo Records had a reputation for supporting local music and for stocking the CDs of SXSW performers, not that I'd ever come looking. But as of this moment, I had a personal interest in perusing their selection.

Rather than poke around browsing, I went straight to the counter, a woman on a mission, and found myself face-to-face with two tall, scruffy, very *interesting*-looking guys.

"Hi. Do you guys know if you happen to carry any CDs by Loch'd In? They're a Scottish band performing at South by Southwest this year?"

"Definitely," said the scruffier-looking dude, coming around the counter to help me in my search. His immediate, positive answer whipped my vital signs into a frenzy, and it barely registered that he was still talking.

"They're actually scattered a couple of places around the store," he informed me as I trailed along behind him. "Easiest to find is right here." His tattooed arm gestured toward a display of CDs. He then flipped through a half dozen jewel cases before he turned and extended his hand, holding out the object of my search.

"Great," I answered, my voice almost unrecognizable as I reached for the CD. My eyes were riveted on the cover, mesmerized by the long, slippery neck of a sea monster surfacing behind the band as they stood on the shore of a loch—and by Sean's face staring back at me.

Two minutes later, I was back in the car, clawing at the shrink-wrap with my short, blunt fingernails, trying to catch an edge in the plastic and rip it off. I could feel an unfamiliar urgency coursing through me . . . and then—*finally*—it was free. Clumsily I pushed the disc into the changer, sparing one final glance for what I could only assume was the Loch Ness Monster. I was 99 percent certain that the photo had been digitally enhanced.

Desperate once again to be *doing* rather than thinking, I shifted the car into gear and pulled out of the parking lot just as the haunting music from last night's Web search filled the car.

Somehow I managed to find my way home with the deep, dark edge of Sean's voice coursing over me, through me, into me. I could picture him, singing these words, and it wasn't so hard to imagine him singing them to me. It wasn't until the CD changer clicked over to the next disc in the queue that I realized I'd been sitting in my driveway, oblivious to the world, for at least a half hour. Evidently the stand I'd intended to take against Fairy Jane had been cut off at the knees, and my willpower was fading fast.

It didn't help that when I walked inside, threw my keys on the counter, and ripped away Saturday's page in the quote-a-day calendar, Sunday's read, " 'Silly things do cease to be silly if they are done by sensible people in an impudent way.' *Emma*." Apparently I needed to get a little cheeky, and everything would work itself out. That didn't exactly sound like a strategy to live by.

9

In which Nic is vexed.
And very possibly hexed.

By Monday I was back to normal, or at least relatively so. I mean, how normal was it possible to be with a magical journal stashed amid your literary classics? Right now I was boycotting the interfering little book, endeavoring not even to glance in its direction. And after my Sunday afternoon marathon whipping up the day's second batch of cupcakes (lemon with Texas "Big Hair" Meringue) with my new CD cued up to repeat, I'd declared a moratorium on *Loch'd In*. The CD was now stashed with the journal, and I was immune to bad influence.

True to ritual, I had checked the quote of the day and been vaguely surprised at how particularly apt it was on this, the day of my performance review: " 'There are people, who the more you do for them, the less they will do for themselves.' *Emma*." But the coincidence was quickly forgotten amid the stress of the morning. I was desperate to hear the final decision on the open management position I'd applied for last month. It would be worth all the crazy uncertainty of the past couple of days, all the magical mumbo jumbo, if just this one little thing went according to The Plan. And then it was back to the antiques store for a chat with the Shop Nazi and a search for a magical key. Talk about living a double life.

Fidgety and unable to concentrate for more than ten minutes at a time, I was up and down all morning, walking off tension, weaving through the maze of cubicles, gravitating toward Brett's cube like an awkward bee to honey. The whole situation was a prickly catch-22: I had no idea what to say to him—how to explain—about the wedding, the sexy stranger, or my unexpected disappearance, and yet I felt like I needed to see him, if nothing else, to recalibrate my thought processes.

But he was MIA. His lights were on and there were curly edged design schematics splayed over his desk, but Brett was disturbingly absent.

Even Gabe wasn't available as a distraction.

I was just back from another go-round when my boss rapped on the door frame of my open-air cubicle and smiled. "Ready, Nic?"

I followed him back to his walled office, fantasizing over the possibility of getting a door and ceiling of my very own. The conversation started out great, with him congratulating me on an impressive slew of accomplishments (his words) and efforts above and beyond. I smiled in a self-deprecating manner and accepted the accolades. It was all very "Hallmark Special."

"I think you'll be pleasantly surprised," he finally said, beaming as he slid a sheet of paper across the desk toward me. "You deserve it, Nic."

This was it! I took a deep, shaky breath and bit my lip, holding it in as I reached for that crisp white sheet of paper that had the potential to change everything. Raising it, I glanced once more at my boss, now lounging back in his chair, a satisfied smile suffusing his face. My anticipation having now risen to a frenzied pitch, my gaze flitted over the page as my heartbeat thrummed in my chest.

A quick scan showed me I'd moved up a pay grade—always nice—and scored a promotion. Woo-hoo! A little more clout was never a bad thing. But there was no hint as to whether it was to be *managerial* clout or just plain-jane engineering clout, and I needed to know. I lowered the page, my smile settled firmly in place, and looked my boss directly in the eye.

"Any news on the open management position?"

His smile fell away, and his gaze scuttled away from mine as he shifted in his chair, and suddenly my heart's thrumming turned to thudding, my climactic moment having taken a disappointing detour.

"The management team felt that right now you're a much greater asset to us as a 'hands-on' engineer."

No doubt. Who else was willing to pick up any and all slack in a blind quest for management? The ultimate irony. He kept talking, but all I heard was a droning buzz, which I suspected was the pressure in my head as I resisted the urge to let fly with a string of curses. When his lips finally stopped moving, I smiled my pissed-but-polite smile, somehow managed to grit out my thanks, and swung through the door.

"Oh hey, Nic," he called, pulling me back. "Probably shouldn't have, but I ate two of those cupcakes you brought in." He smiled, patted his belly, and gave me a jaunty thumbs-up.

Fan-freakin'-tastic. I smiled with teeth, and feeling like a human time bomb seconds from detonation, I focused on moving myself as far as possible from the greatest population density. I was in the hall when I finally went off, a mini mushroom cloud.

Once it was over, I indulged in a poor-baby and spent yet another moment likening myself to Cinderella, the drudge, the girl desperate to go to the ball. Funny thing was, I already *had* a fairy godmother, and I'd been to the ball, albeit another sort of ball entirely. And that had been more than I could handle. I definitely didn't want Fairy Jane messing around with this part of my life—I was having enough trouble reining her in as it was.

Still, I would love to do . . . *something.* I couldn't quit—that would be completely erratic and irresponsible—but *something* . . .

"Ready for a change yet?"

The suggestion, out loud and "out there," ignited a miniature spark in me, and I almost imagined it was coming from the little devil who sat, perpetually ignored, on my shoulder.

I quickly realized I was no longer alone in the hallway. Mark Frasier, division manager for the failure analysis lab, was standing two feet away, his approach having gone unnoticed amid the pity party.

The second I realized his comment had been intended as a legitimate offer, the spark exploded into a wild trail of color, a flare, wending its way through my thoughts, nudging disappointment into rebelliousness. Mark had casually offered me a place on his team more than once before, but I'd always brushed him off, a woman on a mission to management. But today I wasn't in the mood for any sort of brush-off, having just been on the receiving end of a particularly upsetting one myself. Today I was feeling a little dangerous. I took a deep, steadying breath and let confident determination curl my lips.

"I think today I might be ready," I admitted, exhilarated to register the startling effect this response had on Mark and just a little smug in the face of his slow, conspiratorial grin.

"Serious?" he said.

I let my eyes stray a little, nowhere in particular, and then brought them back front and center. "Yep." It actually felt good to admit it. "Do you have openings?"

"We're about to. One of our guys is moving to Phoenix, and you'd save me a lot of trouble, seeing as you're an ace in the hole." And then suddenly his enthusiasm and mine were dimmed somewhat by responsible thinking. "But you should probably take some time to think about it—this seems sort of spur of the moment."

I nodded, exuding good sense but really only thinking how quickly I could have my cubicle packed up. "Well, I'm pretty sure, but if it'll make you feel better, we can wait a couple days to make it official. How about I give you a call on Friday?" Me, I could make a clean break right now, toting along what was left of the cupcakes on my way to making new friends.

"Sounds good. Meantime, I'll work on shuffling things up. We'll get you in and get you to work before you can change your mind." He winked.

I smiled, tossed him a wave, and moved off down the hall on my way back to my cubicle.

In fewer than twenty paces, the warm fuzzy of new beginnings and professional regard had started to fade, and suddenly struck by the reality of what had just happened, I was freaking out big-time.

I couldn't take that job! I had no doubt it would be a fascinating career change and an oh-so-satisfying departure from the life of Go-To Girl, but it was *wrong for me*—it was counterproductive, impulsive, and it *totally* screwed with the big picture (i.e., The Plan). It would be like starting over. Instead of being focused on product testing and production efficiency, I'd be dealing with individual product failures, state-of-the-art analysis equipment, and angry customers. There'd be a significant learning curve, and management would be out of reach for a little while, likely beyond my target age of thirty. . . .

Transferring departments and switching jobs had *never* been on my agenda, but today, just now, it was nearly a fait accompli. Stress reaction? Possibly. Coincidence that it had happened within days of Fairy Jane worming her way into my life? Not bloody likely. You can bet I suspected foul play. How she managed it, I couldn't even begin to speculate.

It had been over twenty-four hours since I'd decided to ignore Fairy Jane's latest advice, putting her firmly in her place amid my collection of favorite fictional romances. Maybe she was a fellow grudge holder intent on kicking things up a notch. Well, I could play hardball too—the shredder was not out of the realm of possibility.

If she could derail The Plan in just a couple of unsuspecting minutes, then what was next?

A nose-pierced vision of myself, belting out "Beautiful" à la Christina Aguilera to a crowd of lesbians in an off-key show of solidarity was just as scary as it should have been. Part of me wondered if Fairy Jane had that kind of power. And part of me was starting to get very nervous.

I'd never planned to "meet him too" either. And look at me now—I'd kissed him, bought his CD, and I was well on my way to becoming a groupie. Could I even take credit for *those* decisions?

I was going crazy!

This shouldn't be freaking me out. I could call Mark right now and tell him to forget it, that I'd been talkin' crazy. Easy out. But honestly, I was still reeling from being passed over for management all over again, and I was afraid of what might come out of my mouth if I tried. Time to make a quick exit, go find that key, and get some answers. I promised myself I'd ask Beck about all this later.

The phone rang as I stepped back through the doorway of my cubicle, and I debated not answering, a little fearful of what I might admit or agree to in this fragile state of not-myself. But crossing my fingers against virtually every eventuality, I picked up and found myself in the middle of a rant.

"A bikini, a mangotini, and a cabana boy?" Gabe blustered.

"Yes, please!" After the morning I'd had, a little fantasy come true sounded very, very good. So long as Fairy Jane wasn't involved . . .

Judging by the silence, Gabe didn't agree. I forged ahead. "Desert isle chick came back with an answer, huh?"

"Seems we weren't *stranded* on the island, just alone, and she had cabana boy plans for *me!*" I imagined Gabe's shouted admission sailing over the open-air cubicles that surrounded him and suppressed a giggle. "A little clarification would have been nice," he complained.

"It wouldn't have mattered—you were proud of that EPIRB."

"True." I heard a muttered curse. "Do they all have to want me only for my body?"

"Ahh . . . the dance of online seduction," I teased, holding back a snort of laughter. "You Photoshopped, didn't you? A little pec here and a little pec there . . ."

"No! I did not. You may be programmed to only see a guy's 401(k) potential, but I can hold my own on both the physical and financial fronts."

This time I didn't bother to hold back my burst of laughter. "Next time I see you, I'll take another look," I promised. "But now I gotta go."

"To lunch? I'll go with you."

"No. I need to run an errand. Sort of a girl thing," I added, knowing that'd stave off any and all follow-up questions.

"Say no more. Hey, how did your performance review go? That was this morning, right?"

"Tell you later," I fudged, really not wanting to discuss it right now. I tried to hang up, but Gabe was evidently undeterred by my dismissive, slightly brusque manner. I yanked the phone back against my ear.

"What?" I demanded, my anger quickly morphing into guilt.

"Did Beck . . . say anything?"

"About what?" I asked, trying to be nicer as I gathered up my purse and rummaged for my car keys.

"About me."

I smiled into the phone. "You're the one who left with her. I haven't talked to her since."

"Well, what'd you think?"

I was standing in my cubicle, hopped up on anxiety, ready to go but for the landline receiver attached to the side of my head, and Gabe wanted to dish like a junior high school girl. Resigned, I pulled out my chair and dropped into it.

"About you two? Well, let's see. She's very pink and a little punk; you're very geek and a little ga-ga. And yet . . . it seemed like you got along great. Just remember you're old enough to be her mentor," I teased. "Why not consider what your computer might think of the match? Seriously, can I go now?"

"Please do."

Halfway to the lobby (and about four hours late) it occurred to me that the journal was spending the morning with the Austen ladies. No question it would take a miracle for me to find the right key amid the dubious treasures crowding Violet's Crown Antiques, but it'd be downright impossible without the journal. Looked like I'd be making a little detour back home. I truly hoped I was in line for some good karma.

Pulling into the driveway in record time, I fully intended to run in and back out again with the journal in my hot little hands, but once it had been pulled from the shelf, a mingling of temper and curiosity double-teamed my typical efficiency. Grabbing a handful of dark chocolate M&M's from the bowl on the counter, I parked myself cross-legged in a chair at the kitchen table.

I'd popped open an Internet window during that morning's fidgety waiting period, typed "fairies" into the search box, and learned way more than I'd cared to. They were quite the little bitches—devious, self-serving, and prone to trickery. Fairy godmothers, on the other hand, were known for having their wards' best interests at heart. So which was I dealing with? It was mighty hard to say.

With fairies of all sorts flitting about in my head, I jotted off the day's entry, short and just shy of sweet.

Okay, what is the deal?! Seriously. I assumed we had some sort of arrangement: You supply the crazy, mixed-up romantic advice, and I let you. On condition that the magic is kept safely tucked away in its own little quiet corner, <u>inside</u> the journal. No spells, enchantments, or charms— nothing devious or underhanded. And that's it. My job has always been <u>positively off-limits</u>.

And yet . . . surprise, surprise . . . when asked today whether I'd consider a job transfer, out of nowhere, I said I would. The funny (you could say suspicious) thing about that is that I won't! I've worked my way up through the ranks of this job, and I'm holding out for management—I've <u>earned</u> management. I don't want to start over on a whim.

You want to know what I think? You're not just omniscient, you're hands-on. A couple of magic words, a sprinkling of fairy dust, a little wave of the proverbial wand, and there I am talking crazy, soundly hexed. Well, I'd like to respectfully request that it doesn't happen again—not ever. I'd like you to keep your charms to yourself. If you need to take a break from all the romance stuff for a little while, how about some savvy investment tips? . . . seriously!

Glancing over my words, I wondered how well Fairy Jane dealt with sass. Feeling a little gutsy, I snapped the book closed, ready for the next round. Honestly, I would have much preferred to banish it back to the bookshelf, but today, it seemed, absolutely everything was outside my control.

And then, on the way out the door, as I grabbed a couple more M&M's, my gaze happened to catch on the little square calendar propped jauntily beside the door. It clearly displayed today's date, but the quote had changed from the one that had been there this morning. Now it read, " 'When he was present she had no eyes for anyone else. Everything he did was right. Everything he said was clever.' *Sense and Sensibility*." I smacked it face-down on the counter and slid it into the closest kitchen drawer.

I guess I had my answer. The crazy was no longer confined to the journal—it was on the loose, in Austin. I couldn't imagine a more dangerous combination.

I tried calling Beck on my way downtown, but it rolled to voice mail. As soon as her class was over, she'd be getting quite the earful. I truly hoped she had a logical explanation for this, although, knowing her, it probably wouldn't be the least bit reassuring—or logical.

Violet's seemed a little less quirky on a Monday at noon, and after parking on the street, I hurried inside, the journal tucked away in my purse. Deciding to risk another run-in with the Shop Nazi before launching an all-out search for the key myself, I headed for the counter. She saw me coming and crinkled her lips into a thin line.

"Is there something I can help you with?" she inquired, clearly hoping my answer was negative.

"I hope so," I answered, exuding friendly, encouraging vibes. "I'm actually looking for a key to fit this lock." I held up the journal and watched as it triggered her memory: me groveling unattractively, Beck being Beck. I couldn't tell her I'd talked to Mr. Nelson—she'd wonder how I'd gotten his name and number, since she hadn't been willing to give it up. This was going to go great. "I really feel like there should be a key." Well done.

"I don't recall a key, but you're free to look." That was evidently all I was going to get out of her.

"Are you the owner here?" I was holding out for the possibility that there was a sweet little lady locked in a closet somewhere in the back. If I could bust her out, maybe *she'd* help me.

"I am, yes."

Wishful thinking foiled again.

"O-kay then," I said brightly. "Well I guess I'll just start looking. Any suggestions on where to start . . . ?" I asked, turning slightly, ready to rummage.

"There is a small collection of keys on the marble-topped console by the door." It clearly pained her to offer up even this stingy bit of information. "And a few scattered about in various vignettes around the shop. Enjoy."

"Oh, I plan to," I tossed back, smiling widely. On the outside chance that I found the key and managed to unlock some magical mojo, at least she wouldn't be there looking over my shoulder.

And so, for the next forty-five minutes, I combed the shop, painstakingly searching through an eclectic collection of hiding spots for a magical key. From silk-lined jewelry cases to cigar boxes, crystal candy dishes to cedar-lined drawers. There was no shortage of keys, but none of them fit and, as ridiculous as it sounded, none of them looked quite right, magically speaking. Whatever that meant. I was just about to give up and resign myself to never experiencing the deluxe version of the journal when my tired gaze caught on a dainty brass key on a thin crimson ribbon, winking in a stream of sunlight. I had the weirdest sense that it had been hiding, lurking as it was amid a jumbled mix of dominos and mah-jong tiles in a carved wooden ashtray. I'd scanned this particular menagerie at least once before and come up empty.

Moving closer, my heart starting to pound and my throat constricting with incredulous wonder, I glanced at the key plate on the journal, gauging the size of the keyhole. And then, suddenly, I was standing in the glare of the sun, fitting the key to the lock, feeling a quivering, tingling excitement as I realized that this was the one. With a gentle twist the journal came to life in my hands.

It was all relatively low-key: no shimmering swirls of fairy dust spiraling crazily, no inanimate objects skittering about, just quiet freakiness. The slim little volume that had once fit in my purse expanded, growing heavy in my hands, becoming a veritable tome as pages crowded into its spine. I was quite proud not to have dropped it like a hot potato and was praying the Shop Nazi wouldn't come looking for me, having been summoned by the pounding of my telltale heart. When it finished its magical metamorphosis, I cautiously lifted the cover to peek at the first page. The page was now blanketed with a familiar old-fashioned script.

> *To Miss Jane Anna Elizabeth Austen*
>
> *MY DEAR NEICE:*
>
> *Though you are at this period not many degrees removed from Infancy, Yet trusting that you will in time be older, and that through the care of your excellent Parents, You will one day or another be able to read written hand, I dedicate to You the following Miscellanious Morsels, convinced that if you seriously attend to them, You will derive from them very important Instructions, with regard to your Conduct in Life.—If such my hopes should hereafter be realized, never shall I regret the Days and Nights that have been spent in composing these Treatises for your Benefit. I am, my dear Neice*
>
> > *Your very Affectionate*
> > *Aunt*
>
> *June 2d. 1793*

Oh. My. God! It *couldn't* be—it couldn't *possibly* be! Beck had suspected, and I had been, ever so slowly, starting to believe that maybe the journal's cheeky bits of advice had been conceived by the mind of Jane Austen, but this, this was proof! Omigod, omigod, omigod! Completely thrown by Beck's utterly implausible theory, I had totally forgotten about the inscription, which, it was now clear, was only an excerpt of a more lengthy dedication to Miss Austen's niece!

I tipped the book closed, releasing a puff of dust—it could have been fairy or otherwise, it was impossible to tell. Then eyes wide, movements jerky, I scanned the store around me in a panic. I couldn't think what to do. This book had historical significance, seeing as it contained some lost writings of literary darling Jane Austen. But at the same time, I was kinda in the middle of something here—my life was in an uproar. To say nothing of my sincere desire to keep my journaling secrets strictly need-to-know. And how would the world handle the whole mystic, paranormal element, the one I was currently struggling with myself? Tough call.

Mired in confusion, I tipped the book open again. Hurriedly riffling past the first few pages, I flipped pages quickly, standing transfixed as one set of tidy handwriting gave way to the next. I was scanning only, trying not to focus on anything too closely, more than a little disconcerted with the journal's latest bout of showmanship. I felt suddenly out of breath and helplessly overwhelmed, my thoughts and uncertainties churning themselves into a sickly stew. These were other people's private thoughts—or else they had been two minutes ago when I was still keyless and blissfully clueless. I kept going, spurred by avid curiosity. Pages whizzed past until I'd reached the end—my handwriting, my turn with the journal.

Miss Nicola James, 1 will attend.

My words were there, but I'd replaced them myself—inconclusive. The next page confirmed what I'd already suspected. . . .

Miss Nicola James will be sensible and indulge in a little romance . . .
Not with a man, with a dress . . .

The cheeky little cleavage excerpt à la Fairy Jane had disappeared just as stealthily as it had arrived. I flipped ahead to check the other entries—all fully intact—and then let the journal thump closed, quickly yanking the key out of the lock. The reverse transformation was no less awe-inspiring, and suddenly the stocky volume had once again turned slim, and I held the key in the palm of my hand.

Glancing casually in the direction of the counter, I made a snap decision: This key clearly belonged with the journal, so by rights, it was included in the original purchase price. I refused to run the risk of Shop Nazi–induced complications for an item that was justifiably mine. What if she insisted I demonstrate lock/key compatibility? I wasn't willing to take that risk. So feeling very cloak and dagger, I slipped out of the shop without a word.

On the walk back to the car, it occurred to me that with the key removed, the excerpts had probably returned to the journal. Which made me wonder whether a new one had appeared in response to my latest rant.

Curious, I tipped open the cover and tried to subdue the pages as they riffled in the wind. Carefully turning past the controversial "pencil him in," I saw that Fairy Jane had struck again. I reread the leftover words with mounting anxiety, feeling undeniably trapped.

10

On condition that you take the romance seriously.

Evidently Fairy Jane was not above a little quid pro quo, and as disturbing as that was, I didn't want to think about it right now. I didn't particularly care to think about the fact that my little plan—*the Nic James Life Plan*—was being systematically dismantled, and I was standing helplessly by, struggling to decide whether I even wanted to piece it back together. My world had gone topsy-turvy.

My favorite cupcake spot was nearby, tucked into a shiny silver Airstream trailer, and right now, I needed a fix—bad. Winking in the sunlight with a giant rotating cupcake on its roof, Hey Cupcake! was a city treasure. I stepped up to the window under the frosting-pink awning, closed my eyes, and inhaled the sweet scent of cake and frosting. Today I needed the Double Dose Whipper Snapper, with its injection of whipped cream, and of course, the requisite carton of milk.

Carrying my order to an umbrella-covered table just beyond the metallic glare of the trailer, I let myself be hypnotized by the sprinkle-topped jumbo replica on the roof, and for five solid minutes just let it be about the cupcake. At five minutes, two seconds, I simultaneously got a "Where are you?" text and remembered the meeting for which I was now horribly late.

Shit! I'd *never* missed a meeting—never even been late—and now all I could think was that I didn't want to leave my happy cupcake place. I wanted to hide out inside the trailer and forget everything that had happened in the last seventy-two hours. I. Was. Not. Myself.

Time to regroup. First I needed to ground myself, because right now I was either floating or free-falling, it was difficult to tell. The answers I wanted—some of them at least—were in the journal, and it seemed like Cat Nelson's entries might be the perfect place to find them. Depending on what I found, I might even want to roadtrip down to New Braunfels to quiz Mr. Nelson in person on what he knew about his sister's experience with an honest-to-God Fairy Jane.

Pulling the journal out of my bag as covertly as possible, I tucked it under the table in front of me and glanced around to see if I had an audience. I didn't—evidently no one went for cupcakes at one-thirty P.M. on a weekday. I turned the key and felt the weight of a hundred secrets on my lap—a couple of hefty pounds.

Riding high on a sugar rush, I flipped to the end, searching for Cat's first entry. It appeared she was already a little sweet on Tyler Honeycutt.

Everywhere I turn, he's holding a door or tipping his hat. Seeing his clean-shaven face smiling down at me underneath the brim of his Stetson, a shiver of excitement runs through me. He's wearing me down, little by little—it makes me nervous to think about it.

The second entry covered the barbeque and dance held at the VFW hall and a corsage of yellow roses.

I don't even pretend to know how you seem to "know" certain things— about me, about him—but I figure this is my life, and I need to make my own decisions. And I think Tyler is the man for me.

The next couple of entries came off as vaguely snide—much like my own entries—as if Cat was getting advice she wasn't prepared to take. I could relate. It seemed as if Fairy Jane was fighting a losing battle. But something must have shifted the balance. . . .

Then I found it.

Tyler's older brother Jameson lost his leg today working on a combine. I'm doing my best to be useful in this time of tragedy and praying for the family, but I can't help but consider how this all affects Tyler and me. I don't imagine that Jameson can manage to run the ranch now, which means the job will fall to Tyler. We had big plans—plans to see the world, to have adventures, and now he'll be tied to the ranch, and me with him if I agree to marry him. I've already said yes, and while, in most cases, I reserve the right to change my mind, I can't decide what to do. I don't want to jilt him, but I don't want to be trapped here either. What can I do? What would you do?

A quick scan produced the relevant words: "don't marry him." And much as I felt for Tyler—not to mention Jameson—I had to side with Fairy Jane on this one. And judging by my brief conversation with Mr. Nelson, Cat had ultimately decided to do the same.

So she'd taken Fairy Jane's advice and seemingly gone on to live a lovely life. Seemingly. I gulped down the rest of my milk, scoped out my surroundings—I still had my picnic table to myself—and kept reading.

I did it—I broke it off with Tyler. It was harder than I thought it would be. I guess I thought he'd understand since he'd had the same dreams I had, but he didn't, not at all. He went on and on about family obligations and responsibility, and I understood that, I really did, but Fredericksburg was never going to be big enough for me. I'd been waiting for as long as I could remember to get out, and I just couldn't stay. I kissed him good-bye and tasted my own salty tears. He didn't shed a single one for me, and when I left, there was only anger and hurt in his eyes. I know I made the right decision, and I'm relieved to have, if not an actual person, then at least a voice on my side, so thank you. . . .

After that, Cat's entries ran to her involvement with the USO, her training in the Army Nurse Corps and deployment to Normandy, France, and other adventures after the war. Her entries were a little spottier as time passed, and they never made mention of another man, which, of course, made me wonder: Had Tyler Honeycutt been her one true love? Had she traded her happily-ever-after for a chance to see the world? Had she had any regrets, held a grudge against Fairy Jane? Had she ever come back to Texas?

I snapped the journal shut and twisted out the key, conscious of a subtle, sucking sound as the secrets retreated back inside the journal.

Cat Nelson had clearly had a rewarding life, but what about love? I certainly didn't want to stick to the Nic James Life Plan if it meant I'd spend the rest of my life as a Do-It-Yourself-er. As far as I was concerned, the matter was inconclusive.

And I supposed, in my brave new world, the next step was obvious: Tomorrow's lunch hour would be spent on a roadtrip to New Braunfels. I'd track down Mr. Nelson and hope to get a few answers.

Resigned, I headed back to work, watching the giant rotating cupcake in my rearview mirror until it disappeared, wondering if it was possible that this was all a really detailed, highly involved dream sequence. Thank God there'd been cupcakes.

By the time I got back to work I was dreading the rest of the afternoon—not to mention a run-in with my boss. Within seconds of dropping into my chair, my phone trilled loudly into the subdued hush of murmured conversation and clicking keyboards, popping my private little bubble.

"Nicola James," I answered, sounding deflated.

"Yeah, this is Steve in the lobby. Some flowers have been delivered for you."

I stared at the phone and frowned. "Some flowers?"

"Yes, ma'am."

"All riiight. I'm coming down." This was definitely a mistake—I was not the type of girl who got roses on a random weekday. But today I was happy for any reason to escape.

I took the stairs down to the lobby and beelined for the security desk. A single bouquet of flowers sat on the black granite counter, and I had to admit, I wanted them. No vase, just a clutch of cranberry red gerbera daisies wrapped up in florist's tape and tied with a skinny sapphire ribbon. The fact that there'd clearly been a mistake was going to make marching back upstairs into a gray-walled windowless cubicle more than a little depressing. Particularly today.

Stepping up to the desk, I flashed my badge to the well-identified Steve, and he announced, quite unnecessarily, "Here they are."

Yearning just slightly for a miracle, the general gist of which was that a certain smitten stranger had managed, despite my evasive maneuvers, to track me down, my heart thumped steadily in my chest. Wanting a little privacy, I shifted to the corner of the desk and opened the card that, oddly enough, had my name on it.

I'm not above a good old-fashioned bribe.
Please come Thursday,
Sean.

I reread the words, disbelieving, and then lifted my hand to my lips, only slightly worried that I might let out an embarrassing screech right there in the lobby.

"Pretty please?"

I jerked at the voice just outside my peripheral vision and whipped my head around in shock. An accent wasn't so uncommon around here, but the voice was unmistakable.

"Sean?" My voice sounded strangled; breath escaped me. Scruffy around the edges in jeans, a SXSW T-shirt, and a three o' clock shadow, Sean was larger than life. He'd found me. Here at Micro. Worlds were definitely colliding. I couldn't speak, couldn't think. This was big—pivotal even—and with the latest excerpt still fresh in my mind, I couldn't help but wonder if this pretty little bouquet was doing double duty.

Sean stepped closer, his presence working like interference on all logical thought processes, and reached for my hand. As his thumb grazed my knuckles, I melted a little. I tried for a deep, steadying breath, but it came out shakier than I'd hoped.

"What are you doing here?"

"A harmless bit of self-promotion to jog your memory."

Very deliberately, he leaned in, his whole body shifting toward mine. For a fleeting, obscenely thrilling moment, I imagined that he was going to kiss me right there in the Micro lobby. I closed my eyes, breathed in his citrusy scent, and indulged in this ephemeral moment.

When my eyes fluttered back open, I realized he'd only been reaching for the bouquet, sitting on the counter behind me. Disoriented and a little disappointed to have misread his intentions, I tried to rally, taking the flowers he was nudging into my hands. Grinning at the daisies' happy little faces, I tipped them up to my nose.

"They're beautiful—thank you!—but they're totally unnecessary. You were *very* memorable."

"They suit you. Now you just need a meadow behind you." His voice was low, half-serious, half-teasing, and I couldn't help but smile. I glanced down at myself in jeans and a ruffle-edged white blouse.

"No argument here." I couldn't figure how it was possible, but he was waaay more charming and fly-away-to-Scotland sexy than I remembered. "But I'm guessing it's not waiting in the car?"

My smile quirked up, a surefire hint that I was kidding about the meadow. A little too late, I remembered my own advice: Geeky girls did not flirt with über-sexy men and come away unscathed. What if he assumed I was interested? *Idiot!* I *was* interested. But what if he thought I was seriously interested? Well, I *was* seriously interested—I just wasn't interested in anything serious. And therein lay the rub.

I dipped my head down abruptly and feathered my fingers over the delicate fringe of petals.

"No room on the back of the bike."

"You *biked* here?" My head whipped back up at this stunning news.

His laugh rolled out like faraway thunder as he gave my fingers a friendly squeeze.

"Nothing quite so crazy. The bike is a motorcycle."

Why was I not surprised? "In that case," I assured him, "you're off the hook—I'll be responsible for my own meadow." Was it just me, or did that sound kinky?

"I was hoping the flowers would persuade you to come out to dinner with me tonight. I brought along a spare helmet."

I was busy being amused by his negotiation tactics when it hit me—he was expecting me to ride on the back of his motorcycle.

"Uh-uh." I shook my head in quick little spastic jerks. "I don't do motorcycles. I like a good steel door, a snug seat belt, and a Freon-powered air conditioner—or on a day like today, a trusty heater."

"You're really quite adorable," he mused, sliding his finger along the edge of my jaw. And I had to admit, at this moment, that finger was welcome almost anywhere. "Right, then. Rain check on the bike," he said, breaking contact. Even in my muddled state I could recognize the tone of his voice—he was totally confident he'd be able to persuade me onto that bike. Poor guy, he had no idea who he was dealing with.

But the motorcycle was the least of my problems. He was looking for a date—for tonight! I'd thought we'd kind of mutually agreed at the wedding that this little mini-crush going on between us was a one-night deal. (I may have been deluding myself, but I wasn't counting my appearance at his band's Thursday night exhibition as anything more than a casual night out.) Yet here he was, looking for night number two.

And he looked sooo good.

And he'd brought me flowers.

And Fairy Jane was essentially blackmailing me into giving him a chance. She fought dirty, but with *very* good taste—I considered that a truly redeeming quality.

I needed a second to think this through. I hadn't exactly had time since discovering the latest excerpt, with its blatant attempt at blackmail, not to mention the calendar, with its eerily timely quotes, to formulate a plan. The fact that I'd decided to see Sean's band on Thursday and subsequently raced out to buy their CD and play it just shy of obsession didn't necessarily justify any sort of "date" between us. Even running the risk of blackmail, I didn't think a date would be a good idea.

"So, dinner?" Sean asked, tracing dizzying circles on the inside of my palm. Before I could formulate a response, he moved in closer, close enough to have me backing up against the security counter, whispering, "I'll pretend to be an investment banker."

My eyes widened in a mix of shock and confusion, and I stumbled over my words. "Wh-why would you do that?"

"To put you at ease. You don't strike me as the type to date musicians."

I tipped my head down and felt the flush creep up my neck. "I'm not actually dating anyone at all."

"Brilliant! Can I assume that you're free, then, it being a Monday night and all?"

The surprise and shock of it all, combined with the slow seduction of my palm, had me sliding into submission despite the clamor of protestations sounding in my brain.

"Sure," I answered with what probably seemed like an overly dramatic exhalation of breath. "How about we meet at seven?"

We agreed on a place and exchanged cell phone numbers, and as I programmed his into my phone, I couldn't help but imagine how bittersweet it was going to be when it was time to delete it.

"I'll meet you there," I said. "Without helmet hair."

And then he flashed me that charming, irresistible smile and began, once again, to lean in. Images fluttered like butterflies in my brain, and for at least two excruciating seconds, I was dizzy with uncertainty. I'd imagined so many different ways to be kissed by this man—all of them quite excellent—and I was darn ready to get on with things.

At long last, his lips pressed softly against my temple, sending the blood rushing to that spot, causing a rhythmic pounding that closely resembled a sinus headache. Feeling the tingle on my skin, I realized that further time spent with Sean was bound to turn my face into a series of landmarks, all branded with his name. When he let go of my hand, I tightened my grip on my perky little bouquet and watched as he disappeared through the lobby's revolving door. And then I climbed the steps back to my cube.

I was beginning to wonder if my fancy little spicy-scented journal worked like the famed wardrobe that secreted a passage to Narnia, as a portal that had sent me spiraling into some sort of parallel universe. The very idea was wildly unbelievable, but lately I felt like a stand-in in someone else's life.

Dropping the daisies into a mug of tepid drinking water, I eyed their innocent little faces, forcing myself to remember that they were not the guilty party here. On edge, I shifted my gaze to stare at the phone, biting my lower lip. I suddenly had this intense need to talk to someone who understood about worlds colliding. I immediately thought of Beck.

She wasn't working today—she had a full class schedule on Mondays—but I'd catch her between bells. I dialed her cell, and it went straight to voice mail, and I heard myself leaving an urgent, angsty message with a final plea to please try to call me before seven.

Conscious of the need to get some work done today, I swung into my lab coat, selected the pertinent binder from a tidily organized row, and carefully collected the tray of parts I needed to get tested that afternoon.

I ran into Brett on my way out—literally ran into him. He was lounging in the doorway of my cube, his hands deep in his pockets. He had an uncertain little-boy look on his face as he eyed the daisies peeping their mischievous little faces up over the edge of my travel mug.

"Flowers, huh?" His eyes swiveled back to me, and his smile seemed a little off.

I glanced over my shoulder and then back at him. "Um, yeah. A friend sent them."

"Nice. Well, I just came by . . ." He breathed out, his shoulders drooping slightly with the effort, and started over with, "The guy in the cubicle across from me told me you'd been by a few times."

Hell. Who knew Brett had spies?

"Yeah." *Think fast, think fast. How can I possibly justify swinging by at all hours of the workday?*

"Thought I'd better come pin you down after Saturday night," he continued before I could muster anything useful.

"Saturday night?" I was seriously confused.

"At the wedding? I thought you were going to come upstairs and hang out."

Oh crap. Saturday night had been an out-of-body experience. But that probably wasn't the best response here. "Yeah," I answered, nodding, "I thought so too." I shook my head a little, trying to convey my inadvertent mishandling of the situation. "I ended up leaving early," I confessed, hoping this little fraction of the truth would satisfy him, hoping he'd never seen me with Sean.

"I figured. I didn't see you again after the one dance."

Shit! He saw me!

Frantically fidgeting with my pocketful of engineering tools, I forced myself not to react, to try to stay mysterious.

"Right. I left right after that. I should never have worn those shoes." I was cringing inside, waiting for him to call me on this ridiculous skirting of the truth.

I smiled up at him and saw his gaze flick over the daisies again. As if he was making the connection I desperately didn't want him to make. *Yes, I'm having dinner with that stranger tonight and planning to see him again Thursday night. But it's just a fling, brought on by a little spot of blackmail!*

"I gotta admit I was disappointed."

This had me whipping my head up and stilling the hand in my pocket.

He was watching my reaction with interest and surprised me with the admission, "I was kinda hoping to talk to you beyond the realm of cubicles and the whole Whac-A-Mole dynamic."

Recognizing the appeal of a padded mallet in my current work environment, I nevertheless tried to stay focused on the words coming from Brett's mouth.

"You free for lunch any day this week?"

"Yep. Pretty much any day. Take your pick," I offered, shooting him a much-relieved smile. Sean was no longer the elephant in the cubicle. Or if he was, Brett was content to ignore him.

"How about tomorrow?"

"That works." I'd have to push back my trip to New Braunfels a few hours. Maybe I could swing an early-evening visit, steering clear of the *Jeopardy!* time slot.

"Okay, well, see you then—unless I catch you skulking around my cube sometime before that." He was clearly teasing, but it was hitting a little close to the mark. I plastered on a grin.

His eyes tipped down, taking in my white engineer's smock, schoolgirl binder, and clunky heel straps, and a slow smile slid across his face.

"I know—it's all very sexy," I said, rolling my eyes.

"And here I thought it was my own personal fetish," he admitted with a parting wink before shrugging off the doorjamb to head off down the hall.

Oh my God, he was serious! I stared down at myself, a shapeless figure in white with a pocket protector. Who knew?

Feeling the warmth of a full-on flush creeping up my neck and spreading into my cheeks, I hurried into the maze with my head down, making a beeline for the test floor. Looked like I'd be spending the remainder of the afternoon worrying alternately over my bumbling flirtations with both Sean and Brett. Not to mention trouble.

By six I'd shucked the smock and sped home to change. My thinking was to dress sensible and act the part. But gazing at myself in a tailored skirt and sweater set and remembering Sean's tousled hair and effortless style, I figured it'd be nice to look like his date instead of his personal assistant. Even though this was not a date-date.

Fully aware that I was going to be late—when did this start?—I yanked off the sensible and scrambled to replace it with something sexy. I did a quick touch-up on my makeup and tamed a few flyaways with a squirt of hair spray. Feeling only marginally overdressed for Tex-Mex, I grabbed my purse and dashed for the door. I absolutely refused to check the calendar and psych myself out any further.

I made the drive in record time, wobbled across the potholed parking lot, and scanned for motorcycles. I didn't see one—maybe he wasn't here yet. I spared a moment to gather my nerve and remind myself that there was no need for me to be suffering all these first-date symptoms when this wasn't a date. The last second before I pulled open the door was spent in calling myself a delusional idiot.

All was momentarily forgotten as I stepped into sensory overload. Mariachi music mingled with the sizzle of fajitas, and punched tin lanterns glinted off neon Mexican beer signs to create a quaint but jaunty ambiance. I approached the hostess with her scary-enthusiastic smile. She greeted me brightly. "Table for one this evening?"

"I'm actually meeting someone," I informed her, trailing off, glancing around.

"There's a man waiting in the bar," she said, shifting her eyes that way, willing mine to follow, and letting hers linger. We shared a smile before I thanked her and headed off in Sean's direction. I couldn't help but wonder where his motorcycle was hiding.

He was staring up at a muted television screen, mesmerized by a frenzy of soccer players. Shaking his head, presumably in exasperation, he suddenly, almost guiltily, shifted his eyes in my direction. And I, just as guiltily, tried to pull mine up and away from his ass, hoping he hadn't noticed. We shared a smile, and he nodded his thanks to the bartender, lifted a booted foot off the brass bar rail, and headed toward me.

He'd switched his jeans for chinos and covered that afternoon's T-shirt with a charcoal gray crewneck sweater that looked suspiciously like cashmere. I had an almost overpowering urge to smooth my palms over his chest and snuggle into him. Not the best of sensible, restrained beginnings.

His lips quirked with some secret knowledge and he pointedly checked his watch. I tried not to squirm. "You're late," he informed me. "I would never have imagined that possible, Ms. James. But good for you."

I had absolutely no response to this—an apology seemed out of place, and he didn't seem to be expecting one. Palming my hand in his and raising an eyebrow that dared me to remove it, Sean led the way back toward the hostess station. We were seated immediately in a red vinyl corner booth.

As the hostess stood waiting with our menus, I lowered myself onto the right edge of the booth, swung my legs under the table, and tentatively started scooting. First test of the evening: Where should I stop in my scoot-around? Before I could decide, Sean dropped down onto the seat opposite and began his own scoot, rapidly closing the space between us.

I forced myself to focus on the hostess as she ran down the day's specials, but a slight dip in the seat cushion had me glancing to my right, only to discover that Sean had, in one fell scoot, repositioned himself almost flush up against me. Our knees bumped, followed closely by our thighs. It was only when they'd finally settled against each other that the little zips and snaps of electricity settled down to a low-level buzz. Glancing up at Sean, I caught the look in his eye and once again felt as if he was daring me to shift away. I smiled warmly, keeping all sharp edges of my personality in check, and glanced again at the hostess, who finished with, "Your server will be right with you."

This wasn't going to work. My body went haywire whenever he so much as brushed against me, and here he was, *pressing*, lingering, driving me crazy. I casually shifted over a couple of inches, pretending to get comfortable.

Sean looked me in the eye, quirked his lips, and in a low voice murmured, "I'll follow you all the way around."

My smile fell away a little, chipped off by the shock of it all, and I didn't move again.

At that moment, it occurred to me that if I didn't drag my nerve out of hiding, he was going to play everything to his advantage and probably end up scoring (in one way or another). At this rate it was only a matter of time before my willpower tanked and my plan to stay detached and project incompatibility crashed and burned.

The busboy appeared, bearing tumblers of ice water, little bowls of chunky red salsa, and a heaping basket of golden tortilla chips. Depositing these, he dodged away without a word.

Sean leaned into me as I reached for a chip.

"Did you notice? I'm dressed as 'Investment Banker on Casual Date.' "

"Very nice." I shot him an amused smile. "But not necessary."

"If it helps you relax, then I'm all in. And next time, you can return the favor by dressing like a rock star. Wild hair, a little leather, lots of skin . . ."

This was a bit of a shocker. "Is that how your band dresses?"

"No, but if we had a female band member, we'd absolutely make her dress like that." His grin was quick and sure, and I was getting a little addicted to it. I decided not to mention that there wouldn't be a next time.

He was quiet for a bit, staring at me. Initially I filled the silence crunching chips, but eventually self-consciousness won the day, spurring me to stop eating and ask, "What are you doing?"

"Picturing you in leather."

My stomach lurched. It appeared the evening would have me floundering in ways I'd never predicted.

Reaching for another chip, I tried to get the conversation back onto manageable ground. "What'd you do today, other than ambush a geek at work?"

He eyed me for a moment before answering, as if gauging whether it was a serious question or merely polite conversation. So

I turned to look him square in the eyes, seemingly riveted with curiosity.

"Fiddled about in Whole Foods," he said, in that patient way of his, with humor creeping in at the edges. "Snitching samples until I was no longer hungry for lunch. Ended up with a bloody puncture wound, courtesy of a prickly little star fruit. The beast."

I nodded in sympathy. "Produce can get pretty rowdy. Are you talking *seriously* bloody or just painful enough for cursing?"

"Both," he admitted. "I worked some too," he informed me as I reached for another chip. At the rate I was going, I'd be wedged into this booth indefinitely. In an effort to slow the pace, I broke the chip into crispy little shards and ate them slowly one at a time.

"What are you working on now?"

"We're prepping for the show now, mostly practicing our current stuff. But my mum's started hinting around for some new songs, so I'm searching for inspiration in hopes of some brilliant new music and lyrics."

"Is she your biggest fan?" He could no doubt hear the amusement in my voice, but he couldn't know that I thought the reality was just adorable.

"Are you kidding? She's a mother. She probably would have preferred male model to pub singer-made-good."

I bit my lip and tried not to snigger. The real difficulty, however, came in not getting distracted by imagined skin shots. "But you've won her over?"

"Not exactly. I bought her an iPod and downloaded all the band's songs and nothing else. She takes it walking with her."

"So you're taking advantage of the fact that she's not tech savvy?"

"Don't tell me you're taking *her* side?"

He was obviously teasing, but I couldn't help but tense in reaction. In my defense, I was confident I'd be just as likely to resist the advances of a calendar pin-up as an up-and-coming rock star. *Seriously! Is something wrong with me?* Taking a deep breath, I tried to steer clear of a doozy of a conversational pothole, hiding behind a little friendly banter.

"Sorry. All I had to hear was 'male model.' "

Suddenly, like flashbulbs going off in my head, images of a scantily clad Sean were making me dizzy.

After an excruciating silence, he finally spoke up. "Sorry—are you flirting with me? I'd got the feeling I was strictly off-limits."

Now he was definitely mocking me, but the wicked flash of his grin easily defused the awkwardness, and I laughed. I couldn't help myself. And I had the urge to ask, "Does your nerve ever get you into trouble?"

"I prefer the term 'Machiavellian charm,' " he informed me with a wink.

So the end justified the means. I knew a fairy godmother with the very same perspective. Nerves pounced on my empty stomach as my smile faltered slightly. If I were braver, I'd ask for the evening's agenda right now, because I was certain there was one. I might have been winging it, but Sean, I could tell, had a plan. A man with a plan . . . be still my heart. Too bad it didn't mesh with mine.

"Is that what's got you so nervy, then—the what-ifs?" he asked.

"You could say that." Or you could say I was suffering a tragic crush on the completely wrong man and no one—best friend, mentee, fairy godmother, nary a lesbian neighbor—seemed willing to take my side. I unhooked the wedge of lime from my glass and squeezed it into my water, suddenly desperate for a distraction.

The waiter came to take our orders and left us to our deceptively casual silence. I couldn't speak for Sean, but I for one was in a bit of a tizzy. I tried to relax and focus on the sombrero-topped mariachi trio as they wound their way through the tables, alternating between rousing instrumentals and sigh-invoking serenades. I barely even noticed my fingers fidgeting with a slit in the vinyl seat cover until I realized I needed to relocate my purse to cover the new tangerine-sized hole beside my hip.

"So what if . . . you enjoy yourself tonight?" Sean prompted, sliding his finger slowly along the cold, wet condensation coating his water glass.

"No biggie," I countered blithely. "Mexican food is a pretty sure thing for me." I swirled my straw and watched the ice spin in circles.

"Fair enough. What if . . . the Mexican food isn't the best part of the evening?"

I stopped swirling, just for a second, before starting up again. He had me there—it had taken him two measly questions to size me up and get me squeamish.

"Then that means you're a good date." That seemed a relatively safe response. I smiled, not quite meeting his eyes.

"What if I turn out to be the best date you've ever had?" He smiled back, his gaze clinging to mine. My tortilla chip turned to dust in my mouth, and I reached for my water glass, relieved to have a distraction, no matter how fleeting.

I took a long drink, probably too long, but I was racking my brain for the safest response.

"Then you'll get a full-page write-up in my journal," I promised, figuring a version of the truth was probably best.

"Not precisely what I was hoping for," he admitted, his head tipped to the side.

"And," I hurried on before he could elaborate, "you will have raised the bar for all my future dates." I was teasing now but urgently hoping he'd drop this line of questioning—I wasn't about to agree to anything beyond this one date.

He smiled then, a cagey smile that had my pulse zipping with nerves.

"I'm a sucker for a good cause," he said, twirling his tortilla chip through the salsa.

Sean and I had been steadily working our way through the chips and salsa during the "what-if?" repartee, and now it barely registered that his chip had been around the bowl before. And then it was like fireworks in my head. I had little doubt that tonight would remain uncontested as Best Date Ever, but it eased my mind just a little to discover that, as amazing—not to mention cocky—as he was, the man wasn't perfect. I'd found a flaw: Sean was a double-dipper.

While I was against this on principle, it didn't particularly bother me: If I was going to get Sean's germs, I was likely getting them right now sharing a communal basket of chips, rubbing elbows (and thighs), and breathing the same spicily scented air. And if he should happen to kiss me tonight (please, God!), I'd be well and truly breached. Still, I wasn't about to let this pass without comment.

"You're a double-dipper!" I blurted.

Sean took the accusation in stride. "I hate to disappoint you, but no. Just good with my hands, luv."

Temporarily thrown by the casual endearment, I quickly recovered, turning to argue. But he was faster. Slipping his hand around to cup the back of my neck and tipping his head sideways to speak directly into my ear, Sean made everything else fall away. His voice skittered over my skin and was the cause of widespread goose bumps.

"And I hope it's not my germs you're worried over, because I have plans for you. And clearly I have my work cut out for me." He was dropping a kiss along the curved line of my neck as the waiter approached. As he presented our food on oversized stoneware, warning us of "hot plates," Sean let his hand slide down, skimming over my shoulder, arm, and finally my thigh as he pulled away.

Every nerve ending was on full alert, so when I stuffed that first oven-hot bite of enchilada into my mouth, my tongue got scalded. I was frantically gulping down ice water when the mariachis materialized at our booth garbed in the traditional black and silver charro suits.

Sean set down his fork and asked, "Are you familiar with the Elvis ballad 'It's Now or Never'?"

"The King?" The guitarist looked a tad affronted by the question. "But of course. We play for you?"

"Just the instrumentals, if you don't mind." Apparently Sean was not too impressed with the vocal stylings of these men. And here I'd thought they were pretty good.

"Not at all, señor." The request became a pleasure as Sean slid a few bills into the guitarist's palm. Pocketing the tip, the trio began their tableside rendition of Elvis's smoothly persuasive ballad.

"Let's kick things up a notch, shall we?" His eyebrow winged up in challenge as mine dipped down in confusion.

And then, as the thrill of the trumpet subsided, the voice beside me rose to take its place.

11

It's Now or Never

My eyes widened, first in shock, then in panic, but I didn't turn to look at him. This was so utterly unexpected that I didn't know what to do. I wasn't wired for a serenade. If anything, the very thought of one made me cringe. It wasn't that I didn't appreciate and admire the sentiment and bravado that went into such an undertaking—I did—I definitely did! It was simply that the very idea of it was over-the-top, unnecessary, and just plain awkward. Still, out of politeness, I forcibly subdued my panic and shifted my gaze to my booth companion.

He was staring back at me, daring me to hold his gaze. Somehow I managed it.

He sang the refrain while I drowned slowly in the deep darkness of his voice. The words didn't even register. It wasn't until he raised a single eyebrow that things started to click, causing me to raise a rather panicked one right back. Was he literally asking me for a kiss . . . for more? *Tonight?* No doubt he realized that I was way out of my element here, but what he may not have realized was that I was not the type to trade a kitschy Mexican dinner and a public serenade for a sexual romp.

One innocent little kiss probably couldn't hurt anything . . . Although, in all honesty, both times this man had put his lips on me, my world had tipped and twirled in reaction. And it had yet to right itself. My presence here tonight was proof of that.

Watching him, I could easily imagine how he'd looked when he was younger—too perfect for his own good. Time, I'm guessing, hadn't changed him all that much; life had just sharpened his features, changing mischief into character, innocence into charm, and sweet into sexy. His confidence had probably always been there, behind everything. And why shouldn't it be? Those eyelashes alone had probably saved him from trouble more times than he'd care to admit.

So, as he sang about my exciting lips and inviting arms, I pondered his and mourned a future absent of sexy little get-togethers. As I watched him, his eyes falling closed on the soulful parts and then flashing open again to gauge my reaction, alternating between serious performer and teasing charmer, playing both roles with gutsy flair, butterflies invaded my heart.

His arm was slung over the back of the seat, and he'd turned into me, seemingly at ease with this whopper of a PDA. The King, believe it or not, had nothing on Sean MacInnes. The song may be a classic, but I'd always felt it belonged to another generation. But now, hearing it sung in the slightly scratchy, very sexy voice of the man cuddled up next to me, it had taken on a whole new dynamic. I'd never felt this kind of pull, this shivery sort of wonder, and for just this one fleeting moment, it was perfect. This, I imagined—I truly hoped—was Romance.

As the song ended with a warning of last chances and a brassy flourish of trumpet, I smiled and applauded right along with the rest of my fellow diners. Impressive talent with an equal dose of daring—watch out, world. Tread very carefully, Nicola James.

After the applause had died down a bit and the mariachis had drifted away, I oh-so-casually reached for a chip, trying to ease us back to normal.

"Investment bankers rarely do that," I commented.

"Excellent." For some reason, this had him grinning. "I take it my grand gesture left you unconvinced?" he prompted. I was having trouble reading him, but he seemed slightly disappointed by this—or hurt, maybe.

"What? No! You were unbelievable! I'm definitely getting your CD!" I didn't think it necessary to admit that I'd not only bought it already but broken it in as well. I honestly had no idea how to play this. At least my gushing merited another grin.

"I suppose it's not a total loss, then. I made a sale, right?"

"Exactly." I smiled at him and realized he was waiting. He was waiting for me to acknowledge that he'd been singing for me, waiting for me to register the words, clearly waiting for a kiss.

It's now or never.

One night of romance. I'd known this all along, but I'd assumed Sean was looking for a bit more than that. A painful little hole opened up in the vicinity of my heart, but I ignored it. This was good—perfect—we were on the same page. This would make things much easier.

I looked over at him, hoping the hurt didn't crack my smile, and realized he was still looking at me with raised brows. Oops.

"I guess you're hoping for that kiss, huh?" I'd tucked half of my lower lip under my teeth and was squirming with nervous uncertainty.

"Right," he confirmed with a smug smile as he settled back against the vinyl and crossed his arms over his chest.

"That was your motivation for such a grand gesture? A harmless little peck on the cheek from me?" I took a sip of water to cool the feverish flush that was running rampant over my skin.

"Come now, don't sell yourself short."

A bubble of laughter escaped me, but his expression didn't change.

"All right. One kiss—you deserve it. I even liked your version better." As his smile widened, I added, "Although, if Elvis himself had been serenading me, it might have been a different story."

"His loss," replied my charming date. He truly did deserve a kiss. Maybe I did too. So I leaned in and let my eyelashes flutter closed.

He stayed very still, so the placement of the kiss was at my discretion, and I decided to heed a lesson from the master. I very carefully touched my lips to the corner of his very talented and somewhat spicy mouth. Hints of the beer he'd had earlier mingled with the fiery pico de gallo and the tartness of the lime to give him an exotic taste, but beneath the subtle flavors, his lips were a long, smooth line that quirked into a smile well before my lips were willing to let go.

When I finally sat back, I couldn't help but lick my lips. And I knew, even as I did, that it wasn't the best idea. Sean was watching me, and as our gazes locked, I wondered how much he knew. I suspected he knew that I viewed this as a token kiss, imagining only one more—a good-bye kiss at the end of the evening—in our future. He likely also knew that deep down, beyond the protective layers of good sense and rational thinking, I wanted much more than one more kiss. What he might not have known was that I was willing to sacrifice supreme (but fleeting) enjoyment for the greater good . . . for The Plan. I didn't relish having to admit it.

With teeth-clenching effort, I shifted my eyes away just as Sean broke the silence.

"Thank you. Thank you very much," he said, in a cheesy Elvis impersonation.

Not long after, as we stepped into the brisk evening air, it was my turn at cheesy. "Elvis has left the building." We shared a smile.

Neither of us, it seemed, was through with the evening, so we found ourselves eating single scoops of ice cream outside in fifty-degree weather, amid fifteen-mile-an-hour gusts. It was insanity. But the really good kind.

Settled back against the well-worn slats of a wooden bench and propping his shoulder against mine, Sean was surprisingly, perhaps even moodily, silent, scooping up bites. I took my cue from him. He finished first, set his cup and spoon aside, and tucked me into the curve of his arm. Or at least he tried. I was proving a little difficult—think Han Solo frozen in carbonite, with a cup of ice cream in one motionless hand and a white plastic spoon in the other. I couldn't help but wonder, what was the protocol here? A sensible girl finds herself in a far-from-sensible situation, and her date makes a move only minutes before the night—and the romance—must necessarily come to an end. And . . . go!

"Do you . . . want a bite?" I asked lamely, twirling my spoon slightly.

"Where?"

My girl parts suddenly started clamoring for attention.

I didn't answer—I *had* no answer—and given the evening's dynamic, I wasn't sure an elbow to the stomach was appropriate, which is how I would have dealt with Gabe. At that point, in that position, I wasn't even sure I could *move* my elbow.

"Oh," Sean wondered aloud, "did you mean a bite of ice cream? I assumed not—isn't sharing a spoon akin to double-dipping?"

Someday I was going to find my footing with this man, but right now, I was so out of my depth my ears were popping. Not to mention my eyes.

"You're right. My fault. And since I don't want you to think I'm a tease, I feel like I should offer you something, so where would you like your bite?"

Now his eyes popped. I smiled and scooped up another bite.

He let his thumb slide down the back of my neck, and this time my shiver had nothing to do with ice cream or the temperature. Turning to object to such cruel and unusual punishment, I was totally unprepared to be ambushed. But with only a few inches between us, there wasn't time to object. And to be honest, I wasn't sure I had that much willpower.

His teeth—those perfect, straight white ones he'd been flashing since the beginning—settled gently into my lower lip for a playful little nip before his lips took their place.

I could feel myself melting slowly out of the carbonite and into him. Incompatibility shamelessly forgotten, I let myself sink into this really stellar kiss, let myself imagine the what-ifs . . .

And that's what did it.

I suddenly realized I had to stop while I still could.

We pulled away at exactly the same moment, and I reached my hand up to touch my lips, careful not to meet his eyes. I needed a distraction, a diversion, anything to avoid a second kiss and the complete annihilation of clear thinking. I didn't think I could handle a second fall into a pool of mind-numbing lust and manage to surface coherent. I was struggling enough as it was.

"So . . . ?" I said, not meeting his gaze. "How'd we get from a mushroom to this?"

His answer was immediate. "Through dumb luck, dogged pursuit, and winning charm. You're so adorably in control, it just makes a bloke want to frazzle you. So here we are. Frazzled yet?"

I figured trying not to blush would be like trying to rein in all that Machiavellian charm, so I gave in to the inevitable, "Yeah, I'd say I'm well and truly frazzled. But I'm confident I'll bounce right back."

Then again, that could just be the bravado talking.

"Very sporting of you, Ms. James. And now, I have a question of my own." I could feel the air between us shifting from silly to serious, and I tensed slightly in anticipation. "Just what exactly do you have against a man in a band?"

Whoa. Did not see that one coming. I supposed my choices were to lie outright or get pegged as a self-important clod.

Tell him the truth! my conscience demanded. *Square hole, round peg, nothing personal.*

I was poised to do it, but I felt my resolve weakening. I was already more than a little seduced and falling further and deeper under his spell. I could hear that little devil on my shoulder again . . . *Maybe I could stand to be a bit more flexible, a little more adventurous. It's for a very sexy cause.* I glanced at Sean, who was still waiting for my answer. *Got lust, Nicola?*

I gave my head a firm shake and started over. I could feel my pulse pounding out the passing seconds, but I couldn't think through the storm of sensation. This should really be it—the moment of reckoning—but if I was really, painfully honest with myself, I could admit that I didn't want this thing, whatever it was, to end.

I opened my mouth, but nothing came out, and this entire situation, in all its awkwardness, suddenly seemed undeniably, almost tragically funny. Thus Sean, waiting patiently for an answer, instead found himself faced with a maniacally giggling buffoon.

I sobered up quickly the second I realized that such a reaction might seem just slightly offensive, given our current situation and the question posed. And this time, I had no problem getting an answer off my tongue.

"Nothing. I have nothing against a man in a band." I added a little dismissive shake of my head to punctuate. "I'm very impressed, and honestly, I'm thrilled for you. And flattered you took the time to stalk and bribe me." The last, I have to admit, came off a little flirty.

"So you'd have no problem then saying yes to another date?"

"No. Yes," I heard myself answering. "Yes to the date." Fidgety with nerves, I stood and walked the few steps to toss away my trash. So much for sensible.

Sean followed, and the triumphant look on his face was very flattering indeed. "How about lunch tomorrow?"

How I remembered Brett amid the fog of infatuation and the haze of lust, I had no idea, but I did, just barely. "Meeting," I countered, trying to look apologetic as we slowly made our way back to the parking lot.

"Fair enough. How about dinner and a film downtown tomorrow night?"

"Are you by any chance referring to a South by Southwest film screening?" I asked.

"I am."

"Do you already have tickets?" I asked him, fully aware that they could sell out quickly.

"I have been known to occasionally plan ahead," Sean informed me with a superior smile. "Shall I pick you up at work?"

We were standing between my sensible little car and his dangerous-looking motorcycle. "How about I meet you," I countered, eyeing the shiny bike.

He smirked; clearly I was an open book. But judging from the way his body began leaning toward mine, he didn't plan to challenge me. His hand tightened on mine, mine tensed in his, and I braced myself for the thrill of yet another kiss.

It shuddered slowly through me, leaving me limp with appreciation and sighing at its end. This kiss was way more dangerous than the others, probably because he'd clued in to the fact that I was, ever so cautiously, caving. I couldn't seem to help myself— around Sean it was like I was no longer "master of my domain." Figuratively speaking.

Fairy Jane was no doubt smirking to herself over the burgeoning success of her twisted little matchmaking scheme. I didn't think anyone could argue that I wasn't taking the romance at least somewhat seriously. Take tomorrow, for example: lunch with one guy, dinner with another. I was seriously in over my head.

12

In which agreements are reached

Stopped at a light on Fifth Street, I realized I should probably head straight home, make myself some hot chocolate, and hunker down with my magical journal and its logic-defying key. I should be curious and eager to do some sleuthing—and I *was*. But right now, I didn't want to read about Fairy Jane's interference in other people's lives—I wanted to deal with her meddling into mine. I needed some girl talk, and not the kind I was used to getting from next door.

Glancing at the clock on the dash—quarter after ten—I was pretty confident Beck was still up, either studying or defying the engineering stereotype in some way or another. I reached for the phone. She answered on the first ring.

"Beck! Hey, it's Nicola."

"Thank God! I left you a message hours ago, after I got your spazzed-out message, and I can only assume you have a *very good reason* for blowing me off?" The implication was obvious. "I'm ready to forgive. So anytime you're ready . . ."

I grinned, then bit the inside of my mouth. "Oh, I'm just calling to check in, see how your classes are going," I lied.

There was a beat of silence on her end of the line, and I could hear funky music from unidentifiable instruments. My imagination ran wild, and I pictured an apartment with lots of jewel-toned floor pillows and dark wood, the air swirling with smoky incense. My nose wrinkled up a little.

"O-*kay*," she said. "Things are good. I aced two exams this week—Control Systems and Lasers. Is that enough foreplay? Ready to get to the good stuff?"

"What?" It came out half-shocked, half-amused.

"I'm guessing you called with something more interesting than the day-to-day dramas in the College of Engineering, so as your *very devoted* mentee, let me just give you permission to gloss over my less-than-exciting life."

My smile widened as I took a moment to revel in my life's recent juiciness.

"Okay then. Way to go on the exams," I said, trying to legitimatize our mentor/mentee relationship just slightly.

"Thank you. Now spill it. Or do you want a face-to-face? Because I'm totally up for it if you are. I'm actually a little burned out on studying, particularly while Talitha is trying her—well, belly, I suppose—at belly dancing. With all those little coins clinking and fabrics shimmying, it's unbelievably distracting."

"I'll bet. Well, if you're positive it wouldn't be interrupting something more important, then in-person would be great."

"Awesome. It's Glow Bowl night at the Texas Union."

My eyebrows came together in uncertainty. "Glow Bowl night?"

"Come on! It's the perfect place to gossip—no one will overhear a thing."

Somehow I found myself agreeing to that, and ten minutes later, I was descending underground, into the din. Between the music (that rock/rap combo stuff), the crack of pool balls, the smack of bowling pins, and the animated conversation, I felt confident my secrets would stay with me. Beck would be lucky to pick up the general gist.

It was just now occurring to me that I wasn't exactly dressed for bowling. I didn't even have a pair of socks. Eyeing the line of worn bowling shoes getting sprayed with aerosol deodorant on the counter, I suppressed a shudder.

When I noticed Beck waving from a lane to my far right, I tried not to react. While it had recently become somewhat socially acceptable, I would never be caught out in pajamas—particularly the sock monkey variety—paired with a thermal tee and a ski vest. Although I had to admit, with her hair cocked out in twin ponytails, the pink streaking through, she looked cute and enviably comfortable. Like she belonged down here. Me? Not so much. News flash from the UT Student Union . . .

Beck hopped up to greet me with a giddy look in her eyes and a mischievous smile curling her high-gloss lips, and I relaxed a little. Giving me a quickie shoulder massage, she turned me toward the lanes and gestured up at the video screen suspended above. Apparently we'd be playing incognito as "Mentor" and "Mentee." I couldn't wait to see which of us was which.

"Go get your shoes," she yelled in my ear, "and come right back here. I'll find us some balls." She wiggled her eyebrows and turned with ponytails flying.

I figured it was going to be virtually impossible for me to tell her about my date in this obnoxious environment. While one of us was on deck, swinging a nine-pound ball in a dangerous arc, the other really should stay out of the way. And I wasn't about to shout the whole thing at twenty paces. It should definitely be interesting.

As I was sliding my stockinged feet into a pair of slightly moist leather bowling shoes, Beck walked up cradling a neon orange ball, its three holes turned toward me. "This work for you?"

Fitting my fingers into the holes, I nodded, and she half rolled/half dumped it into my hands.

"You're just a tad overdressed for bowling." She shook her head dismissively. "Don't worry—nobody cares." Stepping closer and widening her eyes with a very gratifying urgency, she prompted, "Take it from Sunday brunch."

"Now?" I glanced around uncertainly, concerned that someone might be waiting for the lane, ready to step up and complain if we were caught squandering precious Glow Bowl minutes.

"He's up," she said, indicating the six-footer in loose-fitting madras in the lane to our left.

I tried to shake off the *Punk'd* vibe and just go with it. This was less of a girl talk and more of a drive-by. But what did I know? Maybe this was how it was done now. I took a deep breath, ready for launch, just as Beck held up her hand. 'Hold that thought. Your turn."

Evidently I was bowling as "Mentor" this evening.

I turned to face the clutch of ten pins at the far end of our lane. Stepping up, trying to resist the thoughts of Sean that persisted in tickling my concentration, I strode forward with measured steps, swung the ball back, and let fly.

Gutter ball.

I glanced at Beck to see her frantically waving me over.

"Go—you've got a minute before your ball comes back. And we can let that guy cut in if we need to," she said in cavalier fashion.

"Okay . . . since brunch . . ." My normally ordered mind was stumbling over all the unexpected happenings of the last day and a half. Probably best to go chronologically. "Let's see: I got passed over for a promotion—again, decided to switch jobs, found the key to the journal—*you have no idea!*, had a surprise visit from Sean at work—he brought flowers, we went to dinner, I got serenaded. We kissed, and I agreed to another date. The complete nutshell." I glanced back toward the ball return to see my ball waiting patiently. "I'm up."

Feeling slightly more relaxed now that it was out in the open, I stepped up, swung the ball, and watched it glide smoothly down the lane. This time it hit just right of dead center, and with a satisfying crack of pins, I picked up the spare.

"You, my friend, are unstoppable!" The smile Beck flashed had my lips curling up cautiously in response. "Tell me about the journal—is it even better with the key?" Her eyes were impossibly wide and her attitude unflinchingly giddy.

I met her gaze, wondering if Beck was above I-told-you-sos. "Turns out you're pretty in tune with the wackiness in the world.

The journal was a gift from Jane Austen—*the* Jane Austen—to her niece."

Beck's eyebrows dropped into a wrinkle of disbelief. "You have proof?"

That knocked me on my ass. "Proof? Seriously? You need proof, Mulder?"

"I don't *need* proof; I just assumed you *had* proof. Besides," she said with a smirk, "it's not long before I'm a full-fledged, degree-toting engineer. I gotta walk the walk on occasion."

"Okay, fine. My proof is that I saw the signed inscription she wrote, and it looks legit."

She interrupted before I could continue with my seemingly impossible explanation.

"So why didn't you see it before?" she quizzed, hefting her ball from the ball return.

"I needed the key. The key brings back everything that's been written in the book since the very beginning—we're talking a veritable tomb of diary secrets. My entries, the ones that disappeared and were replaced with snarky little instructions? They're back. The book is huge with the key in and a skinny mini with it removed."

"Whoa." After a pause, she said, "I should probably bowl. Be right back."

Despite glancing curiously back at me several times while she waited her turn in the bowling queue, Beck evidently managed to shake off the shock and come back raring to gossip.

"And there's more weird where that came from," I told her. "And honestly, I need some advice."

"Shoot," she said, sipping from a jumbo Diet Coke.

Taking a deep breath, I confided, "I think Fairy Jane may have left the journal. So to speak."

Beck squinted. "She's gone? What makes you think so?"

"No, not gone per se, just foolin' around."

"You're saying Jane Austen is fooling around in Austin, Texas?" Her gaze was unwavering.

"Well, I don't know how else to describe it! She's messing with the calendar in my kitchen, and she's finagling things I don't want finagled!"

"Come again?"

I closed my eyes, digging deep for a calm, rational-sounding response. "Today I not only agreed to transfer departments at Micro, thereby backseating my bid for management, but I agreed to go out with Sean after I promised myself I wouldn't get involved. That doesn't sound like me, does it?"

"You're switching out of Product Engineering? Into what department? Will I stay where I am, or can I come along as your intern, sort of a two-for-one package?"

Hell, I'd forgotten all about Beck. I shook my head. I'd deal with that later.

"Try to stay focused. What I'm saying is, I don't think *I* did either of those things on my own—I think someone interfered, worked some magic, messed with my head. Does that seem possible to you?" I couldn't believe I was asking this. "Is that common for . . . magical things?"

A grin stole over Beck's face. "This is painful for you, isn't it?"

I rolled my eyes. "A little, so could we just get to it?"

"Go bowl. Let me think on it for a minute."

I couldn't concentrate knowing that no matter what it was, I wasn't going to like Beck's answer. I'm lucky I managed to bowl down the right lane. I think I downed a total of two pins in the entire frame. When I got back, her mouth was set in a grim line. "Come up with anything?"

"Well, I should probably preface this by saying that I have no real-world experience with anything magical, other than your journal."

"Lucky you," I muttered.

"And," Beck continued, "any magical advice I'm able to give you is drawn from books, movies, mythology, etcetera."

"Talitha's not into magic?"

"Sadly, no."

"Fine, fine," I assured her. "I'll take whatever you've got."

She held up a finger. "Probably best if I played this frame."

I waited for what seemed an eternity for her to come back.

"Okay," Beck said, "so now that you've actively engaged the journal, i.e., the magical item, it's invested in you. The spirit that's enchanting it—we believe, Jane Austen—clearly has an agenda, which you, in both words and actions, are resisting. So it would appear that she's stepping beyond the bounds of the journal to convince you." She nodded sagely. "Sorta scary shit," she said, grinning hugely.

"So she's not going to let up?"

"I don't know . . . maybe?"

"Maybe? This is my life! How the hell am I supposed to deal with this?"

"Well, how bad would it really be to go along with it? She's not asking you to do anything dangerous or illegal."

I stared at her, taking in her pink hair, sock monkey pajamas, and the bowling alley around her. Honestly, I couldn't believe any of this was happening. She slung her arm around my shoulders.

"Okay, executive decision: Let's put a kibosh on the magic stuff. I'm willing to take a lot on faith, but for obvious reasons, I'd like to see this stuff for myself. Right now, why don't you relax and tell me about Sean. We'll get to the Micro situation later—it can wait."

In no time, Beck and I had developed a rhythm, seamlessly alternating bowling frames and concentrated bouts of gossip as I temporarily tried to overlook the invasion of magic into my well-ordered life.

"What kind of flowers?"

"Red gerbera daisies."

"Definite points for originality."

"As a bribe, they worked wonders."

Beck raised her eyebrow, but I could tell she was impressed. I hurried up to bowl with a blithe smile on my face and remained undeterred by my paltry two-pin showing.

"He drives a motorcycle," I told her in a break between frames. "So we drove separately."

"What? Why? Have you ever been on a motorcycle? It's awesome, particularly in this roller coaster of a city."

New frame, new subject.

"He kissed me in the lobby." I skimmed my fingers over the spot just above my left eyebrow, remembering.

"And?" Beck's grin was as bright as the neon orange bowling ball she balanced in her palm.

"I have very little memory of the afternoon after that. Except," I specified, finger in the air, "that I finally set a lunch date with Brett."

Beck wrinkled her nose, unimpressed with my second bit of news, and rerouted the conversation back to Sean. "How'd he track you down at Micro?"

"I guess he did some sleuthing."

"The man *definitely* gets style points!"

"He's a master of seduction," I concurred, sipping the diet drink we were now sharing. Feeling the kick of caffeine, I realized I wouldn't be going to sleep anytime soon. But there was a very good chance I would have had trouble sleeping without the extra pick-me-up. Such was my life this week.

"How exactly did he work in a serenade?"

"He made a request—specified only instrumentals. And then he just started singing. I bought his CD after brunch on Sunday and listened all day. But this was different." I paused to breathe and, positively smitten with the thrill of girl talk, leaned in and gripped Beck's wrist, willing a vicarious reaction. "He made it clear that he was singing *to* me—the words were for me—he was asking for a kiss and for a chance."

"And what did you offer?" Her smile was coy and curious.

"Cliff-hanger," I teased, before running off to bowl. After downing five pins, I fell into the chair beside her with the much-anticipated answer. "Believe it or not, I offered both."

Beck's eyes widened in surprise but then narrowed in concentration. "First things first: the kiss? How was it?"

"Very, very sexy, and I should tell you, at this point in the evening, it's all still close-mouthed."

"Really?" Beck smirked, probably amused by my G-rated romance.

Which reminded me . . .

"How are things going with you and Gabe?"

She blinked rapidly, switching gears. "Good. Very good." Her smile slid into place.

"Good how?"

"We went out Sunday night." I couldn't tell if she was blushing or if light was bouncing off her hair onto her cheeks. "And really, it's amazing how much we have in common, but you're getting off topic."

My girl-talk buzz faded a little, imagining the comparable simplicity of a compatible relationship versus my thorny association with Sean. Being with him hypnotized me into believing that anything was possible, but when we were apart, my optimism quickly faded, and practicality swooped in like a slap in the face.

Beck jerked her thumb toward the pins. "I'm up."

With a couple seconds to regroup, I was ready to steer the conversation the minute she returned. "Okay, I definitely want to hear about you and Gabe, but I'd like to get a little advice first." I looked her in the eyes. "One logical mind to another."

Beck smoothed her expression into seriousness and sat beside me, bowling forgotten. "First magical, now logical. I'm a busy girl tonight."

I ignored that. "You know how I said I offered both the kiss and the chance? Well, basically I just agreed to another date, which, to most people, is no big deal," I admitted, fisting my hands in the fabric of my skirt, creating wrinkles and smoothing them out again. "But Sean's different, as I think you've probably gathered. A little part of me is in love with the *idea* of him. But the rest of me—the sensible, rational majority—totally gets that it can't work in the long term. So you could say I'm sort of at a personal impasse." And just like that, my sparkly, shimmery evening lost some of its luster.

"Why does one more date signify an impasse?"

With a deep, nervy sigh, I prepped myself to say it out loud. "Because I'm pretty sure that one more date will tip me over the edge. Even being in love with the *idea* of him will wreak all sorts of havoc on my uncomplicated life."

"Uh-huh."

But I didn't get the impression that she really got it. I was evidently going to have to paint my impasse as more clearly impassable.

"And I haven't even mentioned the Brett development."

"Do tell," Beck encouraged snarkily.

"He seems interested. We're going to lunch tomorrow."

"And this affects your decision regarding the charming and unbelievably appealing stranger in what way?" Okay, now she was just being snippy. But before I could respond, she was plowing right over me. "Okay. Let's back up." She swirled her hands counterclockwise, possibly with the thought of hypnotizing me. "You stumble over a magical journal—a journal channeling *Jane Austen,* mind you—that offers you romantic advice that starts coming true, i.e., you meet a guy—potentially *the* guy—you fall for him, or at least the *idea* of him; he, in turn, is big-time crushing on you, and suddenly you're at an impasse. Because of lunch with Brett."

"No, *not* just because of lunch with Brett. Right now Brett's more like a warning beacon: a symbol of logical, sensible thinking that doesn't involve impetuous decisions and magical advice."

"Okay, Nic." She put her hands out, as if to say, "this is it." "I understand the appeal of logical and sensible, I really do, but in this case, in your particularly fantastical situation, I don't think it's the way to go. No," she said, forestalling the "but" on the tip of my tongue, "let me just call it as I see it." Deep breath, exhale. "Like it or not, girl, you have a fairy godmother, and that just can't be swept under the rug. There's no avoiding the fact that this whole thing is a crazy-unbelievable fairy-tale miracle, so why not at least *try* for the happily-ever-after? Your odds are good—the two usually come as a matched set."

I pulled back a little and took in my surroundings. If I were any kind of mentor, we'd be discussing circuit fabrication at the library in lieu of happily-ever-afters at Glow Bowl. We'd be discussing *her* problems instead of mine. And I would appear to have it all together. I was Bizarro Mentor.

"And what about Brett?" I couldn't help but ask.

"Listen, sweetie," Beck said, giving my arm a squeeze, "I'm gonna go out on a limb here and guess that if Brett knew about the journal, the fairy godmother, the serenade, and the kissing, *he'd* tell you to go for it too. Given the whole Jane Austen element, and your little tango with 'Mr. Darcy,' I'm having trouble not thinking of Brett as the evil Wickham."

I blinked at her, not particularly caring to admit that that very thought had crossed my mind.

"That's your advice, then? Just scrap my life plan, along with all rational thinking, and risk it?" I was pretty sure that was Fairy Jane's advice as well. I leaned in and dropped my voice a bit. "I don't even really *believe* in magical journals and fairy godmothers— I've been coasting for the past three days on sheer standoffishness."

"What's not to believe?" This came out at a near-shrieking pitch. Beck's pie-in-the-sky, flaky optimism had crumbled, and from the looks of it, she'd had it with me. "I'm taking your *word* for nearly every damn bit of this, and *I* believe!"

"Shhh," I hissed, suddenly self-conscious to be discussing all this out loud, despite the din.

"Like it or not, it's *happening* to you—despite your comprehensive life plan and very good intentions. Plans change, rules are meant to be broken, and sexy guys with accents are stellar motivation for both! For a girl lucky enough to stumble across a magical journal offering a chance at a happily-ever-after, this romance *is* rational. So why not give the man a damn bullet in the spreadsheet of your life?" She leaned back in her chair, and the drama faded a bit.

The woman had a point. Quite unexpectedly, a casual night of bowling had turned into an intervention.

My name is Nic James, and I have a magical journal and an interfering fairy godmother, a.k.a. Fairy Jane, and I damn well better get used to it. Or she'll find ways of reminding me.

"Fine. I'll keep an open mind—for now. I'll give things with Sean a fair, fighting chance. But I'm keeping my lunch with Brett, and we'll just see how things go."

"Seems a fair compromise. Maybe get his take on all this," she teased.

We finished out the game, consciously not speaking about any of it. Personally, I couldn't help but wonder what Fairy Jane would have to say about the evening's developments.

At home, tucked in bed with my covers pulled up to my waist, I wondered if I should dig out the Ouija board I'd had since junior high and hold a little séance. But it was late, and the very idea was fraught with disturbing possibilities, so instead I slid my journal, the little Pandora's book, onto my lap, ready to get into it.

I'd given in and checked the calendar before turning off the lights. The quote of the day had changed yet again. Now it read, "'Better be without sense than misapply it as you do.' *Emma*." Nice.

The whole situation was mind-boggling. I'd spilled a chai latte onto something that had once belonged, however fleetingly, to *Jane Austen* and somehow summoned her ghost, or spirit, or lingering chi, and inspired her to become, at least for a time, my own personal fairy godmother, a.k.a. Fairy Jane. Her letter to her niece, now visible in its entirety with the turn of a key, clearly laid out her intentions. And yet, as interesting as this discovery was, it didn't even begin to resolve the plethora of questions that fairly hovered around the journal. Beyond the lingering nuisance of how the hell she was getting words to disappear, there were now all sorts of new questions on the table.

Like, how were the words coming back with a simple turn of

the key? And how was she giving relevant advice from the be-yond? *Specific, detailed,* kinda creepy advice. Was it possible that her spirit had lingered on after her death and then flourished with the widespread popularity of her books? Okay, maybe I could coax my brain around that possibility—*maybe*—but for God's sake, how on earth was she reaching beyond the journal to wreak havoc in my actual life, switching the daily quotes on a tacky little calendar, in-sinuating herself into my work life, and blackmailing me in my ro-mantic life?

It seemed that, like it or not, I needed to start facing these prob-lems head-on, starting with the journal.

I may as well tell you everything, even though I suspect that in some way or another, you're already "magically" informed. Today I had an un-expected visit from you know who, complete with flowers and an im-promptu invitation to dinner. As you can probably guess, I accepted both. I also had a pop-in from Brett—remember him? the epitome of sensible romance???—which resulted in an invitation to lunch, which I also ac-cepted. May the best man win, right?

Dinner was lovely—Sean serenaded *me! Cheesy as it is, it pretty much solidified my crush on the man. It was just going to be the one dance, then the one date, but now, suddenly it's mushroomed into more than that. (Don't you just love the pun?) I'd ask you to make it stop, but you wouldn't, and honestly, I wouldn't want you to.*

I let my pen tip back from the page and indulged in a deep, bitter-sweet sigh, remembering the oh-so-sensible "Before." And envi-sioning the sure-to-be-crazy "After" life.

Beck is beyond thrilled and a proponent of my scrapping The Plan in favor of Sean. But what about Brett? I've barely gotten a chance to know him, and already he's getting the magical, not to mention the mentee, brush-off. I think, ultimately, I need to make the final decision, and I want to give them both an equal showing. What can I say, I like to play fair.

With a deep and fairly optimistic sigh, I signed off.

P.S. Now that I've come around on the romance, I expect you to keep up your end of the bargain!

I felt compelled to add this last bit, a not-so-subtle reminder of our deal: She keeps out of my work life if I let her call a few shots on the romance front.

Satisfied, I tipped the book closed, catching quick little glimpses of all the advice to date, all of it focused on a relationship with Sean. From the very beginning, *Miss Nicola James will be sensible and indulge in a little romance*, it had all been leading up to this—this moment. And now I'd caved; I was officially indulging, and "sensible" was not exactly the word that came to mind.

Ignoring the fact that it was far past my bedtime, I slipped the newfound key off my nightstand and sat for a moment, the journal in one hand, the key in the other, imagining a subtle tingling in my fingers. I wanted another peek. I hoped it would take the edge off my uncertainty knowing that I wasn't alone—that I wasn't the only one who'd had her life turned inside out by deciding to blindly follow a seemingly arbitrary collection of fortune cookie–style instructions. You could say I was a little desperate.

Bracing myself against the impossibility of it all, I slid the key home and turned it with a scraping twist, watching as sheaves of old pages appeared to grow out of the book's binding, waiting until my heartbeat slowed to a dull thump. Then, ever a fan of the systematic approach, I started at the beginning, with the Dear Jane letter, and then avidly read on from there.

There is to be a dance, and in as much as that is delightful all on its own merit, I have a better reason to be fidgety, for afterwards, I shall be <u>out</u>! I confess to being both nervous and excited at once. I am to have a new gown and am truly hoping for something lovely. Simply the thought of it will help me to happily endure the days—and moments—in between. Mother will surely endeavor to make use of these golden opportunities to warn me against future folly while at the same time urging me to embrace all that is good and true. But I will endure with high spirits, for I intend

to remain, for as long as possible, pleased with the World in general and
everyone in it, Mother included.

As the first entry following the dedication, I assumed it was
written by Jane Anna Elizabeth Austen herself, and I couldn't help
but wonder what little snippet of advice Aunt Jane had culled from
this optimistic piece. And how the girl had reacted to a little magical interference. There were a few clues in the next entry.

I find myself in quite a conundrum. Despite having written to you,
Aunt Jane, and discovered that, by some strange magic, you are able to ad-
vise me through the pages of this very journal, I cannot claim even a vague
understanding of how you are able to do so. And while you must know the
esteem in which I hold your good advice and opinions, I admit that I can
no longer consider this a private journal in the traditional sense, knowing
that every careful word is on display. I can, however, delight in using it
just as you intended, to record the little dilemmas that life presents, expect-
ing, in response, your prompt and sound advice. I expect I will need it
more than you know, because I have decided to follow in your footsteps,
Aunt Jane, and dedicate myself to my writing, and I fear that Mother will
take very vocal exception to this, a very much unintended path. With life-
long admiration and newfound awe, I remain your loving niece, Anna.

I avidly read through the years of Anna's journal correspondence
with Aunt Jane, attempting to deduce the pertinent "miscellanious morsels" based on the clues provided in each subsequent
entry. Beyond the inherent puzzle, I was fascinated . . . and oblivious as the clock ticked away the hours of my good night's sleep.

Hours later, my eyes bleary and my thoughts tangled with sto-
ries, I tipped the volume closed, twisted out the key, and watched
transfixed as it shrank down again to its deceptively slim self. Hoping for an out-of-sight, out-of-mind miracle, I slid book and key
under my pillow and laid my head down, still completely frazzled.
As I switched off the light, it occurred to me that from Sean's perspective, everything was going precisely as planned.

* * *

The morning started with a near fatality. Refusing to give up after at least fifteen whacks to the snooze bar, my alarm clock became the enemy. I barely resisted flinging it against the wall in a groggy haze of aggravation. But as I blinked my eyes open, desperate to get hold of the little beast, they shifted from fuzzy to focused, and registered that it was already seven o' clock.

Well, technically it was six forty-five—fifteen minutes fast translated to two guiltless snoozes—but still, I was way late. If I wanted to squeeze in a drive down to New Braunfels between a lunch with Brett and a date with Sean, then I really needed to get moving. This was what I got for staying up late (and out late) on a work night. Bleary-eyed and fuzzy-mouthed, I stumbled out of bed and scrambled to get ready. I was an efficient whirlwind, and twenty minutes later I was mixing up some cocoa in my travel mug when last night came avalanching back: the date, the decision, the journal.

My eyes strayed to the calendar on the counter, and I read the day's quote with a feeling of dread. " 'What wild imaginations one forms where dear self is concerned! How sure to be mistaken!' *Persuasion*." That didn't bode well at all. Evidently at least one part of my day wasn't going to go at all as expected.

Sipping the warm chocolate, I walked cautiously back down the hall to my room, my heart pounding out a drumbeat as I considered the fraught-with-crazy potential of an overnight, personalized reply from my very own life coach.

I suspect you know it's mushroomed beyond magical

Et tu, Fairy Jane? It was simply too much to process this early in the morning.

I slid the snarky little book back onto the shelf, to the left of *Sense and Sensibility*, on what I imagined to be the "Sense" side. I was keeping it far, far away from *Persuasion*—it certainly didn't need any help in that quarter; it was becoming quite adept at influencing me all on its own. So basically I'd turned into a superstitious kook, although still sufficiently detached to manage an eye roll for my own crazy antics. That was something, I supposed. Naturally I slipped the key into the cupcake tin in the cupboard beside the stove and pretended everything was normal.

On my way out the door, my eye caught on yesterday's valentine-red daisies now livening up the kitchen table, and a smile curved my lips. On impulse, I snatched a single bloom from the grouping and snipped a few inches off the stem before tucking it jauntily in the top buttonhole of my cropped navy blazer. Who said I couldn't be spontaneous?

13

I suspect you know it's mushroomed beyond magical

I got an unexpected number of compliments on my flower, but that didn't stop me from ditching it behind my computer just before Brett stopped by my cube for lunch. The last thing I wanted was to overshadow our lunch with shades of Sean MacInnes. My intention was not to think about him at all, to tune my romantic antennae on Brett and see how things played out with the Epitome of Sensible Romance. No pressure.

While lunch wasn't quite tinged with the whole first-date vibe, my heart rate was speeding slightly as I followed Brett downstairs, out through the lobby, and across the parking lot to his car. His silver Audi was sleek and spotless, and Brett oozed competence as he slid into the driver's seat across from me. It was slightly awkward to hold my feet in the air while he repositioned my floor mat for maximum coverage, but really, fastidiousness was just fine with me.

"So . . . ?" I finally started, lunging into the silence. "Where should we go?"

After cautiously (and silently) backing out of his parking spot, Brett turned to me with a grin. "Pizza Garden." Not so much a suggestion as a done deal. Luckily it was one of my favorite lunch spots.

"Sounds good," I said.

"They have a great lunch deal," he said, easing into a left turn, more serious than I would have thought necessary.

"They do," I agreed.

Awkward silence, Take One. Luckily the restaurant was only minutes away.

Quickly seating us at a scarred wooden table near the window, our waitress recited the day's pizza specials (today's were Greek, Texas Fajita, and Basilica) and left with our drink orders, promising to return momentarily to take our orders.

"What are you getting?" I asked, flashing a smile.

"Texas Fajita."

"Never tried it. I'm getting the Garden pizza."

My smile faltered just slightly in the face of Brett's disbelieving stare.

"But it's not one of the specials."

"Yeah, I know. It's more expensive, but it's a little bigger too. Six inches instead of four. I take the leftovers home."

"But even if you factor in the additional size of the pizza," Brett protested, "it's not nearly as good a deal. And you don't get a salad."

"You're right." Maybe he just needed to know I'd done the math. "But it's my favorite, and it's loaded with vegetables, so I'm happy to splurge." I could have jumped into a cost breakdown/nutritional analysis, but I didn't think anyone wanted that.

"Okay," he said, with a baffled, slightly concerned little shake of his head.

"Don't worry, I can afford it," I teased, linking my fingers, laying my palms flat on the table, and forcing myself to keep smiling.

Awkward Silence, Take Two.

The remainder of our lunch date was actually quite pleasant (if we didn't count Brett's quickly masked disapproving glance as my Garden pizza was slid onto the table in front of me). As expected, we had a lot in common, both past history and future goals, and I felt the tight coil of uncertainty in my chest begin to unfurl. This was what I'd expected, how I'd imagined my romantic life would be. Two compatible people blazing a sensible trail through life. My grin just kept on giving.

Right up until the check came.

We both reached for it, but Brett snatched it cleanly away.

Biting my lower lip, feeling a little thrill zip through me, it was on the tip of my tongue to thank him for lunch.

Thank God I controlled the urge, because two seconds later, he slid the bill back in my direction.

"Since I got the special, it's not going to be an even fifty-fifty split." Pulling out his wallet, Brett went for one final gloat. "I tried to tell you. . . ."

"You did," I snapped, pulling the bill toward me and retrieving my own wallet. I yanked out several bills, including a generous tip, and placed them on the table, really hoping the topic was now officially closed.

He didn't say a word as I packed up the remains of my pizza in the cardboard to-go box, his jaw busy crunching every last bit of ice in the jumbo-sized glass he'd drained of iced tea. What could I say, the man liked to get his money's worth.

Awkward Silence, Take Three.

But no butterflies, no queasiness, and no surprises. There was something to be said for quiet companionship. But it definitely wasn't "Wowza!"

Trapped on the test floor an hour later, my daisy defiantly back in place, I was bored senseless and figured it was as good a time as any to get the lowdown on Gabe's burgeoning romance with my impressionable young mentee. Fishing my phone from the crowded pocket of my smock, I texted an opener.

NJames: Any luck convincing Beck to show you her tattoo?

Exactly seven parts ran through the full test suite at minus forty degrees before Gabe responded.

GVogler: i'm building up to it. what's up?
NJames: I went out last night.

GVogler: WHAT??? NOT with the dude from the band?
NJames: Beck didn't tell you?

This was my sly attempt at deducing just how chummy they'd gotten in the last two days.

GVogler: i see her tonight. spill!

Interesting . . .

NJames: Yes, him. Where?
GVogler: adh-sxsw

ADH? Alamo Drafthouse? Probably. I glanced up to make sure the liquid nitrogen hadn't frozen up the handler before quickly typing in my reply. I hated that I was going to miss seeing Gabe's reaction, but it couldn't be helped. I was stuck down here indefinitely.

NJames: Me too. Paramount
GVogler: serious!? with Scottie?
NJames: Believe it or not. Any new matches?

Another probe to determine Beck's status.

GVogler: haven't checked. got a meeting. later.

Anyone casually passing my tester might very well have mistakenly assumed I was absolutely thrilled over the effortless testing of a tray of parts at freezing temperatures. And technically, it was good news—a relief, really. But not as good as discovering that Beck might be on her way to vanquishing the One-Date Wonders. Whoot!

Eventually, though, the red light on top of the parts handler started flashing, necessitating some actual work. Dipping my hand into a freezing chamber to unjam a couple of parts, the truth of my work situation hit me full in the face (along with a blast of liquid nitrogen–laced cold). I could either toe the line and wait for management to embrace me, or I could take the escape route I'd been offered and juice things up a little myself. As much as switching from one engineering job to another could juice things up.

I didn't dare risk asking Fairy Jane for advice, and Beck, I'd discovered, was a bit of a wild card. Gabe, tired of my bitching, would most likely vote for a transfer. So I was pretty much on my own, with Friday only a few days away.

Sean called around four to confirm our plans for the evening. The premiere was at eight, so we'd meet at the Paramount at seven-thirty. Apparently it was to be a red-carpet event, some dramedy called *Peas and Carrots*, with a couple of up-and-coming celebrities and likely a mad crush to get in. I was promised very good seats. We agreed to get dinner afterwards, which pretty much guaranteed that it would be a very late night indeed (for a Tuesday), and I spent the remainder of the afternoon riding the thrill of being—just for now—Sean's "luv."

Well that, and trying to squeeze in a mini roadtrip and an awkward chat with an elderly gentleman about his sister's once-upon-a-time love interest.

Misty Glen Assisted Living Community, which I'd Googled and then phoned from my cubicle, was a trio of ranch-style buildings relaxing under the lacy shade of towering old pecan trees. The porches, clustered with rocking chairs and barrel tables holding giant checker sets, were empty, either due to the brisk spring breeze or the fact that my visit coincided with naptime. I asked at the desk for Mr. Nelson, crossing my fingers that he had few minutes to spare before an early-bird dinner at 4:45. I was in luck.

I found him in the rec room, playing Mexican Train dominoes with a trio of other inhabitants. After introducing myself, I was gruffly told that I could cool my heels until the game was over. Fair enough. I plunked myself down on the cushy couch and examined my quarry. A horseshoe of white fuzz clung to his head and crinkly lines edged a pair of faded blue eyes that, by the looks of things, didn't let much slip by unnoticed. I'd have to be on my toes when my turn came around.

I tipped my head back, shuttering my eyes closed. I'd been paged four times on the trip down here, but I wasn't up to returning any of them. Truthfully, I wasn't up for much of anything right now—I was way outside my comfort zone, with no clue as to how I'd ever get back.

Time passed, and I kept quiet inside my little cocoon. Until I was launched like a butterfly as someone collapsed onto the couch beside me, close enough that our thighs brushed on my way back down. My eyes flared open and whipped around to catch the delighted little smirk on Mr. Nelson's face.

"I won again," he told me, I assumed referring to his game of Mexican Train. "Ha! It's almost too easy."

"Congratulations," I said, trying to bring my heart rate back under control.

"You find the key?" He glanced at me from under caterpillar-like brows. He was munching on what looked like a particularly lumpy homemade chocolate chip cookie.

"Sorry," he said, catching me eyeing the cookie, "last one." Then, to himself, "I love how she puts the Raisinettes in." Popping the last of it into his mouth, he dusted his hands on his khakis.

Another cookie would have broken the ice nicely.

"I found the key," I confirmed, then paused for just a second before adding, "and I read your sister's story."

"Hrmmph." He produced a double-six domino, seemingly out of nowhere, and tumbled it, over and over, between his fingers. "So why the visit?"

"I . . . ah . . . needed an answer the journal wasn't giving me."

"Yeah? Which one?" He didn't meet my eyes, and I knew this must be hard on him. I almost wished I hadn't come.

But I *had* come—I'd driven all the way down here—and I was going to ask the question.

I looked down at my own fingers, linked in front of me, and wished I had a domino of my own. "Did she have any regrets? You said you thought she was happy, but after Tyler there was never mention of another man. Do you know if she fell in love again? If she got married? Did she ever wish she hadn't taken the journal's advice?"

"You know that's more than one question, right?"

I smiled. "Noticed that, did ya?"

"Cat never married, and as to men, I couldn't tell ya. Wouldn't even want to know, if it came to that." He cringed slightly. "What I can tell you is that she was happy. Every letter she sent told me that. She may have regretted leaving Tyler behind, but she would have regretted it a whole lot more if she'd stayed." He paused on a heavy sigh. "Despite what I said before—blaming the journal for Cat's skedaddling—that wasn't exactly fair. I suspect Cat would have found her way to leaving with or without that diary."

My gaze held his for several long seconds. It wasn't the answer I'd been hoping for. Then again, I had no idea *what* I'd been hoping for—an easy solution to my complicated situation, I guess. Clearly, I wasn't going to find it here.

"That's good to know," I finally said.

"I may not have agreed with her decisions, but I respected that they were hers to make."

"You're a smart man," I told him, smiling.

I stood up and stretched a bit, dreading the hurried drive back to Austin.

He glanced up at me. "I wrote in there too, you know. Just once—couldn't help myself." He shuffled his feet and shot me a look out of the corner of his eye. I sank slowly back into my seat.

"I didn't know," I told him, my heartbeat thumping crazily in my chest.

"It was right after I'd gotten Cat's things back from England—after she'd died. I opened the diary—never put the key in, mind you—and just started to write."

He had been the journal's previous owner. His entry would have come right between Cat's and mine. Somehow, I must have missed it.

My eyes were so wide they were starting to dry out in the dehumidified rec-room air, causing me to blink excessively.

"So did you . . . ?" I lifted my shoulders expectantly.

"Did I get any advice from the all-powerful journal? As a matter of fact, I did." He smiled.

I thrummed with tension and curiosity, waiting for Mr. Nelson to let me in on his little secret.

He chuckled. "I'll give you a hint. Those cookies came from Ms. Eleanor Stone in apartment 112. We have a 'date' tonight to watch *Rear Window*—she's a big Grace Kelly fan."

My mind whirled. Had Mr. Nelson been the recipient of a bit of personalized romantic advice? Interesting . . . I was now anxious to get back to Austin for an entirely different reason.

"Good for you," I said, smiling. I stood, reached down to help him to his feet, and decided to take my chances with one final question.

"Did your sister ever mention the journal's original owner?"

"Nope. Only said she was lucky that little book had found its way to her."

I nodded and reached to shake his hand. "Well, thank you so much for your time, Mr. Nelson. Evidently I have some reading to do," I said, winking.

"I don't pretend to understand how that diary works its magic, but I'm convinced that it's well-meant. That said, my advice to you, young lady, is to take any advice with a grain of salt. You're the one that has to live with your decisions." He gave my shoulder an encouraging squeeze. "Now if you come back, I'll teach you how to play Mexican Train," he said, nodding.

"I'll hold you to that," I said, giving him a little salute before turning away. My real life was calling.

I was cutting it close and luckily missed much of Austin's horrific rush-hour traffic. And before succumbing to what would likely prove to be a thirty-hanger pile-up in my bedroom as I prepped for tonight's date, I was dead set determined on reading the bit of journaling that had resulted in a batch of homemade chocolate chip cookies with Raisinettes.

I never thought I'd be reading my sister's diary. Then again, there's not much left of her musings. Not sure I could have stomached the original.

*She was gone for a long time, half a world away from central Texas, and
I wish I'd had a chance to catch up a little before she died. Cat had a good
head on her shoulders, despite what some folks thought after she left Tyler
behind to get on with her own life. I only regret that she never came back.
Seems as though her life kept her busy—and happy—and for that, I'm
thankful. I'm relieved that she lived such a full life, far away from small-
town judgment and other folks' expectations—I hope she found what she
was looking for. I know she treasured this diary and its peculiar brand of
companionship through the years, and I'm thankful to have it in my possession. Reminds me of her spunk.*

E. Nelson 01.12.10

Well, obviously I didn't know exactly what Fairy Jane's advice
had been, but I suspected something like, *look for companionship
and spunk in 112.* Crafty, very crafty. And it looked as if things were
progressing very well indeed if the cookies and movie night were
any indication. Nicely done, Fairy Jane.

I was now perilously close to running late for my date with
Sean, and I didn't have even a little time to obsess over what to
wear. I resigned myself to calling for backup. I tried Beck first, but
the call rolled over to voice mail, forcing me to fall back on a very
dubious second choice.

"I can't decide what to wear," I whined to Gabe.

"Not really my area of expertise."

"Are South by Southwest festival goers usually dolled up or
grunged down?"

"It's Austin—there's a mix of both. Some are even half and
half."

The man had a point.

"So jeans are okay, not too casual?"

"*I* plan to wear jeans."

How to say this . . . "I'm talking about *other* people—stylish
people."

"You know, *you* called me."

"You're right, you're right," I assured him. "How about jeans, a
shirt with some shimmer, and a nice fitted jacket?" All three items

were currently in my field of vision, hanging off or draped over some piece of furniture, the jacket having been shrugged off the minute I got home.

"That'll work. Just relax, Nic, or you'll look like a tourist."

I didn't bother mentioning that as far as tonight went, I was pretty damn close.

"Okay, thanks." Deep breath. Good.

"Have fun," he said.

Within ten minutes of hanging up, I'd scrambled into my outfit for the evening, added a sparkly belt and some earrings, and even gone a little crazy with the hair gel, scrunching my hair into what I hoped was a slightly edgier look. One final mirror check—oops! a daisy! Sliding the slightly wilty stem from my button hole, skimming my fingers along the petals, I dipped my face once again into its cheery red center and inhaled the swoony scent of a bad crush. It definitely stayed here.

As I skidded out the door, it occurred to me that I'd managed to go the entire day without Fairy Jane running interference. The little burst of confidence and my smug little smile didn't last, though, because it was still anybody's game. The day was far from over yet.

Sean, of course, was waiting, and I was left to wonder how a girl who prided herself on punctuality could suddenly be late for pretty much absolutely everything. A couple waves of the wand could help with that—green lights, convenient parking . . . Maybe I could put in a request.

As I got close, I raised my hand and offered up a friendly wave, but the second I was within reach, Sean snaked his arm around my waist and pulled me in for a couple of quick, very heated kisses. When he pulled back and skimmed his fingers through my daring 'do, my eyes were drawn up to the Paramount's Old Hollywood–style marquee, its glamorous brilliance setting off flashbulbs in my head.

"I like the dangerous new you," Sean informed me, sliding a festival wristband into place on my arm. I was relieved to see that he'd dressed casually as well in beige corduroys and a chocolate brown sweater.

"It's sort of a special occasion," I confided. "Eight years in Austin, and this is my first visit to the Paramount Theater, my first time at a South by Southwest venue of any sort."

"Well then, I am at your service, my little Virgin Queen," he teased, bowing low, his wicked grin making me think seriously about sexual favors.

And then suddenly I was on the red carpet. Admittedly it was a red carpet in Austin, Texas, where cowboy boots are paired with just about anything and pretty much no one is anyone—or everyone is someone—but still. My eyes were flitting about like hummingbirds, and my fingers were tightly twined with Sean's as I rode the wave of jabbering festival goers.

In the middle of it all, Sean dipped his head down beside mine, his breath feathering hot against my chilly ear.

"Dodge out of work tomorrow and come 'round the city with me."

A shiver ran through me as I imagined the thrill of playing hooky with Sean, seeing the city through the eyes of a "cool kid." But it was quickly squelched. I couldn't just take off without warning—I was the Go-To Girl.

"Very tempting, but I have to work."

A Hummer limo pulled up in front of the theater, and I craned my head to catch a glimpse of its occupants.

"Do you really?" Sean pressed, evidently unconcerned with the arrival of the stars. "Is it an absolute must or just habit?"

My gaze shifted to meet his, and I felt as if I'd been caught in a lie. Sean's gaze was patiently challenging, as if waiting for everything to click in my head.

"No, I really do." Of course I did—it was a Wednesday. I couldn't just randomly not show up on a Wednesday. My face scrunched with uncertainty. *Could I?* I turned back to the Hummer, forced to squint against the onslaught of flashbulbs, and tried to consider this unfamiliar alternative.

"We could come up with a proper itinerary and everything." He lifted his hand to settle on the back of my neck, squeezing gently. "Has no one ever taught you to snatch at opportunities when you can, before they disappear?" Sean murmured.

Those particular words served as the necessary inducement. I suddenly felt a feverish need to race the clock, to make every second of this temporary romance count, knowing that it would, inevitably, come to an end. "Okay." The word just ripped out of me before I could snatch it back, and the inherent hesitancy was just hanging in the air between us. I couldn't seem to stop the flood of stilted sentences that followed. "Definitely. I'll take the day off. Wednesday. Hump day. I need a break anyway."

"I must be even more charming than I imagined to lure the dedicated Nicola James away from the office on a random Wednesday. This definitely calls for a celebration, a toast to tomorrow's adventures. But being short on drinks, a kiss will have to do."

The moment his lips began to skim and slide over mine, the strangeness that had settled over me began to fall away. The uncertainty gave way to compliance, and I began to morph from Go-To Girl to Swoony Girl. Everything inside me began to loosen: melting, unfurling, derailing. I should resist him—I knew I should—but I couldn't bring myself to do it. *Danger, Nic James, danger!* And then suddenly we were swept up in the wave of people flooding through the doors on an urgent mission to find their seats. As we stepped from the lobby into the theater, with its breath-stealing, turn-of-the-century grandeur, my heart hiccupped and my throat closed. I gripped Sean's hand, desperately needing to hold on to something. When he gazed down at me, I'm certain he saw stars in my eyes.

"Brilliant, isn't it?"

"Absolutely dazzling," I agreed. "Thank you for inviting me."

His answer was only a slow smile.

We slid into seats near the back, and as the lights dimmed and the film credits began to wink past on the darkened screen, I felt myself relax. By the end of the movie, my head was propped lightly against Sean's cashmere-soft shoulder, and it felt . . . *nice.* So did linking our fingers as we walked through the chilly evening back to my car.

Sean was first to break the silence. "I am now starving and willing to eat virtually anything."

"Most places around here will be packed with festival crowds. Do you want to widen our search parameters?" Whoa, did that sound geeky!

"Logical to a fault—it's impossible not to love you." Suddenly I was frozen with uncertainty. He'd said the "L" word (not "lesbian," thank God!), and it was up in the air, hanging there between us, unclassified, and I hadn't the slightest clue what to do about it. "I'm game for anything," he added, oblivious to my dilemma.

"Hula Hut?" I finally suggested in a shy, scratchy voice.

"Hold here for a sec. I'll grab the bike and follow you." And then he was jogging off into the darkness.

His absence was palpable, and I caught myself staring into the rearview mirror, straining to catch a glimpse of him. The snarl of the motorcycle engine set my nerve endings on full alert long before I had a visual. Then I was squinting against the glare of the headlight until he pulled up close behind me, helmeted and very competent looking astride his roaring beast of a bike.

Driving up South Congress toward the glowing green rotunda of the Capitol building, the colors of Austin nightlife streaming by like a small-town carnival, I finally felt like I belonged in this city. I switched on my blinker, turned left onto West Sixth, and peeked again at my rearview mirror. I was mesmerized by this whole situation and the fact that, head down, eyes focused, Sean was following *me*. With most of Sixth Street's clubs and restaurants running to the east of Congress, we bypassed the crowds and began to leave downtown behind. As Sixth snaked into Lake Austin Boulevard and the city gave way to tree-lined neighborhoods, my gaze was ping-ponging between the narrow roadway in front of me and Sean behind me.

I was starting to imagine a whole spider/fly dynamic. We were heading into an increasingly intricate, very sticky situation, and it almost seemed as if the motorcycle behind me, cruising along at neighborhood speeds, was poised to pounce. My slightly giddy SXSW/hooky high began to morph into more of a predator/prey nervousness. Particularly as the predator was undeniably sexy and the prey couldn't seem to help herself.

I made a valiant attempt to dial back my Animal Planet–fueled imagination and just park the car. Sean might well be a master of seduction—a grand master, or whatever kung-fu term supersedes them all—and Fairy Jane might have done a little wand-waving here and there. But ultimately I'd made the decisions. More or less. I was going to go ahead and go with that assumption anyway. As the saying goes, I'd made my bed, and I was going to have to lie in it.

Watching Sean dismount, slide off his helmet, and immobilize me with a smile in the dark, it occurred to me that that particular saying was especially thought-provoking. And a quick FYI: It's very difficult to behave normally with a man while you're imagining all sorts of bed-related pastimes. It's also difficult to keep your eyes from roving. And your hands from twitching. And your body from sparking off fireworks or puddling in a heap.

But somehow you manage.

"Come over here a sec," said the spider to the fly. . . .

Even in the dark with the engine off, the motorcycle was intimidating, but I stepped cautiously forward.

"I'd wager you've never even *been* on a bike—never straddled one, leaned in, and pretended to ride."

I swiveled my gaze to his and narrowed my eyes slightly. He looked so innocent, it was impossible to tell whether he was using these particular words on purpose, whether he could read the lurid train of my thoughts. But I couldn't accuse him without giving myself away. So I tried to picture myself flying down Mopac on the back of this motorcycle, fear forging a frozen trail from my head to my stomach. It went a long way toward dredging my mind from its lust-ridden haze.

"No," I answered. "I haven't." And I was pretty sure my placid smile implied that I didn't ever intend to.

Sean quirked his lips, seeming to be working an idea around in his head, and I felt the faint stirrings of nervousness. But as he grabbed my hand and pulled me away from the bike toward the restaurant entrance, the nerves were covered over with fresh stirrings of lust. Clearly distance (from the bike) made the heart grow fonder (of Sean).

It wasn't until we were cozied up under our very own private tiki hut on the patio, overlooking the moonlit waters of Lady Bird Lake, the romance at its zenith, that I was let in on the secret.

"Shall we tackle tomorrow's itinerary, leave nothing to the whims of chance?" We'd already dispensed with the menus, deciding to split the infectiously termed Huli Huli Luau Platter.

"Definitely," I agreed, relieved that we were finally on the same page.

"You're all in, then? You're committed to the hooky?"

Hooky . . . nooky . . . When did simple word association get so dangerous? Clean it up, Nic.

"I am," I admitted, schooling my features.

Sean's knee bumped up against mine and stayed, radiating little curls of heat in all directions. "As I see it, the proper way to go about this is to divvy up the day. You get half, and I get half." He speared me with a look and laid his cards on the table. "My half will be devoted to dethroning the Virgin Queen."

Oh. My. God. Is he talking in euphemisms, or is this the real deal? It was possible I was going to need a translator to make it through this conversation.

"Meaning *what* exactly?" My voice was pitched low; it was difficult to get anything out around the wad of nervousness trapped in my throat.

Sean was clearly reveling in my reaction, smug as a satyr with wicked intent dancing in his eyes.

"Meaning this time tomorrow I'm hoping your list of Austin 'been there, done thats' will be considerably longer."

Okay, *now* I was truly nervous. Forget all those little uncertainties over sex—he was going to try to get me on his *motorcycle*. Deep breath. I looked deliberately away from him, running my eyes along the maze of colored lights strung up on the patio and then out over the sparkles on the water and up the dark cliffs to the mansions hanging on the edge. Austin was bewitching at night—a city of surprises—and tonight, I was definitely caught up . . . but insecurities were hovering, waiting to make an entrance. And this could very well be their cue. . . .

When did my life get so out of control? When did I decide to let Sean waltz in and spin me until my life got dizzy and unrecognizable? When will I make it stop?

My heartbeat was loud in my ears, roaring almost, as my mind sped through the possibilities that might conceivably comprise a day with Sean. This was effectively a dare, and on principle, I didn't do dares, but it was about time I earned my Weird shirt—without any help from Fairy Jane. And really, what was the worst he could come up with?

Nic James Does Austin. This film not yet rated.

"Okay." My voice wavered just slightly. Steady, girl. "I'm game." Sean's grin flared wide, knocking out the dimples, and feeling just a little smug myself, I laid down my conditions. "*However,* I draw the line at getting tattooed, pierced, naked in public"—I figured I'd keep my options open, making it clear I wasn't averse to private nakedness—"drunk, or high." I figured I'd need my wits about me. "And I reserve the right to veto one activity on your list." I let this sink in for a second before adding, "Do we have a deal?"

"We do, absolutely," he conceded with a nod. "I'll just need to get a little creative."

I tried for a blithe smile but wasn't certain I pulled it off.

Probably sensing the chicken behind my bravado, Sean wrapped his hand around the back of my neck and massaged gently. As I started to relax and go fuzzy-eyed, he leaned in and laid his lips softly over mine. He tasted spicy and sweet, like grilled pineapple. I'd never been able to resist good pineapple, and I didn't even bother trying.

It wasn't until I was back home, soundly kissed, that it occurred to me that Brett was getting stomped. Sean was running rings around both him *and* me, and I wasn't sure either of us would ever catch up. It was already midnight, and while I could feel fatigue pulling at the corners of my eyes, a wild, structured urgency was careening around inside me. So many things I needed to do. I needed to call in sick, although it was probably best to leave that for the morning. I needed to talk to Fairy Jane—to pour everything out of me in a jumbled, incoherent blurb and have her shoot back a succinct little shot of advice. And I needed to come up with an itinerary for my half of the day tomorrow. And it couldn't be typical Austin fare, because while I could safely (if perhaps unchivalrously) be termed a Virgin Queen, Sean had obviously been around the block. I needed to shoot for the extraordinary, the bizarre, and the downright odd.

I was so not equipped for this.

I could call Beck or go next door—talk about your bizarre—but it was late, and either option would be a cop-out. I was just going to have to hunker down with my laptop and do a little surf and search. We'd agreed to meet for breakfast tomorrow at ten. Just maybe I'd have enough time to do everything and still sneak in a little time to sleep.

I tackled the journal first:

Two dates in one day. Quite the statistical improbability for me—and a rather guilt-inducing situation. I feel like these guys are auditioning for the part of Nic James's Love Interest. But everything is scarily unscripted. Sean's invitation to play hooky and spend the day together having an impromptu "virgin adventure" took me completely off guard. And while I probably shouldn't have, I said yes—I wanted to say yes. Sean has a way of making even the ridiculous seem irresistible. So it seems I've agreed to be somewhat of a guinea pig, hustled around Austin according to the whims of Sean's big dethroning plans. I really don't want to think about what he has planned—I may have laid out my conditions and insisted on a veto, but I suspect he'll find ways of getting around all of it. I fully expect to spend half the day in a constant state of anxious uncertainty.

Then the other half is mine. Seeing as it's already midnight, and my exciting friends are off-limits, I'm going to have to really dig deep—otherwise Sean's going to find himself inveigled in a city-wide search for the perfect cupcake. So far, my mind hasn't moved past the idea of insisting that Sean don a kilt for at least part of the day—it's pretty firm on that point. In fact, I plan on calling him in the morning to shock the pants right off him.

I'm nervous, but lately I'm nervous over just about everything. Sean should come with a warning label, because the truth is, if I had to venture a guess, it would be that by tomorrow night, life as I know it will have changed irrevocably. I'm not sure how ready I am for that eventuality.

I reread the words out of habit, wondering what sort of advice this magical little journal would squeeze out this go-round. Part of me was yearning for the shakable (and re-shakable) simplicity of a trusty Magic 8 Ball or the sweeping near miracles of a dusty old Ouija board. Fairy Jane's offerings were whimsical at best, but her opinion was clear: Sean was precisely what my life was missing. But could I trust her? I hadn't decided yet.

Tipping the cover shut on my entry, I reached for the key, slipped it into place, and watched the magic unfurl all over again, amazed anew at the hidden depths of this little book. And then suddenly it was heavy on my lap, the lost and found-again pages brittle and crinkly with secrets. I settled in to read.

Taking up where I'd left off the night before, I discovered the first entry written by a society miss in love with a servant. Reading between the lines, I'd say that Fairy Jane was quite the progressive instigator, encouraging the romance as well as a daring adventure or two. The second entry was really quite juicy:

I met him, just as you suggested, in the folly. No one would imagine the crumbling structure, long vacant, might harbor the most illicit of romances, but it did, and it most definitely will again. Passionate deeds are definitely addictive. I have responsibilities and a life that requires my attention, but it doesn't preclude me from wishing for the impossible. I daresay I'm no longer certain the word even applies. This journal has convinced me that there is magic lurking about, and henceforth, I vow that I will endeavor to search for it most strenuously.

The next few entries had me vicariously enthralled, shocked, and slightly guilty to be reading such personal, passion-filled thoughts. But not sufficiently to stop. Talk about your bodice-rippers . . .

I am sure I surprised him, waiting as I was when he arrived. And the manner of my greeting no doubt surprised him even more. To anyone watching as I set off from the house, I'm sure I looked every bit a lady out for a walk and picnic, but my basket was crowded with other things . . . I'd sneaked into the bedroom reserved for the seamstress and stolen away yards of tulle that would now be conspicuously absent from the wedding dress I never intended to wear. My trousseau had been pilfered as well, and I shivered with the secret thrill that the lacy confections would be worn solely for the man I intended. All week I'd been setting off in the chilly dawn light, a down pillow concealed beneath my cloak, and, ever so slowly, the folly had been transformed. When Luke stepped through the door, I watched his eyes darken with appreciation as I lay nestled amid all that stolen luxury. We indulged ourselves for hours, touching and exploring, until finally, while he lay sated, I convinced him to run away with me. . . .

By the end, my mouth was gaping, my breathing erratic, and a sense of wonder had settled over me. Despite the odds, the obstacles, and the implausibility of it all, the pair had found their happily-ever-after.

It was pretty easy to tell which of the journal's previous owners had been willing to take a chance on a little magic and which hadn't. The squeamish ones wrote one, maybe two, even three entries, but no more. The believers kept coming back, chatting up Fairy Jane in pursuit of the fairy tale. I fell somewhere in between: an obliging skeptic, willing, at least for now, to play the odds.

It didn't escape me that the underlying theme running through these vintage journal entries was that some occasions called for a bit of conscientious rule breaking. Cat Nelson had left her love behind, but I was hoping to go forward, and even willing to deviate from The Plan, to find mine.

Life with Sean might seem like a pipe dream, but life without him now seemed eerily hollow. I'd try to keep that in mind during the enthusiastic corruption he no doubt had planned for tomorrow.

Removing the key, I waited for the magic to seep away before flipping the pages back to my latest entry. Fairy Jane had already done her homework.

an adventure shouldn't be planned—otherwise it's just a venture

On that note, I decided I'd forgo the planning altogether and go to bed. I was still the Virgin Queen—at least for tonight—and I planned on dreaming of my own folly.

14

an adventure shouldn't be planned—otherwise it's just a venture

"As requested, a kilt-wearing escort for a day of hooky."
Sean was waiting for me outside Juan in a Million, balancing Austin's fine line of fitting in while standing out. Likely the fact that he'd paired a black "Keep Austin Weird" tee with his knee-skimming plaid had something to do with it. Or it simply could have been that he was heart-stoppingly gorgeous even in a skirt.

After fibbing on the phone to my boss's voice mail, I'd called Sean and laid out my first request. Not surprisingly, he hadn't balked.

The kilt had been nonnegotiable, and the fact that I'd planned that aspect of the day didn't make the reality of seeing Sean in a kilt any less of an adventure. Besides, I had no idea what he might be wearing underneath. And that had adventure written all over it.

With that single exception, I'd taken the advice. Weird, yes. But today, by its very nature, was deviant from the norm—a Wednesday without work, a day of surprises with a sexy Scotsman . . . Why not do the opposite? It had worked for Costanza. I do admit to balking slightly when faced with the latest quote-of-the-moment: " 'It was, perhaps, one of those cases in which advice is good or bad only as the event decides.' *Persuasion*," but I tried to let it roll off me. So while I was about to eat breakfast tacos with a man in a kilt, beyond that, I had no plans.

A nervous shiver crawled up my spine, and I suddenly felt very *Rain Man. No plans . . . not good . . . not good . . . not good at all.* But then Sean leaned in, laid his warm hand against my shoulder, and kissed me on the top edge of my cheekbone, and I felt instantly calm. Well, calm-*er*.

"I'm glad to see you've gotten into the spirit of the day, but fair is fair. You chose my clothes, so I've chosen yours."

My eyes flashed wide, swung up to meet his, then dropped to zero in on the package he was holding out to me, wrapped in purple paper and tied with black ribbon. I reached for it slowly, simultaneously desperate and afraid to open it. I had, after all, agreed to all of this.

As Austin's breakfast crowd streamed into the restaurant around us, anxious for their first cup of coffee and the aroma of homemade flour tortillas, I tore into the paper, finding more purple beneath, in the form of a T-shirt. Holding the edges, I let it drop down before me, a spike of shock zooming straight to my stomach. I glanced at Sean to see a smug smile lingering on his lips.

He'd bought me the shirt I hadn't had the nerve to buy myself: "Keep Austin Weird." I'd never mentioned it to him, and yet, after nearly a week-long trial by fire, on the day I imagined I might deserve it most, he had it wrapped and ready. At this moment, I could almost believe that Sean knew a bit of magic himself. Biting my lip, I glanced down at my pale pink T-shirt and charcoal gray hoodie and vowed to change at the first possible opportunity.

As I stepped closer to wrap Sean in an impulsive hug, he shifted slightly—I suspect deliberately—setting our lips on a collision course. I kicked the unexpected PDA up a notch, clinging to him with a strange urgency for the day ahead.

"Like T-shirts, do you? Good to know," he said, grabbing my hand, tossing the paper, and pulling me into the restaurant.

Seconds after we ordered I was dragging off my hoodie, draping it over the back of my chair, and heading for the bathroom to change. By the time I got back our breakfast was already on the table and Sean's coffee cup was being refilled. Evidently the time I'd spent admiring myself in my Weird shirt had flown by, and now I was eager to dig in to my huevos rancheros. The shirt, it seemed, had taken the edge off my squeamishness.

"Let's have a look at your list for the day," Sean suggested, dousing his taco with hot sauce.

I sat up a little straighter before revealing, "I didn't make a list."

"Sorry?" Sean looked up from his plate, turning his head slightly, bringing his ear around.

"I decided to go a little crazy today. The kilt is the whole plan."

A great big watermelon smile spread across Sean's face. "It is, is it? Were you hoping the lack of pants might somehow thwart the success of my plan for the day? Or is it just that little thing you have for me rearing its lusty head?"

Despite the blush creeping up my neck, I managed to answer coherently. "*Will* the lack of pants trip you up?" Curious minds wanted to know.

"Does it matter?"

"It depends on what you have planned." And whether or not I'm chicken to go through with it.

"Shall I tell you?" The man was a flirting fiend.

"Please do." My heart had started to beat a little faster in nervous anticipation.

Sean wiped his mouth with a napkin and settled his hand loosely around his coffee cup. "I thought we could stop off at Central Market, put together a picnic lunch, then drive up to Mount Bonnell. When we've squeezed all the romance out of that, I imagined us strolling through Zilker Park, possibly dipping our toes into Barton Springs, and then renting a canoe to row out on the lake to watch the evening exodus of bats. All very tame. But there is, naturally, another list."

My blood pressure suddenly spiked, and I forced myself to ask, "Why is there another list?"

"Well, I see no reason to trek all over the city separately. Gas is ludicrously expensive, and the two-car-length separation puts me at a distinct disadvantage." He paused, his lips curving into a rueful twist, but I didn't rise to the bait, instead waiting for the big bang. "Sooo, I had this brilliant idea: You could clap on the spare helmet, and we could ride together. On the bike."

I opened my mouth to object, trying to get the words out around the pulse pounding in my throat, but Sean was quicker. And clearly not hampered by frenzied nervousness.

"You can, of course, veto the motorcycle, but you only have the one veto, luv. And I am determined to inject a little daring into your day."

I tapped the tines of my fork against the edge of my plate in a bit of a temper. "You're stooping to blackmail . . . really? What about my half of the day?" I demanded. I might not have had a plan, but if nothing else occurred to me, I could always stall.

"Don't think of it as blackmail—more as a call to adventure. And as the only one with a plan, I thought we'd run through that first and leave the evening—post-bats—to you."

Post-bats. Twilight and after. I was in charge of the after-dark activities. Damn Fairy Jane! When was it *ever* a good idea not to have a plan! So it was going to be left to me to either plan a seduction or circumvent one. Not only that, but I quickly needed to decide whether or not I wanted to risk vetoing the motorcycle and having Sean come up with the threatened alternative.

Sean waited patiently as I glared. He'd done this on purpose. Crowding my mind with two separate and distinctly worrying topics, he'd hijacked my thought processes and sent me into a tizzy of uncertainty. As deviousness went, it was very clever—I was impressed, and I wasn't.

I lapsed into a silent pro/con debate as I worked through the rest of my breakfast. Sean, wisely, did not attempt to sway my decision.

Con: It's a motorcycle! No seat belts, no doors, just open air and pavement.

Con: This is Texas Hill Country—everywhere you look are roller coaster roads!

Pro: It's an excuse to wrap my arms around Sean and hang on tight.

I flicked my gaze up to make sure he wasn't watching me, watching a new wave of flush ride up my neck.

Pro: Only one of us is wearing a skirt, and skirts tend to whip about in the wind. . . .

Whew! I could feel the blush crest at my cheeks and then flood onto my forehead, but I had the salsa as an alibi. I reached for my water glass and took a long, cool sip. My eyes shifted to look at Sean, and the white words on his shirt seemed to be shouting at me. It might not be weird to trek around Austin on the back of a motorcycle, but it was weird to do it with a man in a kilt, it was weird for me, and it was definitely weird to have to assemble a pro/con list about it. Seeing as I'd dedicated the day to the business of getting weird, how could I say no?

"Okay, fine. We can drop my car back by my house."

"Brilliant! You'll love the bike."

Judging by the worrying view in my rearview mirror on the drive back home, I rather doubted it. To take my mind off my upcoming "adventure," I decided to call Beck for a little pep talk. Seeing as I was shortly going to be pressed up against Sean, holding on for dear life on the back of a motorcycle, it was looking like there might not be another opportunity.

"Mmmph. 'lo?" Obviously she wasn't awake yet.

"Beck? Wake up for a sec! It's Juicy James, and I need to talk!"

"What? I'm up. What's juicy? I really hope you're not calling from your cubicle, because you probably don't want a nickname like 'Juicy James' going around."

"I'm not at work. I called in sick, and I'm spending the day with Sean."

"Wha—"

"Long story. I'll hit the highlights. We split the day fifty-fifty, each of us in charge of planning our half. No problem, right? Well, I stupidly took Fairy Jane's advice and *didn't plan*—except to make him wear his kilt. So now I'm in charge of *tonight*." I gulped in a huge breath of air, hearing the whole thing lingering, ridiculous, in the air between us and wondered anew, *How did he ever get me to agree to this?*

Thankfully, Beck broke the silence before I started hyperventilating.

"Hold up. I'm only half-awake, and this isn't making a whole lot of sense. He's wearing a kilt? What's on *his* list?"

I tried to settle my breathing while relaxing my foot on the accelerator to cruise through the timed lights on Cesar Chavez. "A *motorcycle* ride up to Mount Bonnell," I nearly shouted into the phone. "And that isn't even my biggest problem."

"What's your biggest problem?" Beck soothed.

"My biggest problem is that *I'm in charge of tonight!*" Big, deep breath. "Sorry."

"I'm not getting it. This is Austin. There's plenty of stuff to do. What's the problem?"

This was a tad awkward. "Well, we eventually have to come back to my house . . . and he *is* wearing a kilt." Surely that should say it all.

"Ooooh . . . I getcha. Let's see . . . What if you ordered in and cuddled up on the couch with a movie? That's bound to lead to something." Something in her voice made me think it might have already led to a little something with Gabe. But with only a minute left to talk, I didn't have time to press her for details.

"Maybe. But it lacks even a whiff of creativity—no offense. I want to deliver my own dare, and I want him to squirm a little before he decides to take it."

"Got it. Do you own a collapsible pole for a little performance piece?"

Cell-phone silence wasn't quite the same as a steely-eyed stare or a V8-inspired conk in the head, but it seemed to get my point across.

"Sorry. Just a little hooky-day humor. Hmmm . . . You've got all day, right? Let me think about it, and when I come up with something, I'll text you. Is that good?"

Seeing as I was pulling into my driveway and couldn't exactly sit locked in the car to wait out Beck's brainstorming session, that was going to have to do. "That'd be great, thanks. Assuming I'm not completely shell-shocked after my day on a motorcycle, I'll definitely be looking for advice. Think subtle," I urged, picturing her pinkness, fully aware that I was charging her with a very likely impossible task—subtle was not exactly Beck's forte.

"Gotcha. Good luck. Take full advantage of the situation, and call me when you can, prepared to dish! Bye!"

And then it was just me, alone, with Sean and the bike parked beside me on the driveway purring quietly. I stared at it through the car window, the swoops and curls of chrome and leather, with its jaunty leprechaun green accents. It almost seemed friendly. Almost. Much as I dreaded it, I felt compelled to get out of the car.

"Ready, then?" Sean asked, irritatingly chipper.

"No." My attitude could best be described as petulant. I was already thinking of reneging on the whole deal to scurry back to the safety of my cubicle.

Sean laughed, which didn't help, then quickly sobered.

"Right, then. Why don't you try just sitting on it? We'll slide your helmet on, and you can just sit until you're ready to move on."

Sitting in a helmet. That had a safe ring to it. "Fine," I mumbled, cautiously edging forward.

Bracing his left foot on the driveway, Sean swung his right leg over and off the bike in a smooth, competent motion. He then unhooked the spare helmet from its spot on the seat and slowly slid it onto my head. I was officially a bobblehead. He dipped his head down to look at me and grinned. "Ready to climb on?"

I managed a nod that seemed to go on long after I'd stopped consciously moving my head and, gripping the handlebars, swung my leg up and over. After a couple of uneventful seconds I turned toward Sean, a shaky grin creasing my previously starched face.

"You're a natural. Ready to start her up and take a little ride?"

The grin slid quickly away, right along with my tact. "No."

"Just to the end of the driveway and back," Sean pressed. Before I could reject this idea, he'd slid onto the bike behind me and brought his arms around to cover my hands on the handlebars. "Trust me, luv," he urged.

Rather than comfort me, his words derailed my confidence. The truth was I couldn't figure out who to trust: myself, Sean, Fairy Jane, or any of my life's little cheerleaders. But that was a bigger issue. This was just about a motorcycle—everything else could wait. I concentrated on Sean's arms, and the warm contact points where our bodies met, and the fact that I did trust Sean to get me safely down the driveway and back.

Relieved that he couldn't see my face, I nodded once, bobbing the bobblehead.

Wordlessly, Sean revved the engine and walked the bike around to face the street. Then he lifted both feet from the pavement and puttered us down the gently sloping driveway all the way to the street. He turned us neatly, and with a little twist of his wrist, we rocketed forward a little faster, shooting up the driveway with a buzz and a hum to stop once again beside my safe and quiet little car. Sean shifted the engine back to neutral and climbed off, leaving me to settle into the idea of whipping around the city on a breezy *Wednesday* morning in March.

"You're hooked, aren't you?" Sean taunted, dragging a smile out of me.

Our mini test drive might not have fazed me, but I had no delusions that our driveway jaunt would be in any way comparable to zipping around Austin at ten times the speed. But butterflies or not, I needed to risk it. Because if there was any chance of making things work with Sean, I was going to have to learn to be open to compromise and the occasional outlandish adventure.

I turned to Sean to give him the thumbs-up and spotted Leslie sauntering across the lawn in some sort of tangerine caftan, a pale avocado mask smeared over her face. Super.

Before launching into the inevitable commentary, she gave Sean the once-over, flicked her eyebrows up as if to say, "Where were *you* when I decided to switch teams?" and settled her gaze on me.

"My, my, my," she started, feathering a hand to her ample bosom in an "I do declare" sort of way. "Do my cucumber-soothed eyes deceive me, or is that our own sweet Nicola James atop that monster of a motorcycle? Surely not." She seemed oddly flirty. I kept my guard firmly up.

"Hi, Leslie. Late class?"

"I don't need to be on campus till noon on Wednesdays. But I can't imagine what sort of apocalyptic situation lured *you* away from work." Her gaze, dragged inexorably back to Sean after each whiff of a glance at me, finally settled in to stay. "Are *you* the emergency?"

"Guilty as charged," Sean admitted, oozing charm. "Sean MacInnes, Bad Influence." This came off as simultaneously cocky and self-deprecating.

Leslie shifted sinuously forward, and I almost expected a little forked tongue to slip between her lips and flicker about in intimidating fashion. But she merely extended her hand, palm down, the picture of silver screen moxie, particularly with the green goo. "Leslie Innerbock, *Original* Bad Influence," she purred.

Insert eye roll.

"She seems relatively uncorrupted," Sean pointed out after dutifully bestowing a kiss and releasing Leslie's hand.

Leslie's lip curled; I could tell she was grudgingly impressed. "What can I say? Perhaps you have more persuasive . . . *tools*"— her gaze raked down and lingered before whipping up again—"at your disposal. And what woman can resist a man in a kilt?"

I turned away to hide the grin I could no longer hold back. But conscious of the unpredictability of both participants in this showdown, I knew I'd have to intercede before things got hideously embarrassing. For me, that is. I schooled my features and turned back.

"Whoa. Down, girl. Just think of this motorcycle as that mechanical bull you were telling me about, and it can all be your idea." I gave the cycle a little pat, willing her to remember her little Friday-night pep talk.

"That *is* true," she conceded, as graciously as she'd ever conceded anything. "It doesn't matter anyway. What matters is you found a man, got yourself a Weird shirt, and damn if you're not sitting astride a great big vibrating—"

Vvvvvrrrrrrooooovvvvmmmmm!

Sitting there, caught up in Leslie's runaway monologue, visualizing it streaking toward its train wreck of a conclusion, I was at a loss. My reaction? A cringe with a twist. My hands had curled reflexively around the handlebars, jerking just enough to rev the engines in one big guttural growl, the mother of all reprimands.

Leslie's mouth rounded to an "o" and popped shut, a virtually unheard-of reaction.

Sean's head whipped around in surprise, but then he dimpled me with a knowing grin. I was as shocked as anyone and becoming more and more fond of this bike.

Leslie recovered quickly, and rather than hold a grudge at such a garish interruption, seemed more than a little impressed with my sudden burst of spunk. "In case she doesn't mention it herself . . ." Leslie shot me a look. "Nic comes for karaoke every Friday night. She brings the cupcakes. Get her to invite you along, and we'll see if you can keep up. And if you can get Nic to sing, I'll know you're a god. Wear the kilt."

I suddenly had an urge to ram her, but before I could act on it, she was sauntering back the way she'd come, giving me a fluttery finger wave and a devilish grin.

Sean watched her go but quickly turned back to me. Before he could comment—I didn't even want to guess what he might have said—I blurted, "I'm ready." I'd deal with Leslie's impromptu invitation later.

I scooted back, giving Sean room to climb on in front, and suddenly outrageously shy, I wrapped my arms loosely, tentatively around Sean's waist. I managed to make it to the end of the street with my relaxed grip, but once we'd slid into traffic, with cars whizzing by on either side and the pavement stretching in front of us, potholed and bumpy, I quickly traded it for the infinitely more comforting full-body clamp technique. With blustery-crisp wind on my cheeks, I shamelessly spooned him on the streets of the capital city. From chin to knee, every last inch of my body was pressed against the inches of his. I was jittery and shivery, and, sur-prise, surprise, a bit of a potty mouth. But the roar of the engine and the rush of the wind carried all those words away.

Just as I was getting used to it, we were slowing down, easing into the Central Market parking lot, and killing the engine. I'd done it! I'd trusted and survived. And it hadn't been so bad. I re-fused to picture the roads we'd have to take on the next leg of the trip, instead reveling in this one triumphant, exhilarating moment. I felt a bit like I'd conquered the world—and deserved a celebra-tory cupcake.

We wove our way through the maze of Central Market, stocking up on standard picnic fare: a baguette, a bit of cheese, an eclectic selection from the olive and pickle bars, strawberries, and bottled water. It wasn't until we were lugging the picnic supplies out into the sunlight in an environmentally conscious canvas bag that I realized the bike didn't have one of those cool storage compart-ments or hipster baskets—it was pretty much "what you see is what you get" as far as I could tell. So if Sean was driving, and I was sprawled over the back of him like a bug on the windshield, where exactly did we plan to stash a baguette? Not to mention its accompaniments.

"Has this bike been on a picnic before?" I asked.

He aimed a quizzical look in my direction, covered it with a smile, and lifted his hand to circle the back of my neck. No answer was forthcoming. I tried again.

"Where are the groceries going to ride?" I pressed.

"Between us, where else?" His reply was automatic and posi-tively reeked of male ego. Evidently he'd forgotten how I'd had to peel myself off him, a regular pudding skin, after the first ride. I hadn't a doubt that this second leg would be considerably more frazzling than the first, given the dips and curves in the roads that led up to Mount Bonnell, and I fully intended to reprise my role as pudding skin.

We would see who fared better: me or the picnic.

15

In which Sean succeeds
in toppling the Queen

That is how we came to be zipping down West Thirty-fifth and bouncing along Mount Bonnell Road with an edible bazooka resting on my shoulder. The groceries had *not* fit between us, and I fully expected to have bruises on my butt where the water bottles had thumped in a steady beat all the way there. I'd have to keep that in mind while making my plans for the evening.

Pulling myself off the bike at the base of Mount Bonnell Park was another matter. I'd been coiled in a pseudo-fetal position for the last fifteen minutes, and my fingers had been curled, talonlike, into awkward clenching claws. Likely I was also deathly pale and ornamented with a curious array of kamikaze insects. It was entirely possible that the Juan in a Million moment, the gifting of the Weird shirt, was destined to be the day's highlight.

I turned away slightly and made a show of stretching and surveying while surreptitiously pulling out my cell to check for messages. I was in luck—a text had come in while I'd been swooping along like a superhero with a grocery bag cape.

Mssg from Beck:

Strip poker??

I was rolling my eyes in exasperation when Sean's voice startled me back to the reality of right now. "Ready?"

This seemed to be the day's recurring theme—Was I ready? Hard to say. Today was mapping out to be one of those "kill you or make you stronger" sort of days, and so far, for a squeamish little chicken, I thought I was kicking some serious ass. I did dread the thought of a final elimination round, though. . . .

"Yep," I answered with an enthusiastic nod, glancing at the trail of limestone steps leading up to the park.

Sean took over as pack mule, and I couldn't help but notice that the top of the baguette was drooping, a little limp from the journey. I knew the feeling.

The rough-hewn limestone steps seemed to go on forever, and I lost count at a hundred. We reached the top together, Sean having tangled his fingers with mine at the bottom, maybe to keep me from looking up his skirt.

The steps led to an open expanse of patio laid with the expected limestone and covered with a partial wooden trellis held up by, surprise, surprise, limestone posts. Rather coincidentally, the spot put me in mind of an old-fashioned folly. I deliberately shook that thought from my head.

We drifted together toward the overlook of Lady Bird Lake snaking a beautiful, reflective blue through the surrounding hills dotted with scraggly cedar and scrunchy live oaks. Sean looked away first—I could feel the tug on my hand as he twisted his body around, scanning the area.

"Relatively secluded this morning."

"Well, it is Wednesday," I reminded him (and myself).

"Lover's Leap," he murmured, reading a mounted plaque and leaning his torso far forward and then whipping back with startling quickness. "Nothing romantic about death and disfigurement, in my opinion, but then I've been told I'm dreadfully dull."

"Who told you that?" I demanded, shocked and rather appalled.

"My younger sister." Judging by his grin, he'd been pleased with my reaction.

"Speaking as a younger sister, I'm sure it was justified," I said sweetly.

"Brothers?" he asked.

"Just one."

"He has my sympathies," Sean parried with mock seriousness.

"He managed," I countered, spearing him with a defensive glare.

"Against what was no doubt a carefully considered, meticulously organized, deviously clever assault. The man is a hero."

"*You* seem to be managing just fine," I retorted, scuffing my shoe through the pale powdery dirt.

"Ahhh, but we've already established that I'm a hero. And I'd wager you've mellowed slightly."

"I'll take that wager," I countered, letting one eyebrow kink in challenge.

Sean's grin flashed quick, the sun glinting sharply off his perfectly straight teeth. My eyebrow relaxed as he demanded, "Truce! Even now it's clear I'm no match for a little sister."

He held out his hand and I took it, for once not second-guessing anything. Filling my head with thoughts of Sean, careful not to leave room for anything else, I managed just fine. The effect was a floaty, serene sense of light-headedness. Perfect for a wandering hike along the limestone cliffs and a sunny picnic on a vast sloping slab of rock facing out over water and sky, both the same Easter egg blue.

I managed somehow to forget about everything—all of it but the two of us together. I might have fallen asleep on that flat, warm rock under the sun, but with nothing more than the tail end of a baguette for a pillow and a Texan's fear of sunburn, I opted instead to wrap my arms around my knees and tip my head back for five blissful minutes of heat without the burn. It was a tricky balance, an art form really, much like the way a fugitive knows precisely how long to stay on the phone to beat the trace.

It was impossible to say when Sean switched his gaze from the glorious Texas Technicolor to me, but when my eyes finally blinked open, he was staring. Flustered, I took refuge in common sense, struggling to sit up despite my limbs feeling like warm wax. "We're going to need to pick up some sunblock if we're going out in a canoe," I reminded him. "Otherwise we'll crisp up and hurt like hell."

"We don't want that, do we?" he asked, sounding very James Bond and looking the part with his carefully banked smoldering gaze. He kept it trained on me as he pulled me to my feet.

"No-ooo," I answered, suddenly obsessed with dusting off my bruised bottom.

"In Scotland we pack umbrellas, not sunblock. No sense in being overly optimistic." We were climbing slowly back toward the limestone-paved patio, the sun beating warmly on our backs.

"You only have to burn once. After that you remember: getting aloe vera gel sticky-slathered all over you, cringing at every touch for days, peeling and itching until you resemble some sort of queer albino reptile. After that, you don't leave home without it." I looked at him quizzically. "You've never gotten burned?"

"Funnily enough, this is my first good opportunity. And now I'm wondering why *you* didn't bring the sunblock," he teased.

Something triggered in the back of my mind but got shuffled away in the face of unadulterated exasperation. "Possibly because I wasn't privy to your plans, and I never expected to be flitting about, exposed to the elements, not to mention the pavement, on the back of your motorcycle." I could hear the panicky edge to my voice and knew exactly what was causing it. Sean had touched my biggest nerve—today, I was flying blind.

"I'm teasing, luv. The sunblock was clearly my responsibility, and I bungled it. I'm just relieved you thought of it before we shoved off into the lake, pale and exposed as sitting ducks."

"Well, we'd have had your umbrella, right? You *did* bring an umbrella . . . ?"

I was almost positive—you could say 100 percent certain—that the man wasn't packin' an umbrella.

"I'm afraid not," he admitted, looking chagrined, the slightest bit of pink staining his cheeks. Quite possibly the onset of sunburn.

"I'm only teasing, luv." I mimicked him, looking away quickly before he could see the onset of my pink.

"I deserve that," he said, tangling his fingers with mine.

My jeans brushed against the velvety leaves of a Texas sage, and I let my fingers skim the lavender blooms. My breath was suddenly coming in pants, and not from exertion. If I was truly honest with myself, I had to admit that the hardest part of this whip-fast romance was stepping further and further outside my comfort zone with each baby step I took toward Sean. Made me wonder how I'd feel about the "new me" after the first blush of romance had paled.

Thinking to aim us down a scrub oak–lined hiking path and detour the century of steps, I shifted right. Sean shifted left simultaneously, and we collided on the uneven rock. He caught me, and for the space of a hundred rapid-fire heartbeats, we were only inches away from . . . who knew what . . . something good. But then the wind whipped up, high on our little outcropping of rock, fluttering Sean's skirt.

I glanced down—I couldn't help it—and Sean, glancing down too, moved his hand to that little pouch hanging over his . . . hanging over the front of his kilt. Black leather trimmed with three jaunty tassels, it matched nicely against the colorful plaid of pine green, true blue, and black, shot through with streaks of yellow, pale blue, and red. But the colors all blurred together as I stared at that little pouch and Sean's hand on it. I waited with bated breath (really!) and tried to ignore my heartbeat, building in silent crescendo. Unsnapping the pouch, Sean reached his hand down inside. I was blinking rapidly now, and my lips were twitching with the minor hilarity of the situation.

When his hand reappeared, it was holding a disposable camera, and it took my detoured mind a second to register that Sean had probably brought it along to commemorate this Day of Dares.

"Let's take a photo, shall we? No one will believe it otherwise—you, out on a Wednesday." He scoffed.

We hiked back to the overlook and posed beside Lover's Leap, Sean holding the camera at arm's length as the two of us grinned, the moment captured.

"Did you get our T-shirts in the picture?" I asked.

"Hard to say. Why don't I get one of just you and your shirt? Then we can stop off at Hippie Hollow and get one of you without it," he teased with a wicked smile.

I posed, framing the white words emblazoned on my chest like a handsy spokesmodel, and he snapped a second picture. "One more," I insisted. I extended my hand for the camera. "It's possible you're the first man to climb to the top of Mount Bonnell, skirts fluttering. Doubtful, but possible."

Handing over the camera with a grin, he was quick to pose with his hands on hips and a rakish gleam in his eye. Hoping Sean wouldn't notice, or at the very least wouldn't comment on it, I stole a second behind the camera to marvel at this latest surreal moment in my once-predictable life.

Coming back to stand beside me and slide the little twenty-four-shot camera back from whence it came, Sean ever so casually suggested, "How about I race you to the bottom."

He wasn't joking. In two seconds I was scrabbling over limestone, heading downhill, making for the path in lieu of the stairs. I left Sean in a white puff of dust, his hand still in his pouch.

My grin was imperturbable as I navigated the path, dodging live oaks and ducking around the curves, skidding on gravel and getting hung up for a nervy eternity by an older couple meandering downhill with walking sticks and single-minded determination. But mere seconds had passed when I glimpsed the blacktop—the far edge of roadside parking at the bottom of the hill—and only seconds stood between me and victory.

And then I was there, my feet skimming off the slippery gravel and onto the tar black . . .

And then lifting, spinning in the air in a dizzying swirl that had my adrenaline bubbling over and my stomach plummeting in panic.

The thrill of victory crashed into defeat as I realized Sean was below me, around me, everywhere: He'd beat me to the bottom.

"Trounced you fair and square, darling, despite your head start and the slight disadvantage of my regalia." Our makeshift whirli-gig had finally slowed to a stop, and Sean was making no move to let go.

"If I could think of a way you could have cheated, I'd accuse you. But since I can't . . . congratulations." I admit it—I'm a bad sport. But for God's sake, the man was wearing a skirt!

"Come on. That was hardly sincere. And while we didn't wager, I think I've earned a prize. One kiss," he demanded quietly, a sin-gle eyebrow raised in yet another challenge.

I let my shoulders slump slightly in defeat and puffed out a sigh. "Fine." And while he slid me down the length of his body, letting the tips of my toes settle on the blacktop, I kept my arms twined tight around his neck and tipped his head down for a kiss.

As usual, it sprang out of my control, pulling at me, twisting in-side me, urging me to indulge, to steal this shady roadside moment under the twittering trees and careless clear spring sky. I'd meant to skim my lips over his and leave it at that, but within seconds I was nipping and sliding my tongue along the seam of the lips that had taunted me mercilessly for going on four days now. I heard the hum and roar of cars on the road, and Sean shifted, shielding me from passersby or possibly distraction, and I let myself let go and fell into him, swooping and sailing, my own little "lover's leap."

Practice for tonight. Possibly.

With his breathing distinctly hitched, Sean casually suggested a rematch. I suspected his motives were ulterior. I politely declined and we climbed back onto the bike. As we glided down the winding, bumpy roads back into the city, it was clear—at least to me—that things between us had shifted. Into considerably more dangerous territory.

We made a quick stop at the drugstore to load up on sunscreen, despite my suspicions that I was at greater risk alone with Sean than at the mercy of the afternoon sun, and I took advantage of the moments alone to check my messages. I ignored the voice mails—it was likely they were work-related—and focused on the single text:

Mssg from Beck:

Strip Truth or Dare?

Well, someone had a one-track mind. Although, in her defense, it wasn't a *horrible* idea. Knowing Sean, he'd take the dares and get bored quickly. I'd take truth and he'd know way more than he cared to in under thirty minutes. Tucking my phone away, I just happened to look up and notice Sean snapping a photo of me astride his dark, glossy bike. I couldn't even imagine my expression: Had I been picturing him naked or bored?

Now that I'd somewhat overcome my fears (I was not so much a limp pudding skin as a living, breathing pudding skin), I was urgently conscious of the fact that I was draped over a very sexy, very ripped man with an accent. It was a tingling ride south on Mopac, over the river and along the shaded, serpentine curves of Barton Springs Road, and it was over before I wanted it to end—shocker, I know. With both of us still playing strong, silent types, we pushed our rented canoe away from the creek bank and paddled out onto Lady Bird Lake.

I'd vetoed the proposed chilly dip into Barton Springs Pool, so with a couple of hours to kill before sunset, Sean insisted that I dump my oar in the belly of the canoe, sit facing him, and soak up the chivalry. It was all I could do not to stare at the man, captaining a canoe in a kilt, his skirts draped suggestively. Thank God for dark sunglasses and a little privacy for roving eyes.

When we'd slid out of the shade and into the full-on, glittering impact of the lake, I pulled out the sunblock, smearing it liberally on the pair of us. And then we just floated, beside a city at work. On a Wednesday.

Shading my eyes against the glare, I peeked at Sean, who seemed perfectly content to paddle us up and down the river with a single oar. "It's so peaceful. Even crossing over the bridge every day, I forget how nice it is to come down here and just laze about. It's been years since I've been in a canoe."

Sean smiled and asked, "Was your boss very upset that you dodged out?"

"Hard to say. I left a voice mail, and I haven't checked my messages." Except for Beck's.

"Do you imagine he'll be upset?" The question was fuzzy and faraway sounding. The rhythmic lap of the oar on the lake was lulling me into a pleasure-filled haze.

"Maybe not today . . . but soon enough." I almost had the urge to giggle.

The rhythm slowed. "You've lost me," Sean said.

Closing my eyes, I tipped my head back and let the sunbeams dance over my face, let my thoughts play with possibilities. Dragonflies buzzed into the silence, and eventually I came back to myself. "I'm considering switching jobs. Maybe."

"Why is that?"

"I'd thought to stick it out, hold out for management." I was skimming the tips of my fingers through the water. "But I'm not so gung-ho anymore."

"I wouldn't necessarily peg you as management material."

My eyes flashed open and my spine immediately abandoned its comfortable slump for a defensive, ramrod posture. The canoe rocked with the sudden movement.

"Before you settle into your grudge, you might hear me out."

I was a fair person. He had a right to have his say before I tore into him.

"You're relatively shy and rather intimidatingly competent with, I imagine, a desire to get your hands dirty. I suspect a management position would smother your sparkle with office politics and general tedium." His eyebrow winged up, as if to say, "Fair enough?"

The fledgling grudge, hanging in the air between us, ready to do its worst, dissipated into nothingness. And I found myself with nothing left to say. I was used to people trashing The Plan; I was *not* used to people couching their objections in candid compliments.

"What's the other job?" Good to know he wasn't a gloater.

"It's in failure analysis. Basically I'd be deprocessing the micro-controllers that fail in customer applications, then pinpointing where a failure occurred and how we can screen for it in production. Solid engineering work rather than the babysitting I've been doing. I'd have a new boss, a clean slate. And I'd get trained on all these cool machines . . ." Out here, floating on the murky water with my cell phone switched off and responsibility far away, it was all starting to sound very nice indeed.

"So what's the vote—pro versus con?" Sean asked. I flipped my sunglasses up to squint at him in disbelief. What a seriously mind-boggling turn of events. I rallied.

"I haven't formally tallied things up, but there's at least one con—a biggie. The whole point of getting my MBA was to get into management. And if I switch jobs now, it'll be a considerable setback for my career. Not to mention The Plan," I mumbled.

"What plan is that?"

I looked up at him, calmly rowing, passing the oar from one hand to the other, patently curious. Tipping my head down to stare at the puddle of lake water in the belly of the canoe, I told him.

"I've had my life pretty well mapped out since I was around thirteen years old. There've been a few changes here and there, but generally speaking, I'm on track."

"I'd wager I was a surprise," he interrupted, dimpling.

"You definitely were," I admitted, nodding, feeling a bit bobble-headed, even without the helmet.

"Well, if something as stunningly perfect as this can just happen, then why bother with a plan that'll just slow you up and limit your view?"

"*Is* this stunningly perfect?"

"It's bloody damn close!" There was an edge of exasperation in his voice, and his perfect, lulling rhythm turned jerky. "You're fighting it, but I intend to be merciless in my pursuit. I've discovered I have something of a thing for geeky girls—one in particular. And this is fate."

Or possibly magic . . .

Long moments passed, and neither of us broke the silence. The sun shifted, the light softened, and the sky switched from crisp spring blue to pale lavender. We drifted, watching the cars on the First Street Bridge speed over the lake and the city begin to switch on, incandescent and neon. We scrounged for chitchat, balking at discussing *Us* any further, at pushing too far.

Eventually crowds began to gather along the grassy banks of the downtown hotels, and chattering tourists mingled with Austin locals to wait: the city's own bat signal.

Sean rowed us cautiously under the Congress Avenue Bridge, and the two of us stared silently up into the dark crevices that housed the city's bat population. Despite the lively voices carrying over the water, this little stretch of lake seemed shrouded in creepiness. And as I glanced over at the small flotilla of boats passing under the bridge with us, I could tell I wasn't alone in my impression.

"I've never actually been out on the lake to watch the bats come out," I confided in a whisper, rubbing at the goose bumps that had sprouted on my upper arms.

"Makes two of us." Sean's answer was clipped—he was either still ticked at me or else he was distracted with trying to keep the canoe turned so that we both had an easy view of the bridge.

"It would be easier if we were both facing the same direction, wouldn't it?" I asked, already knowing the answer.

"It would, yeah." Skepticism was clear on his face.

Damn. I really didn't want to be shifting around in a canoe out in the middle of a lake, particularly with an audience, but I would. I didn't know if this was my olive branch or what, but it felt like it was my turn to make an overture. It was my move.

So I made it. I started to anyway. Halfway there, karma decided to make its appearance in the form of five hundred thousand hungry bats.

I could hear the gasps and amazed outbursts from the gathered crowd, but I couldn't turn, couldn't look—I was immobilized in this ridiculous in-between position. And then I felt the canoe shift beneath me. Whether it was the wake from the other boats or a mini gust from a million vigorous little wings, I couldn't say. But whatever it was, it was freakin' me out big-time.

Before I could decide what to do, Sean snagged my hand and yanked me from my crouch down onto the hard middle seat of the canoe. Crisis averted.

"I didn't want you to miss it," he said, as a continuous frenzy of wispy black emerged from beneath the bridge to waft out over the city in search of dinner. Twisting my head around, I caught Sean snapping pictures of the bat-riddled sunset. When he finished, he pulled me back to lean against his chest.

"Smile," he instructed, aiming the camera back on us and snapping a second picture of the two of us together. It occurred to me that this one could be classified as the "After" photo. Our recent chat had shifted things into stunningly perfect focus. I'd decided to take a chance on fate . . . or magic—whichever. I'd decided to take my chances with Sean.

16

In which The Plan is
unceremoniously debunked

Having definitively decided to seduce Sean within the hour, I should have been a nervous wreck. But evidently Weird Day was working its own magic, because I wasn't the slightest bit nonplussed, even *without* a plan—I suppose you could say I was surprisingly plussed. I was lucky I didn't jump him right there in the canoe and send us both tumbling into the water. Somehow I kept it together.

It was mighty difficult to sit patiently and keep my hands in platonic positions while we zipped up Congress Avenue on the last ride of the day. The vibe of Austin nightlife buzzed in my veins, and Sean's words thrummed in my head. Just before he'd fired up the engine, he'd said, "Where to, your highness? I'm yours to command." The answer was easy: "My house."

By the time we glided up the driveway, I was a woman on a mission, poised to drag Sean into the house. The one thing getting through the fog of lust curling relentlessly through me was the knowledge that if I didn't get Sean locked down in the next twenty seconds, Leslie was going to be out on the lawn looking for a piece of him. And I was hardly in a sharing mood.

Taking his hand, I pulled him along behind me, unearthing my house key on the way to the door. I thought of my cell and the possibility of text messages full of advice but figured I was past that. As of right now it was all me. Fairy Jane was right about one thing—this would definitely be an adventure.

"Should I be nervous?" he teased.

I turned to look at him, his face in shadow, and let a slow smile creep across my lips. "Uh-uh." The key clicked, and I pushed the door open.

I kept a night-light in my kitchen for late-night forays in the fridge, but tonight it was being repurposed for a different sort of foraying. I didn't want to turn on the lights—tonight I wanted to be a daredevil in the dark. Sean had pulled off his helmet on the path from the driveway and now set it on the counter, watching while I did the same, heedless of helmet hair. I admit I was a little curious to see what Fairy Jane might have to say by way of the calendar, but it was too dark to see, and I wasn't about to ruin the moment by turning the light on to check.

"Have you come up with a plan yet?" he said, his curiosity clearly piqued. The element of surprise definitely had its advantages.

"Nope." I grinned up at him, realizing I'd finally found my feet with him, and that I was on the verge of something amazing.

I stepped forward, closing the space between us, making a conscious decision not to second-guess anything, to just enjoy every minute. I settled my palms on his shoulders and looked into his eyes.

"It's now or never," I whispered before curling my left hand around the back of his neck, spearing my fingers into his hair, and pulling his lips to mine.

It was impossible to tell why this kiss trumped all the ones that had come before. Maybe because it was riding the heels of a thrill ride of a day. Maybe because of the kilt, what might or might not lie beneath, and my plan to do some sleuthing. Maybe because I'd decided one Wednesday wasn't going to be enough, and The Plan was just going to have to get screwed. For whatever reason, this one was in a class by itself. Right up until it got tangled in a fine frenzy of mushrooming love and lust as I marveled at how we'd gotten to this moment—he'd picked me!

And today—tonight—it was my turn to return the favor.

Neither one of us was particularly chatty or inclined to tease, and no objections were raised—quite the opposite—so once we stumbled over to the couch and dispensed with tops and bottoms (the kilt stayed!), we were a very serious pair, striving to make up for lost time.

While Sean had most definitely been going commando, quite thankfully he'd had the foresight to pack a condom or two (crossing my fingers for two!) in the little leather pouch on top, which I'd since ascertained was called a sporran. I looked forward to a very educational evening.

"You wear a man out, luv. What with the hiking, the racing, the rowing, and now this? I hope you plan to feed me." Sean was lying with his head beneath the coffee table and me sprawled alongside him, the pair of us having slid to the floor at some point during the festivities.

"I've only been calling the shots for the last forty-five minutes, *luv*. I hardly think I'm to blame," I answered, nipping at his earlobe. "But I'm sure I can rustle up something. If nothing else, we could make cupcakes."

"Cupcakes?" Sean queried, reaching for his T-shirt while simultaneously tidying the couch. "Would those be chocolate?"

"Could be," I said, swallowed up for a moment inside my very own Weird shirt.

"You'll likely not want my amateurish hands meddling—I'll just keep myself busy."

"Your hands are hardly amateurish," I muttered, yanking my jeans up over my hips. I was working the snap when the rest of his words registered. My head jerked up as I realized that Sean had moved out of my peripheral vision. Curious, I shifted and watched him wander, examining the occasional knickknack that I'd displayed either for sentimental or aesthetic reasons, running his finger across the spines of my keeper bookshelves . . . only two feet from where Fairy Jane was hiding. I held myself still, trying to think, then lunged for the TV remote, the perfect distraction.

"The TV can keep you busy! You've got your pick of ninety-something channels!" I scrambled for the cheat card that helped me keep track of which channel was which and waved it in the air.

Sean's progress momentarily came to a halt as he stared over at me, amusement lurking under the surface. "No, thank you," he answered. "I'm quite content just browsing through the textbooks on lasers and semiconductors . . . and semiconductor lasers." He glanced in front of him, at the shelves to come, and his eyes lit up a bit. "Aha! A few books I've actually heard of—one I've even skimmed."

Instantly, goose bumps cropped up all over my body. While I might have just abandoned The Plan I'd been clinging to for the better part of my adult life and celebrated by having sex with the man who'd put me up to it, I definitely wasn't ready to discuss my resident fairy godmother. Baby steps . . .

I lunged forward, my jeans gaping, nearly tripped over the coffee table, and rather fortuitously, collided with Sean just as his hand brushed The Collected Works plus one.

He was momentarily taken aback, and I honestly couldn't blame him. I'm sure I looked like a psycho, eyes wide and haunted, pulse jumping at my throat.

"You're not a proponent of the praying mantis style of relationship, are you?" Sean asked, looking slightly concerned.

"Are you asking whether I plan to devour you now that I've had my way with you?" I found this oddly amusing.

"Pretty much," he confirmed, glancing at the respectable row of Austen novels and my hand dramatically plastered up against it.

"It's your lucky night," I told him, lifting my free hand to settle at my stomach, suddenly conscious that my underwear was still on display. I smiled widely, with teeth, and tried to rally while I zipped up. "I'm in the mood for a cupcake." I tried to relax. With my other arm tensed and locked in position over my big little secret.

"Don't tell me," he said, the corner of his mouth edging up. "You're one of those Jane-ites." At this point, I was thrilled he was amused and not uneasy. Keeping his eyes fastened on mine, and lifting a single eyebrow in challenge, he extended his arm to the shelf above and pulled down my Jane Austen action figure.

It had come complete with a miniature writing desk and quill and had been a gift from Ethan. While he'd intended it as something of a gag gift, I'd recognized it as a subtle reminder of good sense, sound decision making, and perfect romance. I'd bought *Dating with Jane Austen as Your Wing Woman* shortly after that and promptly classified Ethan as a Willoughby. It wasn't long before Ethan realized his blunder: Jane Austen was a formidable nemesis.

"Maybe a little bit, but it's not that," I admitted, rolling with a sudden flash of inspiration. "This just happens to be where I hide my diary—in plain sight, so to speak." Relinquishing my grip on The Collected Works, I snagged the little black leather journal and held it against my body, on display but out of reach. "Honestly, I'm a little embarrassed." That much was true; I'd said some weird things in this journal, and Fairy Jane had managed to out-weird me at every opportunity.

"Ah . . . a diary, huh?" He glanced down, running his eyes over the shabby little book with the vintage hardware, likely taking in my iron grip as well. Lifting his eyes, now sporting a wicked gleam, to mine again, he waggled his eyebrows and said, "Am I in there?"

"I will admit that you've made the occasional appearance." I sincerely hoped that this modest admission would help him forgive the earlier wild-woman behavior.

"I happen to know that women aren't always completely honest when it comes to their diaries," he said, carefully putting Jane back on her shelf.

I promptly abandoned all modesty. "Do tell."

"Younger sister, remember?" Clearly he wasn't the slightest bit embarrassed by this behavior.

"You should be ashamed! Girls keep their most private secrets in their diaries. They are *not* for prying eyes, particularly those belonging to nosy brothers or potential love interests," I said point-edly. "I am going to hide this somewhere else in the house. You are going to stay here and out of trouble until I get back. Got it?"

"Yes, ma'am."

I decided to forgive him the ma'am. His grin sent nervous shivers up my spine, and with shaky legs I turned away and quick-stepped out of the room. I detoured into the kitchen to retrieve the journal's lovely assistant, the Magical Key, and then locked myself in my room to stash the pair in a shoe box with some long-forgotten burgundy satin bridesmaid heels. Satisfied with my ingenious hiding place, I hurried back to the kitchen to whip up some cupcakes and frozen pizzas and act normal. The quote, I was to discover, read, " '. . . why did we wait for any thing? why not seize the pleasure at once? How often is happiness destroyed by preparation, foolish preparation!' *Emma*." On this one thing, Fairy Jane and I were in complete agreement.

A couple of hours later, heady with chocolate cupcakes and re-quited lust, Sean was persuaded to stay the night. Of course that meant his motorcycle was revving in my driveway at seven-thirty in the morning, right after he'd kissed me senseless, sans bra and makeup, in the kitchen.

And the revving, in turn, was why Leslie was pounding on the door fifteen seconds later. Quickly donning yesterday's hoodie, I swung the door wide.

"Why, Leslie," I drawled, "you know how I love the not-yet-decent morning pop-overs!"

Leslie, as usual, ignored me in favor of inquisition-style tactics.

"I assume I just heard the triumphant getaway of yesterday's bad influence." She was sporting the proud my-daughter-lost-her-virginity-on-Prom-Night look.

"Never assume, Leslie."

"Funny," she said. I couldn't help but find her reaction amusing, and my own smile settled in to get comfortable.

The stare-down was her next plan of attack, but two seconds after leveling me with a stubborn glare, she abandoned the tactic to play the pity card. "You would seriously deny me the chance to share in this proud moment?"

"Okay, fine. I may not have been cobblered exactly, but I definitely had a little 'Brown Betty' action going on, if you know what I mean." It was very hard to keep a straight face. Leslie, however, had no trouble at all.

"Fine," I conceded, just wanting to get this over with. "Sean spent the night. Heterosexual activities ensued. Good enough?"

Leslie's face slumped right along with her shoulders. "Do you seriously not know how to tell a good story, or are you just out of practice?"

"Could be either," I admitted, completely serious.

She uncrossed her arms, and her boobs slumped in delayed reaction to my subpar storytelling. "Try to work on it." Seeming to realize her reaction was a little off, she quickly rallied. "Brava, chickadee! You rode the bull!" I got a thumbs-up, and she got fodder for a gossipy breakfast. She was halfway down the steps before she called back, "Bring him over Friday night!"

How could I possibly resist?

Flicking the lock on the door, I made myself a cup of cocoa, fully intending to play up yesterday's imagined illness with a late start today. Seeing that it was now somewhat of a ritual, I couldn't help but check the chunky little calendar block. Turns out I'd gotten used to its conveniently updating itself. And reading, " 'How wonderful, how very wonderful the operations of time, and the changes of the human mind!' *Mansfield Park,*" on this sunny morning was a pleasure—I couldn't help but smile. Fairy Jane was back in my good graces, and I needed to rescue her from yesterday's impromptu hiding place. It seemed a little thank-you was in order. . . .

My room was full of fresh distractions, not the least of which was the tousled, tangled state of my bed. But my eye caught on the purple wadded Weird shirt flung over the nightstand.

I guess it was sort of official: I was weird—and happy.

Admittedly, I wouldn't be claiming weirdness right now if it weren't for Sean. If it weren't for Fairy Jane and her magical abode . . . If it weren't for the spilled chai latte and that wild mushroom with a mind of its own. I wouldn't be weird without any of those things, because without them, I hadn't been ready. But I was ready now—as ready as one could be for a life of weirdness.

Smoothing the wrinkles from the shirt, I laid it on the bed, conscious of the unexpected kink I'd put in my life. It was eight o' clock on a workday, and I wasn't at work. I'd never even bothered to check my messages from yesterday. Crazier still, when I did finally get to work, I planned to make things official with the job swap and avoid Brett if at all possible. Then tonight, it was back to Sixth Street for my second SXSW first. The music portion of the festival had kicked off, and crazy as it sounded, I was sort of "with the band." Wowza—weird.

Palming the journal, it occurred to me that Beck still hadn't seen the magical transformation. I'd work something out soon. After this week SXSW would be over, and things with Sean would start to calm down a little. I assumed. Right now though, I needed to hurry.

Okay. I admit it. You were right, and I was wrong since the very beginning, and I apologize. I just never imagined life included chatty journals and fairy godmothers. But now I know and will make every effort to keep an open mind in the future.

Likely it comes as no surprise to you, but Sean finally charmed his way in. Yesterday played out somewhat like a quest, and I slayed the dragon— also known as "The Plan." I admit I've had a mad crush on Sean since that very first moment with its unexpected mushroom surprise, but I'd been more than willing to ignore the feeling and let it burn itself slowly out. It took a whole day alone with him before it finally sank in—nothing is ever going to go back to normal. Welcome to Austin!

The ride to work felt different, as if the city was suddenly sparkling with possibility. My secret—not that it was a secret, more of a "nobody knows yet"—was crowding my chest, threatening to spill out in the form of strange squealing noises. More significantly, I wasn't stressing. The Plan was now crosshatched with motorcycle skids, and I still wasn't having even low-level second thoughts. First test would be a little chat with Mark Frasier.

I didn't even bother with a heads-up phone call, choosing to go with the pop-in instead. Mark was turned away from the door, reviewing something on his computer, and I spared a moment to take stock: no sudden squeamishness, no shortness of breath, no cringes or qualms—I was good. This was it. I raised my hand to knock and relaxed.

"Hey, Mark. You busy?"

He swiveled in his seat and then leaned forward, resting his elbows on the desk between us. "I didn't expect to hear from you till tomorrow." His eyes shifted sideways behind his glasses, and before I could answer, he asked, "Or are you here checking in on a customer return?"

I smiled, stepping farther into his office. "You were right the first time—I'm here about the job." Big deep breath. "If it's still available, I want it."

This earned me a wide grin. "Awesome. I'll call Human Resources and get things going. Does David know yet?" Mark looked vaguely guilty about stealing me away.

"He's my next stop." And I wasn't particularly enthused. If an e-mail wasn't considered a shabby way to end a relationship, it would be my communiqué of choice.

"Good luck." His smile was commiserating, mine was resigned. "Let me know if you run into any problems."

"Got it." One down, one to go.

I really had to work for that second one. Trying to sever ties with my boss was like trying to cancel a magazine subscription, but in person. He managed to glamorize my job so significantly that I began, for a fleeting moment, to have doubts. He inundated me with the pros while my brain buzzed with the cons. He offered incentives, alternatives, even a new computer, a regular Wile E. Coyote, grasping at thin air. Because in my head I'd already gone.

Finally it was done. We agreed on two weeks to wrap things up, and I slipped out of his office, planning to while away the day in transition tasks. But first I needed to call Gabe. There'd been a lone message from him amid the slew of work-related calls I'd ignored yesterday. He wasn't in his cubicle, so I went back to mine and texted him instead.

NJames: You called?

I'd tackled my e-mail—a whopping sixty-three new messages—by the time I got a response.

GVogler: yesterday

Evidently he was a little peeved. I tried again.

NJames: Are we still on for tonight?
GVogler: far as I know. i'm picking Beck up on campus
NJames: What time?
GVogler: around 8
NJames: I have the passes from Sean, so meet you there at 8:30?
GVogler: that works—so is yesterday a 'lost wednesday'?
NJames: Ask me tonight.

With any luck Beck could de-grump him before I had to deal with him. And if I was lucky, I could get to her first. Gabe might be my best friend, but I was balking at discussing yesterday's "queen toppling" with him. I dialed Beck's number, and she answered on the first ring, her greeting a sort of muffled hiss.
"Shhhh! What's up?"
My eyes narrowed in confusion. Was she shushing me?
"You go first," I insisted.
"I'm in class, scrunched down in my seat, hoping no one notices me—cell phones are taboo in here, but you're bound to be plenty more interesting than Differential Equations."
"Gee thanks," I muttered, remembering D.E. "I don't want to get you in trouble. Gabe says he's picking you up on campus around eight. Can you meet me at sevenish to chat?"

"Without Gabe, you mean? Sure. He's picking me up under the bridge on Dean Keeton. Why don't I meet you there, and we can swing up to the Law Library, and then you can drop me back under the bridge?"

"Sounds like a plan."

Then she just faded away.

"Drive," Beck demanded, slamming the car door at seven on the dot. I turned to look at her as a Capital Metro bus roared past on my side, swooping to the curb in front of me to pick up and drop off.

Her smile was mischievous. "Sorry. Just wanted to see how that felt."

I pulled into traffic and then glanced back at her. Her hair was wound into two messy magenta coils on top of her head, a modern take on Princess Leia's cinnamon buns.

"So . . . is Gabe proving nerdy enough for you?"

"More than," she confirmed with a nod and a playful smile. "And while I'm excited to see him tonight, I've gotta admit, I'm just as anxious for the chance—*finally*—to meet Sean. How'd it *go* yesterday? I tried not to call, just in case, but I've been absolutely quivering waiting to hear. I can't believe I had you on the phone earlier and didn't get the deets."

"You were in class," I reminded her as I slid into a parking spot on the street, somewhat in the vicinity of the Law Library.

"You know we're gonna have to whisper in there," she said. "And knowing them, they probably frown on squealing. Wanna go somewhere else?"

"We could. Or we could chat here, wait for campus police to show up before we put money in the meter."

"Perfect." She rooted around in her backpack. "I was going to try to smuggle them in but now I don't have to." She pulled out two giant chocolate chip cookies in paper sleeves and handed me mine. I could totally get used to these girl talks.

"Perfect," I agreed, wishing I had a Coke.

"So? Yesterday? Did you go with either of my suggestions?"

"No. But you get points for effort and consistency." I sank my teeth into the soft cookie and chewed appreciatively.

"Girl, I will take your cookie hostage," Beck warned.

"Okay, okay." I held my cookie out of Beck's reach and commenced with the telling.

It was a shame we didn't bother with the Law Library. The two of us getting kicked out would probably be the most excitement they'd seen in . . . possibly ever. Beck was loud and effusive and agog. I managed to finish off my cookie while she worked through her first wave of reaction.

"So 'The Plan' has been vanquished, and you're hitching your wagon to a rock star?" She licked a smear of chocolate off her thumb, her eyes smiling.

I laughed. "Only you would phrase it that way."

"And you're not even hyperventilating! Impressive, Ms. James! How do you account for this wild change? Could it be magic?" She leaned in to position her imaginary microphone for my response. Even in the dark, our conversation lit only by a streetlight two car lengths away, I could see the twinkle in her eye.

"It could be," I finally admitted with a smile.

"You've come a long way, baby," she said, crumpling the cookie bag.

"Been there, done that, got the T-shirt." We grinned at each other until I looked away to glance at the time. Five minutes to eight. "Yikes! We're cutting it close. Ever the eager beaver—at least as far as women go—Gabe's probably already waiting."

"Just drop me a block away—I'll hoof it."

I stuck with this plan and sailed past Gabe's Honda, letting Beck out on the next corner.

"See you in thirty." She waved before darting out into oncoming traffic.

"Drive," I told myself, heading toward Sixth Street and an evening of watching Sean at work.

17

life will surprise you—
surprise it back

After dashing off my entry that morning, I'd broken my own rules, stuffing the journal into my bag and slipping the key onto my key ring. Chalk it up to impatience. I was curious to see whether my little fortunes would change now that I'd essentially given in. I was hoping for more straightforward and less, well, cheeky.

Evidently it was not to be.

Parked downtown, with a few minutes to spare before eight-thirty, I decided to take a little peek. And judging by this morning's leftovers, it looked as if the gummed-up cliché was here to stay. And while I now realized that all those previous fortunes did eventually make sense, hindsight wasn't a whole lot of help right now.

It was impossible to tell whether "life will surprise you" referred to the little shockers of the past week or new ones still to come. Which meant I was stuck playing defense. I hadn't the vaguest clue how to go offensive with my life and "surprise it back"—although I would have dearly loved to one-up Fairy Jane. Talk about your double whammies! So rather than dwell on something that would, I had no doubt, come clear eventually, I decided to sneak another peek into the past.

Hunching down in the semidarkness of the front seat, I let the magic happen and then flipped through the pages until I'd found my place. Reading by the pearly glow of streetlamps, I lost myself in someone else's life. . . .

27 February, 1908

I've been called the family changeling as long as I can remember. And it isn't simply my chestnut locks and deep brown eyes that have garnered me the nickname. While my siblings are each elegant, accomplished, and engaging, I am clumsy, overly candid, and unfashionably academic. They worry I will end up a spinster, and honestly, I can't fault their assumptions. The men who interest me are much the same as I, and consequently, we are bound never to move past an awkward introduction, for neither of us have a fondness for small talk or dancing. Somehow, I need to sift through the glamorous trappings of New York society to find a kindred spirit. And once I've found him, decide precisely how to seduce him. It seems best to treat this as any experiment, recording both successes and failures on the path to getting practical results.

I couldn't help but admire her strategy. I hurriedly flipped the page, eager to read on.

1 March, 1908

I've come to wonder whether my nickname might be more literal than I could have possibly imagined. What other explanation can there be for a diary in which some words disappear and some are left, seemingly for the purpose of offering advice? Is it possible that fairies are at work here? Surely not—this is New York, not the wilds of Britain, and yet no other solution presents itself. . . . I've not yet felt it necessary to use the diary's key, but today, I think I must. I wonder if it will be any use. I need some time to consider this mystery—perhaps an afternoon in the library might shed some light on the matter. I look forward to discovering a plausible explanation. My only regret is that my proposed experiment must unavoidably be put on hold.

This could have been me a century ago! I glanced at the clock. I would have loved to keep reading, but several minutes had already passed, and I didn't want to miss any of the band's SXSW performance. I was going to have to come back to this later. Talk about your riveting reading—I was hooked!

I joined the parade on Sixth Street, thronging along with festival music-lovers in search of a great band and a couple of adult beverages. Maggie Mae's was already crowded, and I hollered for my rum and Coke, rather surprised to be heard over the din, paid my tab, and spent the next ten minutes worming my way through clusters of people, looking for any kind of breathing room.

When Gabe and Beck finally did show, holding hands and tipping their heads together, I lifted my free hand in a wave, feeling quite delighted with the world.

Gabe dropped Beck with me and beelined for the bar to order their drinks.

Beck leaned in and said loudly, "Gabe never suspected a thing." She tried for the smoldering gaze of a femme fatale but came off more Cyndi Lauper.

Then Gabe was back, toting a couple of Guinnesses, as a voice sliced through the dull roar, stretching out to reach every corner of the bar. "Ladies and gentlemen, Maggie Mae's is proud to host South by Southwest Showcase Artist Loch'd In!"

Standing on tiptoes, I'd only caught the barest glimpse of the band when a tall, sturdy cowboy of a man in a black Maggie Mae's T-shirt, Levi's, and boots showed up at my elbow, tipping his head down to speak into my ear.

"Nic James? There's a table reserved for you and your guests at the front."

Surprise flustered me, had my eyes darting toward Gabe and Beck, both of whom were staring curiously back.

"Hello again, Austin!" Sean's voice piped through the speaker system had me whipping my head around to see him, center stage, guitar in hand. "Welcome to South by Southwest!" The only hint that Sean even noticed the Texas-sized helping of cheers and applause was the hint of a smile as the drummer synced them up with the one-two-three clicking of sticks. Opening with a pounding-loud drum solo and a sizzling guitar riff, the music held me in its thrall. This wasn't the first time I'd heard the song—or even the fifth—but hearing it here, amid the noise and the lights, live and in person, with memories of last night zipping and twirling through my mind, I was lost. I didn't even realize the cowboy had lingered, waiting patiently for me to get it together.

"This way," he prompted, gesturing toward the stage. Beckoning Gabe and Beck with wide, "do you believe this?" eyes, I turned and let him lead the way.

As we wound our way closer to the stage, the music was building to an impossible crescendo, and my pulse was struggling to keep pace. When the words finally came, overlaying the music, I wasn't prepared, and nearly stumbled into someone's lap. As distracted as I was, it was lucky I didn't settle in.

The same voice that had serenaded me with backup from a mariachi trio was now singing his own wildly seductive lyrics at a professional venue. And people *loved* him. Seeing him like this, immersed in the music and the crowd, it was impossible to look away. In scuffed jeans and an emerald green polo, he looked like a celebrity. And then I realized—here he *was* a celebrity.

I was vaguely aware of Beck tugging on my sleeve, urging me to sit, so I sat, still staring, mesmerized by Sean's fingers skimming, impossibly quick, over the guitar strings. He made it seem effortless, and it was obvious that his focus was reserved for the crowds. He wasn't grudging with his dimples either.

An unfamiliar little curl of jealousy was quickly and thoughtfully tamped down. Evidently I needed to get used to the idea that when Sean was performing, he belonged to the crowd.

Certainly I never thought I'd find a man who'd reserve *all* his smiles for me, but maybe I thought they'd be given out more sparingly, or with less obvious sex appeal. I realized I was being unreasonable, feeling slightly dizzy and overwhelmed, like a little girl at a carnival watching the rides spin in the dark with a tummy full of funnel cake.

Deliberately I let my eyes fall closed and pretended, just for a minute, that I was the girl I'd been a week ago, with a life relatively free of complications. I could feel the bass vibrating into me as the guitar notes hung in the air and the last lyrics skimmed the surface of my consciousness. And then the song ended on a long lonely note, a promise hanging in the air, echoing in Sean's voice. My eyes fluttered open and came into focus, homing in on the Complication himself.

The band played a couple more songs, wowing the crowd and ratcheting up my qualm-o-meter, before breaking for a quick intermission. They'd demonstrated they could shift seamlessly from edgy rock to British band punk to haunting melody, and it was all brilliant. I had no doubts that this band—Sean's band—was going to make it big. The rest of the world was going to know their names. Sean's voice would be forever imprinted on the minds of many. He'd never belong only to me.

"Fill us in on the 'lost Wednesday.' " Gabe's voice broke through my subconscious as I pondered my dubious sharing skills.

"Um, okay," I agreed, blinking the room back into focus. "I'm now the proud owner of a Weird shirt." I smiled, oozing forced optimism. "Sean bought it for me, and I wore it yesterday. I'm official!"

Gabe cut his eyes around at me in disbelief. "Lucy! You've got some 'splaining to do!"

A laugh bubbled out of Beck as I answered. "What?"

"You've never worked up the gumption to buy your own Weird shirt, but suddenly you're letting some guy—a virtual stranger—do the deed?"

I glanced at Beck, whose lips remained sealed despite the unexpected euphemism.

"Yesterday tipped the scales."

"But you were already wearing it yesterday."

Damn. I'd hoped that little detail would slip by him.

"True." Stalling . . . stalling . . . "But my whole week has really been kinda out of the ordinary. I figured I'd earned it."

"Good enough," Beck pronounced cheerily, leaning in on her

elbows. "So Sean's the lead singer slash man on guitar, right?" Her eyes were dancing, her lower lip was tucked between her teeth, and she was glowing a radiant, otherworldly pink.

I nodded, returning her smile. "That's him." Then I darted in with a question of my own. Letting my eyes flick back and forth between them, I said, "Looks like you guys are getting along pretty good."

Gabe shot Beck a glance of irritable affection and answered first. "We are," he said, "but Beck wants me to keep my membership active on We Just Clicked and quiz her with the same questions I fire at potential matches. Naturally it's irrelevant that I have no interest in any of these potential matches."

Beck slid her index finger through the condensation rings on the table and countered with careful nonchalance. "I'm just curious to see whether he would have picked me out of a lineup," she clarified, faced with Gabe's and my blank stares. "And so far, I'd say it's going pretty well . . . ?" She made this into a question and lifted her eyebrow, waiting for Gabe to weigh in.

"It's hard to say since you won't 'lock in' your answer," Gabe said with a wry twist of his lips.

"I'd think that would impress you, Mr. EPIRB. I want to weigh my options, choose wisely. The question isn't quite as cut and dried as Olga seems to think."

Faced with my avidly curious stare, Gabe elaborated while Beck sat quietly, her lips pursed and waiting. No doubt for my condemnation of Olga.

"*Olivia's* question," Gabe informed me, "was, 'If you had to be an animal, which would you be?' "

Evidently unable to stand it any longer, Beck leaned in to interject, "She also asked, 'Which flavor of *ice cream* would you be?' An animal I get, but *ice cream?* What's the underlying question there— 'Would you choose to be whirled with nuts, fruits, or some other ill-conceived mix-in before being frozen and eventually consumed?' "

Grudging smile from Gabe, twitching lips from me. "She probably meant to ask my favorite flavor, not which one I'd be. And what's wrong with a dolphin?" Gabe was clearly smitten, not giving a flying fig about the questions so long as Beck kept answering them.

"I don't particularly care for that high-pitched squealing way they communicate. Imagine listening to that all day."

Gabe and I shared a look, neither of us really believing we were having this conversation in a Sixth Street establishment during a SXSW showcase intermission. But Beck's voice was ringing out through the din with you-better-believe-it attitude.

I couldn't help it, I had to ask, "What sort of creatures are on your short list?"

"The naked mole rat is currently a front-runner," she informed us. Faced with our no-doubt matching expressions of horrified curiosity, Beck added, "What? Hairless and buck teeth doesn't appeal to you? Fine. I'm joking. But you know, they live in colonies—one queen and bunches of little worker mole rats doing sexual favors. Doesn't sound too shabby."

"Picture yourself as the queen," Gabe insisted. "I dare you."

Beck smiled sweetly and started shaking her head, as if she could avoid the image locking on by simply staying in motion. "I'd rather picture you as a worker rat. Stick your teeth out," she insisted, grinning, reaching up to cup her hand under Gabe's chin to pull him in for a spontaneously happy kiss.

I tried to hold back my smile as I waited for Gabe to look my way. Once upon a time we made a pact outlawing PDAs, particularly in the company of each other. And while I might have broken it many times over in the course of the past week, I hadn't yet broken it in front of Gabe, so I was still one up.

But my smug smile fell quietly away as they were both instantly distracted by something behind and above my head. As I tipped my head up and around, I got a sudden, unexpected view of Sean's face before he swooped down to bestow an impressively thorough PDA of his own.

When I finally tipped my head back down, I was gasping, shaky and unsettled. Looking deliberately away from Gabe and Beck, I noticed there were any number of other pairs of eyes gazing at me with amused interest. Note to self: A PDA with a rock star is like polishing off a huge hot fudge brownie sundae—unbelievably decadent, sweet and satisfying, but capped off with a queasy, what-did-I-just-do sort of feeling. Not for the faint of heart.

"Sean MacInnes." The words went right over my head as his hand settled around the back of my neck, his fingers skimming through the little wisps of hair there. He reached his hand out first to Beck, then to Gabe. "Good to meet you. Glad you could come along with Nicola. We're set to do one more song tonight, and then shall we all have a drink? On me."

Gabe's "Sounds great," and Beck's "Definitely" were garbled in my head.

"Excellent." Sean's voice speared through my mental fog, and I turned again to look at him, realizing too late that I might be carelessly tumbling into a PDA ambush. "Back in a sec, luv," he said, offering only a wink this time. A wink that made every nerve ending stand up and salute.

Thank God the happy couple didn't try to chat, because I was ill equipped for small talk at the moment.

Back up on stage, Sean stepped up to the microphone. "This is a new song for us, recently written, hardly practiced, so I'll ask that you bear that in mind."

As his voice carried through the crowds, softly persuasive and achingly beautiful, it occurred to me that Sean was like a magnet working on my personal compass, throwing me off, sending me in directions I'd never intended to go, with no guide to follow. I could only assume that eventually there'd be a point at which I could go no farther. And there'd be no going back to the way things had been. It was that day that worried me.

After Thursday's journal overload, Friday morning was refreshingly Fairy Jane Free. I'd stayed up late last night, poring over the entries outlining the Changeling's experiments and discoveries—her thoughts on Jane Austen and the magic of the journal (inconclusive), and her scientific approach to finding a man (success!). Fascinating reading.

Personally, I wasn't yet ready to go another round with Fairy Jane, having not yet cracked the code on her last little directive. And beyond that, I didn't have anything to say, at least nothing I wanted to reveal. I wasn't too proud of the fact that I'd choked a little my first night out of the gate with Sean, the two of us as a couple. I'd been overwhelmed and hadn't handled things particularly well. But that was a thing of the past. Today I was once again swept up in the wowza factor of this relationship, and it was infectiously exhilarating.

Even running into Brett in the hallway didn't faze me. Admittedly I didn't spout off about Hooky Wednesday, the Weird shirt, the sex, or SXSW, but I almost wished I could. It all sounded so good in my head! We even made plans to go to lunch next week—as friends (at least on my end). I figured I'd just play things by ear. And in the event that those awkward silences had a flirty undercurrent, I'd decide which part of the fairy tale to tell him over our separate checks.

In honor of the changes in my life, I whipped up papaya-coconut cupcakes with mango pastry cream after work, and I must admit, they were very tasty. I felt very tropical parked in the purple papasan, beneath the odd assortment of novelty lights and that perfect ice cream scoop of moon. The Pendleton blanket I was curled beneath was sort of cramping my style, but you have to roll with the punches. That might as well be the motto of Friday night karaoke at Laura and Leslie's, and yet, I had to admit the calendar's latest quote had me a bit on edge. It read, " 'Surprizes are foolish things. The pleasure is not enhanced, and the inconvenience is often considerable.' *Emma*." I couldn't agree more: I'd never been big on surprises simply because you couldn't plan on surprises. I did my best to just sit back and relax. Sean had been thrilled to come along with me tonight, and the girls took to him from the get-go—he even managed to snag Leslie's approval.

"Tell me this," she demanded of Sean, "are your intentions with regard to Nicola honorable?" With raised eyebrows she warned, "Consider your answer carefully."

I missed his answer, but judging by the cacophony of laughter and Leslie's "that'll do, pig" attitude, it was spot-on. Hardly a surprise.

It seemed my fledging relationship was nearly perfect. And yet . . . I had this odd feeling that something was off.

Sean was in his element, effortlessly charming and at the same time strategically self-deprecating. Listening to him work the patio, one could almost imagine that he understood these women's frustration with men and that he empathized with their decision to switch teams. And then he'd offer up an encouraging wink, a boyish grin, or a playful lift of his brows, and it seemed—to me as a spectator—as if they froze a moment in frantic, ponderous thought, wondering if they'd made the right decision. It was like magic . . . or momentary hypnosis . . . just how far a dollop of charm could carry him.

It had definitely gone the distance with me. But as devil-may-care as he appeared, I got the impression that Sean hadn't abandoned that original "now or never" mind-set and its associated urgency. He'd seemed anxious to tell me something earlier, but Leslie had shanghaied him the moment we'd crossed the fence line. I hadn't had a moment alone with him since. With the whole weekend stretching empty ahead of us, he should have plenty of time. For lots of things.

It was during a pleasant little daydream that Leslie sidled up and perched herself onto the edge of my papasan. For anyone unfamiliar with papasan geometry, it's a circular chair with spherical depth—no edge and no perch. Leslie started sliding immediately. And speaking as the girl at the bottom, it was a slippery slope indeed.

"He's got a cute ass," she informed me, gesturing with her margarita glass. A bit of the rim salt tumbled down to join the cupcake crumbs on my blanket.

Glad to have settled on a topic we could both agree on, I turned eagerly in his direction. My gaze fell first on the profile of his face, etched with shadow and light against a twilight sky. He turned at that moment, as if sensing our eyes on him, and sent a curiously amused smile back in our direction, toasting us with a longneck beer.

Leslie leaned in farther until she was hovering over me, precariously balanced on her hipbone. Avalanche conditions.

I'd psyched myself up for the papasan extrication—one fluid motion, up and out—when Tawny Brown, a rare talent in the backyard karaoke set, stepped up to the microphone.

"Okay, ladies. I know you've been waiting. Our token male of the evening, Mr. Sean MacInnes," she swept her hand around him like he was a showcase on *The Price Is Right*, "is going to give us a little sample of what a man can do with *our* equipment."

Wild and wolfish whistling ensued, and Sean took up the gauntlet, accepting the microphone from Tawny. I took the opportunity to extricate myself from the papasan.

"I'm gonna go warm up by the grill," I told Leslie before scooting quickly away.

Selecting his song from the machine's playlist, Sean turned back to his audience, the quirk of his lips hinting at unrepentant cockiness. Not really wishing to have this performance interrupted by a chat on what sort of havoc animal fats could wreak on a person's system, I didn't quite make it all the way to the grill, instead choosing a spot midway between the Ls.

When the music started, I didn't recognize it, and Sean seemed to be reveling in his little mystery. His lips stayed quirked with the secret right up until, with a clear, bright voice, he launched into the jaunty, unfamiliar lyrics, singing of sailors and marines.

Now I was definitely baffled. But as Sean kept singing the lyrics he clearly had memorized, I kept thinking it was going to come to me. And then, just before the refrain, it did. *South Pacific*.

Leave it to Sean to come up with a song that playfully paired "dandy games" with "dames." My hand fluttered to my mouth as I let my eyes stray from Sean to gauge the gals' reactions. Mostly they seemed impressed. Whether with his voice or song choice, I couldn't say.

And as he finished the last, rapid-fire verse with a flourish, down on one knee with his hands spread wide, the lesbian karaoke crowd went wild. Sean was an undeniable success.

"Not too shabby, mister," Tawny praised with a good-natured

wink, once she'd taken back the microphone. "Now if you could just get our karaoke virgin up here . . ."

Sean's eyes beelined to mine, and Tawny's followed leisurely, confident in the failure of this casual challenge. It only took one lift of his brows and one single shake of my head for that idea to die a dismal death. Tawny was the first to accept it.

"Don't sweat it, sweetie," she told him. "It's an impossible dream. Girl ain't never gonna sing." And with a good-natured tsking of her lips aimed in my direction, Tawny set her sights elsewhere. "So who's up next? Seems Laura and Leslie have all the show tunes—who knew those girls were so *gay?*" I was off the hook, out of the spotlight, right where I wanted to be.

Free of the spotlight himself, Sean headed in my direction, his grin sliding over me as lovely as twilight.

"You a big fan of show tunes?" I couldn't help but inquire.

"Big enough. And I know a little something about playing to the crowd." Despite his wide grin, a touch of the defensive seeped into his voice.

"I've seen you in action," I answered, conscious of a dual interpretation.

Dimpling adorably, he leaned in and lowered his voice to a seductive whisper. "Suppose we continue our evening somewhere else?"

My reaction time impressed even Sean, and within seconds we were back in the darkness on my side of the fence, whispering and giggling, wondering how soon we'd be missed. But as I was fumbling with the keys, babbling about my impressive collection of take-out menus, Sean clarified his original suggestion.

"I thought we'd go out, hit a few pubs, hear a few bands."

I was still registering my misunderstanding when his words began tumbling out, over and around each other in helpless irritation. "I'd meant to tell you earlier—I'd hoped to get my flight pushed back, but I've exhausted all options, and I'm afraid I have to leave *tomorrow*."

Wiry branches of live oak shifted above me in the wind, and I was conscious of a rushing in my ears. "Wha-aa-t?" It was all I could manage. I was having trouble processing every bit of it: the leaving, the fact that he was springing it on me in the manner of a pesky obligation, and rather critically, the *tomorrow*.

"I'm flying back to Scotland tomorrow. My flight's been arranged for six months now at least, and despite—"

"Flying back to Scotland to . . . *visit?*" Surely this should have come up before now.

Sean looked slightly befuddled by this question. "I suppose you could say that, but—I thought you realized that I'm—the band— we're an actual Scottish pub band—*from* Scotland. We flew over for South by Southwest."

Scotland? . . . Home of the mysterious, fantastical Loch Ness Monster. And, it seemed, my own fantasy as well.

Images from our Technicolor, whirlwind week flashed in my mind, a study in confusion. Had I known this deep down? Had Fairy Jane had me so distracted that I'd missed the warning signs—or deliberately ignored them? Surely he didn't think he could just drop this bomb on me now—today—*the day before tomor-row!* "But . . . you seem to know Austin as well as a local."

"I've come for the festival several years running. And I Google." This had him quirking an apologetic smile, and I felt the tiniest little flicker of anger licking at my insides.

"What about your motorcycle?"

"I borrowed it from a mate—the one at the wedding, with the pregnant wife."

"And your Weird shirt?" I demanded.

He actually seemed puzzled by this question. His eyebrows drew together in confused concern, and he reached for my hand. "It's a souvenir, luv. When in Rome . . ."

I tugged my hand free as his words pelted against my heart and then fell like stones into the depths of my stomach. *Oh my God.*

Shades of Austen in Austin, with Fairy Jane playing the role of matchmaking Emma, Sean as the unpredictable Mr. Elton, and me as naïve and silly Miss Smith.

No, scratch that, Sean was the Henry Crawford I'd first imag-ined—worldly and charismatic, and I was a more gullible Fanny

Price who had fallen for him against my better judgment. Not exactly flattering to either of us.

I was so utterly frazzled that my Austen metaphors were getting all tangled up in each other!

I felt strangely betrayed. Not so much by Sean as by my journal. I'd played along, kept writing, kept reading, an odd take on that trust exercise where your partner stands behind you, and you fall backward, confident that this person will catch you before you thump ignominiously to the floor. Well, stupid, trusting me, I let go and fell hard. And now even the ground beneath me had disappeared, and I was plummeting. My relationship with Sean had already been stretching every one of my limits. To add a long-distance, pond-crossing element was simply beyond me.

"Nic." Sean's voice pulled me back and reminded me that the pity party would need to wait. Right now I needed to buck up and get through the good-byes, rip away the fairy tale like a Band-Aid, because there was absolutely no chance for a happily-ever-after now.

"Nic, it's only—"

Gulping in a lungful of cold, dark air, I let my eyes flicker closed for one courage-gathering second and ruthlessly interrupted him. "I need to just say this . . ." It was obvious he wanted to cut in, but I hurried on, not entirely sure how long I had before I began to fall apart.

"You make me feel like a girl at a carnival—like everything is just lying in wait. But eventually carnivals pack up and move on, and everyone goes back to life as usual. I think I have to do that too."

"Or you could become a carnie," he teased. I glared up at him. "Seriously, Nic, there's no one right way to do things. I thought I'd convinced you of that this week. It seems I'm not as persuasive as I imagined." His voice had sharpened and now had an edge.

In the week I'd known him, the only other time I'd seen his eyes darken dangerously was while sitting in the canoe when I'd hinted that our little liaison was iffy at best. And it occurred to me, fleetingly, how undeniably sexy he was, even fierce with anger. I stepped closer to kiss him once, urgently, on the cheek, marveling that two minutes ago my plans had been lazy and much less chaste.

The moon was shimmering now, more than before, and I knew it was only a matter of seconds before those tears started to fall. "I thought I could change enough to make things work," I told him, my voice rough with emotion, "but when I'm with you, I'm always playing catch-up, always wondering what's coming next. Today's little surprise just happens to be that you live in Scotland. Not sure how I missed that," I murmured with a forced laugh, fighting to keep my focus. "What I'm trying to say is that I need just a tad more structure . . ." In an effort to lighten the mood, I held up my hand, a half inch separating my index finger and thumb, and forced out a brittle smile. "I want the fairy tale and the happily-ever-after as much as the next girl, but it has to make *sense*."

He stared at me for too long. I was yearning to fill the silence, but I couldn't think what else there was to say. Dipping my head down, I watched the first two tears fall as his answer finally came.

"Fairy tales are magical, Nic—they don't ever make sense. I didn't plan for this—I flew in for South by Southwest and just happened to find you with a mushroom down your dress. You enchanted me. We've only had one week together, and I, for one, want more than that."

I tipped my head down and didn't answer, didn't know if I could answer. I wanted the same thing, as evidenced by my thoroughly debunked Life Plan, but where our relationship was a little rough before, now it was impossible.

There was a beat of silence as Sean waited for my response, but when it didn't come, he pressed on.

"You can't seriously imagine that a life plan orchestrated at age thirteen is going to go off without a hitch, Nic." I could hear the exasperation in his voice and couldn't help but get defensive.

"So what if I did—*do!*"

"Really? And what exactly did your thirteen-year-old brain have planned for you, romantically speaking?"

"Plenty!" I fired back.

"Uh-huh. Anything to compete with what we had this week?" He didn't wait for an answer. "Let me see if I have this right: It took you a week to decide that I might be worthy of the grand scheme of your life, and now that you've discovered I don't live in Austin, I'm voted off? I don't suppose this is reality TV, is it?" His smile, when it came, was tight.

My shoulders slumped, and suddenly my whole body felt heavy and listless. "It wasn't like that." But truly, it was, and I didn't know what to say.

"So change your plans—edit me in," he insisted, but I could already hear the defeat in his voice. "Come on, Nic. It's not that far off—"

"It is, Sean," I said, my jaw tight. "It's too far. I can't make that work."

"Have it your way, then. You're still selling yourself short, Nic, and I can't put it right because you're calling all the shots."

My head whipped back up in time to see him unpinning the clan pin from his collar. I couldn't help but remember the MacInnes motto: *By the grace of God and King.* Even the cheeky efforts of a fairy godmother hadn't been enough for the two of us.

"I'd ask that you remember how magical it was," he said, dropping the pin into my palm and curling my fingers protectively around it. "All of it, madcap and reckless. And it bloody well worked."

As I stared down at my fist, the cold metal tingling my palm and gradually radiating outward, Sean unearthed a second offering: the disposable camera, proof of the lost Wednesday that now seemed a figment of my imagination. "I'd thought we could talk about this, but I don't imagine that's possible just now. Just remember, luv, you're not the only one with a plan."

When the kiss came, hard and bittersweet, I wasn't expecting it. And before I'd even recovered my breath, he was gone.

18

In which the regret
sinks its teeth in.

After that I refused to speak to Fairy Jane and slid her tidily back onto the shelf with The Collected Works, nudging them close together and pinning them in with a makeshift bookend. The calendar, by association, was shunned in equal measure, and slid back into the darkness of the kitchen drawer. The banishment wasn't nearly as satisfying as I'd hoped. I would have liked to return to "life as usual," but the trouble was, I'd changed. I'd quit my job, I was starting fresh, and I owned a Weird shirt after eight years in this city. The Nic James Life Plan had been obliterated.

I had decided to spend my suddenly free Saturday moping in my shirt, but soon came up with a better idea. I'd develop the pictures from the disposable camera and then treat myself to a signature Keep Austin Weird cupcake from a bakery on North Mopac. I suppose it was sort of a statement: me in my Weird shirt, with my Weird cupcake, perusing pictures of the Weirdest day of my life. I was hoping for a little closure.

Intentional or not, the camera had been a diabolical touch, and every last picture proved a bittersweet reminder of a magical week and a perfectly charming, irresistibly sexy, never-ending surprise of a man. Sean couldn't have engineered a more wrenching parting gift if he'd made a concerted effort.

The cupcake helped—the fusion of mango, citrus, and cayenne was definitely a distraction, and the chocolate ganache provided enough of a sugar rush for me to want to give Fairy Jane forty lashes with a poison pen. I settled for a ballpoint.

While flipping pages in my quest for an empty one, my gaze fell on the most recent excerpt, a definite contender for the most confusing: *life is full of surprises—surprise it back*. The fragile reality of my current sucker-punched state—surprise!—just fueled my ire. And I wielded my pen like a weapon.

You're suddenly bearing a remarkable resemblance to the interfering, bitchy fairy godmother in Shrek. *Although, I'll admit, I can't imagine how the kerfuffle you made of my life fits into any kind of agenda. The man you've been hyping for the past week is gone—back across the pond (really a ginormous ocean) to Scotland. Color me surprised! My little adventure is over. What else could you possibly have in store??*

One solid benefit of a ballpoint: It barely smears when wet—the words just go a little wobbly. I'd never before had to dash away angry tears, but here I was, dealing with another first.

But before you answer that (or not), I should probably tell you flat-out that it's going to be damn near impossible for me to trust you now, seeing as you've proven yourself woefully untrustworthy. I've considered giving up on you entirely, but I just can't bring myself to do it. Lucky for you, I never figured out how to work my Ouija board. But just so you know, this time I'm on to you, and blind acceptance of your particular cheeky brand of advice is a thing of the past. You, Dear Journal, are on probation indefinitely. . . .

It felt very empowering to snap the journal closed and banish it once again to the bookshelf, pushing it far, far back this time until it was completely hidden from view. Best I'd felt all day, not counting the time I'd shared with a cupcake. So I suppose it was a tie.

The rest of the weekend was consumed with a *Lord of the Rings* marathon, my objective no more well considered than to crowd my mind with Aragorn and leave no empty spots for Sean. Success eluded me, possibly because I could smell Sean on the pillows—and because I could imagine him speaking elvish sweet nothings to a pointy-eared version of myself. It was late into day two when I finally dredged my groggy, tear-stained self from the sofa to trudge off to bed.

As I crowded the popcorn bowl onto the counter, along with a trio of cups from my hours in front of the television, my eyes strayed guiltily to the bookcase. Damn it if I didn't want to look. I couldn't help it—I wanted to see her response to my little on-paper outburst. So stalking across the living room, I yanked the charming little book with its little brass doorknob and key plate and all its secrets and attitude out of hiding, and I looked.

life surprised you, and You . . .

I could actually feel my body clench, ready for a fight. This little snippet was more in-my-face than any of the others—it was taunting me. What did *I* do? Well, let's see. Life *surprised* me—you could say knocked me on my ass—and I did what I had to do. I did what made sense—the only thing I could do. What could I say, nobody would be making a cobbler out of me anytime soon. Luckily I preferred cupcakes.

"What the hell was I supposed to do?"

Yep. I'd reached the point where I was actually *talking* to the beastly little book. It occurred to me that I might not be dealing with a fairy godmother at all. Perhaps I'd been ambushed by an actual fairy—the bitchy sort, the kind inclined to play tricks on unsuspecting humans. Sounded about right.

Well, either, or. I was ready for a throwdown. Before I could change my mind, I snatched up the key and thrust it into the lock, watching the journal's transformation with a cynical eye. As the book's binding stretched and new pages filled the space, I waited, wondering if Fairy Jane would come out of hiding, urgently hoping she would, and at the same time desperately hoping I could deal with it. When the journal once again lapsed inanimate, I waited patiently for one solid minute. Nothing happened. I suppose I never really expected it to. In fact, now that I considered it, it was kind of a huge relief that it hadn't. I suppose I'd been imagining a sort of "genie in the lamp" confrontation. Thank God I'd been spared. Points to Fairy Jane for coddling the nervous skeptic.

Left with only one sure-fire way to communicate, I flipped to the now-unabridged version of my latest entry, skipped down a few lines, and wrote:

You tell me—what <u>should</u> I have done? Dropped everything and followed him? Offered to make a go of a long-distance relationship that's doomed to failure? Begged him to stay? None of those options seemed quite right at the time. And I don't regret my decision—like it or not, it was mine to make!

As my chest swelled with a cleansing intake of breath, a fraction of my anger and resentment fell away. But as I watched my words slowly fade from the page beneath my shocked gaze, my breath caught, almost choking me. One by one, it was as if they were being sucked back into the journal, perhaps never to return. Sitting in the dark, hopped up on Tolkien and witness to some arcane magic, my life suddenly felt terrifyingly Gothic.

Line one had disappeared completely. Four more words and line two was gone as well, with line three slipping away fast. I couldn't help but wonder if she planned to erase all traces of my lippy reply. But suddenly her intention was clear, because two words stayed even after the final lines were obliterated. Two words I'd hastily scribbled just two minutes ago shimmered in front of my eyes all alone. Blinking them away wasn't an option, because I definitely tried—they were there to stay.

regret it

Shit! I slammed the book closed, yanked out the key, and watched wide-eyed as the journal shrank to normal size. *Shit, shit, shit!* Was this a warning, a dire prediction of bad things to come? *Oh my God!* I didn't want to be holding the journal right now, but at the same time, I wasn't comfortable with it palling around with The Collected Works either. Charging down the hall to my bedroom, I tossed both journal and key in with the maroon bridesmaid heels and then buried the shoe box in the laundry bin and slid the closet doors shut for good measure. I wanted the perfidious little book out of my sight—I wanted to forget every last bit of magic that had gotten me into this heartbreaking mess. But I couldn't. And so I sat cross-legged on the bed, my mind whirling with crazy, mixed-up thoughts of fairies, magic, regrets, and Sean.

I woke up dressed, slumped over on the pillow, with the lights still on. Needless to say, I wasn't ready to face work, but I figured it was the best medicine—if anything could wrench my thoughts away from last night's freak show and this weekend's pity party, it was a day of logical thinking and problem solving.

By eleven I was inclined to think distraction was a pipe dream, and I decided to pull out all the stops. I dropped what I was doing, ducked out of my cubicle, and navigated the maze toward Brett's. Not too long ago, I'd thought he was the one. Maybe, with time, he still could be. It was worth giving it a shot. But as I approached his cube, my steps started to slow as my heart started to pound with urgent warning. I could hear his voice, chatting with someone invisible, and suddenly I was in a panic. I didn't want that voice, that face, sitting across from me at lunch, droning on about the specials and reminding me that I hadn't chosen him. The fact was, I'd chosen someone else and then let him go. I felt like Lizzy Bennet, standing in the rain, without the happily-ever-after.

Pivoting quickly, I ran on tiptoes back down the corridor, praying Brett wouldn't tip his head out, wouldn't see me, wouldn't ever know I'd come by. Once in the clear, I detoured over to Gabe's cube, texting him on the way.

NJames: You up for lunch?

By the time his reply came in:

GVogler: sure. what time?

I was already there, so I answered.
"How about now?"
While this sort of surprise drop-in would have jolted my heart rate sufficiently to require resuscitation, Gabe took it in stride, turning in his chair, flicking his gaze to the phone in my hand, and finally shrugging.
"Works for me."
Lunch with Gabe was comfortingly familiar, despite the fact that we'd mostly been dealing in teasing jabs and text messages ever since Sean and Beck had bulldozed themselves into our lives. One of us had gotten scooped up, one of us had gotten flattened— I hadn't been the lucky one, and I didn't want to talk about it.
"How is Beck faring with the Q and A?" I probed once we'd ordered.
"Is that all we're ever going to talk about?" he countered, one eyebrow raised, swirling his iced tea with a straw.
"Right now it's the most interesting thing about you," I told him honestly. Surely he realized that Beck was a colorful force of nature.
"True," he conceded. "Okay, fine. The most recent question, from potential match Jana, was 'What two celebrities, living or dead, would you invite to dinner and what would you serve?' "
"Match-up's answer?"
"Martha Stewart and Katie Couric. Pumpkin-sage ravioli." Gabe's opinion on this inspired a curled lip and a couple of quirked eyebrows.
I made a face. "And Beck?"
"Jane Austen and Colin Firth, buffalo wings, sweet potato fries, and coleslaw. And key lime pie." Gabe shook his head slightly,

whether in confusion or disbelief, or a combination of both, I couldn't tell. But I could totally relate: It was downright mind-boggling how Ms. Austen was suddenly popping up everywhere. I wondered if her recent run-in with Fairy Jane had anything to do with Beck's top picks.

"No contest. So things are going good, huh?"

With a rueful smile, he confided, "We've sort of decided to keep things 'friendly' until she graduates. And then we'll see where it goes."

"How friendly?"

"That's a little personal, don't you think?" He was giving me the eye, implying, I guessed, that he too could get personal.

"You're right. Sorry." I'd rather back down than deal with a possible trouncing later. "Whose idea was it to be 'just friendly' for another year plus?"

"Mutual. But I was just being chivalrous."

"That's admirable, Gabe. But if you step back, someone else is bound to step forward."

His eyes held mine for a long moment before he came back with, "Is this the voice of experience talking?"

Refusing to meet his eyes, I answered quickly, "You could say I have some recent experience in stepping away." Suddenly parched, I reached for my lemon water and gulped.

Gabe's eyes speared me. I couldn't tell if he was still playing the chivalry card or if he was busy deciding how best to broach the subject of Sean. I broke under the pressure.

"Sean and I are done. Turns out, he's from *Scotland*." I sounded bitchy without intending to.

Faced with Gabe's puzzled stare, I widened my eyes and nodded.

"Seriously? You didn't know that?" he said. "They're a Scottish band, Nic—they're an import."

"*Yeah!* I know that *now*." The bitchy just kept on coming. "I assumed that they were *originally* from Scotland and were inexorably drawn to the sunny weather and quirky melting pot lifestyle of this, the Live Music Capital of the World!" After this little tirade I promptly shut up, pressed my lips together, and fought against the onslaught of tears.

"Aw, Nic. It never occurred to me that you didn't know. Then again, maybe I'm off my game—I'm still reeling from the news that The Plan is waving the white flag. I'm planning a victory parade. With baton twirlers and marching bands."

I could see the tears edging my lashes, but Gabe managed to lure a smile out of me without one falling.

"I thought about resurrecting it, but it didn't take."

"Thank God." The sentiment came punctuated with a sympathetic smile.

Our food showed up rather conveniently at that moment, and we each concentrated on keeping our mouths full for a very long time.

I'd expected to feel a sense of relief to have my life back on my own terms, but ironically, I was constantly cranky and on edge, overwhelmed by the feeling that everything was just "off."

I'd set the calendar back on the counter on Wednesday morning, the front page curiously current with the day's date. I can only assume that the displayed quote, " 'Friendship is certainly the finest balm for the pangs of disappointed love.' *Northanger Abbey*," was largely what compelled me to agree to go to dinner with Laura and Leslie. Only a bit of quick thinking saved me from untold awkwardness—I invited Beck to tag along. As far as I knew, the Ls were unaware of Sean's sudden disappearance, but it was bound to come out over dinner, and I was relieved to have a little backup. Beck agreed to swing by early to get the whole story.

Hunkering down at the kitchen table, we dove right in.

"Wow. So he just left? And you just let him?" Beck was obviously as crushed as I by the fairy tale gone awry.

"We hit a snag," I reminded her. "It was all I could handle when he was a phone call away. A continent is out of my league."

Leaning toward me, eyes wide, she whispered, "What does Fairy Jane have to say?"

"Plenty. And none of it helpful."

Her eyes grew impossibly wider, but glancing at the clock, real-izing we were already running late, I pulled the journal and the key out of hiding and hustled her out the door as she queried, "Why do you still own maroon bridesmaid pumps?"

In the pale glow of twilight, under the spotlight of streetlamps, Beck turned the key. And judging from the sparkle in her eyes, she was thoroughly enchanted. Making *one* of us. I indulged her as long as I dared, but eventually we had to step away from the magic and into the restaurant. And mum was most definitely the word.

Leslie took Beck's appearance in stride, promptly putting out feelers as to the nature of our relationship. I could tell she was op-timistic that our "friendship" would mutate into something more to her liking eventually.

Shortly after dispatching that topic, Leslie's trademark "touch of crass" invaded the dimly lit elegance of our little corner of China-town, hitting on the subject I'd most been dreading. "I haven't heard the roar of a motorcycle on a booty call recently. Trouble in paradise?" Beck's eyes flitted toward me in silent shock, and I smiled blandly, hoping to convey that as chats with Leslie went this was relatively tame.

"Paradise lost," I confirmed matter-of-factly. "Well, technically I suppose not *lost,* just out of range."

Laura gaped at me, and Beck's eyes were sad. Rather than look at them, I let my eyes blur, watching the candlelight flicker and wink. For a single exquisite moment, even Leslie was stunned speechless.

She quickly recovered.

"Is it possible you've decided to transfer your name to another team's roster?" Across the table, Leslie's eyes were twinkling with mischief.

"For God's sake, Les! Give the lesbian press-gang tactics a rest, will you?" Laura turned back to me oozing supportiveness, clearly waiting for the story.

"That *can't* be your actual team name," I insisted, tongue firmly in cheek. No reaction.

The arrangement of Leslie's lips put me in mind of an old-fashioned snap-closure coin purse. Her eyes were snapping too. I optimistically assumed it was with amusement. And judging by her eventual response, she wasn't holding any sort of grudge.

"Which one of you got squeamish?"

"Neither," I snapped before collecting myself. "We just weren't . . . geographically compatible."

"In the bedroom?" This, naturally, came from Leslie.

"Will you get your head out of your vagina for *one* second, Leslie, and let Nic tell the story?" It was not until the words were ringing in the air around us that it dawned on Laura that this might have come out a touch too loud. Our little group was suddenly garnering a *lot* of attention from surrounding tables, and Beck and I could barely hold back the bubbles of laughter. Meanwhile Leslie was highly amused at Laura's expense.

"And the hits just keep on comin'." Leslie laughed, not the slightest bit put out that she happened to be the evening's punching bag. "Bring 'em on!" She lifted her glass of Merlot and toasted us all. Swallowing down a gulp, she trained her eyes on me, waiting.

"He went back to Scotland," Beck inserted, punctuating her statement with a sip of water.

All eyes swiveled toward me. Whether they were looking for confirmation, a reaction, or a breakdown, I couldn't say, but I kept my expression carefully neutral.

"Well, that sucks," Laura grumped.

"You know you could go cavewoman on his ass. Haul him right back here . . ." Leslie had dropped her voice and was rearranging her silverware.

"Tempting as that sounds, I don't think I'm that girl."

We were all quiet for a moment before Leslie raised her glass. "On to the next one, then! May he be fully compatible—with no bugs. Little computer humor for you."

I clinked my glass against theirs but felt oddly disloyal. Sean was still too fresh in my mind. But luckily, he was no longer a topic of conversation. Chatter turned to weekend plans—Beck and

Gabe were going on a roadtrip in search of finger-lickin'-good Hill Country barbeque, and Laura and Leslie were attending their costume party as Austin Powers and Dr. Evil. I was doing nothing of note.

Dinner proceeded without incident, and for me, without meat. With Laura on my left, pressuring me to eschew (i.e., not chew) beef, chicken, pork, and shrimp in favor of tofu, I struck a compromise and ordered the spicy green beans. It wasn't until the waiter brought the little silver tray of fortune cookies that the trouble started.

Desperately wanting something other than a green bean, I reached for the first cookie.

I dispensed with the crinkly wrapper and cracked open the smooth, crispy cookie, separating the halves, freeing the fortune. I tugged it out, suddenly craving a random, ambiguous bit of wisdom completely unrelated to Fairy Jane's little orchestrated fairy tale. No such luck. She'd had her fingers in the cookie jar too.

An optimist sees the opportunity in every difficulty.

My thoughts flashed with heart-wrenching images of Sean in the moments before I let him go.

Without thinking, without even considering, I dropped my cookie and its shitty fortune onto the green beans and reached for a second cookie. Wrenching that one open even faster, a woman on a mission, my eyes scanned the string of red words.

The heart is wiser than the intellect.

Fairy Jane had struck again.

"Shit!" I tossed that one down too and grabbed a third, scrabbling with the cellophane wrapper.

"Nic?" Beck sounded concerned, but right now, I couldn't be bothered.

As I was cracking open my third cookie, I noticed Leslie's arm snaking past the soy sauce and snaring the last one on the tray, her wrist skimming dangerously over the candle flame. I noticed, but didn't particularly care. Right this second, it was all about the fortune I had in my hand.

Of all forms of caution, caution in love is the most fatal.

Oooh! She was just toying with me now!

I let both fortune and cookie fall from my fingers and eyed Leslie and that last cookie, suddenly obsessed with finding one fortune that didn't make my stomach roll with nausea. One optimistic fortune that didn't make me cringe with regret. One whimsical, unrelated fortune that could keep me from spewing curses on the interfering, intangible head of my resident fairy godmother!

They couldn't all be like this. There had to be at least one cookie on this table that was meant for me—one cookie to confirm that I hadn't made a truly terrible mistake. There simply had to be.

"Give me the cookie, Leslie."

I knew I wasn't being polite, or even sane, for that matter. But I'd put up with a lot from Leslie, and dammit, it was my turn.

"Give me a reason," she said with a maniacal smile, clutching the cookie like it was a grenade, and she was about to lose it. Her mind, I mean.

I took a deep breath and then another. In this semirelaxed state of pseudo calm, I figured it couldn't hurt to come clean. "I just want to read the fortune."

"What's wrong with all the other ones?" she asked, gesturing to the cookie carcasses strewn across my plate.

"They're not mine," I told her, feeling like an idiot but unwilling to back down. The woman was holding my fortune hostage, and she was pissing me off.

Laura's eyes were flicking between my face and the discarded little fortunes, and I could tell she was itching to ask why not. Beck was agog and very likely wondering if Fairy Jane had gotten to the cookies before I did.

"Why is that?" The epitome of polite, Leslie was either trying to talk me down off my personal ledge or else she was just desperate for a cookie. I'd say it was fifty-fifty.

"They just aren't," I said. "Just give me the cookie. I'll open it and hand you back the pieces."

"Why don't I open the cookie and hand you the fortune?" Rarely one for a compromise, Leslie was clearly digging deep.

"Because it doesn't work like that. You can't just hand over a fortune—they're not transferable." It occurred to me that I was digging myself a hole.

Leslie stared pointedly at the crumbled pile in front of me.

"Well, then what are you going to do with those?"

Dropping my gaze from its lock with hers, I eyed the votive candle positioned between us, in the center of the table. I'd never been the sort of person who burned things, and even in my current wacko mind-set, I was pretty sure I didn't want to be that person, but desperate times . . .

Luckily, Leslie offered to make a deal.

"Tell you what," she said, holding the still-wrapped cookie between thumb and forefinger, positioning it temptingly at eye level. "I'll trade you the fortune in this cookie for the other three." Pointing to the mess on my plate, she added, "I get to keep the cookie." Her gaze shifted to mine. "Deal?"

I spared a moment to glance around the table, cringing inwardly, before eventually turning back to my plate. The reject fortunes were arrayed on top, barely stained with spicy sauce.

"Fine," I agreed, gathering the slips. I extended both hands, being careful of the candle. The fortunes were in my left hand, closed inside my fist, and my right hand was open, waiting for Leslie to drop the cookie into my palm.

She let her hands hover over mine, her fingers primed to grab the fortunes at precisely the same moment she relinquished the cookie. The exchange went without a hitch, the cookie dropping cleanly into my palm and the fortunes quickly, greedily gathered into hers.

I felt calmer the instant I had the cookie in my hot little hand. But still riding a desperate streak, I figured it couldn't hurt to harness the power of positive thinking. Closing my eyes, I inhaled a deep, cleansing breath and imagined the fortune I'd like to see:

Congratulations, your instincts are dead-on.

Admittedly, that would have been the ideal fortune in this situation, but having selfishly seized and strip-searched every last cookie on the table, I was finally getting the fact that these were just random fortunes. It was sheer coincidence that we'd ended up with these particular four—it meant nothing. Except that Fairy Jane had turned me into a superstitious wacko.

And yet . . . at this very moment, wacko or not, it meant *everything*.

With considerably more intense concentration than a cellophane-wrapped cookie should merit, I ripped into it, while at the edges of my peripheral vision, Laura, Beck, and Leslie perused my rejects. But as I cracked open that last cookie, all eyes were on me, waiting to see how I might react. With my pulse pounding insistently in my ears, I pulled the fortune from its cookie confines and smoothed it open between my thumbs and forefingers.

My eyes scanned the words, tumbling them out of order, and leaving me with a nonsensical jumble. It was possible too that my synapses were sluggish and out of sorts and were refusing translation. Blinking rapidly, I tried again.

Love is the triumph of imagination over intelligence.
H. L. Menken

Everything fell away but that misshapen parallelogram of paper—the fourth in a series—that read like a message from above . . . or beyond. Was it *possible* I was reading too much into these trite little sayings? That I was letting my obsession with Sean and his abrupt departure, not to mention Fairy Jane's involvement, twist words and meanings in my mind? Was there a chance I was seeing hidden meaning where there was none? Or had Fairy Jane's magic wand truly extended into innocent little cookies?

I would have killed for the ever-popular, always ridiculous *You love Chinese food* fortune right about now.

I could feel the regret starting to close in, its clammy hold grasping at everything. It came over me with the stunning power of a tidal wave, and its undertow was brutal. I regretted ever trusting in a magical journal, letting my guard down with Sean and then yanking it back up at the worst possible moment. And I regretted tearing into all four fortune cookies and the fact that I was now going to be subjected to a sympathetic but rousing pep talk when all I wanted was to slink away on my own, curl into a ball, and decide what to do.

Because clearly, I had to do something.

"It's only a fortune, Nic." Laura's voice was quiet, soothing.

"Well, four," Leslie clarified. "Pretty big coincidence, if you ask me." Judging by the quirk of her lips, Leslie was both impressed and befuddled by the whole situation.

Wrinkling her nose a little in consideration, Beck suggested, "Maybe today holds some sort of astrological significance for you."

"Like sexy planet rising over shy and quiet little moon?" Leslie cackled at her own joke, earning herself a collection of dirty looks from the rest of us. "What? I think writing horoscopes could be a blast."

"I've known him less than a week." The words came tumbling out, and I was too overwhelmed to stop them. "I wasn't looking for anyone and certainly not him, but he charmed his way in. He made me imagine how it could all, just possibly, work out, and I just followed trustingly along." My shoulders slumped in remembered defeat. "But then it became an international incident. If I were to go for it now, I'd have to contend with airlines, passports, customs, time zones, exorbitant cell phone charges, driving on the wrong side of the road, incessant drizzle . . ."

"Pick me up a couple Toblerones and a bottle of Scotch whisky at duty-free." I shifted my gaze to Leslie, marginally derailed. "When you get it all worked out," she clarified.

"I like to stop at the duty-free shop." The little *Seinfeld* ditty was Beck's contribution to the muddle.

I decided to put a stop to it just as Laura chimed in. "Okay, enough!" A little karate-chop motion, and the table fell silent. "I never said I was going to Scotland. I was expounding on the fateful twists my life has taken in the last week, pondering what to do, and all you three can contribute is commentary on duty-free!"

"It's only a matter of time, sweetie. I'm just trying to get my order in early," Leslie said, sitting back to sip her wine.

"What makes you so sure—and smug?" I demanded.

"You're in love with him, and you let him go. Now you've got four fortune cookies busting your ass, and you're waffling." Damn, was she smug. "Sean is your sexy coincidence, Nic. You know Lizzy would agree with me." Raising her eyebrows in that "you know I'm right" way she had, Leslie waited as I mulled this over.

"Lizzy who?" Beck had switched from pity-partygoer to avid curiosity seeker in the space of a second.

"Elizabeth Bennet," I clarified, grudgingly admitting to myself that for once, Leslie was spot-on: Sean was my sexy coincidence. *He* was my Mr. Darcy. Fairy Jane had been hyping him all along.

Beck pondered this a moment and then said, "I think this would blow Lizzy's mind." She leaned in, nudging her plate with her hands, and added, "You know, you're like a character from one of Austen's novels now."

"No, I'm not." I shook my head, bobbleheading again.

"Oh yes, you are, and it's your turn for a happily-ever-after and a Darcy of your very own. You have to go!" Beck insisted.

"And stop at duty-free," Leslie reminded me.

"Who would have imagined you'd end up with a Brit?" Laura added.

"But what about all that other stuff?" I asked desperately.

"Trivial in the face of true love," Leslie answered. "Didn't *The Princess Bride* teach you anything? Sheesh."

Is this true love? I'm not sure. But there's only one way to find out.

"But what if he doesn't want me back?"

"Seduce him." It was Leslie who answered, but the other two nodded in sage agreement.

"But what if I start to resent him and—"

"Don't do that," Laura interjected in a voice she might use to talk to a three-year-old.

"But what if I'm not ready?" This was really the crux of it all.

"I have an idea," announced Leslie, a huge grin settling over her face as her eyes twinkled with mischief. All eyes swiveled in her direction, braced against the very worst. "Do a test run—try something you wouldn't have before Sean but that isn't too terribly out of range for you now, in your . . . chrysalis of Weird." It was evident she felt as awkward saying that last bit as we did hearing it.

As an idea, it wasn't half-bad. As an idea from Leslie, it was outstanding: nary a crude, unmentionable, or objectionable aspect in sight. Within seconds suggestions were flying around the table: a tattoo. A piercing. Body shots. Cliff-diving. Hippie Hollow. It was at that point that I felt compelled to intercede.

"I'm shooting for a mini-adventure, Leslie. I think a visit to the city's token nude beach is more than I care to take on right now. And I'm afraid that's all the time we have," I announced in the mellow slide of my game-show-hostess voice. Not counting my little bribe to foot the bill for dessert at Amy's Ice Cream, that was all it took to turn the conversation.

I had much to consider.

19

In which Cinderella
storms the castle

Believe it or not, I'd settled on getting my navel pierced. Right up until I'd Googled it. Turns out the healing process runs from four months to a year! Considering the possibility of infections and a selection of less-than-desirable diseases, the adventure du jour promptly fizzled flat. With no particular fondness for any of the other outlandish suggestions, I skittishly considered the option of going for the whole enchilada, chips all in. Within seconds I was typing "Loched In" back into the search window.

I'd memorized the band's URL, but with all this talk of Scotland, I was in the mood to see that photograph I'd stumbled over days ago—the ethereal castle poised on the edge of silent lochs, hovering serenely between the depths of sky above and water below. Lingering over it again had my thoughts turning to fairy magic, making me wonder whether it was foolish to fight it. And even downright dangerous to bury it in the laundry bin.

The spell was soon broken, though, and shaking free of those wispy thoughts, I typed in the band's URL, prepared this time for the musical onslaught. As the site cycled through snatches of various songs, I pored over every detail, every picture, every word, rather startled with myself for not having indulged in this little vicarious thrill while Sean was still on my home turf. Then again, he'd kept me pretty busy.

I tried not to let my mind linger overly long on certain, particularly fond memories, but it was a definite tussle to stay on track. Navigating back to the band's bio page, I reread Sean's blurb. He hailed from the picturesque village of Dornie and began singing in the local pub as just a lad; he played guitar, piano, and if sweet-talked, the bagpipes as well. He was also a firm believer in the famed monster of Loch Ness and hoped the band's music shared a little of the magic of Scotland with the rest of the world.

Suddenly I wasn't just lusting over the man but the country as well.

What if I went?

Out loud (and straight from Leslie's mouth) the idea seemed absurd. But I wasn't the same girl anymore—I'd outgrown a lot of things, I'd changed. And with the haunting music of Loch'd In niggling at my subconscious, a little international adventure seemed like an exhilarating possibility.

Pulling up Google Maps, I typed in Dornie, Scotland, and searched around a bit, zooming in and out, checking for airports, calculating distances. The village was on the edge of three lochs: Loch Alsh, Loch Duich, and Loch Long.

Something was skirting the edges of my memory. I pulled up the castle again and read the artist's description. Eilean Donan Castle sat at the join of three lochs—the very same three! My fingers skimmed over the keys as I Googled the castle, and as I read, they begin to shake ever so slightly. That glorious, steeped-in-history, edged-in-mystery "Loched In" castle was just outside the village of Dornie, home of the band "Loch'd In." I couldn't decide whether it was coincidence or fate. Or possibly even magic.

My mind started zinging with what-ifs.

I'd visited Scotland once, about two years ago, for work, and it had been wet, green, and chock full of rowdy, rosy-cheeked, laugh-a-minute, deliciously accented people. I'd lived in a hotel for seven days, sick for six of them, ordering room service and longing for ice cubes. On that last day, I'd trudged out, taken the train to Edinburgh, and indulged in a gorgeous adventure via window seat. As lilting conversation buzzed around me and the hedgerows whizzed past, my thoughts had run to the filmed-on-location BBC adaptations of Miss Austen's masterpieces. Staring out into the drizzly gray, I'd daydreamt of country dances, frilly bonnets, and curly haired gentlemen.

Those remembered mental images had me newly wondering whether Fairy Jane's competency was sufficient to direct my own whirlwind romance nearly two hundred years beyond her expertise. In her defense, Jane had ensured, in each of her novels, that things had all come out right in the end, romantically speaking. Not to mention the fact that she'd somehow found a way to provide happily-ever-afters for those intrepid journalers in the years in between. With Sean in Scotland and me in Austin—and a vacuum between us—this was hard comfort. But given a couple minutes, I just might get around to fixing that.

I tried for a moment to imagine a longer stay in Scotland and pictured myself schlepping about in wellies and hand-knit sweaters, making up peat fires and spending casual evenings at the pub. Hmmm. It all sounded very cozy, but I didn't know how I'd feel after a few weeks of rainy, chilly days with no quick runs to Target and the closest Mexican restaurant hundreds of miles (or more!) away. But Scotland had marvelous, melt-in-your-mouth butter toffees. And well, Sean, of course. There'd be Sean, with his sweet-n-sexy grin, his smooth, velvet voice, all wrapped up in a kilt . . .

Spurred into action, I dashed into the kitchen, grabbed hold of the quote-a-day calendar with both hands, and scanned the top page. " 'What is right to be done cannot be done too soon.' *Emma.*" I grinned, grabbed for the phone, and dialed Gabe's number. He answered on the fourth ring, and unable to contain myself, I blurted, "I'm thinking of giving chase."

"Huh?"

Closing my eyes, priming myself to start over, I explained. "Sean's in Scotland, I'm here. Ergo, I'm thinking of giving chase."

"Who *is* this?" The jocularity was coming through loud and clear.

"Get it out of your system, Gabe—this is a serious call."

"Okay, fine. But who knew you'd give up the 'thrill of the 401(k)' for the 'thrill of the chase.' " Gabe's laugh was barely contained and so was my temper. I didn't answer. "Okay, seriously?" he said around a chuckle. "That's awesome. When are you leaving?"

Wishing we weren't doing this over the phone, I begged, "Just play pro and con with me. Subject: Compulsive International Travel. I'm pro, you're con."

"Really? I have to be con? I think I'm much better suited to pro."

"But shouldn't I be the one fighting for him?"

"Point taken," Gabe conceded. "Me first?"

"No, me. If I go, I have a much better chance of getting Sean back."

"And an equally good chance of embarrassing yourself to within an inch of your pride."

"I'll have made the grand gesture, followed my bliss . . ." I envisioned all sorts of pride-numbing endings, and my conviction faltered a bit.

"You'll be out the cost of the plane ticket, transportation, accommodations—not to mention the cost to your pride."

"You've mentioned that," I reminded him.

"It's a biggie. You know, you could just call him."

"I can't. We're way beyond that. I think I have to go for the grand gesture, if only to make the point that I can be flexible and spontaneous in a pinch."

"But it's an eight-hour flight—over an ocean—and unplanned time off work. That's a whopper of a gesture for a man you've only known a week."

True. As gestures went, it was big. I quickly squelched that train of thought, not about to let my sensible side get a foothold here. I countered, "There are perks over and above just seeing Sean. I haven't had a vacation in almost a year, and Scotland is drenched in history, culture, and glorious scenery. The castles alone would justify the trip."

"Drenched being the operative word. And I don't think you'd much care for the castles 'alone.' I'm sure they're better with a friend."

Damn, he was good. I gritted my teeth and tried again.

"There's the toffee and the tartans and the cashmere." It was a desperate, last-ditch effort.

"All of which can be purchased with minimal effort over the Internet. And the shipping costs are nothing compared to the monumental cost of flying over to pick them up." I could hear the smugness in Gabe's voice as he added, "Keep 'em comin', 'cause we haven't even touched on the flighty irresponsibility of ditching out of your first day on a new job."

Gabe was irritatingly, excruciatingly good at this, but I'd realized it didn't matter. The whole time I'd been trying to convince him, I'd convinced myself. I was going. I'd find a way to work out the job thing.

"Your work here is done," I told him breezily.

"How'd I do?" he asked, the interest clear in his voice.

"I plan on making my travel arrangements as soon as we get off the phone."

"I'll score it as a win."

"That doesn't surprise me."

"Yeah, well, bring me back a souvenir—if you end up coming back. I'm a large if you're shopping for cashmere—same for toffee."

"If you're lucky, I'll bring you a kilt. Beck will love that, trust me."

As promised, within thirty minutes it was done. I decided it was positively providential that my passport was up to date. I booked a one-way flight into Inverness, a seat on ScotRail over to Kyle of Lochalsh, and accommodations for two nights in a cottage with a view of Loch Alsh. With luck, Sean was somewhere in the vicinity and could be unearthed simply enough, leaving me free to focus my efforts on an all-out seduction.

The flight was costing me just over nine hundred dollars, not to mention many long coach-trapped hours, but none of it was fazing me—at least not yet. I was excited, thrilled even, eager to fast-forward through two days of waiting until Saturday morning and the start of my big adventure. I used a good chunk of the time to back off my grudge and lose myself in the pages of *Emma* and *Pride and Prejudice*, marveling at how elegantly everything in the novels worked out. I definitely had a few things to learn.

I called Beck to give her the news. She was thrilled, of course, and insisted I take a vow of "full disclosure." Evidently spurred on by my gutsiness (her words), she had decided that she and Gabe should go ahead and "give each other a whirl." I insisted on an identical vow from her.

Besides the requisite packing and a little chat with my new boss about this impromptu but nonnegotiable vacation, I considered it prudent to call a truce with Fairy Jane, step one being a full pardon and retrieval from the laundry bin. I wouldn't want her to exact revenge at inopportune moments. That would be bad. So basically I needed to suck up.

I took my time, paging slowly through the notorious little journal, reading over the scattered words of the now-poignant messages left behind. I'd changed a lot since finding that first little scrap of fortune cookie wisdom. I'd been stubborn and close-minded, and a bit of a bitch, but Fairy Jane had been just as stubborn, and she'd won the day. I still didn't understand it—really *any* of it—but that part of the picture no longer seemed to matter.

On the cusp of my wild and reckless adventure, I'd take any help I could get, magical or otherwise. Where I was going, what I planned to do, I figured I needed a posse. It couldn't hurt to go back and read the letter that had started it all—the dedication from Jane herself.

". . . I dedicate to You the following Miscellanious Morsels, convinced that if you seriously attend to them, You will derive from them very important Instructions, with regard to your Conduct in Life."

"Miscellanious Morsels"—wasn't that the truth! Fairy Jane had definitely stepped in and stepped up when I needed her. With only a few select words, she'd helped me realize that I simply needed to let go, to relinquish my white-knuckled grip on life and go after my best chance for a happily-ever-after.

I could do that. I *would* do that—no regrets, no looking back.

This whole thing could go down any number of ways, from the downright depressing to the cringingly embarrassing. I preferred not to dwell on those possibilities, let alone write about them. For now at least, I was hopped up on optimism, and in a surprise turn-around, looking for affirmation from my journal. Her banishment days were over—she'd been upgraded to trusty sidekick.

I admit it—you've converted me—truly this time. Logic is out; magic is in. On a trial basis. I'm incontrovertibly in love with him, and I plan to give chase, across the pond, to the land of fairies, not to mention kilts and toffee. My flight leaves Saturday, and despite the very real possibility of failure, I'm oddly psyched by the hugeness and spontaneity of it all. Maybe I have a touch of the adventurer in me after all. I have a plan—obviously I have a plan—but it's simple and straightforward and not likely to go as expected seeing as Sean is just the opposite. The plan is to find him and lure him back—back to Austin would be preferable, but—and here's a shocker—even that isn't a requirement. I'm hoping for an Austen ending—my very own happily-ever-after—but with a dollop of scorching sex thrown in.

Obviously I don't want to jinx it, and I certainly don't assume it'll be a cakewalk, but I'm not going to let that get me down. I'm going to play it weird, live juicy, and just do it. How's that for a strategy? And I'm letting you, Dear Journal, tag along, just in case I need some last-minute advice. Or a little bit of magic . . .

I decided to leave Fairy Jane's reply for a bit of in-flight reading.

We were cruising at thirty thousand feet before I let myself peek. And there it was . . .

magic is flighty—find it and don't let go.

A slow smile snaked across my face, expanding, curling, rounding as it went, until eventually I felt like a goon, grinning at nine little words that two weeks ago would have earned a dismissive scoff from me. I liked it—it summed up my new attitude: motivated *and* open-minded. And it hinted at the fact that I was not the only one who'd changed. As far as I knew, Fairy Jane had never before had to resort to chopping up words to piece new ones together. I was quite sure I hadn't used the term "flighty" in my entry (although it certainly wouldn't have been out of place), but I had mentioned my "flight" on "Saturday." And judging by the spacing between the "t" and the "y," she'd spliced as needed. I had to admit to being impressed with her Machiavellian techniques. Reminded me of someone else I knew . . .

Letting the journal fall closed and my eyes with it, I tipped back in my seat and let my dreams waft me across the Atlantic.

I slumped off the British Airways plane in Inverness a little bleary-eyed, but focused on finding the ScotRail counter. Wobbly as I was, I felt ready for anything—in a tentative, baby-steps kind of way. I'd made it this far, and that had to count for something.

On the train I watched through the window as spring unfurled across the Scottish countryside. It rained—naturally, it rained—but it was a light drizzle, zigzagging over the windows and making the world just beyond glisten and shimmer. I could imagine Fanny Price, riding out in the rain, cursing her hurt pride and the circumstances of birth. And Elizabeth Bennet, happening to run across Mr. Darcy, only to find herself irrevocably smitten. Clearly I was content to lump Scotland in with England, and Austin in with Austen.

We zipped along the racing River Ness, and I couldn't help but feel a little disappointed that I'd not be getting a peek at the mysterious waters of Loch Ness, not to mention their infamous occupant. Not that I necessarily even believed that he (she?) existed . . .

But there were plenty of other very real distractions as we sped past a glistening green blur of mountains and forest, straight into the station at Kyle of Lochalsh.

The trip so far had been a study in logistics, but it was about to get personal real quick. I was closing in, and getting more nervous by the minute. I'd need to somehow find my way to Dornie and, once there, find Sean. Sad to say, but that was pretty much the extent of the formal plan. Still, I figured I had a bit of time yet to work out the details. Right now I was still in big-picture mode, content with simply having made it this far.

Or so I thought.

"I'd like to visit Dornie while I'm here," I blurted at the check-in desk of the quaint little highland inn I'd picked out on the Internet.

"Naturally," came the innkeeper's cryptic reply. I had only a moment to wonder over it, because with her next comment, it made perfect sense. "There are tour buses and guided car tours to take you over to the castle. When were ye wanting to go?" Turning to reach for an enormous binder behind the check-in desk, she kept her eyebrows raised as she flipped through the pages, waiting for my answer.

The "Loched In" castle. Beyond my online infatuation with this photogenic stunner, I hadn't really given it much thought. But now that my nerves were starting to twitch and fidget, memories of the enchanting castle were enticing me to procrastination. I could rest today, tour the castle and its grounds tomorrow, and then leisurely find my way to Dornie, maybe for lunch—or dinner—in the pub.

"What about bright and early tomorrow morning?" I answered, hearing the question in my voice. Satisfied, she glanced down again, I assumed to scan the schedules for workable options. Three-quarters of the way through my massive sigh of relief, my throat closed up, leaving me to grapple with more of a last gasp. A sudden inexplicable urgency surged through me, heedless of my unpreparedness and outright squeamishness.

"Wait!" I demanded, my hands splayed over the counter. "Is it too late to go today?"

We glanced at our watches in synchronized harmony, and I realized I had no idea what time it was. I'd not yet troubled to set my own watch to adjust for the considerable time difference.

"It's going on four o' clock now, so with the drive, you'd have but an hour. Not really enough for a proper tour, more of a little jot about. Will that suit ye?"

"Perfectly," I told her, nodding. But behind my grateful smile was shock, plain and simple. I'd lost control, and it seemed I was spiraling faster and faster into the unknown perilous world of grand gestures and uncertain futures. And there was no end in sight, I realized, as I stuttered out one final request. "I'm actually hoping to locate someone in Dornie—a man, Sean MacInnes. Do you know . . . ?"

Her smile was the knowing kind and made me wonder what it was she knew. "Most evenings he's like to be found at the Dog and Bagpipes, that one."

My heart suddenly felt worlds too big for my chest. Self-consciously, I pulled my hands from the counter and awkwardly crossed my arms to cover the painful pounding. "Is the pub within walking distance of the castle?" I'd imagined there'd be a bit more sleuthing required, but it looked as if my search could only get any easier if Sean turned out to be driving the tour car to Eilean Donan. *God forbid!*

Giving me the eye, the innkeeper made a point of leaning her deep bosom over the counter to stare down at my feet.

"Have ye some other shoes, miss?"

"I do." I tacked a little smile on at the end, but it felt watery. *I* felt watery.

"Be sure to switch, and you'll be fine. It's maybe a twenty-minute walk. Impossible to miss."

"And getting back?" Clearly I should have stayed in Dornie, but I'd been too chicken, and of course I'd been desperate to avoid any potential awkwardness . . . or any more than strictly necessary.

"I'll ring up one of the innkeepers down the road from the pub and ask them to drive you back 'round." She waved away the uncertainty plain on my face. "It's not a bit of trouble. We do the same for them. Not as often, mind, but who's counting?" She winked merrily. "You're all checked in here, so ye just have time to go on up to your room, freshen up a bit, change your shoes," she paused for effect and eyebrow raising, "and get back down to the lobby before the car pulls 'round outside." Now she smiled, no doubt waiting for me to obey.

A change of shoes (and underwear) and a slick of deodorant and lip gloss took longer than expected, and I missed my chance to tag along on the last castle tour of the day. But not yet ready to venture off to the Dog and Bagpipes, I chose to wander the castle grounds on my own.

The green of the hills and the showy flare of sunset colors was breathtaking, but my eyes were drawn to the mirrored beauty of Eilean Donan caught—trapped—beneath the water. Locked in. And then it clicked, and my brain went numb, thrumming with the frightening truth that in this spot, at this moment, I'd locked *myself* in. Tonight it really was *now or never*.

I could already see the moon, a bright crescent, rising in the sky, and a matching one reflected far away beneath the surface of the water. Like two separate worlds, one real and one imagined. Like my own schizophrenic whirlwind of real life versus dreams come true. Standing in the misty chill of early evening thousands of miles from home, the luster on my grand gesture was beginning to tarnish amid the harsh climate of fear. But there were hours yet till the clock struck midnight, and in an odd twist, I was off from the castle to find the prince.

Time skittered past, and like magic, I ended up in front of the Dog and Bagpipes, staring in disbelief at the pub signage, decorated, as one might expect, with a dog playing the bagpipes. There was no mistaking the place—how could there be? Music was filtering out through the slightly cracked door, and a warm yellow glow shined at the windows, beckoning me in out of the twilight and chill. Into a world of awkward. I stepped back, wrapping my sweater more tightly around me. I wasn't ready.

I needed a little boost, a little inspiration . . . a sign.

Unzipping my bag, I pulled out the journal and ran my hands over its familiar cover. A little chat with Fairy Jane was probably impossible—who knew how long I'd have to huddle outside waiting for an answer. Digging deeper, my hand closed over my cell phone, which I'd neglected to power on after the flight. I remedied that oversight. It was midmorning in Austin, and I could probably catch Gabe or Beck, but there was nothing left to say. Honestly, I just needed to cowgirl up and get 'er done.

A tiny red beacon started winking at me—the message light. A text message had been sent a couple of hours ago, as I was whipping through the Scottish countryside on my merry way to here.

Mssg from Leslie:

Text us with Darcy deets . . . L&L P.S. And demand make-up sex!

Believe it or not, it was the nudge I needed. Taking a deep, courage-gathering breath, I let it go and watched it billow out on the breeze, sparkling in the pearly glow from above.

Turning to face the pub door, I said a little prayer, offered up an appeal to Fairy Jane and any and all magical creatures willing to intercede on my behalf, and with a fluttery breath, pulled it open.

20

In which Nic does the unthinkable

Even standing in the shadows, just over the threshold, the awkwardness hanging heavy over my head right beside the huge potential for failure, I could feel the tension start to ebb away. For now I was still anonymous, but I felt welcomed just the same. The flickering glow of a peat fire, the raucous laughter of pub regulars, the clink of glasses raised in toast, and the lilting sound of a young female voice accompanied by a fiddle—all of it felt right. The chill slid out of me, but I stayed by the door, cursing my lack of planning for the second time in recent memory. I hadn't a clue what to do now. I admit, I'd been hoping I'd catch a glimpse of Sean and suddenly be struck with an ingenious segue between our awkward good-bye and this, the unexpected hello.

But I didn't see him.

My hands darted about like dragonflies, feathering over the clamoring parts of my anatomy in their turn. My throat, with its jackrabbiting pulse, my chest, with its runaway bass drum beat, and on to my stomach, where anxiety was starting to churn things up . . .

And then I saw him.

Time stopped for just a moment, and then the room was spinning once again in a kaleidoscope of color and sound, all of it a blur but him. He looked exactly as I remembered, but sooo much sexier. My nausea spiked with the memory that I'd let him slip through my fingers and must now hang my future on the hope that he—much unlike me—wasn't a grudge holder. Holding court across the room, he was relaxed and confident, the apparent golden boy of Dornie village.

Whereas I was skulking in a corner, a full-fledged stalker. We didn't fit, the pair of us. Two people could not possibly be more different. And yet, I wanted him. And I needed to convince him, right here, tonight, that I'd bobbled things and really and truly deserved a do-over. Because if I walked out of here now, I wouldn't be back; I wouldn't have the courage to try this again. This was it.

As the ballad ended amid much whistling and applause, my eyes strayed toward the band and quickly recognized Sean's band mates.

"Anyone else now?" called the drummer—Ian, if I remembered right—in a clear, carrying voice. I scanned the pub as he did, looking for takers, before glancing back to him. Eyebrows raised, he warned, "Otherwise you'll be having to listen to Sean again, and I wouldn't trust him to have any new material."

Widespread groans, hearty jokes, and shouted encouragement were offered up all around, but I barely noticed. It had just occurred to me that suddenly I was in a time crunch: If I waited any longer, Sean would be on stage and out of reach indefinitely. Never mind the suspense, I honestly didn't think I could handle the grueling physical symptoms of waiting any longer.

As if prompted by an awfully pushy invisible hand, I shuffled forward and felt my heart rate soar, pounding out its objection. Too bad. This was it—I was going to do it! Newly determined, I headed toward the makeshift stage where the band was waiting to accompany the vocal stylings of the next performer. Which I'd just now decided was going to be me. That's right: *I* was volunteering. To sing. In front of complete strangers. No doubt bearing a striking resemblance to a zombie in a sweater and sensible shoes.

Within seconds I was facing a couple of Sean's band mates and a complete stranger with a fiddle, slightly slack-jawed (me, that is, not them) and stumped as to what to do next. Recognition flick-ered in their eyes (except for the fiddler), and slow grins seeped onto their faces.

"Are ye here to sing, then?" This from Ian (I think).

"If that's all right?"

"It's bloody great," he assured me, and his cohorts seemed to agree. I stared for a moment, thrown a bit by their effusive encour-agement, before forcing a smile on my face. My shocking lack of talent would melt those grins off their faces soon enough. "Do ye have a song in mind?"

I opened my mouth, ready to blurt anything just to move this along, but nothing came out. Probably because nothing came to mind. Out of all the karaoke songs I'd memorized against my will over the last six months, none of them seemed appropriate for this moment. My mind flitted over show tunes, one seeming even more ridiculous than the next, and I briefly considered—and ve-toed—a Katy Perry tune. I was stumped and losing courage fast.

I glanced away from the band, out toward the crowded pub, where strangers were whispering and wondering. Whipping my head back around, focusing hard on not hyperventilating, I let my mind tumble over possibilities.

What songs did I even know all the lyrics to? And which of those did I have a prayer of not massacring? I couldn't think of a single one . . .

And then I did.

I blurted it to the band before I could change my mind, and while my request garnered a few smirks, no one questioned it. This was really happening.

I felt suddenly compelled—honor bound—to give them a little heads-up. So before I turned around to face the music (so to speak) and my first audience (who knew it'd be on foreign soil?), I screwed my face up a little in apology and admitted, "This isn't going to be pretty."

"I can assure you, we've heard worse." As words of encourage-ment, they sucked, but at least they came with a wink. I shrugged. Nobody could say I hadn't warned them.

I watched them count it down, poised on the balls of my feet, quivering with nerves and fear and queasy anticipation.

And then my time ran out. And I spun. And started to sing.

Obviously I felt like an idiot belting out the theme song from *Shrek*, particularly surrounded by musical talent and following a lovely, lilting Scottish ballad, but what could I say? I knew the words, and that was a huge plus.

I'd blurred my vision so I wouldn't have to look at any one person's full-body cringe, but my hearing was disturbingly sharp, and I was fully aware that my pride was in the middle of a smackdown. I could literally hear my voice being stretched beyond the bearable limits. But I couldn't stop now, and besides, how could things possibly get any worse?

Somehow they found a way.

As the song started to quicken and move into the chorus, my head bobbing along, keeping time with the music, I felt the rest of my body start to twitch, impelled by the beat, or the exhilaration, or reckless, rampant insanity to *dance*.

I was not a dancer—I had no skills, no moves, no rhythm. Then again, I wasn't a singer either, but here I was, microphone in hand, belting out the lyrics of an ogre. As an argument it was weak, and yet it proved sufficiently convincing. Before we'd hit the next bit of the chorus, I had moves, and I was sharing them with everyone. All I could do was hope to God no one had a camera phone. Not to mention the cold-blooded cruelty to post this little indiscretion on YouTube.

Suddenly, through my blurry haze, I heard clapping. Not appreciative clapping, mind you. Sympathetic, rousing clapping—the sort inspired by subpar performances, intended to offer up encouragement. I took it as a sign of good karma and readjusted my eyes to eliminate the blur.

Skimming over faces, some with wide eyes, others with wide grins, my gaze finally settled on Sean, his eyes riveted on the spectacle I was making of myself, just as I sung, a little desperately, about needing a little "*chaaange*."

It took only that one line to make me realize that somehow—

magically, maybe—I'd chosen perfectly rather than arbitrarily. This kooky song felt like it should be part of my life's sound-track—my "big moment" track. Because even if Sean refused to take me back, even if he was appalled at my singing voice (how could I blame the man?), I'd done this. I'd taken a chance, taken a risk, gotten wild and weird all on my own. And I was proud of my-self. My world was literally on fire.

Two more seconds, and it was over. I was done. The band wrapped the song, and I thumped ignominiously back to earth, a regular girl with post-performance anxiety, the fairy dust gone.

Ian's voice replaced mine on the microphone. "Let's have a round of applause for Miss Nicola James, everyone!" So much for anonymity. Tossing the crowd a jaunty little wave and a pained smile, I decided to make my escape before the morbidly curious decided to approach.

I turned to murmur my thanks to the band, shaking each of their hands in turn, and retrieved my bag from the floor beside me. I made my way back to the door in the same trancelike state I'd come through it and pushed out into the cool night air, gearing up for a full-on panic attack.

What just happened in there? Why did I . . . ? How could I . . . ? I couldn't go back in there. Forget that I couldn't catch my breath, couldn't slow my pulse, couldn't stop the goose bumps popping up willy-nilly, nothing to do with the cold. This hadn't been how it was supposed to go. I'd wanted magical, not mortifying. And Sean had witnessed every horrific moment. *God, how awful.*

I heard the door to the pub open behind me and realized I hadn't run far enough—I hadn't been ready to disappear just yet. I was praying it was a kind soul on his way home for the evening, unin-terested in making conversation with a whacked-out foreigner like myself.

"Nicola?"

Sean. And no escape.

I dropped my head down on a sigh. This was not at all how I imagined things would go when I rode a whim all the way to Scot-land looking for one more chance. But if this was all I was going to get, then dammit, I was taking it. I spun on my heel, a cordial smile plastered on my face.

"Karaoke Queen, in the flesh," I countered.

My smart mouth bought me a grin, shooting a slug of warmth straight down into the pit of my stomach. "Stellar performance," he said, but his eyes quickly shifted from amused to bemused. "You on tour?"

"Just the one stop," I confirmed, leaving it at that. What could I say? I was flummoxed. Sean stood only a couple feet away, gorgeously limned in moonlight, and in this pivotal, romantic moment, he seemed tragically out of reach. I was aching to touch him, to kiss him, to be told all was forgiven and nothing had changed, but I didn't, and I wasn't. And he clearly didn't intend to make it easy for me, judging by the way he was standing, eerily silent, simply waiting.

A gust of wind swirled around us, sending the dog and bagpipes swinging, prickling the air around us. I could almost feel it crackling with interference, and I suspected the fairy sort. I shuddered to think what could be coming next and how a little fairy magic could send me careening into the wild unknown. But hell, I was there already, so I braced myself and gave in, yanking down every last defense I had standing.

A second passed, and I didn't feel any different. Perhaps a little lighter, a little less inhibited, a little more urgent . . .

Stepping forward one step, then two, I tipped my head to the side a bit and let the truth unfurl, gliding through the air between us like the tail of a kite. "I was convinced you were out of the realm of possibility for me. You swooped in, a regular Prince Charming, and worked your magic. You seduced me—and how could I help myself?—I let you." My lips quirked, curved at the memory. "You made me believe we could work out all the kinks. But then I discovered you *live* in Scotland—whew!—and I stopped believing. I let you leave and cursed myself for a week." Now that I was getting to the meat of things, I stepped closer still. "I missed you—awfully—and booked a flight, a spur-of-the-moment, one-way ticket. And here I am, on a quest to seduce you back."

There. I'd said it. I'd said it all out loud, and it hung, hovering there between us, waiting for Sean's reaction. And waiting still. He said nothing, did nothing, and the enormity of failure loomed hideously before me.

The buzzing urgency swelled inside me and seemingly all around me, reaching a frenzied pitch, and I couldn't help it . . . I blurted out an imagined enticement, hoping to lure him in. "I packed thongs!"

The words seemed to echo, hanging in the air around us, the death knell of my pride. I barely resisted the urge to clap a hand over my mouth and give in to the hysteria bubbling up inside me.

"I'm a big believer in second chances," Sean finally answered, a grin spreading slow and wide across his face.

Exhilaration whipped through me, and caution skittered away. Needing to touch him, I lifted my hands to cup his face, feeling my way along his jawline and skimming my fingers over his dimple. When I felt it deepen, I went up on tiptoes and pulled him forward for a kiss. I tried to infuse everything into that kiss: relief and hope, and of course, love. There was a healthy helping of lust mixed in there too.

Several moments later, with his arm tucked warmly around me, Sean let me in on a little secret.

"I should probably confess . . ."

My body stiffened automatically at these words, but Sean tightened his grip. "As flattered as I am to be chased across an ocean, tracked down, and serenaded in my local pub, you could have saved yourself the trouble—not to mention the airfare. I'll be flying back in three days, luv." At this point his sincerity turned to teasing. "Does Guinness post a record for irresistibility? Because I think I just might be a contender."

My body suddenly felt like a train wreck—everything suspended, and carnage all over my insides. None. Of. This. Had. Been. Necessary. Not the trip, the heartache, the urgency, and not the damn performance that would likely live in infamy in this sleepy little village for generations to come. Tourists would come over from the castle to have a pint, and villagers would regale them of the evening in early April when a strange woman appeared just long enough to massacre a single ridiculous song before she disappeared into the darkness. I'd be the stuff of legend. Awesome.

"You're coming back?" My voice was brittle and breathless.

"Ahhh . . . you didn't know that." I couldn't decide if I appreciated the sympathy in his eyes or not. Nor could I tell if he was faking it. "Because you heard 'Scotland' and panicked. You said good-bye before I could tell you about our record deal." My eyes widened, a thrill whipping through me, and I opened my mouth to respond. He cut me off. "Uh-uh. This time you're listening, Ms. James. After our showcase Thursday night, we got a call and an offer to have our next record produced in the States. The chaps and I discussed it and voted unanimously to relocate to Texas. Austin specifically. We'd actually discussed that possibility before getting the offer, so when the deal came through, everything was damn near perfect, it being 'the Live Music Capital of the World' and all." He smiled. "I'll admit you sweetened the deal a bit yourself."

He paused and leveled me with a meaningful gaze. I wondered if I should tell him that I was willing to move to Scotland, trudge around in wellies, and spend the rest of my life coexisting with the fairies. I promptly decided against it. *I* knew it, and for now, that was enough. Instead I gushed and squealed my congratulations until I found a better use for my mouth entirely.

Minutes passed quite delightfully, but Sean eventually pulled back, obviously with more to say.

"The return tickets were already booked, and there was packing to do here, and good-byes. Funnily enough, I'd thought I'd convince you to come along," he told me, starting to get adorably huffy, "but you never even gave me the chance to ask."

It occurred to me that the man *could* hold a wicked grudge. For some reason, that little surprise had me grinning like a fool despite the reprimand. Nevertheless, I was effusive in my apologies, soothing and patting. Nothing, not even my own bad behavior, could trouble me now. "So you punished me," I accused him. "Made me sweat a little—okay, a lot—and come haring after you.

I'd say you got what you deserved." My lips curved into a playful smirk, remembering my impromptu performance.

"Do you, now?" Sean's mouth quirked into a matching smirk, and we stared at each other, smitten. "Turns out, I agree with you." His arm snaked away from me, taking the warmth with it, and I stood waiting, oddly bereft, as he rummaged about for something in his wallet. I was fervently praying it wasn't a condom and that he wasn't about to spring a one-with-nature fantasy on me.

A not-so-subtle breath whooshed out of me and hung shimmering in the cold air between us as his palm extended toward me, holding only a narrow rectangle of paper.

"What is it?" My voice was barely audible, fraught with nerves and ponderous with possibility. And I waited for his answer despite its being unnecessary.

"My fortune," he confided with a cocky grin that tingled along my nerve endings.

Flicking an uncertain glance in his direction, I reached for it. Tilting it first toward the moonlight and then toward the pub lantern, I could just barely make out the tiny typed words.

> *"The only way to get rid of a temptation is to yield to it."*
> *Oscar Wilde*

"I don't get it," I insisted, wondering if it was possible at this stage in the game that another fortune could possibly be a coincidence.

"I cracked it out of a cookie my first night in Austin—a comforting bit of British wisdom deep in the heart of Texas." It was kind of cute how amused he was with the cliché. "I liked the sound of it. Then I met you, a damsel in distress, and you became the embodiment of that quote."

My mind wrapped instantly around the negative. "If you want to be rid someone, I'd advise against stalking, flowers, and serenades," I retorted, pulling away a bit.

"Don't pout, luv. You're missing the point. I wanted you, so I set about getting you."

Oh. Well, phrased like that, it sounds perfectly lovely.

I stepped closer again, tucking my arm into Sean's and looking out over the shimmer on the loch. For him, one cookie made all the difference. I, on the other hand, needed a magical journal, a considerable amount of nudging from a medley of friends, and *four* cookies before things finally clicked for me. Who knew that first bit of advice was so particularly profound . . .

Miss Nicola James will be sensible and indulge in a little romance.

Not to mention prophetic.

Huddled beside Sean, gauzy bits of cloud sailing above us, wispy grass twittering in the breeze, and the air laden heavy with mystery and barely veiled giddiness, I could admit that none of this—not one bit of it—made sense. And yet . . . it was imminently sensible, perfectly juicy, and a real-life fairy tale.

Score one for Fairy Jane.

And one for me for going chips all in.

All tied up.

A little gust moved toward us across the surface of the loch, ruffling everything in its path. As it tousled my hair and tugged at my sweater, I imagined it intent on whipping up mischief. Content to let it, I went up on tiptoe, letting my lips brush against the curve of Sean's ear as I whispered, "Wanna score?"

21

In which a bit of dandelion fluff is well and truly caught

It seems that in an odd confluence of fortune cookies, fairy magic, and "weird," Sean and I have ended up together. I should probably say thank you, Dear Journal . . . Fairy Jane . . . Miss Austen. You've been quite the interfering busybody, and yet . . . without you I'd still be daydreaming of Brett, baking the same old chocolate cupcakes, and listening to Leslie rant about men and rave about women. You swooped in, an honest-to-goodness, no-nonsense fairy godmother, grabbed me by the ear, and shook some sense into me. Evidently you're not a fan of the pumpkin carriage/glass slipper method, but whatever works, right?

And sitting here, on the shore of the mysterious and truly magical Isle of Skye, watching Sean skip stones over the water, I have to admit, it worked like gangbusters. The thongs are in play, and tomorrow we're flying back to Austin and a new and different weird life. I can't wait . . . if for nothing else than an ice cube and a cloudless sky.

Turns out Sean is a sensible investor in not only his pension but a slew of stocks and mutual funds as well. How sexy is that?? Evidently the man is destined to surprise and delight me at every turn, a situation I'm finding increasingly appealing. Clearly I'd been mistaken in classifying him as a Henry Crawford—he is most definitely a Mr. Darcy, my Mr. Darcy. I must admit, I don't know quite what to do with you, Dear Journal, and yet I suspect you would agree that your "unique powers" are better suited to the individual rather than the collective world of Jane Austen devotees. In particular, my own perfectly happy ending makes me wonder how Beck is faring with her current romantic entanglement and whether she might welcome a little magical interference. That is, if you're up to it . . .

On that note, I tucked the journal back into my messenger bag, eager for this last chance to spend time with Sean on this side of the pond—at least for a while. We hadn't had the "journal talk" yet, but it would need to be soon, for the sake of my sanity. Besides, I rather suspected Sean would take it all in stride.

Fairy Jane's response I once again saved for the plane. With Sean napping beside me, his hand warm on my thigh, I skipped through the pages till I found the one I was looking for.

You have to admit, weird is sensible and sexy, and a happy ending is magical.

A Note from Alyssa:
How Jane Austen Edited My Book

In 2006 I became obsessed with all-things-Austen, and despite my relatively blissful ten-year-to-date marriage, that obsession manifested itself in part with the purchase of *Jane Austen's Guide to Dating* by Lauren Henderson. I was fascinated by the premise of the book—that Jane Austen's six novels, written two centuries ago, could offer relevant and adaptable romantic advice to modern-day women looking for Mr. Right—and I wondered whether I could work a similar concept into my current work in progress.

Jane Austen's Guide to Dating is broken down by chapters, highlighting ten key points of timeless Austen advice, each supported by anecdotes from her novels and modern-day examples. And then at the end, there is a quiz . . . well, two: "Which Jane Austen character are you?" and "Which Jane Austen character is the man you like?" Naturally I took the quizzes. Who wouldn't?

Based on my answers, I am "Anne [Elliot]—quiet, composed, and cautious." My best matches are Captain Wentworth, Colonel Brandon, and Edmund Bertram, according to Ms. Henderson's compatibility matrix. I can definitely see that. . . . I am all of those things. (Once you get to know me, I am also funny, direct, and outgoing, like Elizabeth. Just FYI . . .) My husband is characterized (based on my answers) as "straightforward, happy, and looking for love," and might be a Captain Wentworth, Henry Tilney, or Mr. Bingley. So, generally speaking, we're compatible. I may have already figured that out for myself, but it's good to know that our relationship is Jane Austen–approved.

The early brainstorming stages of *Austentatious* are a little fuzzy.

Nicola was at all the meetings, as was Sean, looking very sexy indeed. The journal was there, too, not yet corrupted by the advice and magic of Jane Austen. What I do remember is being struck by the perfect, world-altering moment in which it occurred to me that maybe I should squeeze a little Austen into my Austin-set story. Maybe the journal, somehow channeling the still-spunky spirit of Jane Austen, i.e., *Fairy Jane*, could offer up useful bits of modern-day romantic advice. Bits that would throw a kink in the romantic works of the ever-so-sensible Nicola James. I *adored* this idea, and I was thrilled to get back to work.

After that, Jane pretty much took over. She nuanced her way into every aspect of the book, and I just went along for the ride. *Austentatious* is, in part, a (loosely interpreted) modern-day retelling of *Pride and Prejudice*, and part homage to the wit and timelessness of Ms. Jane Austen. The dedication on the first page of the journal attributed to Ms. Austen was actually written by her, in a similar (although presumably not magical) journal given to her niece. Cool, huh? Stumbling across it and having it fit so perfectly with the story line of *Austentatious*, I could not help but consider it a little bit of magic from Fairy Jane herself.

Keep an eye out for Alyssa's next novel, coming next year!

1

"What does it say about me that I'm jealous of the lives of fictional characters?"

I posed the question nonchalantly as I nudged my Scrabble tiles around on the stand.

"Given that you're a high school English teacher, referring to eighteenth- and nineteenth-century British lit, it says you're glamorizing an era before indoor plumbing and takeout," Ethan said in his calm, rational manner. He glanced up at me, over the top of his tortoiseshell frames, gauging my reaction before refocusing his concentration on his own tiles.

I smiled ruefully and supposed in some ways, he had a point.

"Besides," he continued, "what do you have to complain about?"

"Not complain, exactly. More lament."

Prefacing his turn with an eyeroll and playing off the "T" from my wildly impressive "TRAMP," he neatly laid down all his letters to play "INTRIGUE," on a double word score, earning him a whopping seventy points to my seven. It was doubtful I could come back from this, particularly given the slew of vowels I'd just drawn, but I tried not to let it bother me. I never won against

Ethan. Besides, I didn't need the distraction, being as I was in the middle of my own pity party.

Ethan tallied his score and slid his hand into the bag of remaining tiles. "I'll bite. . . . What are you *lamenting?*"

"The reality that I may as well be wearing a tracking anklet, for all the excitement going on in my life. Then again," I said, looking out into the yard at the Bradford pear tree that had stripped down to bare branches, "the FBI would never bother to issue me an anklet, because I've ceased to be a 'person of interest.' Literally."

"You either deserve the anklet or you don't, Cate. Pick a side."

I wasn't particularly interested in continuing our Scrabble game, both because I was losing badly and because I was trying to make a point, so I ignored the board—and the fact that it was my turn—and focused on the pita chips I'd "borrowed" from my mom's pantry.

"Fine. I'm lamenting the fact that my life would never make the cut in publishing. I don't have any big moments—no cliffhangers, no happily ever after, no thrilling action sequence—just filler."

I crunched a chip loudly, feeling violently frustrated. Yep, that was me: violently frustrated and taking it out on a pita chip. My shoulders slumped.

"This isn't about *Pride and Prejudice* again, is it? Because that book is a menace."

"We've already determined that you, Mr. Chavez, are jealous of Mr. Darcy, so your opinion is moot. Besides, you're well aware that *P&P* isn't on the district reading list this year—this year's graduates are going to go off to college without ever experiencing the wit of Lizzy Bennett and the serious sex appeal of Mr. Darcy." I gazed off into the distance, hamming it up for Ethan's benefit, before getting back to business. "They did substitute *Emma,* so at least we know they're not completely uncultured." Willing myself back from the tangent, I grabbed another chip and swiped it through the hummus I'd found in my own refrigerator.

"Are you planning to play your turn?"

I looked up at Ethan, exasperated at his inability to focus.

"Are you here for the Scrabble or the company? Because if you're just here for the Scrabble, then maybe we should stick with the iPhone app and save ourselves the face-to-face." I knew I was starting to sound snippy, maybe even a little hurt, so I abruptly stopped talking.

Ethan reached for the Corona beer, sweating and forgotten, in front of him and sat back in his chair. He lifted one eyebrow in invitation for me to continue to talk my heart out.

I stared at him, with his tousled dark hair and weekend stubble, his deep brown eyes worldly wise behind his glasses, and I instantly regretted my snappish words. Scrabble notwithstanding, I would hate it if I missed my Sunday evenings with Ethan. He was the yin to my yang—or, more accurately, the squelch to my whine, and I needed that more often than I cared to admit.

I sipped my own beer with its tang of lime, puckered my lips, and prepared to make my point.

"Much as you'd probably hate to admit it, you're living the male version of my life. We both work in a high school—I teach English; you teach French and German. You live alone; I live alone, although admittedly in my mom's backyard. You haven't had a girlfriend for as long as I've known you, and you never talk about the women you're dating. I can't get further with a man than the first Saturday night date because you pick him apart over Scrabble on Sunday. Why I continue to confide in you is beyond me." I stopped, letting that all sink in.

"That's what friends do," he said, taking another pull on his beer and keeping his tone matter-of-fact. "They warn you off unsuitable men. Men have a way of impairing your judgment—I call it the Darcy Effect. Bad manners and mediocre good looks and you think he's a worthy specimen. Turns out he's more like a bug. So I dissect him."

"I'm so glad we're friends."

"If you're looking to change things up a little, friends with benefits would be acceptable to me." He grinned, a boyish, mischievous grin that convinced me he was definitely kidding. Which was a relief. Because that would be weird. So weird.

I needed to meet someone before . . .

I blinked and shook my head slightly, hoping to dislodge that train of thought.

"I need to do something," I finally said, glossing right over his provocative suggestion.

"Dare I suggest finishing the game?" He lifted an eyebrow and tilted his head, indicating my little row of vowels.

"I wouldn't if I were you," I said, sour-sweet.

"Okay, does that mean you'll pay the forfeit? I'm thinking pep-peroni pizza."

"Fine. I'll trade you the pizza for an honest answer."

"That's gonna depend on the question."

I pierced him with a quizzical stare. "What have you got going on in your life that has you looking so self-satisfied all the time?"

Ethan's mouth hitched up at the corner, putting the smug out on display. "That's pretty personal."

"Interesting comment coming from the man who just suggested we upgrade our Scrabble matches to include benefits."

"I meant pizza," he deadpanned.

"Evidently you're not so much a man of mystery as a man of mystery meats." I shook my head, biting back a smile, and looked away from him out over the darkened yard. Obviously Ethan was keeping his secrets close—assuming he had any that didn't involve hot cheese.

Sitting here under the brightly decorated Japanese lanterns I'd convinced my mom we should string up under the oaks, the possibilities seemed endless, the world glowing—I just needed to hold on to this feeling and find a way to have a little adventure. It couldn't be anything too risqué—one amateur videographer with a camera phone was all it took for things to get very hairy indeed. A good friend of mine had learned that the hard way. I needed a buffer, a way to keep my real, respectable everyday life separate from a little after-hours adventure.

An alter ego would be perfect . . . sort of a secret identity. I could be the kind of girl who would wear red lipstick and a secret smile and agree to a "friends with benefits" arrangement without batting an eye. Or maybe batting them madly . . .

"Want me to order the pizza?"

My gaze whipped back to Ethan, his face fringed in shadow as he searched his phone for the number of the pizza place. I blinked rapidly, trying to get my thought processes back on track, hoping the darkened twilight hid the flush in my cheeks and the nervous whites of my eyes.

"Knock yourself out," I finally agreed.

As we waited for the pizza and I considered, and discarded, a number of "alternative" options, opportunity e-mailed an invitation.

Derring-Do and Savoir Faire . . .
presented by Pop-up Culture
Join us for an evening inspired by the films of Alfred Hitchcock.
Suspense, my dears, is key, and so the evening's menu must remain
a mystery. . . .
The cast of characters: charismatic men, intriguing women,
and glamorous, grown-up drinks.
When? Sunday, All Hallow's Eve, 9:00 p.m.–midnight
Where? Location to be revealed on confirmed reservation
Entrée? $40, suggested donation
RSVP to this email address by Tuesday, October 26

Chills edged up my arms as I scrolled through each consecutive line. This was *it!* A perfect departure from my bookish, Darcy-obsessed self.

Pop-up Culture was the current business venture of my good friend/bad influence Syd Carmelo and fellow food junkies Olivia Westin and Willow Burke. It was a sort-of culinary underground, hosting über-cool, invitation-only "pop-up" events all over the city. Austin was cooler than ever. I'd been on the mailing list from Day 1, but had yet to make it to an event—I either had a parent conference, a family commitment . . . or a long-standing Scrabble match. I ended up getting the details with the rest of the city in the paper's Lifestyle section. Halloween was only a week away. And this time, I was going.

Not as myself, though. I was in the mood for a little "mysterious."

Maybe I'd be a Hitchcock blonde . . . with a long, slow smile and a whiff of suggestion. The blonde aspect, I had covered. The rest might require a little practice. I hurried to RSVP before I could lose my nerve. Next Sunday . . . I glanced at Ethan, who was randomly arranging tiles on the Scrabble board. Sundays were currently reserved for my "friend sans benefits." I could either ask him to go with me or I could strike out on my own. Chances were we'd be done with Scrabble in plenty of time for me to transform myself into a blond bombshell.

I'd started to type in my RSVP, single lady attending, when car doors slammed in the front yard, signaling that the pizza had arrived. Pocketing my phone, I grinned to myself, smirked in Ethan's direction, and nearly skipped through the gate at the side of the house. Only to stumble across my mother, holding a large white pizza box up over her head.

"Mom!" I glanced at the pizza dude, collapsing back into his tiny car, counting the bills in his hands.

"Hi," she said, dodging carefully around me. "I took a chance—thought maybe if I sprung for the pizza, you'd let me share."

"Sure," I agreed, trailing along behind her. "Where have you been?" Somewhere casual, I assumed, judging by the charcoal gray track pants and raspberry Polarfleece pullover she was wearing.

"Just out," she answered, vaguely waving her free hand, seeming to encompass all the options the city had to offer for an active fifty-something.

"Hello, Ms. Kendall," Ethan said, politely rising to his feet while surreptitiously eyeing the pizza box currently being held out of reach. He'd been a quick study, clueing in early on to the whole "recently divorced, taking my life back" attitude my mom was projecting. As far as he was concerned, "anything goes" was a bit of a watchword when it came to my mom.

My mother smiled at him. "Final score?"

Ethan glanced over at me, leaving me to answer.

"He's waiting for you to relinquish the price of my forfeit," I confessed, not even the slightest bit embarrassed. "Mom paid, so you're going to have to share," I informed him.

"Okay if we rough it and eat straight from the box?" he said, hurriedly gathering up the Scrabble board to make room for the pizza box in the center of the table. "I'm starving."

"A picnic under the stars—lovely," said my mother, smiling approvingly at Ethan before turning to me to flash the twinkle in her eye. "I'm not interrupting anything, am I?"

Honestly, I think my mom would be thrilled if I answered Ethan's teasing booty call.

The next ten minutes were blissfully quiet as we devoured gigantic greasy triangles of pizza with single-minded determination. I noticed a few bats winging gracefully overhead, but otherwise I was distracted by the opportunity burning a hole in my pocket. Suddenly I worried that a flood of people would jump at the chance to attend a Hitchcock-inspired party and edge me out with their quick-fingered RSVPs.

"Anyone need anything from the kitchen?" I yelped, standing suddenly, my legs pushing my chair away from the table. "Napkins have become necessary."

The pair of them eyed me quizzically but declined my offer. But as I neared the French doors leading into my mom's kitchen, she called out, "Cate, I've changed my mind. Will you pour me a glass of the Cabernet on the counter?"

"Got it," I said, stepping into the dim kitchen. The desk light in the corner was on, pooling a warm glow, so, preferring to keep my little secret from the pair outside, I decided to make do without additional lighting. It seemed irrational, but I couldn't help it; I wanted this one little secret for myself. My life wasn't just an open book with these two, it was an interactive free-for-all. Mom had been running interference in my life long before Dad and Gemma had left two years ago, within three weeks of each other, leaving us only to breathe an anticlimactic sigh of relief.

Gemma was sixteen months older than me and had long wavy auburn hair—twins we were not, but we'd had a whole *Parent Trap* dynamic going since early childhood. Photos scattered around the house told the story and hinted at the inevitable ending. Gemma always posed beside my father, in his lap, or on his shoulders. I, on the other hand, was my mom's shadow. Gemma and Dad were outgoing, outdoorsy, take-a-chance, make-it-happen types, while Mom and I were crafty, bookish rule followers, taking it on faith that magic would happen precisely when it was meant to, a personality type crafted initially by fairy tales and honed by Jane Austen.

Starting her third year of grad school in North Carolina, Gemma came home as school holidays allowed. Dad was happily entrenched in his new life as owner of a Texas Hill Country zip-line outfit, and despite being only a quick day-trip away, we rarely saw him. As for Ethan, the pair of us had hit it off around the same two-year mark, glommed on to each other, and hung like sticker burrs . . . impossible to shake. And I didn't want to shake him . . . him or my mom. I just wanted something of my own. I wanted a secret. A little desperately.

I quickly gathered up the napkins and pulled a favored wineglass down from the kitchen's open shelving. Then, with my back to the door, I made a slow effort of pouring the wine and cleaning up an imaginary spill—just in case anyone was watching. With my free hand, I texted my RSVP and credit card number and felt the thrill of derring-do ricochet through my veins.

I returned to the table, barely able to suppress a scary sort of smile—the sort where it's obvious you're hiding something particularly juicy. This subtle sneaking around felt good—liberating—but I couldn't very well flaunt it unless I wanted to risk Ethan anteing up his two cents. I was über conscious of their mildly curious gazes, but I stayed focused on my pizza and beer until a text came in, instantly disrupting my carefully arranged calm. I hurried to pull the phone from my pocket, my blood pounding crazily through my veins as I urgently wondered if I'd been too late.

Syd Carmelo: So thrilled you rsvp'd! Finally! Going to be awesome! Expect a call. . . .

I smiled down at the screen, my pulse slowly returning to normal, and casually sipped my beer.

Judging by the banked look in Ethan's eyes, he could tell something was up. He no doubt assumed that it was my mother's presence that kept me from blurting my secrets.

"Do you two have any plans for the evening?" my mom quizzed us, staring intently at Ethan.

Mom had been gunning for Ethan ever since I'd brought him home for our first Scrabble game a year and a half ago. She assumed that eventually one of us would realize that this thing between us could be so much more than a little word game with beer. As a romance reader, she couldn't help it—he was perfect hero material. Charismatic, clever . . . debatably sexy—it had, in fact, *been* debated, with Mom talking up his finer points and me la-la-la'ing my way through.

Ethan and I caught each other's eye, simultaneously shook our heads in one quick negative, and let our gazes swivel away again.

"I've actually got a few errands to run before tomorrow. Not to mention a little work to catch up on." He stood, eyed the pizza box splayed open on the table, and looked to me with a question in his eyes.

"I got it," I told him. "Seeing as I didn't buy the pizza, I'll pay the forfeit in cleanup. Sorry to rob you of another Scrabble trouncing."

"It had its benefits," he said, winking.

I glanced at my mom, hoping she wasn't picking up on any of this.

"Thank you for dinner, Ms. Kendall. See you at school, Cate." And then he disappeared into the shadows at the edge of the house. Minutes later, all car sounds had faded, and Mom and I were alone in the dark.

"Does he have a girlfriend?"

"No, and neither do I."

Mom's laser stare bored into me. I may as well have been splayed out on the table like James Bond.

"Kidding, Mom. But Ethan is just a friend."

"He could be a friend with benefits. . . ."

I turned the laser back on her, wondering for a moment if she'd been eavesdropping earlier and merely glossed over it by paying the pizza guy.

"Where did you say you were today, Mom?" I countered.

She clammed up immediately, which, while slightly suspicious, was just fine with me at this point.

"Do you have time this week to come in after school and help me decorate the store? I'd like to get the Halloween stuff up by Thursday at the latest."

Mom owned a vintage clothing and jewelry store down on South Congress called Mirror, Mirror. It irked her that fall retail tended to be one big blur of holidays, so she determinedly decorated for just a few days surrounding every holiday. I was always conscripted to help with window displays and ladder-top duties. Halloween, as I was now well aware, thanks to my invitation to a Hitchcock soiree, was only one week away.

And I needed something to wear.

I mentally rummaged through my closet, trying to think if I had anything at all with a Hitchcock-blonde vibe, and I couldn't come up with any hits. I'd have to cross my fingers that there was something in the shop I could borrow—something that wouldn't raise questions I didn't particularly want to answer. I hadn't decided quite how to play this. Spies and superheroes didn't go around outing themselves, confiding their secret identities, and handing out invitations to their secret lairs. Except maybe to a sidekick.

I hadn't really considered a sidekick. Ideally there'd be one trusty soul who had my back and could save me from the laser table. But seeing as this was just a little role-playing experiment, I really didn't need a sidekick. At least not yet.

"I can do that," I agreed, flashing back to reality. "I'll come by after school, but it might not be until Thursday—this week's busy." I stood and started gathering up the bottles for recycling. "I'll get this, Mom, and then I'm going to bed."

My cell phone chirped. I glanced at the display and then took my time answering until Mom and her wineglass had moved out of earshot.

"Hey, Syd," I said, closing the pizza box filled with crusts and wadded napkins.

"Hot damn! You're coming to my Hitchcock party!"

Here, finally, was someone who could share my secret. A smile quirked my lips as I finished clearing up. "You can bet I'll be renting *North by Northwest* this week—for research purposes."

"Wait, are you coming as a character?" Judging by the thrill in her voice, this was more than she could get her head around.

I flipped the switch for the lanterns, now bobbing gently in the breeze, and crossed the yard to the garage and the steps up to my apartment. "I'm shooting for seductive spy-girl Eve Kendall from *North by Northwest*," I said, having decided just moments ago myself. "And I'm coming alone, so you can bet I'll be looking for a Cary Grant sort to finish out the picture."

"Um, sweetie, if we get any men of the Cary Grant persuasion, your competition will be fierce. But good for you—way to ratchet up the sexy! Will, Oli, and I are going dressed as cat burglars à la *To Catch a Thief*. Sorta . . . ninja-sexy."

"I need something that will stamp out the 'schoolteacher by day' vibe coming off me in waves. I'm planning to visit the shop this week, so hopefully I'll find something perfect in my size." Letting myself into my little apartment, I leaned backward against the door, dropped the Scrabble box on the hall table, and scanned the room's potential as a superhero/spy lair—the sunflower yellow bowl of Dum-Dum lollipops on the coffee table was way too Doris Day. Although, come to think of it, she'd been a Hitchcock blonde. . . .

"You just need to get your blonde on, and you're gonna rock this party."

My understanding of the logistics involved in that suggestion was a little vague, but as a little fizz of encouragement, it was awesome. Trouble was, with a week to second-guess myself, I couldn't vouch for my confidence next Sunday night.

"It'll definitely be an adventure," I agreed.

It was about damn time.